"CAPTAIN! LONG-RANGE SCANNERS HITTING US, SIR! THEY TRACKED US!"

Helmsman Sulu hunched over his controls. Beside him, Ensign Chekov spat out, "There has never been a Romulan this close to Earth!"

"Not our Earth," James Kirk said. "Sound general quarters. Ready photon guidance. This may not be the Earth we know, but we're here and we're going to defend it. Gentlemen, arm phasers. Prepare to fire . . ."

Look for STAR TREK Fiction from Pocket Books

Star Trek: The Original Series

STAR TREK®

FIRST FRONTIER

DIANE CAREY
and
DR. JAMES I. KIRKLAND

POCKET BOOKS

New York   London   Toronto   Sydney   Tokyo   Singapore

This book is a work of fiction. Names, characters, places and incidents are products of the author's imagination or are used fictitiously. Any resemblance to actual events or locales or persons, living or dead, is entirely coincidental.

An *Original* Publication of POCKET BOOKS

POCKET BOOKS, a division of Simon & Schuster Inc.
1230 Avenue of the Americas, New York, NY 10020

A VIACOM COMPANY

STAR TREK is a Registered Trademark of Paramount Pictures.

This book is published by Pocket Books, a division of Simon & Schuster Inc., under exclusive license from Paramount Pictures.

ISBN: 0-671-52045-8

First Pocket Books printing August 1995

10 9 8 7 6 5 4 3 2 1

POCKET and colophon are registered trademarks of Simon & Schuster Inc.

Printed in the U.S.A.

Foreword
by
Dr. J. Kirkland

STAR TREK and dinosaurs . . . what a combination! Each brings forth visions of adventure and fantastic worlds—one in the vision of a promising future, the other shadowed by the mists of time.

But what is the connection? STAR TREK is science fiction, stories of a boundless future with infinite possibilities. Dinosaurs are science fact, an extinct group of diverse animals that dominated this planet for 160 million years. Each is a glimpse into an unattainable world.

As a child, I owned every dinosaur toy on the market, which in the mid-sixties was a very limited selection. My mind was filled with images of great beasts fighting it out on a landscape loaded with volcanoes. On one of my trips to the library, searching for another book by one of the great dinosaur hunters like Edwin H. Colbert or Roy Chapman Andrews, I stumbled into science fiction.

Soon I was reading every SF book I could find. I began to liken the alien world of Earth's Mesozoic Era to an alien world in deep space, each attainable only through my imagination.

When STAR TREK hit the airwaves in 1966, I was hooked. The stars were ours to explore, a new vista revealed each week. STAR TREK has become a lasting success because of the interplay of real characters in this marvelous unexplored panorama. Like the very best of science fiction, STAR TREK examined mankind while mankind examined the universe.

As I pursued a career in science, my perception of dinosaurs matured. I began to see a lot more than a bunch of giant reptiles. The Mesozoic Era was not just one world, but an immense succession of worlds, with ever-changing atmospheric, oceanographic and climatic condtions to rival an alien world. Life was as diverse as today, but alien and unique. If we went back a billion years, we couldn't even breathe Earth's atmosphere.

I realized dinosaurs have no more in common with reptiles than do birds or mammals. They were the most successful creatures in history, but not just because they happened to be there. They were dominant because they outcompeted all others, including mammals. In fact, they're still not extinct. They survive today in the form of their descendants, the birds.

Dinosaurs were too successful to have died out because of any earthbound mechanism. They were driven out by an extraordinary event—the impact of an asteroid ten miles or more in diameter. During the past decade, evidence has led to discovery of "the bullet hole," a crater 185 miles across and more than 12 miles deep on the north side of the Yucatan, known as the Chixulub crater.

This changing view of the Mesozoic world has caused a revolution in dinosaur paleontology. It is my good fortune to have witnessed and to now play a role in this revolution. As far as dinosaur paleontology is concerned, these are the "good old days."

As my perspective of the past has matured, so has the STAR TREK universe—through books, movies, and new TV series. I've followed all these permutations. Many a night around the campfire, discussions of the ancient world would shift gears as the stars above beckoned, and we would start talking about STAR TREK.

After graduate school, I became a gypsy scholar and hoped for a permanent job. For a popular subject, paleontology has always offered few jobs, so I considered myself lucky when I landed a job actually doing paleontology.

The Dinamation International Society (DIS) was the brainchild of Chris Mays, President and CEO of the Dinamation International Corporation. DIC is world famous for its traveling robotic exhibits of which the dinosaurs are the most famous. Chris formed a nonprofit organization dedicated to promotion of earth, biological and physical sciences, and particularly that most interdisciplinary of all, dinosaur paleontology. I was hired by Executive Director Mike Perry as DIS's first employee, to oversee a participant-funded dinosaur research program. Dinamation's Dinosaur Discovery Expedition program provides manpower and funding for dinosaur research and gives the amateur public a chance to dig dinos. We've worked with host institutions in Colorado, Utah, Wyoming, Arizona, Mexico, and Argentina, and have programs pending in England, Indonesia, and perhaps Morocco. We're now the largest organization conducting dinosaur digs. Now, I'm teaching people from every walk of life who love dinosaurs and the process of discovery. There's nothing more fun than watching someone uncover something new to the human experience.

If you'd like to know how you can get your hands and knees really dirty and live to tell about it, call 1-800-DIG-DINO.

Even more exciting than working with such an enthusiastic audience is the fact that we've made several important discoveries. It was excavating a new dinosaur discovered by amateur fossil hunter Rob Gaston that unexpectedly led me, Don Burge, and my other colleagues from the College of Eastern Utah Prehistoric Museum to the discovery of Utahraptor.

Now, here's the kind of dinosaur to discover if you want to make a big splash with the public! One of the most sophisticated hunting machines the world has ever known, the dromaeosaur—or "raptor"—was a terrifying dinosaur. At twenty feet long and 1,000 pounds, Utahraptor was the largest raptor ever found. We released the story and were feeling pretty pleased with the worldwide coverage, when I got a call from Diane Carey.

Diane had read an article about Utahraptor in *Discover* magazine and wanted to know how the heck I knew that this animal hunted in packs. Now, I knew here was someone who wanted the inside scoop. Not many people will call the editor of a national magazine and harass him until he gives up the phone number of a source. In fact, Diane is the only person ever to phone me as a direct result of an article.

I explained that raptors were fast and coordinated, as anything that killed with knives on its feet had to be, and that the best-known raptor, Deinonychus, was known from a site where five were buried with a much larger prey animal. Certainly they were specialists in killing animals much larger than themselves.

If you'd like to see the life-sized robotic Utahraptor in all its gory splendor, visit us at the Devil's Canyon Science and Learning Center in Fruita, Colorado, just off Exit 19 on I-70, by the entrance to the Colorado National Monument.

The conversation with Diane ultimately strayed to her line of work, and for me this was too good to pass up. I told her about a story line I'd come up with during one of those long nights around the campfire. The story was based on an intellectual exercise proposed by Dr. Dale Russell of the National Museum of Canada, who noted that the most intelligent of dinosaurs, the troodonts, may have had the potential to evolve into a technical species had their stay on Earth not been cut short by extinction.

I related my idea to Diane, who suggested we collaborate. She and her husband, story developer Greg Brodeur, and I molded the original story line and finally developed the story you now hold in your hands.

FOREWORD

A percentage of the royalties from *First Frontier* will go to Dinamation International, to help continue our explorations.

We've merged the STAR TREK universe with that of Earth's past, and in our own way expressed my long-held belief that, when we look closely, deep time is not at all different from deep space.

See you in the future, and in the past. . . .

James I. Kirkland, Ph.D.,
Dinamation International Society,
1-800-DIG-DINO

FIRST FRONTIER

Prologue

A SCENT OF ENEMIES over the ridge.

Sounds. Scents. Vibrations on the harness sensors.

Even before the instruments told her, her instincts were there to tell her. Living things over the ridge.

Not many, but enough. A science outpost wouldn't be populated by very many.

The real question was not how many, but how many *what*. And how strong, how determined, how armed.

Mythology blistered the air. Whispered rumors, legends of an opportunity so outlandish they had barely spoken about it even among themselves during their entire voyage to this region of space.

There was no room for failure. Even after the loss of nearly half their crew, she pushed them on, searching for a technology older than any known settled planet, a place so out of the way that no one wanted it.

If it still existed.

I insist in my mind that it does.

"Oya, . . . don't . . . *lag!*"

The technicist bowed her head in acknowledgment of the director's snap. A silent answer to buoy her silent doubts.

Until now the terrain had been spongy, pierced with rocks. As Oya's footpads would sink into the moss, a stone would press up and push her off. Her bad leg would buckle, and she would thrash for balance. The others had been struggling, too, twenty-two thick tails swinging in exaggerated arcs.

Now the ground was hard, but her feet were sore and her thighs ached. She wished there was more cover. This whole planet was barren, ugly and gray.

At least they had left their bright livery on the ship. These polished utility harnesses, launcher gauntlets, spatterguards, and shell belts were the least color she could convince them to wear. They were on a stealth mission—entirely against their nature. Spikers didn't like to be quiet. They were too young and so impatient that it had become custom to paint only two colors on their faces, and in time the two-colored face had come to identify them.

And Oya disdained being in back, but that's always where she was. Always behind the ones who got to fight first, to eat first, and to rest first. Instinct needled her forward, to slash and kick her way up there, to be a leader. She watched the bright yellow, red, and bronze necks and heads of the female directors, and she let envy chew at her.

The males were hungry. There was no eating before a maneuver, but no males had ever gotten used to that. Their heads were low with frustration. Their necks curved and swayed. They swiveled their eyes back and forth, willing to snap at rodents in the rocks or anything else they saw. Hunger crowded their minds.

"Rusa." She waited, but there was no response. Again she said, "Rusa."

The director nearest her glanced back. On Rusa's face three bands of colored paint identified her quickly, even in the oblong shadows cast by these ruins.

Oya hissed, "Keep control of them."

Rusa arched her neck. "Don't tell me my work."

The scent of prey teased Oya's nostrils, and she caught glimpses of movement beyond the rocks . . . not rodents.

Enemies were there, real ones, very close, shifting back and forth, talking, working.

"They must not eat," she said, pushing a growl on the end of every word. "We'll never have this opportunity again. You keep control!"

Rusa drew up sharply, her eyes dirty with resentment. "You are a technicist. That's *all.*"

"This is my mission."

"I don't care about you. This place doesn't look like the legends say. We're in another wrong place. If we get a fresh meal out of it, good."

Oya took a long step to draw herself out of the rear, lowering her shoulder to push the spiker in front of her down and out of the way. "This is the right place! You know how difficult it was to hold orbit!"

"So what?"

"You know the theory! The doorway is on a dry planet with—"

"Theory, legend, all the same."

"It's not the same." Oya had to draw her voice inward just as she wanted to spit. They could be heard from here. "This is the place! You *must* keep contr—"

Her bad leg folded, and she stumbled, but she was able to right herself without falling. Two of the spikers and one of the other female leaders glanced back at her, but none made a sound. They didn't care about her any more than Rusa did. They hated her authority, that she could tell them to retreat or order them onward, outpost after outpost, until they found the right one or ran out of supplies and died in space.

Or until they were caught and humiliated before the civilized galaxy even more than they already were.

Two-thirds forward through the silent, swaying line of brown bodies and bright necks, Rusa twisted her long neck and made motions with her tail and hands, gesturing the spikers into position. The single file broke up. The spikers fanned out. One by one they sank into hiding places among the rocks.

Oya drew her head downward and lowered her tail. Her legs folded, and her body settled down onto them. Cool rock cradled her thighs. The scent of their targets entered her nostrils, flowed back into her sinuses and down along the rims of her tongue, and now she could taste them, too. Sweat. A touch of salt.

The taste made her want to pump forward, attack, rip, and gulp. What must it be doing to the young males?

They were panting, shaking, shifting their weight more than they should be on a stealth mission.

Carefully she moved her head enough to look down at her readings on the harness-mounted sensors. A handful of living beings, moving casually . . . scattered temporary dwellings around a large ellipsoid rock formation . . . massive, sprawling ruins, very old . . . some concentrations of metal and synthetics—probably scientific equipment.

Upright beings, bipedal, about the height of the spikers, a head smaller than the females of her team. No tails.

Keeping low, Rusa moved back toward Oya and kept her rough voice low. "What are they?"

Oya kept her own voice low and her head down. "Mammaloids. Could be Vulcan . . . Klingon . . . Terran . . . Romulan. Can you see their heads?"

"We will smash their heads," Rusa hissed. The fire in her belly shone in her bright eyes. "Easy kills."

"They have no precautions against attack," Oya confirmed. "Keep one of them alive for me."

Rusa's bright yellow throat rippled. Rough abutting scales flickered above her armored vest. Her eyes were heavily shaded under their protective brow plates, but the excitement glared through.

"I'll keep one head." She folded a clawed hand and motioned Oya back.

Oya straightened her neck until her eyes were on a higher level than Rusa's. "The mission is mine. I have authority, too. I deserve to provoke."

"You're not in training as a spiker leader anymore." Rusa's expression flared. "You sucked on six or eight generations of respect because of it, but those days are shrinking. This batch of youngsters has no respect for you. To them you're only a technicist. They won't follow you. I won't follow you either."

"Then they must do exactly as you tell them. You must keep control of them!"

"I will."

"That's what you said the last time!"

Rancor boiled in Rusa's face. "I'm saying it again. Go away, thinker."

"Make them use weapons," Oya persisted. "And take prisoners." She turned her head and angled back into the rocks, taking the chance that Rusa wouldn't slice her team technicist's head off and call it a casualty.

Anticipation shuddered through the crouching spikers, each a mottled ball jutting from a crevice. Hunger enflamed their young eyes, left their mouths slightly open. Their lips quivered and showed the tips of ivory ripping teeth. Beyond the rocks, the prey were moving.

The spikers twitched, hunched their shoulders, dug their claws into dry dust. Rusa raised her large head and stiffened her stance to hold them back.

Oya watched with ripening envy. She remembered how it had been, training to lead the spikers before the accident that crippled her leg. Now, all she could be was a scientist, to sit around day upon day and think.

And she had thought up this mission. Presented it before a leadership desperate enough to listen. And here she was.

She pressed to the cliff abutment and wallowed in umbrage. If this mission dissolved, her people would slip back again to living in the bushes just as they had before—cycle after cycle for millions of years. The ugly image grew crimson in her mind. At least as a technicist she was a valuable evil, a modern necessity—one of those who sit and think. A step above those who only sit.

She would eat humiliation raw if she could be the one to keep the backsliding from happening again.

"Attack," she murmured. "Attack!"

Rusa and the other female leaders cranked their long necks around to glare at her, but too late. The spikers erupted around them and didn't care who gave the order. They were young, their blood was hot, and they were no good at stealth. Hissing and snapping as their senses took over, the males flushed over the rocks and jumped into the arena around the big rock formation.

"Weapons only!" Oya bellowed.

As soon as she cleared the rocks, she saw their targets and the research outpost they had established. A dozen or more mammaloids, small eyes wide with shock, some frozen in place, others diving for cover.

The mammaloids scattered. The spikers shot incendiary darts from their cuff launchers as they had been so carefully drilled to do. Flames skittered on the tents and on some of the mammaloids' clothing, driving them to the ground.

Head crests bristling, tails whipping, slash-claws flexed, the heavy-legged spikers pounded into the camp. From where Oya stood back against the rocks as ordered, she saw only two of the spikers but could hear the others and the panicked noises coming from the victims.

The mammaloids were maneuverable beings, quick to understand what was happening to them. They were good fighters. Oya thought they were all male, but she couldn't be sure. This slim upright anatomy was common in the settled galaxy, and these could be any of a hundred species, a thousand races.

Can there be so many of the conqueror kind, and so few of us?

The spikers whirled in calculated half-circles, balancing in a beautiful way, one foot at a time on their two walking toes, and they fired a volley with each pause.

The mammaloids were good hiders and quick with their own weapons—phasers. Recognizable. Very effective. Needle-thin and unforgiving. *Phasers . . . that's right.*

Streaks of glowing energy lanced from the fog. Oya kept her head low and tried to sift the scene for more clues, but the confusion and spurts of movement blended to make this almost impossible. She held her breath and reassured herself with what little she already knew.

So far the spikers were channeling their aggressiveness

into extreme speed and risk. They moved in plunges and rushes, more foolhardy than the pause-and-fire method of the female directors.

Bodies littered the ground, stunned and heaving with effort. *Weapons only, weapons only.*

She chanted the order in her mind and thought it might hold, until one of the mammaloids—a thick, muscular one whose eyes were dark and mane nearly black—pounded from a hiding place with some kind of knife in his hands. The blade was short but sharp.

"Bring him down!" Oya shouted to the spiker he was running toward. "Turn around!"

The sound of her voice startled the mammaloid, and he veered away from her but didn't stop his charge. He raised the sickle blade and swung it high, forward.

But the spiker had heard her, too, and to him her voice was more than just the hissing roar it was to the alien guard. He swung around, arching his tail outward in a reflex that would sweep the area clear by the time his throat and chest were in line with the charging enemy. The tail came in contact with the big blade.

The mammaloid saw that he had lost his chance to slice the spine of his target and managed to control his blade as it struck the spiker's swinging tail, putting all his weight into redirecting the attack. His blade made a hollow whistle as it swept downward at an angle. The spiker dropped back a step, and only that saved his life. The blade sliced across the spiker's shoulder, rode across his throat, and was deflected finally by the heavy harness covering his chest.

Red blood sprayed the mammaloid in the face. He was driven to one knee by the inertia of his attack and had no time to raise the heavy sickle again. The spiker bellowed, a passionate thanks for breaking him free from standing orders. Pain acted in his favor and made him move faster toward the alien who had attacked him.

He roared over the being's head and reached down.

"Hold back! No slashing!" Oya called to him. When he ignored her, she swung around. "Rusa! Control them! Control them!"

But the spiker plunged forward in ram-slash style, spread his hands wide, extending the claws on his fingers, and got the mammaloid by the face. He slashed his victim from throat to groin with the big claw on his foot.

Torn fabric rolled back and entrails pushed out the gash. The creature's white eyes widened.

Oya charged forward. She had to separate them.

The spiker slapped her aside. Before she could recover and use her greater mass against him, he pushed his snout into the mess and shook it back and forth. His growls were answered by the roars and thrusts of other spikers suddenly ram-slashing other victims. Contagious wildness blurred their minds.

The leaders didn't bother to stop them. Blood had been spilled, and the females were hungry, too. As the craving clouded their thinking, they stopped caring about how a feast would leave them or about why they were here in the first place.

The scent enticed Oya and made her want to join the young fighters, to club-kick and slash her way to that succulent passion she smelled and heard from the spikers and their leaders.

She raised her bad leg and lowered her mouth to it, taking the crippled foot in her teeth. The taste of skin and dirt . . . the scent of free-flowing blood . . . If she could bite off her own foot she would taste what the spikers were tasting and push herself into the riot. In a few moments wound-shock would set in, and she wouldn't care whether it was a victim's limb or her own.

Suddenly, there was blood everywhere. The males roared and plunged, driven by their own pain, every pierce of their own hides or their enemies' thin skin, every thunderous volley as the victims fought back against the headlong attack. Salvos of phaser fire still skittered along the hard ground, answered by shells from the spiker leaders' leg-launchers, but the scene was under domination by the spikers now.

Battling for control over her own mind, Oya used her

tongue to push her foot out of her mouth and gritted her teeth hard. The smell of blood and shredded flesh muddled her thoughts, but she clung to her purpose. She had to move and function, or her instincts would make her forget why she was here.

Blood sprayed and ran along the rocks. Strangled screams bounced across the clearing. Limbs of the butchered mammaloids littered the ground. The dwellings were on fire, giving the mammaloids no cover other than the rocks, and they couldn't run fast enough to outrun the spikers.

Two spikers were using their ripper claws to hack at a small standing structure, probably a supply bin, and Oya realized that one of the mammaloids had locked himself inside it. A flash of hope punched through the daze of instinct. She dodged and barely missed the ripper-plunge of one of the spikers who had lost his ability to distinguish between friend and foe. He took a sidelong hack at her with a foot claw, but she whacked back with her large hand.

He got the message and angled away. Ignoring the phaser volleys streaking across the clearing, he pushed his blunt snout into a mass of slaughtered enemy and began to gorge.

Oya stepped over the young spiker and his lunch, ducked through pulsing cross fire, and struck out toward that supply bin. Two other spikers were tearing at the bin with their hacking claws and pounding at it with spent launcher casings. She would have to fight them off if she was to save that mammaloid inside the bin for questioning.

Had there been time for a distress signal? Why was this outpost here? What were the purposes of these old rock formations? Were the legends right?

The questions caused her to salivate. She clamped her mouth closed and banished the heavy scent of blood and bowels; she was nearly there. There were fewer screams now. Almost all the victims were finished. The silence triggered a deep afterkill hunger, and she had to battle that down, too.

She fixed her eyes on the variegated tails of the two spikers pounding on that bin. The creak of metal spurred her forward, and she jumped. A touch of that old spiker training surged back and even her bent leg responded. Pain belted through her hips, but she slashed her way between the two spikers.

A yellow and black tail struck her across the face, driving her down. Her knee cracked against the base of the storage bin, but as she went down, she lashed out at one of the spikers. He fell sideways, she fell forward, and the metal bin vibrated against her harness.

The downed spiker lay on his side and kicked, confused about whether he was standing or not. Oya shoved her elbow into his thigh, levered herself back onto one foot, and blunt-kicked the other spiker in the ribs. He staggered back, red-rimmed eyes blinking at her like mechanical flashes.

Oya vaulted up and reached inside the gashed supply bin. The creature inside hacked at her, but her arm was long enough that none of the blows reached her neck or face. She would pull him out, save him for—

She was hit from behind, a blow across the neck. One of the spikers bumped past her, then the other, both hissing and snapping, to the torn metal opening in the bin and they fought over the captive inside.

One of them put his foot on Oya's neck and pressed her to the dirt. Energy shells sheeted the ground near her legs, and she realized other victims were still fighting. Their screams told her the spikers were earning their name.

Not many weapons here, not a heavily defended outpost. Could this be the right place? Doubts chewed at her. The place they sought—anyone with sense would defend it to the extreme. Or someone might come and try what she intended to try. But could such a dry, dead place be the portal to paradise?

A wild scheme, but her people were half wild and willing to snatch at a chance. She would give them that chance if she could.

If she could get past these two brats.

The creature inside the bin had some kind of weapon to fight with, a club or shard of metal. The spikers flinched as their faces and arms were hacked every time they reached inside, but they kept grabbing. Suddenly one spiker got a metal point in the eye and stumbled backward, half his face torn. Blood pumped out of the eye socket. Oya pushed him out of the way. In spite of his injuries, his instincts had hold of him and he tried to punch forward again, but she kept him back with her own outrage.

She grasped the shoulder of the other spiker and pulled. He arched his back and neck, keeping his head inside the hole. His shoulders flexed as he pushed deeper, and the bin shuddered with the gasps and thrashing of the mammaloid inside.

"No!" Oya roared. Again she scrambled up, this time aiming for the spiker's legs. He felt her grip his lower leg and kicked at her.

Intoxicated and combative, the spiker beat her back with three limbs and his tail, with the other arm buried in the bin, slashing at the captive.

Hope fled as Oya heard the screams from inside dissolve to gagging, then chop to silence. A dirty kill.

She dropped back. The spiker kicked maniacally at her, then turned to concentrate on his task. He pulled away from the bin and with both hands pulled out his winnings.

The captive was now carrion. Its body was cleaved almost in half, its head unrecognizable, sliced at least three times from ear to chin. One of its arms was missing. The spiker drew the corpse out and was chewing on its ribs even before its feet cleared.

Blood splattered Oya as the spiker whipped around with his prize and retreated to indulge. The bywords of her culture throbbed through the scent of blood and entrails. *Full belly, empty mind.*

She still didn't know what species this was. She still didn't know if they had raided the right outpost.

It didn't fit the legends of lush scenery, vaulted mountains, temperate air, and burgeoning prey. Here there were only rocks lying against a yawning sky, with air made stale by so little plant growth.

Around her the spikers and their female leaders crouched over gushing lunch, overgorging themselves on their victory. It would be hours before their heads cleared. If a distress call had been sent and another enemy group came, all these would be dazed and helpless.

Oya clamped her mouth shut. The smell of blood, bile, and discharge made her mind sizzle, but she forced herself to beat down her desire to eat.

These others wouldn't get their minds back for hours after surfeiting themselves. She had been afraid of this since first rising from her saddle in the spacecraft. The seats weren't as comfortable as everyday furniture that supported their necks and tails, too, but comfort wasn't the idea. Space travel was only a purpose, not a luxury, and it was the most advanced of their sciences—to be able to leave their home planet and trundle out into space, possibly to take advantage of one technicist's crazy idea, a chance to give their race the great destiny promised by nature.

After months of living on blocks of frozen meat and nutrient tablets, could she beat them back from fresh, salty, wet meat when they got it?

Well, she could *try,* if she wanted a look at her own innards.

She moved cautiously across the stinking clearing, battling to keep her mind, to survey the large rock formation at the center of the outpost. Frustrated and doubtful, she shook her head and turned back. She moved toward Rusa.

The big female leader had pushed her large head almost inside the stretched, gaudy corpse of a mammaloid who had been cut lengthwise from neck to knee, and she was wobbling back and forth to force the guts out. Staying out of tail-slash range, Oya circled around into Rusa's periphery. Rusa's eyes were glazed as if drugged, her face pasted red with the blood of the vanquished. Her large face turned slightly toward Oya, and she blinked. Through the glaze her eyes focused a little. Oya made a motion with her hands— nothing overt—but enough, she hoped.

Rusa seemed to go back to her meal but then reached up, punched the dangling head of her victim until it snapped loose, and batted it toward Oya.

Oya scooped the head away from Rusa, then picked it up

and moved well out of hacking range. The smell filled her senses. Just one lick . . .

She brushed the blood-matted hair away from the ear. Not Vulcan . . . not Romulan.

Saliva dribbled from her back teeth out the corners of her mouth. She pressed her tongue hard to her palate and shuddered. She pushed the hair away from the top of the victim's head. Not Klingon.

The open eyes were blue. Not native Rigelian.

She smelled it. The scent rolled back into her skull and turned into taste.

Terran. Probably Terran. *Human.* She lifted her head to fill her nostrils with the scent. And there against the sky she saw the circular formation of stone that would be the saving of her race.

"This is the place," she said through a convulsive shiver. "*This* is the place . . ."

She looked closely at the round formation again and forced herself to think like a scientist, past all the trappings of legend, to the facts before her.

"Rusa," she said, "this is the place. Say good-bye to everything you've ever known. No more shame for us. Today, everything will be different."

The spiker leader tilted toward her, looked at her, but kept chewing at the ribs of her headless meal. Her eyes were glazed.

Oya tasted in the air all the primitive instincts that had curtailed her culture and the bitterness of their slow development.

No more. There would be domination as nature intended.

She looked down and turned the head in her hands until the face no longer gaped up at her. The passion rolled through her. Her thoughts swelled and turned to fog.

Dreaming of the coming hours, she gave up and pushed her snout into the exposed flesh.

PART ONE

HIGH WARP

Limitless power mad with endless rage
Withering a soul; a minute seemed an age.
He clutched and hacked at ropes, at rags of sail
Thinking that comfort was a fairy-tale . . .

                                        —John Masefield

Chapter One

"BATTLE STATIONS. All hands ready for incoming fire."

Apprehension needled the ship's bridge. Something about that old-fashioned way of using *ready* as a verb. Worked every time.

The captain heard his own voice throb through the dozen-plus primary decks and the dozen more engineering decks far below, but he felt detached from the sound.

The communications officer would gladly have done that job—probably should have—and announced general quarters, but at times like these the captain liked to do it himself, let the crew hear his voice just before he plunged them into thunder. It was almost an apology before the fact, testimony that he was here, on the bridge, putting his own hand into the fire first.

Trying to be deadpan without being spiritless almost broke his neck. Battle stations. Battle stations. Okay, people, general quarters. Cool, not hard-hearted. Controlled without being soulless.

There should be a class at the Academy on this. Dispassion 202.

He almost stuck a finger in his ear to rattle out an itch,

then thought about what that would look like. "Raise shields," he added. He tapped the communicator on his chair's arm console. "Engineering, confirm you have shield control."

The voice of an assistant came through, a little cocky. *"Shields confirmed routed through warp engines, sir."*

"Stand by."

He'd never had to practice being an inspiration in emergencies—he could do that. His natural ability to rouse a crew had won him both awe and contempt. But this was different. This was inviting destruction to come on over and take a potshot.

Yellow alert lights creased the bridge's upper level, casting amber slashes upon the half-dozen faces most familiar during day watch and three or four others assigned to subsystems stations by their department heads.

The captain drew a breath into his muscular, compact body and felt it almost immediately pushed back out. He needed another dose of medication and almost turned to the ship's surgeon standing behind the command chair, but his mind was on the incoming fire and that's where he insisted it stay.

"This is Captain Kirk of the *Starship Enterprise,* authorizing full-impact attack. You may fire when ready, Gridleys."

"Gridley One, aye. Starship Exeter *preparing to fire, Jim. Gridley Two, take position and acknowledge."*

"Gridley Two, Captain Phillips, U.S.S. Farragut, *acknowledging."*

"Captain Phillips," Kirk said, "congratulations on your first field assignment."

"Thank you, Captain. I'm ready when you both are."

"I think we just said we were ready," Kirk muttered flatly. "Stay sharp, everyone."

He leaned hard on his right elbow and glared restlessly at the forward screen. The black rectangle showed a beautifully generated picture of space before them—well, maybe a little down and to the right—where two starships hovered on two different planes of attack.

It was disquieting to look at the other ships, perfect

—if slightly newer—echoes of the *Enterprise,* with starlight flickering on their dish-shaped primary hulls' white plates and the stiff spines of those nacelles going back like strong chalk marks above the low-slung engineering hulls.

They'd been in war games before. *Enterprise* had always shown herself a tough customer, taking more than she was designed to take. One of only twelve in a mighty big galaxy, the first of her kind, older, more battered, and more hardened than any—their starship was their life. Letting somebody take shots at her plied against the grain of any crewman's mettle.

So let's get to it. Ready, aim, fire. What was taking so long?

"Lieutenant Uhura," he began, swiveling to see the woman at the communications console, "cut off the chatter. I don't want to know when they give the order to fire. That cancels out the worth of the test."

"Yes, sir," the graceful woman said and had the noise blanked before her own voice finished.

"Actually, it doesn't, Captain," a low voice drummed from the upper deck at his right. "The new shield technology's reception of impact from any angle has no relation to surprise."

Kirk glanced up there. "But it has a relation to *me.* Thank you, Mr. Spock."

His Vulcan first officer regarded him with those unaccommodating dark eyes set in angles beneath gunshot-black brows that were also angles. The face of a thousand subtleties. Not grim exactly. Earnest, with spice. He didn't look like anybody else here, hovering above them with his helmet of black hair and that blue uniform shirt the only science entity on the bridge. Everybody else wore the command gold or the bright red of engineering—

No, that wasn't right.

Kirk swiveled and glanced to his left at Leonard McCoy. The doctor was also in blue but wearing a short-sleeved, tight-fitting, glossy medical smock.

Well, so he couldn't count his blues today. Or maybe Spock just wore it differently.

McCoy was looking down at him as though he could read

his mind. "Want another treatment, Jim?" the doctor muttered, holding his voice down. No sense blurting out to the bridge crew that their captain was under the weather.

Though no one said anything or even glanced at him, Jim Kirk knew they had all registered his reddened eyes, the glaze of fever on his cheeks, his Academy-trim sandy hair now sweat-drenched and flopping in his eyes, and the bulb of swollen leg he tried to hide under the other boot. That's what he got for going first into inclement planetary conditions instead of letting some brawny yeoman go first.

"Not now," he said.

"You can't fight this off," McCoy insisted. "This is the bite of a hairy thrillkiller scorpion. Now, how do you figure that animal got its name? This isn't a hangover. You know what this means?"

"Means it hurts."

"Means it's seventeen times as toxic as the bite of a king cobra and about forty times harder to cure, and the victim had better cooperate with his friendly dockside physician. What you're feeling is inflammation of the joints. You should be convalescing."

"I don't even like the sound of the word, Doctor. I'm not that sick."

McCoy waggled a writing stylus at him. "Only because we live in these times. That bug thinks he killed you. He'd be right if I wasn't around."

"The test first." His elbows were shaking. He drew them closer to his ribs and tried to position himself casually in the command chair.

"Well, what's keeping them?" the doctor beefed.

Kirk pivoted his chair back toward the main screen. "That's a good question. Ship to ship."

"Ship to ship, sir," Uhura echoed.

"Kirk to *Exeter*. Is there a delay?"

"Newman here. No delay—we're just coordinating our firing sequences."

Kirk glanced up at Spock for that flicker of tacit agreement that was always there. Almost always.

"Understood . . . but I would suggest, gentlemen, that enemy fire is rarely coordinated."

"Point taken, but, we don't want to hit you with too much too fast."

"I wish you would." Hearing the crab in his voice, he glanced at McCoy. His plundered leg throbbed. "Field testing these warp-powered shields with starships would be a waste of time if we didn't throw all we had at them. Especially considering the next step."

"Since you're the man who's going to take that next step," Douglas Newman responded, *"we'll do it your way. Prepare for random fire."*

"Acknowledged. Kirk out. All right, everyone, this is it. Let's not have anyone get carried away and start returning fire."

A faint thump on the lower starboard deck beside him drew his attention, and turning his head displayed a sore neck that hadn't been sore a minute ago.

"Captain, if I may"—Spock appeared beside him, hands clasped behind him—"respectfully suggest I relieve you for the duration of the warp-shield testing."

His expression was mild, or maybe Kirk just saw the mildness under the severity of Spock's reputation. "Thank you, Mr. Spock, but either I'm up on the bridge with a bad leg and a fever, thinking about the tests, or I'm in my quarters with a bad leg and a fever, still thinking about the tests. Since I can't get away from it, I might as—"

The fever took him by the brain and blurred the screen before him. Fever? With one hand thrust out and down, he kept himself from rolling.

It was a phaser hit. McCoy was picking him up.

As he was stuffed back into the command chair, Kirk noted with gratitude that the doctor had the sense not to ask him out loud if he was all right.

"Friendly fire," he grumbled, his eyes fixed upon the wide forward screen.

"Pardon, sir?" In front of him, Helmsman Sulu leaned toward him without really turning.

Kirk pressed his back against the warm black leather of his chair. "Nothing, Lieutenant. Present all shields to them in random sequence. If there are any weak points in this technology, I want them found right now."

"Aye, sir. Executing."

Spock bent over his panel's viewers and warned, "Second volley incoming."

"Brace yourselves," Kirk snapped. This time he clung hard to his chair.

The phosphorus blue lights of two—three—full-strength phaser bolts bloomed from *Exeter*'s outer hull, made a true line to the *Enterprise*, struck their new shields, and crackled around the ship.

Dipping far to port with the seizure of the hit, the ship fought against the artificial gravity that was their unseen lifeline. She righted herself almost immediately, compensators howling.

Kirk wiped his brow. "Good shields."

The two other ships veered off their positions on separate angles, one sideways and one on the z-minus. He suddenly envied their moves, the action of the game. His job was to be the sitting duck and take the hits.

"Sulu, hard port, one-half impulse."

The helmsman's shoulders tucked a fraction; the *Enterprise* moved.

"What are we doing, Jim?" McCoy asked quietly.

"Might as well make the lesson worthwhile on their sides, too. Let them hit a moving target."

The other ships didn't hail them. They just responded. There seemed to be an extra lilt to the phasers crashing along *Enterprise*'s shield envelope now.

"Mr. Nourredine, shield status?"

At the engineering subsystems monitor, a gangly mideastern ensign said, "Mr. Scott reports no drains and no sign of overload whatsoever on the warp tie-in. Space-time element seems to be working right along with warp theory as—"

"Thank you. Uhura, notify *Exeter* and *Farragut* that we're warping out. I want to see how the tie-in works when there's a hyperlight drain on the warp engines."

Spock straightened and turned. "That is not in the test program, sir."

Kirk looked up at him.

Spock tipped his head. "Logical."

"Go to warp one."

"Warp one, sir," Sulu responded.

The starship hummed around them, more a feeling than a sound, and dipped gracefully through open space. Salvos from the other two Starfleet vessels pounded against the new-tech shielding at undiscussed angles, causing the phasers to distort as they skittered across the impact plane. Starfleet phasers at this proximity were terrifying weapons and Kirk sensed his crew's fears. No one knew better than Starfleet people how exterminatory their own weapons could be. It was easy under enemy fire to believe those doing the shooting were insufficient or behind the times, but today they were ordered to take a full-power pounding from their own science and that was different. Big different.

Kirk indulged in a few glances to measure the expressions of his bridge team. Of all Starfleet, the twelve starships were supposed to be the best, strongest, tightest operations in the flying galaxy, by attrition their crews the best of each profession. But the reputation, implied or earned, didn't provide much armor at times like this. He saw them bury their personal fears by keeping their faces cool and blank. It was a dead giveaway. Spock had more expression right now than anybody else.

So Kirk got up and hobbled over there. "Report, Mr. Spock."

The first officer didn't turn this time. He responded only by changing his posture as he gazed into his readout screens.

"Warp tie-in stable, forward shielding unfazed . . . Midships and aft shielding show fluctuations within the one one-thousandth percent range, stabilizing now." He moved to another part of the computer complex, summoned a readout with a fanning touch, then said, "Hyperlight compensators show nominal strain."

Kirk leaned on the bridge's circular red rail and turned. "Engineering?"

"Mr. Scott reports the strain is negligible, sir," Nourredine said. "He'll have numbers for you within five minutes."

"I'm not waiting for it. Helm, reduce speed to sublight. Advise *Exeter* and *Farragut* to cease fire and regroup. All departments report any changes to the first officer. Ladies and gentlemen, prepare for stage two. Fifteen minutes from now we'll know exactly how much these shields can take. Assuming we survive."

"A fifth-magnitude sun, one of the most powerful natural forces in the galaxy. The gravitation is strong enough to hold twenty planets the size of Jupiter. Megatons of debris move at extreme speed as they are drawn inside. As we pass near the blue giant, they will have to absorb that intense gravity, ward off any solid objects, plus deflect heavy X-ray bombardment. The problem with conventional deflector shielding is that overload can occur. These new shields, powered through the warp engines, can dissipate energy through space–time. Extreme gravity tends to change the physical laws of space–time, magnifying uncertainty in any equation. At this point, physics will be based not on certainty, but on probability. This will be the final step in the test, the culmination of years of lab testing, field testing on drones and modified cargo vessels. We will be passing closer to a blue giant than anyone ever has. If the warp shields can stand up to this, we will consider them a success. Only a heavy cruiser starship is powerful enough to engage the phenomenon at this proximity with any hope of survival."

"Thank you, Mr. Spock. Is that clear, gentlemen?"

"*Very clear, Captain Kirk.*"

"*As clear as a nonphysics major can soak up, Jim. I'm glad you have Spock on your side, since you're the ones going across that monster.*"

"Appreciate that, Doug. It'll be good to know you and *Farragut* are out there in case anything goes wrong."

"*I hope we're completely useless, otherwise we'll be here to record your extermination. And I don't like that idea very much.*"

Jim Kirk stuffed a groan back down his throat and willed his swollen foot to stop hurting. He won with the groan, but the foot ignored him. He refused to let the pain show on his face.

On one of the monitors over Spock's station, Newman looked a little older than the last time they'd had contact, around the eyes mostly, but that was forgivable. *U.S.S. Exeter* had been supporting a line of defense on the Klingon Neutral Zone almost singlehandedly for eighteen months, and that was aggravating service. Not war, but a very tense peace.

On the other screen, *Farragut's* new captain showed another kind of strain—guilt, maybe—at not being the ship to go into the big fire.

Kirk knew that little guilt, and he hated it. He'd volunteered all his life for the dangerous missions just to avoid that feeling, the sensation that he should've gone instead of somebody else and didn't . . . and somebody else died.

McCoy was observing him. Kirk swiveled the chair away from the doctor's ice-blue incising eyes. "We're not betting on extermination," he said, "so don't call up your ship's logs just yet."

On the port-side screens, both captains smiled. "*No, we won't,*" Newman said. "*I didn't mean that the way it sounded.*"

"No difference," Kirk told him. "My ears are clogged up anyway."

"*Captain Kirk,*" Phillips said, "*it's within our mission schedule to give you time to recover from that injury if you like.*"

"And have you two tell headquarters that I let a six-inch scorpion slow me down? Not on your life."

"It was nine inches," McCoy muttered.

"Captain," Sulu interrupted, "we're approaching the vicinity of the blue giant."

"All stop."

"All stop, sir."

"Adjust forward screens for safe visual. All hands, yellow alert. Stand by, Captains."

He didn't wait for their responses before motioning to Uhura to cut off the communications. He wanted to sweat a little and wince a couple of times without their seeing it.

Both screens went blank. On a third monitor, *Exeter* and *Farragut* wheeled around to *Enterprise's* starboard bow and held position.

"Engage main screen to show us the blue giant."

Sulu glanced at his board just to make sure the compensators were on line and he wasn't about to blind what might be the finest bridge crew in Starfleet, then activated the screen.

"There it is," the captain uttered. "Izell."

"One of the brightest stars in the heavens," Spock filled in. "Fifty-one thousand five hundred times as powerful as Earth's sun. Its diameter is roughly ten million kilometers."

Before them, a ball of neon blue-white energy, glowing with mindless, unthinkable power, incapable of comprehending its own beauty.

Maybe that's the mark of nature, Kirk thought. *The line that divided man from everything else—that we appreciate ourselves.*

With its center of strontium-white and its electric-blue rim, the star shined with such perfect violence that it created the illusion of having another sun inside and the sensation that they could hear it sizzle. A constant flow of debris washing toward it from open space to disappear inside the licks of blue fire.

For a moment, the captain and his crew were caught up by the raw dumb triumph of the thing. No one said a word. They stood at their posts and let it burn.

For centuries artists had struggled to convey the stunning presence of a blue giant on everything from canvas to glass to crystallized fabric. No one had done it. Tourist agencies still ran shuttles of high-paying sightseers out here, because there was nothing like the real thing.

Kirk cleared his throat. "Adjust for ultraviolet spectrum."

Spock made one of those barely there motions with one hand, and the main screen changed. Ultraviolet waves flowed outward from the great mass, delineated in what appeared to be beet red pulses.

"X rays."

Another change. Flowing pulses of green to silver.

"That's a sight to see," McCoy murmured. "It's laughing at us. If we explode during this test, we won't even register on that thing. It has the power to rip a neighboring star to bits."

"It probably has," Kirk muttered. "That's all the debris gushing in and being burned up."

McCoy leaned on the command chair in a moment of commonality. "It's even bigger than Rigel."

"Yes," Spock confirmed from up there, as if anybody had asked. "However, unlike Rigel, which supports fourteen worlds, ten of which are habitable, Izell supports only eight planets, none of which bears life or has been colonized."

"We wouldn't want to tamper with somebody's sunshine," Kirk clipped, then tossed over his shoulder, "Bones, if you want to give me a treatment, now's the time."

"You should come down to sickbay for treatment," McCoy said. "You know it's a thirteen-minute process."

"It only takes thirteen minutes because you stop to give me your mission philosophy every four minutes. Just get me through the next ten, and all this will be over."

McCoy put his stylus down on the command chair's arm and wrestled in his medipack for a hypo. Obviously he hadn't expected to win this one and had come prepared.

"Hold still." He pressed the hypo to the inside of Kirk's elbow.

The captain held his breath. Shots didn't usually hurt, but this one burned going in and kept burning all the way up his arm and into his neck. At least it distracted him from his throbbing foot and its unhappy ankle.

"That'll hold the fever and infection down for about forty minutes," the doctor said. "Enough for you to get us in real trouble." He pointed at the captain's glazed face, then at the turbolift door. "You, sickbay. As soon as this test is over."

Kirk felt his mouth pull into a grin. "Understood. Now for the hard part." He shifted again and eyed the figure hovering over them on the upper deck. "Mr. Spock."

"Captain?"

"Come down here, please."

Spock moved to the captain's side but stayed a step farther back than usual. His patinaed features were strained.

Ignoring McCoy's silent curiosity and what the third presence might cost Spock, the captain lowered his voice. "All right . . . what is it?"

The Vulcan hesitated, glanced at McCoy, then drew his slashed brows together. "I beg your pardon?"

"Whatever's bothering you."

Spock looked as if he'd been blindsided. "Sir . . ."

"You haven't slept in six days," Kirk said. "You've downloaded all the information available about this test and run it again and again in your quarters. Yes—I know you're thorough, but seems to me you're also uncertain about this. I assume you've found nothing wrong with the tests up until now, because you haven't stopped us. As science officer, that's your prerogative, but you haven't done it. But everything you've said is laced with . . . let's call it suspicion. So there must be something else."

Resistance plied Spock's face. He went from one foot to the other, put his hands behind his back again, and spoke with particular deliberation. His voice was low, almost gravelly.

"There is always a frontier of science," he began, "especially in physics, which can only be understood through experience. Very often the experience does not match the theory. Extreme gravity and intense energy conditions change our equations by changing space–time around us. The more elements thrown in, the more unknowns, and the more the equation may distort."

"Are you objecting to the test?" By asking, Kirk gave him the option to get them out of this, just as McCoy could supersede the captain on medical grounds—and looked like he might any minute.

Spock paused, seemed almost to be considering that, then made a decision he wasn't happy with. "I have no basis on which to object. There are certain assumptions dealing with quantum probability matrices, but while a 'guess' will occasionally be correct and may even allow a shortcut, it will more often provide the reverse. I prefer a system of thought."

"In other words," Kirk added, "you think that in the long run we're better off with the facts in hand?"

McCoy leaned forward. "You won't admit you've just got a hunch, will you, Spock?"

Spock looked at him as though the question were serious. "I cannot countervail the test based on unease," he said. Now he looked down at Kirk, and his eyes turned decidedly sympathetic. "Unless, of course, *your* unease, Captain."

"Thank you," Kirk told him, "but I've already decided to ride it out. After this is all over, I can put my leg up and read a good book without preoccupation."

"Usually," McCoy needled, "it's you, Mr. Spock, with that hybrid physiology of yours that's so susceptible to exotic bugs."

He waited for the smart response, the cutting comeback, the intellectual razz—usually the best show on the ship—but seconds ticked by, and . . .

"Yes," Spock said. "Excuse me, gentlemen."

They watched him go. He didn't look back at them but reached for his computer consoles with both hands and sank against the units, eyes fixed on the readouts, one knee bent against the bulkhead as though to push events his way.

McCoy continued to watch Spock as the first officer fine-tuned the ship's computers. "Well," he sighed, "I guess everybody's entitled to a little forbearance now and then."

"He'll trust my hunches," Kirk pondered, "but not his own."

The doctor came forward and leaned closer. "Should we postpone the blue giant?"

No matter the doctor's low voice, no matter the distracting and horrific beauty of the great star showing its spectra like a dance hall girl flashing her petticoats before them, the words somehow carried. Kirk sensed the attention of the crew around him, though no one looked at him. They didn't have to.

But they were listening.

"This is our job," he spoke in measured tones. "We're explorers, but not only of the concrete area of open space. We're also a tool for the most hair-brained plots of Federation science. It's our job to run these gauntlets, to court disaster on purpose. To be rash with dignity."

"We're plucky," McCoy chimed. "Willing to prove we're red-blooded . . . Oh, sorry, Spock. Red and green."

"I should be writing this down," Uhura droned.

McCoy cast her a look. "This is how Zephram Cochrane stumbled onto the space warp. While looking for something else."

"Which he never found," Sulu added.

"I don't think he missed it any." Kirk pushed out of his chair and with his tone brought them back to the task of the moment. "Mr. Chekov, Mr. Sulu, plot us a course across the equatorial region. Feed the engine control directly into the navigational computers. Plot three alternative elliptical courses and two more courses directly away from the blue giant at thirty-degree angles."

"Aye, Captain," Chekov said just as Sulu said, "Aye, sir."

Kirk tapped his chair's communication panel. "Bridge to engineering."

A few seconds ticked by. That told him they were busy down there, and the engineers and assistants had been told not to answer the bridge hails themselves, but to leave that to the chief engineer.

"Scott here, sir." A solid voice. That Caledonian know-what-I'm-doing rumble.

"Mr. Scott, we're putting as much on automatic as possible on the bridge, and I want you to do the same."

"Agreed, sir."

"We're plotting two angled courses away from the blue star in case we get in trouble. Coordinate your engines to trigger with those navigational lines and give us a surge of power in order to break out of the gravitational pull."

"Makes good sense, sir. I'll feed it through to the bridge within two minutes."

"Acknowledged. Sulu, make sure the forward screen is adjusted to go black if the light becomes too intense for us to tolerate and still do our jobs. We're going to get . . . rather close."

He slid the thigh of his good leg onto the black mat of his chair but didn't settle too deeply. Moving only his eyes, he communicated wordlessly with Spock on the upper deck, then fixed his attentions forward. "Let's march up the cannon's mouth. Warp factor two."

"Warp factor two, sir," Sulu echoed.

As the ship turned into the face of Izell and jockeyed for position to run across the dangerous belt, Kirk heard the echo of his own words and clung to them for all they were worth. This was part of their job. To be dauntless in the face of nonenemies as much as enemies. To die, if necessary, for a test. To follow orders so others could call them valiant.

Chivalry?

Not exactly.

The screen went dimmer, though the blue giant burned nearly white as they turned toward it. They vectored across its equatorial region on a great arch that closed kilometer by kilometer.

Energy and gravity yanked at them and tried to push them away at the same time. The ship began to shudder as the new shields channeled all that energy through the warp effect and dispersed it into space—time like the flickering of candles in an infinity mirror. Readouts started to change so fast that the crew couldn't follow them.

Dizziness washed over Kirk's body and fogged his mind. Maybe he should've taken that treatment.

Then he looked up and saw McCoy sway, and Nourredine at the station above had his eyes closed and was shaking his head. McCoy's stylus slid off the command chair's arm. Kirk looked down at it, and his gaze locked there. Suddenly he couldn't move his neck, couldn't look up again.

He spread his fingers, leaned on the chair, and reached for the stylus.

In the middle of all this, why was he reaching for a writing implement? Leave it on the carpet—

Two frames of mind collided in his head. One said they were fine, hadn't even started the test yet. The other pushed forward into his imagination—they'd started the test and were skimming the vast blue equator.

But that was real. Wasn't it?

He straightened his back, tried to move his neck so he could look at the main screen. The stylus held his attention. He wanted to look at the main screen, but his neck still wouldn't move. Had the scorpion bite won out? McCoy said something about joints freezing up—

Kirk swallowed a couple of times to see if he had control over his muscles. He pushed a groan up through his throat to check on his voice. Still something there, but all he could do was look at the stylus as it lay there on the command chair's arm.

It tipped over the edge of the chair arm and fell again.

Again . . . *again*.

Kirk tried to turn his head, but he might as well have been sculpted from granite. Unhinging his jaw was like manipulating iron.

"Spock! Time . . . warp!"

Chapter Two

"LAUNCH MUST BE DONE from the highest ground. We must keep them moving."

"You do your science. I will keep them moving."

The spikers had eaten, so they were still lazy. The key was to get them to work just when they were getting a little hungry again but before they lost their minds.

Rusa had said that three times already. "I'll keep them moving."

But Oya was plagued with doubts and tensions. This place . . . they could lose their minds here. Such a different place from where they had begun, yet somehow just a step away.

Midheight mountains, continental fragmentation, heavy plant life, at least two major continents separated by a seaway. Much animal migration going on. Very hot air. Super tropics dripping with moisture and life. High sea level. Warm saline water carrying less oxygen than cold water, deep, sluggish, oxygen-starved ocean basins.

If only there were time to study!

But there would be. There would be.

This was spiker paradise. In a few days, they would all be able to pour themselves into this land and live here without effort. Paradise. No more rocks, no more ruins. They had come through the doorway and the galaxy would be theirs.

If only the spikers could be kept from losing their minds before that. Rusa would keep control of them.

Oya pushed herself onward through the lush vegetation, demanding of herself that she ignore most of what she saw around her and that she only glance from time to time at the sensor equipment on her harness. There would be time. All her life.

Heavy scents of animals swarmed around the team as they hauled carts overladen with equipment. They had brought everything with them when they stepped through— launchers, backup launchers, firing mechanisms and sequencers, computers and sensors, mapping equipment, nutrient rations to keep the spikers from hunting, antenna grid, guidance system, beam emitter, loading plate, crystal housings, particle accelerator, focusing shell, arming console, intermix chamber—

"Technicist! Are you *thinking* again, or are you walking? You're falling behind."

Oya was shaken brusquely from running her roster of equipment for the tenth time. The spikers and leaders could keep up a pace without strain, but for her to keep that pace required concentration.

"Yes," she mumbled to herself, "I'm walking."

Heavy air. Wet. A smell of life. The taste of it rolled on a thrifty breeze. With every step, the spikers grew hungrier. Already the males were snapping at insects, from time to time getting one. Every few minutes a domed head would lash out to the side or even directly behind, long muzzle leading outward, snaggled teeth clashing, and each time a tail went whipping out or up to compensate. They wanted to stop, set up the equipment here, and be done with it. Each time they growled and paused, Oya would have to insist for higher ground, fewer trees.

Before her, Rusa and a couple other female leaders trod through the bushes, then the line of young spikers struggled on, some trailing a loaded rig, and in front of them two more females. Their heads shifted fore and aft with each stride, arms folded tight against their chests, hands hanging limp at rest. Their legs were doing all the work today.

Here, in this uncivilized place, there was room to stride and stretch, a relief from the ordeal of getting here. Space travel had always been uneasy because of their bodies' wide turning radius. Some career spacefarers, what few there were, had their tails amputated for that reason but inevitably paid for it in loss of balance.

Not a bad place. Hot, wet, overgrown, volcanic. Frogs, lizards, salamanders, were everywhere. The spikers were snapping up a few of those here and there, too.

There would be plenty of food here after the mission. They could survive on fleshy animals, on fish, shellfish, insects, plankton—any other treats this environment could provide the healthy carnivore. There were plenty of hot-bodied animals. Smells of them, in life, in death, were everywhere. Plants could be spices and flavorings, but food was best fresh-dead and still warm.

Something came out of the sky and flapped down to whack across the line of spikers and sent them all snapping and hissing, but the creature swirled back into the sky even before Oya could get a good look at it. Small, fast, and apparently curious. If it tried to strafe them again, its curiosity would make it lunch. With luck, only one spiker would catch it. If two got a grip on it at the same time, there would be a fight.

That would take time. Oya sighed in aggravation and admitted to herself that she wasn't sure enough of her calculations. How much time would they really need to set up the launcher? Would the automatic targeters work? She either had a few minutes or a million years, and only her mind, her wild calculations that couldn't be put together on any machine held her accountable for today's success and the future's wonder.

Suddenly two of the spikers dodged to one side, both snapping at the bushes. Leaves rattled, and before Oya could see what was happening, a shapeless piece of bloody flesh spun through the air and slapped her in the eye ridge. Had they attacked each other?

"What happened! What is it?" she demanded. An aroma of raw meat and red blood swelled her nostrils as she pawed strings of ripped-up muscle off her face.

Rusa whirled toward the attraction, smacking the young males out of the way, forcing them to stay in line.

"What is it?" Oya asked again.

Pausing and looking downward at the base of a spikey plant with one lonely flower, Rusa said, "Carrion."

Desperate, Oya raised her head. "Don't let them eat!"

Too late. Three of the spikers were already picking at the carrion around Rusa's massive legs. Their eyes began to glaze as they licked, gulped, and forgot their purpose.

"This is new kill. Whatever did it," Rusa said, raising her own head to look down into the valley, "is still nearby."

"Let's hunt them," one of the female leaders said.

"No time!" Oya protested.

Rusa swiveled her head to look at her. "You don't know that. We could have a thousand years."

Oya shook her head. "This is how we lose chances."

"No," Rusa said. "This is how I keep loyalty. There's no harm in letting them hunt. If they turn on me in a bloodlust, there'll be no leader to push them forward, and your mission will be over. They'll give up and satisfy themselves with gorging and sleeping. Then where will you be?"

"In a few days, that will be all they have to do forever," Oya grumbled. "Why can't the males think beyond instinct?"

"They're good at what they do. Mind your business."

Despite the contempt her species often held for technicists, thinkers, designers, Oya realized the faith that had been put in her to devote an entire field team to her theory and for Rusa and the others to donate their lives to this cause. No matter how they leered at her or bit off her attempts to explain, they had all given themselves up. They would live out their lives here.

The divine superiority would be the Clan's, as those who had borne them to their planet first had always intended. Until now, they had failed to achieve their foreordination. Until today, there had been nothing but stalled prosperity for them, for they were contained by their lessers. Today, at last, they had a future.

An animal roared in the distance—a large one—a sound like metal grazing against gravel. A twinge of apprehension rattled through Oya's chest. The rest of their lives, here . . . Eventually their food would run out, their equipment would break down, and they would sustain themselves on the abundance of life here, unless the abundance decided to prey upon them.

She shuddered from harness to footpads. The Clan had been called primitive by many in the settled galaxy, called unevolved, underevolved, even devolved. She and her kind knew it wasn't true. No matter the likeness between Clan and creatures in the distant past, no matter what the others thought, the Federationers, the Klingons, the Romulans— the Clan knew who they were.

From now on, everyone else would, too.

Oh, she dreamed! She let her thoughts roll with the scent of blood. She dreamed of knowing what would happen, of seeing all the wondrous revelations that would occur—the magnificent accomplishments, conquests, superiority that would release upon the Clan after today. Such a future! At last, at last.

"Look!" One of the spikers raised his long hand and pointed. "There they are!"

In a shallow valley to their left, a rustling in the leaves rippled through wide-leaved undergrowth and all at once they saw a half-dozen small faces. For a moment Oya thought they were looking at a flock of birds, but the faces were leathery and greenish brown, eyes-forward and toothy.

"What are they?" one of the other females said. Her name was Aur, and she didn't talk much. There was a shudder in her voice.

"I know what they are," Oya said.

Rusa swung around, her tail echoing the movement of her head with less than grace. "Then what?"

"Flocking predators. In books, I've seen fossils of them."

"Let's take them on!" a spiker gushed, hunger in his eyes. "We can make them fight us."

The others bobbed their heads and gargled a cheer.

Oya pushed forward. "Rusa, Aur, I'm begging you."

"Spikers need sport as much as they need food," Aur said.

Without waiting for the females to argue among themselves, the spikers shed their harnesses. Moments ago they had been sluggish and exhausted, but they suddenly discovered an energy reserve. The taste of blood and meat had done that to them.

"Half of you go," Rusa said. "Front of the line, stay here."

The front spikers howled and argued. Rusa waved them down and they complied, rumbling with dissatisfaction. Even as females went, Rusa was large and had a mastering nature.

In seconds the spikers were down to bare skin and crowding the edge of the incline.

"No, Rusa, this is bad!" Oya shook her long, narrow hand in the air. "Those are advanced predators. This isn't a game to them! Don't you see what they are?"

"Animals." Rusa shook her heavy head. "Mind your science. The rest of you, go. Bring meat back, and we will not stop again until we find the place to set up the launcher."

Half the line of young males rushed over the edge of the incline and scrambled down toward the valley. They had worked for months on this project, traveled weeks in space, willingly given up their place in society and sacrificed their futures for this, and now they wanted only to play.

Ten spikers shuffled in a rush down the incline, their broad backs warmed by the envy of those left behind. The others folded their heavy legs, settled forward upon their resting bones, retracted their arms, and lined up to watch.

In the bushes below, a flurry of heels and tails answered the spikers' rush. Whistles and squeals of effort chased them like the attention of wild admirers. The spikers rattled through the brush, teasing, snapping, stomping, and breaking as many branches as they jumped over, making loud noise to attract the quick little predators. When they reached the bottom of the valley, they turned abruptly to the right and pounded toward open ground.

The small predators launched into broad pursuit, as

though they too thought they had fallen on playtime. But there was a ferocity about their play. Their necks were extended fully out, their teeth gritted and leathery lips pulled back, eyes wide beneath bony protective plates, forearms reaching and long claws touching at the air before them. They had crescent-shaped claws on their feet also, held back as they ran, but theirs were much larger in comparison to their body weight than the spikers', and the sight of the claws clacking against rock gave Oya the shiver of the lame. They would've been on her by now. They would've torn her to pieces by now.

"Rusa," she said tensely, "get the spikers back."

"It's a game, Oya."

"No, it's not."

Below, the running spikers divided into two groups and drew the predators into division also. But they failed to confuse the smaller ones. Several Clan males glanced behind, expecting to be gaining range, yet gaining none. The predators hadn't so much as paused. They separated in almost perfect symmetry, dividing like a leaf torn in half by the wind.

The spikers gargled a reaction and ran faster, enticing the predators into the open.

"At least," Oya began again, "draw your weapons."

"On lizards?" Rusa spat. "Primeval."

Oya pushed sideways past other hungry spikers chomping as they watched and made her way to Rusa. She lashed out toward the valley with one specifying finger.

"Those are not lizards! Those are warm-bloods! Intelligent! Look at the resting bones! Look at the position of their eyes! How their brains are set upon their necks—Rusa, take your weapons out!"

"It's a game. They're animals. The divine nature of the Clan is to dominate. Sit on your bone, relax, and watch."

It was Clan nature to feast on the vanquished, to waste time eating the conquered. This was part of the strong instinct that had slowed them down scientifically and let others take control of the galaxy. The Clan were good hunters, the top of the food pyramid on their planet, and had to force themselves to use intellect. Once bellies were full, they would fall behind.

Oya was a thinker and most of her life had lived with the stigma of that. The Clan could be more brilliant, pound for pound, than Terrans or Romulans or Orions or anyone else, but instinct had always overwhelmed them. Most of their science had been borrowed, kept alive by types such as her, the lower caste, the necessary evils. The most admired were the ones with blood-cunning. The superior eat.

Since she had never been able to compete physically, Oya had developed her mind. She had studied societies that developed faster, discovered that not every other living thing was only food. The deities had put her people on their planet to be the top eaters, and as such they had never been eaten.

They had never been able to find a genetic link between themselves and their own planet. They had been put on their planet without ancestors. They were the children of a higher purpose.

But when they first ventured out into the galaxy to conquer there too, they'd been driven back, held away from their purpose, their destiny as the chosen ones left unfulfilled.

Held back for generation after generation by the Federation. By the humans. Humans . . . who tasted the same as the little scurrying, crawling animals on the Clan planet.

A flush of humiliation made Oya's skin ripple. It was the same flush that had driven her to conceive this plan, to go before the leaders, explain, then explain again, then wait until after lunch, then explain again.

These young spikers were just right for this. They'd been chosen from among the hatchlings five years ago and raised to be here today. The strongest legs, the leanest bodies, not too big—just right for space travel, then long hikes through jungle, wilderness, or this hot, crunchy land.

Only she herself, Oya knew, was not up to this. But she was the one who had thought of it.

Yet, as she watched the spikers rushing through the bushes

below, she still felt the tug to be one of the hunter-chasers, one of those who always had enough to eat.

Around her, the nine remaining spikers were foaming at the teeth and quaking with excitement. Would Rusa be able to hold them back? They wanted their turn.

She screwed her eyes shut. She would never have her chance. Forever she would rely on the scraps tossed by others.

The carrion was making her wild! She glanced at it and at Rusa standing guard over it.

Oya settled down on her bone and pressed her chest forward almost to the ground. Cold anticipation crawled through her body until she shivered in spasms.

The predators were anxious to get to the open area. The spikers let themselves be driven forward, whistling with the rapture of the game. In a moment they would turn on their pursuers and attack.

The bushes fell away and the running spikers came out into the bowl of the valley, an area with scrubby growth where sand was kicked up in great puffs by pounding feet and slashing claws.

"Rusa!" Oya shouted, vaulting to her feet. "They're being eaten! Rusa, go after them!"

Even in the early tribal wars, before the planet squared away against the galaxy, they never ate each other. They even burned their enemy's dead. *None shall be devoured.*

"Rusa!"

But Rusa was staring, too, entranced by a spray of blood and slashed skin rising out of the dust cloud. "Weapons out!" she shouted. "Go down! Weapons out!"

The shocked males here on the ridge looked at each other, at Rusa, at the valley—they didn't understand. Below, the dust began to spread, to flatten against the land, giving rise to the heads and thrashing tails of the spikers.

Bloody heads, shredded tails. The scene opened to view, parting in a dozen places as a flower opens and releases its scent, but this flower was blackened, soured. From before them and from the sides, the spikers had been corralled by more than twenty predators—twenty *more*. Chased to exhaustion by a fleet they thought they were leading, the young males were trapped in a flurry of coordinated attacks. Every few seconds, one of them reared from the dust cloud, skin shorn and punctured, throats slashed, and they were drowning in the dust.

Paralyzed, Oya gasped at what she saw, her mouth open. Dust collected on her tongue and the rows of her teeth.

Rusa fired wildly across the valley, sending a stream of energy spiraling over the scene of carnage below, serving only to scatter a few of the predators. Almost instantly they realized they weren't hurt and whirled around to leap upon the panicked spikers again. The attack was brutally coordinated, quick. There was nothing of the arbitrary here, nothing of individual animals seeing to themselves. This was teamwork, and that took intelligence.

The spikers were falling to their knees, each covered with five or six small slashers whose crescent-shaped hind claws sliced between the spikers' ribs, creating lacerations like gills that wheezed precious breath out. The spikers were going down on their forearms like puppets whose strings were being cut.

"Go! Go!" Rusa roared, slamming her fists upon the backs of the spikers around her. Each time she struck, one of the young males came to his senses, brandished his weapon, and rushed down the hill into the flurry of whipping tails and arching spines.

When five were gone, Rusa held back the rest. "Use your weapons!" she called to the fresh team. "Fire! Fire!"

Two of the young ones skidded to enough balance to use their weapons. Spirals of energy blurted into the slaughter, blasting the small predators away from their prey, but not enough.

"Look!" Oya shouted. "More!"

Out of the bushes, ten, twenty, twenty-five more predators came flooding at the fresh spikers, some only to be slaughtered in the beams of the weapons. But even the fresh males couldn't move fast enough to take down so many organized attackers. The energy weapons whined and spat. Flesh blew away. Shattered bones flew off and dug furrows in the sand.

The dust cloud rose again. Weapons clunked to the ground, spent, useless. Others fired with blunt, spitting deliberation.

Gradually the slashers gave up and scrambled for the cover of heavy overgrowth. The spikers gained control over the site.

"Come back! Hurry!" Rusa waved her weapon over her head to break the trance of the shocked youngsters below. "Leave them and hurry back here!"

The confused, horrified spikers scrambled up the hill, flushed with panic as they turned their backs on the bushes below and were wheezing when they reached Rusa and huddled behind her, peeking out at the valley floor.

Within moments, the bushes rattled again. The gaggle of slashers nosed their way out, eyeing the top of the ridge, and made their way to the site of the slaughter.

And they began to feed casually upon the twitching bodies of the dying youngsters.

Shivering with violent energy, heart pounding and mind aflame, Oya reached across the backs of two spikers, nearly climbing them as she did—and she might have pierced skin herself had she not realized at the last instant what she was doing—and managed to snatch Rusa's weapon out of its holster.

"We can't let it happen!"

A blunt force cracked across her face. The impact rolled down her long neck into her shoulders and sent her staggering.

"It's done," Rusa raged dreadfully, her voice sibilating. "It's over. We'll lose even more if we try to save them. Spikers, in line—*in line!* Harnesses on! Double the rigs; discard the camp equipment. Take only the science gear; stop looking over the edge! Do your jobs! Aur! Take the lead! Oya, stop looking down there. We'll go to your high ground now."

Here on the ridge, dumb with shock at what they saw below, the terrorized spikers slowly gathered their harnesses and doubled their loads, slipped into the hauling yokes, and took on the duties of those who had gone off in sport and ended up cut to pieces. Rusa, Aur, and the other females goaded them forward, anxious to get out of here before those fast devils below decided to climb the ridge.

They weren't used to this. None remembered any age in which Clan had been overtaken by predators. They had always been the toughest on their planet. Now what? Even with weapons—what? How long could their weapons last? History had just changed below them.

No paradise. For the first time in their history, Clan were being eaten.

Legs shaking like winter twigs, heart shattering in her chest, Oya rested downward and lay her extended hands upon the ground, wracked with hate for what they were being forced to do. This was a decision she knew was beyond her. She would have committed every last spiker, every last leader, until all were shredded by those smart killers below.

They would all be dead. The mission would be over. The future would be set. Rusa was right.

Oya took her place at the rear of the line, eyeing the guard at her side, who was eyeing the feasting predators below. Ahead, the familiar shuffle of doubled rigs full of equipment began again as if nothing had happened.

Limping forward, she stepped over discarded equipment that now was too much for the shrunken team to haul. She scooped up one of the rig yokes and drew it over her own head.

As she pushed forward, her head hung low and her feet moved to the cadence of spurting blood below.

Chapter Three

"WARP—TIME—WARP—WARP—"

Jim Kirk heard the ship's emergency-disengage switches trying to cross over from the new shields to the old ones, but the switch wouldn't complete. He kept trying to reach for them, to help or confirm the override, but the movement kept repeating. Yet he was aware of doing it. Each movement wasn't *entirely* new. He felt each occur, then recur.

His hand hovered over the stylus again, down there on the carpet next to McCoy's black boot.

McCoy was trying to move. Kirk sensed the attempt but couldn't look. The doctor's hand passed in front of him, and for an instant there was a hint of touch on his arm, then things changed again.

Lights from separated spectral bands passed across the carpet and McCoy's leg and what Kirk could see of his own nose as he looked down. The reflection off his own checkbones nearly blinded him. For a moment he saw the main screen as though he were still standing straight—the first few seconds of passing across the blue giant. Then he was looking down again, but no sense of movement lashed the perceptions together.

The stylus tipped and fell again.

His innards puckered as he realized what was happening. Some slices of time were caught like eddies on the banks of a rocky river, but others were moving forward, and the moving ones were hitting the stalled ones.

Now that he knew *what* was happening, *why* was it?

As human beings they had trouble accepting hopelessness, the concept that their lives might be unsalvageable, their ship irrecoverable. They'd cheated death so many times, maybe they didn't believe they could be killed. Maybe they wouldn't work hard enough against the confusion and repeats of the immediate moments. He'd have to talk to the crew about that.

He squeezed his eyes. These thoughts weren't threading together right. This wasn't the time to get philosophical. They had to get away, gain space—

The engines howled louder now, fighting for the ship's life, shutting down system after system and stealing the power, demanding of her own guts that she not be sucked past the point of no return. She'd rip herself inside out to keep that from happening. Kirk sank all his hopes into that one chance—the ship. She had no perceptions to confuse, no vision or hearing to be distorted, and didn't care how many times she noted the same thing happening. She'd fight the scrolling events again and again until she escaped or was crushed.

He would have to talk to the crew about that. Talk about that.

The stylus fell again. This time McCoy stumbled and landed on top of it. Kirk reached out to catch him but only brushed his knuckles against the doctor's bare arm before things started to change again.

Talk to the crew—

The ship bellowed so loudly he thought his eardrums would burst. Again he looked up—and this time his neck moved. Vermilion lights damned his every motion. Spock was crossing the upper deck, plunging toward the stabilizer monitors. The urgency of his plunge was offset by Kirk's damning knowledge that there was almost nothing they could do. Everything was up to the ship now, and her ability to override each surge of time within microseconds. That was the only way ground could be gained. They were down to measuring their movements in half-centimeters, and only the ship could count those as progress. What felt like recurrence to him might be progress to the ship.

That goddamned *might*—he hated it. How many times had he clung to it?

He'd have to talk to the crew.

Suddenly he fell on one hand and a knee on top of McCoy. With the other hand he caught the bridge rail. The howling of the ship changed. The engines picked up a roar of confidence and the ship tilted to starboard, enough to throw everyone sideways.

The peal of red alert knelled against the braying of hull strain and engine's bull roaring. The sounds started pulsating in his head.

"Captain!"

Spock's voice.

Kirk turned. Turned again. And again. Finally he saw Spock in his periphery and managed to keep him there.

"Accretion disk!" Spock called, forcing every syllable. "Accretion . . . disk!"

The tone told Kirk that his first officer wasn't having time glitch his words into repetitions. He had said it twice on purpose. Forcing his neck to twist until his muscles felt twice their length, Kirk pulled toward the forward screen.

The composition of Izell had changed. A ten million-kilometer-diameter blue giant star . . . had *changed*.

Great arms of pearly fire had been blown off the star in blue and white streaks and were being sucked into what appeared to be a swirling disk in space. The only definition of the disk was the matter and energy it yanked off the star by the megaton, but this was nothing like watching the natural beauty of a nebula or a swirling cluster. This was pure violence. The star was being pulled apart before their eyes—by something that hadn't been there a few seconds ago.

Nourredine crawled forward on the bridge rail and gasped, "Impossible!"

"Source, Spock!" Kirk shouted. His tongue felt like a wad of glue. "A black hole?"

Spock managed to shake his head once, very deliberately. "No source of collapsed mass—"

"Then what is it?" What he was really asking was, How do I fight it?

And Spock knew that.

Whatever it was, even if they couldn't find it, the force was behaving something like a black hole—except that there wasn't any black hole. How could there be enough gravitational force to form an accretion disk without a black hole?

"Impossible—impossible—impossible!"

The young engineer crawled forward twice more, three times, then recoiled from what was happening to him and shoved himself aft toward his post, shocked by the repetition.

"Captain!" Spock had miraculously moved from his station to the steps between the upper and lower bridge decks and was hanging on to the rail. "Speed of light—gravity—"

Kirk pulled toward him. "Say it again, Spock!"

"Gravity reacts at the speed of light," the Vulcan struggled. "If we turn into it at high warp—"

Kirk cranked around. "Sulu, comply!" he called, speaking fast, determined not to let time repeat itself before he could save his ship. "Turn into it, emergency warp factor nine!"

The order didn't make sense: turn *into* the accretion disk instead of angling away? Head into it just as those streams of crackling blue fire were doing?

Would Sulu believe him? Or think it was more distortion and do what he was trained to do?

Summoning his will muscle by muscle, a finger, a joint at a time, Kirk shifted one hand to Sulu's chair and dragged himself toward the helm. He went through the motion twice but got there.

Sulu's eggshell complexion had gone to white shellac. His hands spread over his controls as he tried to pinch the ship harder starboard. He knew what Kirk was thinking, but his hands kept repeating the motion. "Setting automatic—engaging high warp—"

48

On the screen before them, the accretion disk's fabulous gravitation yanked off solar flares the size of entire solar systems, cutting into the Izell's surface and peeling off strands of steely fire as if that was easy.

"Keep doing it," Kirk choked. "Keep doing it . . . do it again—"

"Aye, sir," Sulu rasped. "Aye, sir, sir, sir, ayesir—"

"Push your . . . velocity."

"Warp seven, sir, . . . warp eight . . . nine . . ."

Kirk pulled back toward Chekov. The young navigator's eyes were fixed on the forward screen and he was working his controls by feel, resisting the urge to use one of those preprogrammed escape angles. He had been asked by his leaders to do the insane, and that's what he was doing. His face was screwed into a grimace.

At this point physics is based not on certainty, but on probability.

"Work at it," Kirk uttered not too loud, or they might try to glance at him, and that could be fatal. They might spend their last moments glancing over and over again instead of pinching the ship out of this mess.

The *Enterprise* clung to her reputation. Strong and defiant, able to take those body blows with dispassion, she shot toward the accretion disk even as it ripped the giant star's gorgeous inferno off like a cheap wig.

A maneuver like this could peel the hull and melt the structural members. She howled as she climbed successive tiers of compensation. Now that she'd gotten her orders straight, she was scrambling to obey, slamming forward into the intense gravitational field at immeasurable speed. Caught on the side of a slippery hill, she scratched and bit her way toward her master's voice.

"Come on," Kirk murmured. "Come on."

All at once, time snapped.

Jim Kirk swore he heard the *crack.* Suddenly the star was behind them and they were plunging through open space.

A sharp mechanical howl pumped up from the engineering bulkheads on the port side, then dropped off. With it went the pulling sensation holding them all down.

Kirk stumbled—his weight was suddenly cut by nine-tenths. He caught himself on the command chair and shouted, "Shipwide compensation! Safe distance, Sulu!"

The helmsman only managed a nod, but it was the right kind of nod and freed Kirk to turn his back on the helm.

At engineering, Nourredine was crawling along the bulkhead, pulling himself toward the controls. Engineer Scott would be doing the hard work many decks below.

"Minimum safe distance, Captain!" Chekov gasped.

"All stop! Stabilize!"

Ten seconds later, the red alert's hunting-horn bawl was all that was left of the screams of near death.

Breathing like an old man, Kirk hobbled up to the engineering subsystems on the upper deck and helped the lieutenant bring down the top ends of his readouts.

Gradually the starship settled down around them, though twice as many lights were flashing as usual as the root system of mechanics throughout the ship clamored for attention, each fiber seeing itself as the most important.

Around him, Kirk's crew was gasping and groaning. Luckily, Sulu had let the ship coast on impulse past the minimum safe line and into a better zone of stability, and Chekov had kept them from piling into any debris on its way to a close encounter with that blue monster back there.

"Good work, both of you," he tossed off as he reached down for McCoy. "Bones?"

"Fine, no problem," the doctor coughed. "Just a minor broken neck . . ."

"Damage control."

Sluggish, Uhura nodded. "Aye, sir, . . . damage control parties, this is the bridge . . ."

Stumbling past McCoy and favoring his bad foot, Kirk used both hands to drag himself, limping and sweat-drenched, to the starboard upper deck and to his first officer's side.

"Spock? All right?" he asked.

"Ship's condition seems stable for the moment, sir."

Kirk paused. "Good, but I was referring to you."

The Vulcan met his eyes in a blunt but candid fashion. "I am quite well. Thank you very—"

"What happened to us? How could there be an accretion disk with no source of collapsed mass? Do you know?"

Spock seemed to take security in having been asked. He held his finger out to a scale that came up on one of the monitors. "I have yet to isolate the cause of the accretion disk, but when we reached the point at which our conventional shields would have collapsed, the force of gravitation and warping of space–time went off all scales. Our conventional shields would have shut down at this point, but the warp shields allowed us to approach the apex of the star's equatorial region. Then the warp drive weakened, and the shields started failing. The engines were bombarded with X rays, therefore could no longer support the shields. We were plunged into an effect of almost unreality as the shields broke down. Somehow, space–time was distorted by our actions."

"It's that 'somehow' that bothers me," Kirk said. "At times even the hull looked transparent. I kept seeing myself doing what I'd done five seconds before."

Spock nodded. "When the shields started failing, they not only stopped acting as shields, but began acting as a lens, focusing energy back upon the ship rather than dissipating it, and trapping it inside the shield sphere. The ship was nearly incinerated. Only veering into the . . . 'object' within four seconds saved us. Because we could move faster than the gravity moving at the speed of light, we actually passed through it before it had a chance to crush us."

"That's pretty good for a ten-second analysis."

Looking tired and relieved, Spock tilted his head graciously. "Thank you, Captain."

Burying a shudder, Kirk allowed himself a long breath. "So much for warp shielding. Intense gravity seems to throw all our probability equations out the window."

"Obviously there are unforeseen flaws," Spock said quietly. "A minuscule probability became nearly a certainty, and the technology broke down. It will take years to unravel exactly what happened to the shields."

"Somebody else's years, Mr. Spock, not ours." The captain glanced around at his people as they coddled the ship into turning off some of those bells and jangles. "That's what tests are for." He pivoted toward Uhura. "Go to yellow alert. Report all major damage up here."

"Yellow alert, sir," Uhura answered. She pressed back a flop of black hair that had twisted into her way and gathered her composure. "Secure from red alert . . . Repeat, secure from red alert. All hands go to yellow alert . . . yellow alert . . . Report minor damage to department heads, all major damage to the first officer."

Kirk listened to the sound of her voice and let the regulation evenhandedness crowd out little fears that still shivered in the corners of his mind. "Spock, see if you can figure out what happened."

"I will, sir."

Stunning how sharply something like this could be on them and then over with. As Kirk and Spock stood together and waited for those damage reports, the bridge crew began to move with more control, burying their shaken nerves in the therapy of their work. The crisis had hit, they'd fielded it, it had flown, and now there was nothing to do but coil lines and tidy the deck. They had lived. One more time, they'd pulled out at the last second and earned solace.

And the damned stylus was finally staying on the deck.

"Captain!"

Irritated, Kirk looked sharply down at Chekov. "Ensign?"

"*Exeter* and *Farragut*—Captain, they're gone! They're both gone!"

Chapter Four

"EXPLAIN THAT."

"No vessels of any kind within sensor range, sir," Sulu confirmed, scrambling to cross-check the navigator's discovery. "Not even at extreme range."

Unclamping his finger from the edge of the library computer housing, Kirk pushed off the console. "Spock, confirm that reading. Sensor failure?"

Spock squinted into the readout hood. "Sensor systems are somewhat scorched but accurate. No vessels registering at all, sir."

Squinting until his eyes hurt, Kirk drew a breath. "Red alert."

Uhura looked at him for an instant, then turned away and funneled that pedal-toned voice through the ship. "Red alert . . . all hands, red alert. Man general quarters . . . Red alert—"

The amber flashers on the walls suggesting that they were on the edge of trouble turned to bright electric red.

Prowling the main screen, Kirk became abruptly suspicious of everything. The blue giant was still out there, spooling merrily its blazing gases, so the *Enterprise* hadn't been thrown light-years away by some unguessed power.

So what happened to the other ships?

"They can't have run out of our scanning range so quickly, not even at high warp. Full search pattern, all stations. Wide-range sensor scan of the area." He paused, his instincts twitching, and added with great deliberation, "Adjust for disaster beacons or wreckage."

McCoy was watching him, face white and eyes wide. Everyone else was working, putting out a thousand feelers through space. That wide black expanse before them teased their awareness of how fragile they were out here without the protective islands of their vessels to keep them alive.

"Lieutenant Uhura," Kirk began quietly, "audio scan of subspace. See what you can hear."

"Aye, sir." She pivoted to her station, adjusted, listened, adjusted again, frowned, touched the earpiece linking her to the outside galaxy, adjusted some more, but didn't like what her instruments drew in. "Captain, this . . ." She paused and fine-tuned again. Dissatisfaction creased her dark eyes. "This doesn't make sense." She swiveled around and looked at him. "I'm not picking up any subspace noise on conventional channels at all."

He moved toward her. "Garbled?"

"No, sir, not garbled. Just . . . nothing. Empty space. I can't explain it. I can't even catch drifting residual signals on Starfleet or Federation channels at all. Not at *all.*"

She turned from him long enough to run an emergency flash-diagnostic just to make sure her systems were at least talking to each other. There was nothing worse for a communications professional than to hear nothing. "This simply can't *be.* Subspace signals linger for years sometimes!"

"Keep searching, Lieutenant," Kirk said. His calm was a lie. "Prepare to send high-warp hails, emergency scramble. Call for immediate rendezvous, these coordinates."

"Aye, sir."

"Captain," Spock said, stepping in behind him, "no disaster beacons, no propelled or drifting wreckage of any kind, and no life pod carrier loops."

"Then they didn't collide with each other."

"Space is unthinkably large for such an occurrence, sir." Spock's way of agreeing.

"Jim!" McCoy gripped the command chair. "Could that incident have done something to *us?*"

Kirk shot the same glare at Spock. "Time warp? Have we gone either forward or back? Have we been thrown any distance?"

Spock looked embarrassed that he hadn't thought of that but vectored back to his station, tapped his panel with three or four touches, then hovered over the readout hood. Its frosty blue light washed across his eyes.

"Calibrating relative position of stars. Negligible changes. We experienced a time shift of only . . . four minutes, twenty-one seconds. Our location is also stable, since Izell is still within sensor range."

"All that was only four minutes?" Kirk moaned.

"Four minutes during our encounter with the blue giant."

"Then where are they? If this is Doug Newman's idea of a joke, I'll have his hide."

Still bending over his station, running program after program through the computer, eliciting the machine's help in coughing up possible causes for a four-minute vanishing of two ships, Spock dealt with his own subtle incredulity. "I doubt even Captain Newman could engineer the total disappearance of two starships. Even a cloaking device produces a ripple effect."

"Can they be hiding behind the blue giant?"

Spock frowned at the idea. "Certainly not in four minutes without residual trail from their warp drive."

"I know. I just wanted to hear you say it."

"Sir, long-range sensors snapping on," Sulu interrupted. He squinted into his own readouts. "Large vessel approaching."

"About time. Identification."

Their flashing hopes and assumptions cracked to pieces when Spock said, "Unknown configuration . . ." Suddenly he looked up. "Romulan signature."

Levering on one hand, Kirk leaned on the bridge rail to get his bad leg out of his way. He dropped to the command deck.

His jaw hardened. "Battle stations," he said.

Chapter Five

"RAISE SHIELDS."

Sulu turned. "Warp shields, sir?"

"Negative. Conventional shields. I'm not taking that chance until we know what happened to us. Arm everything we've got."

"Phasers armed . . . Photons armed . . . Ready, sir."

Diagnostics flashed across the upper rim of the bridge, sifting the incoming ship, but there was heavy shielding on that ship, too, and every little detail became a win.

"Captain, they're attempting to scan us," Spock said.

"Jam it. I want to know who they are." Kirk swabbed a clammy hand across his face and blinked the sweat out of his eyes. The bridge was hot, muggy. "Confirm that signature, Spock," he said. "I want to be sure."

"Standard warp drive . . . Slightly richer formula than usual . . . Vessel is double-hulled, double-shielded, heavily armed . . . Communication echoes specifications . . ." Bent over his console, Spock half turned to meet the captain's eyes. "No doubt, Captain."

Gritting his teeth, Kirk grunted, "All right, then . . . maximum visual. Let's have a look."

The forward screen shifted its star pattern, and suddenly they were staring head-on at a pit bull of a space vessel. Even at this distance, the ship looked twice the size it should have on this magnification. That made it almost twice the size of the *Enterprise*.

Kirk pressed his spine against the black leather of his command chair. The vessel was shaped like a crouched cat, with arched weapon launchers for muscles and two forward viewports for eyes, dark blue with yellow markings disguised as lights, so only a close look showed where the lights really were. There were great stylized wings painted onto the hull, arching up in contrast to the shape of the ship itself. A war bird's wings.

Those, at least, were familiar, but all the reassurance of familiarity was a lie.

The rest of the paint, the nondecorative colors, was designed to make the ship look smaller than it was and to confound the eye during visual targeting, angled where there were no angles, dark where there were no shadows, except for those two glowing portals, like an eagle's eyes in the dark.

Pretty good effect. "Romulans in a ship like that?" McCoy blurted. "Since when?"

"Could be renegades," Noureddine suggested.

Tight as a drawn bow, Kirk pulled forward. "Display all Starfleet codes, pennants, and signals. Imply minor distress so they don't take us as hostile. Request flagging and home system I.D."

"Aye, sir." Uhura's voice, like Noureddine's, pretended to be calm. She was a lot better at it than the engineer.

"Open hailing frequencies, audio only."

"Frequencies open, sir."

Kirk cleared his throat. "This is Captain James T. Kirk, commanding *U.S.S. Enterprise.* You are in Federation jurisdiction. Stand down your weapons and identify yourselves immediately."

He paused and waited. This was always the bad time.

Uhura perked up suddenly. "Receiving response . . . Seems to be some kind of warning or challenge . . . Definitely native Romulan, sir." Having confirmed that, she touched her earpiece and frowned. "But I don't think they understand what we said."

McCoy leaned toward him. "If they're Romulan, they should know passable English. Why can't they speak to us?"

The pain in Kirk's leg was pumping for attention again. "Uhura, universal translator."

"Engaged, sir. Go ahead."

"This is Captain James Kirk of the United Federation of Planets. You are in violation of—"

"This is the Imperial Guard. You are in the war zone. Identify yourselves and your purpose."

The alien voice thrummed across the bridge.

"I just did," Kirk muttered. "This is James Kirk, commanding the Federation *Starship Enterprise*. You are in Federation space. Explain yourselves."

"We have never heard your language. What is your homeworld?"

Kirk and McCoy exchanged a glance, then, just for security, he looked up at Spock. Spock looked down at him and all but shrugged.

With a silent nod, Kirk passed the shrug on to the alien craft. "Earth," he said, more flippantly than he meant.

On the upper deck, Spock appeared more troubled. He bent to double-check what he already knew—and he almost never did that.

"There is no 'Earth.' What is your true homeworld?"

Kirk ran a finger along his lower lip and allowed himself time to think. He motioned Uhura to go silent and leaned on an elbow. "Well, hell," he murmured.

Why did it seem so long since he had a captain to do his worrying and thinking and make decisions for him? He was so tired today . . . He tried to think. Large, heavily armed alien ship, apparently Romulan, hadn't heard of Earth—

"Chekov," he said, "man the defense subsystems station."

The Russian navigator jumped up from his chair with a faint "Aye, sir" and hurried to the starboard bow quarter, up the walkway from Spock's station.

Kirk glared at that big ship coming at them and drew a deep breath. His chest hurt now, too. "Uhura, take navigation."

Her chair made a faint squeak as she turned, then stepped down and slid into the helm chair at navigation.

"Spock," Kirk began reservedly, "opinion. Are they lying? Testing us for some reason?"

The first officer kept tight to his instruments but glared with plagued fascination at the encroaching vessel. "I cannot conceive of any such reasoning. Federation space has been well marked for decades."

"What can it get them?" McCoy offered. "Maybe they're trying to foment a dispute."

"There's no dispute here, Doctor," Kirk said. "They're well inside our territory. The question now is whether or not they represent the Romulan Empire as they claim to. I've never heard of anything called 'Imperial Guard,' Romulan or otherwise. All right, we'll do it the hard way. High frequency all-points display. Warn them off. I want a sphere of clear nonentry. Range?"

"Five hundred thousand kilometers, sir," Uhura reported.

"Sir!" Sulu blurted. "I'm getting a firing sequence. They're opening fire! Quadramegaton salvos!"

"Evasive action. Emergency warp five." Kirk pushed to the edge of his chair, intending to stand, but at the last second his foot sent pain stabbing up into his hip and kept him down.

Huge white globular bolts were launched from the Imperial ship and bore down toward the *Enterprise,* but the starship wasn't waiting around. Sulu angled the ship off and pressed her into high speed.

"Photon torpedoes," Kirk ordered. "Narrow dispersal."

"Targeting, sir," Chekov said.

"Fire torpedoes one and two."

The ship bucked twice, buffeted by her own firing system coming into action in the middle of a very tight turn.

Bright salvos plunged in on some kind of acquisition program, dodging after them no matter how the starship plunged and veered. One salvo was losing power, but the second held integrity and flashed in at them. The bulkheads shuddered, structural members hummed. Straining to hold course, the ship skidded to one side and sent her crew smashing into their consoles. Kirk held on to his chair and managed to grab McCoy and hold on before the doctor stumbled into the helm.

"Engineering section!" Nourredine choked. "Possible structural rupture—"

"Another incoming, sir!" Sulu shouted over their voices.

A heartbeat later the second hit struck. The ship jogged slightly to one side, then continued building speed.

"Glancing blow off the port nacelle, sir," Spock called over the noise. "Stabilizing."

"What about our shots?"

Spock straightened and turned. "Both direct hits. They made no attempt at all to evade our fire. Damage is uncertain."

"Has their speed increased?"

"Negative. They seem to be topping off at warp seven."

"I'll take it. Mr. Sulu, warp factor—"

"Captain, another contact!" Uhura interrupted. "Dead ahead!"

The screen dropped the departure angle and flashed to a garish picture of what could've been the same ship, but stationary in front of them. Kirk pushed to his feet.

"Same as the ship behind us, sir," Sulu confirmed.

"Sound collision."

"They're blocking us," Sulu said, effort rising in his tone.

Kirk gritted his teeth. "Ram them."

The helmsman didn't dare turn from his instruments because things were happening too fast. "Say again—"

"Ram it!"

"Aye, sir!" Sulu gasped, raising his voice over the whine of instruments and warnings. "Brace for collision!"

Everyone grabbed for a handhold as a moment of horror reared itself that even a starship couldn't survive.

Holding his breath as they relapsed into danger, Kirk made a mental bet on his helmsman that Sulu knew better than to ram anything head on and would find a way to glance off that monster.

Get out of my way. He grasped the arm of his chair and hung on.

Chapter Six

THE HULL PUSHED up at him, the carpet pressing upward into his aching foot. On the screen, the big menace tilted at a bizarre angle. A turbolift nausea worked on his stomach. He held on to the chair with both hands and damned the lights flashing in his mind. The hit went straight to his bones.

Where had the two ships struck? The primary hull could take a lot, but those nacelles—if they were knocked off alignment by so much as a centimeter—

He leaned forward, found the back of his chair, and wrapped an arm around it as though clinging to a friend. The forward screen was full of stars. Open space!

"Status!" he choked.

"We're clear, sir!" Sulu gulped.

"Aft view!"

The main screen shimmered and brought them a picture of the second enemy ship, spinning awkwardly, driven by the impact, one of its big weapon-launch arches sliced open to reveal sizzling veins of energy pouring into space, crackling with the change in temperature.

"Damage report," Kirk demanded.

"We grazed the underside of our primary hull, sir," Uhura said. "Forward port quarter."

Spock quickly straightened. "No compromise in maneuverability or thrust, Captain."

"Mr. Sulu, get us out of here," Kirk gasped, holding his tone down. "Warp eight."

Sulu swallowed a lump. "Warp eight, sir!"

A sharp turn to starboard threw them all sideways, but they'd heard the order and everybody managed to cling to something. The ship's massive warp engines vibrated through the hull and into the crew's bodies as speed piled upon speed.

"We're leaving them behind, Captain." Spock's deep voice was not only the knell of security, but a plain relief.

"At least we know we can outrun them," Kirk said with an involuntary shudder.

At engineering, Lieutenant Nourredine stared at the empty screen, breathing hard. "We ran . . ."

Looking up at him, Kirk noticed for the first time the youth and freshness up there. He hadn't really paid attention before. He'd never questioned Engineer Scott's choice of post assignments or the crusty department head's habit of shuttling very young engineers to the bridge for instant experience.

Sometimes they got caught in a vise. Like now.

"Of course we ran," he said.

Paying the price of bridge duty, the engineer blinked. "No . . . no disrespect intended, sir. I just thought—"

"You thought the good guys never retreat. As a matter of fact, it's the good guys who know *when* to retreat, in my experience." Kirk settled back in his chair and let his shoulders ache. "All through history there are episodes of clever saves."

"I . . . didn't know that, sir."

"I'll tell you the stories sometime."

"Thank you, sir."

"Damage report, anyone?"

"Oh—" Nourredine shook himself and cloyed to his work. "Minor damage across almost the whole port side of the engineering section. No major hull ruptures discovered yet, but sensors have taken a beating. Long-range sensors are reduced twenty-two percent, but looks like short-range sensors are down completely."

"Put the hull stability on priority."

"Yes, sir."

"Captain," Spock interrupted quietly from his post, "if you would, please."

Kirk glanced up and anchored himself to the complex, solid expression of his first officer. There were answers up there, he saw in the black eyes and the frictionless posture. Troubled answers, but answers.

He pulled himself up with a grip on the back of Uhura's chair.

"Lieutenant, take your post and see if you can contact Starfleet Command on a scrambled frequency. I want to know what's going on. If they don't know, I'm going to tell them."

"Yes, sir, I'll try," Uhura murmured, moving behind him.

Spock waited until the captain limped to the steps, then reached down to help him to the upper deck. He kept his voice low, private.

"We're most fortunate that we evaded head-on strikes by those salvos," the Vulcan said. "Quadramegaton force is sufficient to break our shielding and possibly inflict major damage with one blow. I am at a loss to explain the Romulans' access to such a weapon. There are no reports from Starfleet Intelligence of any such possession."

"I'm aware of that. What else?"

"I believe I know what happened to us."

With a disbelieving smirk, Kirk asked, "You analyzed what happened to us at the same time as we were under fire?"

Spock looked perplexed, then a little guilty. "I *had* begun the analysis when the other vessel—"

"Never mind. Let's hear it."

"If you would attend monitor number three . . . the ship's automatic recording system captured this series of events. The pictures are not the usual quality. Energy was being tapped from this system to the hull plate shields when the warp shields began to break down."

"Yes, it saved our lives." Kirk couldn't help a little squint, as if that would help. The accretion disk was there as well as miles-long licks of blue solar flares and solid mass being torn off the giant star.

But there was an added element. Something the big forward screen hadn't registered the first time around.

This time there was a slice through the picture, as though a scalpel had been drawn from top to bottom at dead center of the accretion disk.

Kirk leaned forward. "What's that?"

"Computer analysis revealed this central spool," Spock said evenly. "As we arched across the blue giant's heavy gravity field at warp speed, with the new shields operating as they did, we began to generate a change in the gravity, in fact yanking material and energy toward ourselves. We created the accretion disk, which then began to drag us toward it. In essence, we created a *node*."

He paused, letting the word sink in.

"Do I have to ask?" Kirk prodded.

"No, sir. A node—theoretically—is a period of stabilization for cosmic string."

Kirk actually backed off a step. Even the talk of this kind of blind power made him nervous. A kind of scientists' tall story.

Spock watched him. "As you know, cosmic string exists between layers of space–time. Our new warp shields work by displacing energy through space–time."

"And we catalyzed it . . ."

"Yes."

Turning, Kirk motioned to the center deck. "Doctor, come up here. I want you to hear this."

McCoy's eyes were already fixed on the small monitor. He moved toward them, keeping one hand on some part of the bridge—a chair, the rail, and finally the captain's elbow. "I'll bet you're going to describe to me how many broken bones and concussions are waiting for me in sickbay," he muttered, but he wasn't being funny.

"Did you hear what Spock was explaining?" Kirk asked.

The doctor nodded vaguely. "Something about . . . cosmic yarn."

Indulging in a sigh, Spock clasped his hands behind his back. "Cosmic string. Primordial matter so tightly spun that it manifests itself in immeasurable gravity slicing through the levels of space–time, much as a knife might go through paper. It is so dense that it actually bends space and time. In the proximity of cosmic string, nothing works as we know it. Thousands of trillions of tons per centimeter, traveling at nearly the speed of light, it is indescribably small—"

McCoy glared at him suddenly. "Try."

The challenge lit Spock's black eyes. "It could pass through a planet and not collide with a single molecule."

"So what? What's a molecule, more or less, among friends?" The doctor glanced at Kirk. "So it passes through."

"As it moves," Spock went on with false tolerance, "it would crush the planet to the size of a walnut. The poles would rush toward each other at ten thousand miles per hour. If an atom were as large as a nebula, cosmic string would still be the diameter of a bacterium—"

"That's enough." The doctor looked like he'd been slapped. "I got those last two—"

"This doesn't make sense," Kirk interrupted. "There's no string in this solar system. We would've picked up its X-ray and gamma-ray distortion—or at least we'd have seen its gravitational effect on every star in the area as it passed by. If it just passed *near* a planet, it would yank off the atmosphere and half the surface mass."

"That is precisely what it did, sir," Spock said, "to Izell. It consumed nearly a quarter of the star's mass."

"Yes, but space is a vastly empty place, Spock. You said that earlier. It's filled with mostly nothing. The odds of string appearing here, at this time, this space—they're trillions to one."

With damning ease the Vulcan said, "And we are the one."

Every now and then, when two like moods were in the right equinox, Spock would make a joke, but as Kirk and McCoy gazed at him, they realized quite abruptly that this wasn't one of those times.

"In fact," Spock went on, "we attracted the string to this

space–time by creating the node of stability for it. As it traveled through dimensions, it was momentarily caught . . . here."

"Sounds to me like it's almost the same as a black hole," McCoy said. Some of the color was coming back into his face.

The Vulcan nodded briefly. "True. But unlike a black hole, it has no dimension."

"But how did we survive being so close to it?"

"By moving at hyperlight speed," Kirk said. "Gravity moves at the speed of light. We were within a million miles of the string. At warp nine, that distance was traveled almost instantaneously. The crushing waves tried to act on the ship at the speed of light, but by turning into it we were actually dragged into the string and passed through it faster than its gravity waves could crush us."

McCoy stared and shook his head. "That's phenomenal . . . I can't conceive of that!"

"Neither can I," Kirk said bluntly, "but that's what saved us and I'll take it." With a bitter knot forming in his gut, he lowered his voice. "Spock, could the cosmic string have destroyed the *Exeter* and the *Farragut?*"

The prospect reared its inhumane snout and cracked them like a whip. All of a sudden the speculation had a foul solidity.

Finally, under the eyes of the whole bridge crew, Spock faced the captain. "I am only assuming that physics acts as we know it under such circumstances, Jim," he admitted. Worry showed in his eyes. "I am not that sure of these details." At least he was brave enough to say it.

Kirk freed him with a nod. Something on the bridge was starting to whine, and the forward screen was losing its picture.

"Captain," Uhura said, and only then did he realize she'd been watching them, trying to catch his attention and find a good place to interrupt.

"Report, Lieutenant."

"Sir . . ."

"Say it."

"Sir, I can't pick up Starfleet on any channel. In fact, I can't pick up anybody at all on any Federation channel."

"You mean there's complete silence?"

"Oh, no, sir, I'm catching ragged signals on other channels, but it all seems to be scrambled. My translators aren't recognizing a single code. I'll . . . keep trying."

He saw the fear behind her confusion and her determination to reach out into space and find *something*.

That expression on the faces of his crew—that decipherable fear, asking him to take care of them, to come up with the missing piece to the puzzle—the burden seemed iron hard today.

"Tampering with space–time," he murmured, "dimensions . . . We could've caused any number of wild things to happen . . . Did those two alien ships slip through a dimensional crack when that string paused here? Have we loosed them on our own galaxy without even—"

"But they were Romulan!" Chekov bolted.

"Yes, sir," Sulu added. "Even though we didn't recognize the ship, they weren't from some other dimension. We know who they are."

"Yes," the captain uttered. "Romulans."

The whine got louder. It was blocking his thoughts.

"Course of action, sir?" Spock asked.

He could barely hear now. He fought to think. "Course of action . . . We'll go by the book. Starfleet Catastrophic Response Code, Section A: when all forms of communication fail to establish a link between Starfleet vessels and any Federation outpost, all personnel and ordnance—"

"Will attempt immediate rendezvous at Starfleet Command," Spock completed.

"Yes. Uhura, open all frequencies . . . Scan continually for any Federation contact at all. Sulu—"

"Jim!" McCoy caught his arm on one side, Spock on the other. Kirk registered that his legs weren't holding his weight. His thighs pressed back on the computer housing.

"You've got to let me treat you," McCoy insisted, "or you're not going to be conscious to deal with this."

The doctor had gone no-nonsense, and there wasn't going

to be any more putting off. Medical authority had just kicked in.

"All right," Kirk wheezed, "all right . . . Spock, do it."

Still holding him up, Spock turned to the helm. "Mr. Sulu, set a direct course for Earth, warp factor eight."

"Warp eight, sir." Sulu's response was a buzz.

As his head wobbled and the carpet reeled before his eyes, Kirk tried to nod to Spock. "Good . . . be sure to keep us out of trouble—"

The last thing he registered as they carried him off the bridge was the life-buoy voice he would cling to in his encroaching nightmares.

"I will, Captain."

Chapter Seven

"APPROACHING THE SOL SYSTEM, Mr. Spock."

"Thank you, Mr. Sulu. Still no response from Starfleet, Lieutenant?"

The first officer didn't turn for Uhura's answer. He knew she wasn't ready to give it. The clicking and straining of her computer complex told him she was still reaching into space for messages, codes, symbols, something familiar.

Yet he had asked. As the words left his lips, he tasted the illogic of asking. An inefficient habit he had picked up after nearly two decades of service in the company of humans. She would have told him if there had been a change. All the way here, past planets colonized by the Federation, outposts, starbases—there had been nothing but silence. No response to any search or hail. Starfleet Catastrophic Response Code demanded that they not stray to investigate but head straight to Earth to rendezvous with anyone else who might also find themselves alone in the silence.

"Nothing, sir." Uhura's voice was heavy, soft with trouble. "No nearby subspace communication of any kind, Starfleet or private. This area should be teeming with transportation. I don't understand it, sir."

Spock felt stiff, empty. "Understanding will come with time, Lieutenant," he said. "For now we deal with only the facts."

He leaned forward in the command chair, his brow tight as the planets of the Sol system floated by in brainless innocence—and utter lifelessness. Not a light, not a signal, not a single colonial satellite. He spoke of facts, but his hands were clenched, elbows pressed hard to the chair. His chest felt hollow, and he did not possess the logical answers with which to fill it.

"Status of tactical sensors now, Mr. Nourredine?"

"Only up to thirty percent, sir. Mr. Scott wants six hours."

"Acknowledge that."

"Yes, sir."

"Sir, we're approaching Earth," Sulu said.

Everyone paused and looked up. Before them the familiar solar system they'd all cut their teeth on scrolled out, planet after planet, moons, asteroids, and the tolerant yellow sun far beyond.

And Earth, home to them all in one way or another, home to Starfleet, core of the Federation, a sedate blue ball marbled with clouds and dashed with spice-colored land masses—

"Mr. Spock," Chekov began, "where are the space docks?"

"Where are the orbital stations?" Nourredine echoed. "I don't pick up any lunar installations—"

"Go to the dark side of the planet, Mr. Sulu," Spock interrupted.

Ordinarily, this would have been a beautiful sight. Moving from the sun-bathed side to the comforting nest of shadow, where glittering cities shone their prosperity through mindless patches of cloud.

No cities . . .

Sulu turned, his face blanched. "Could it all have been destroyed somehow, sir?"

For a moment Spock didn't respond. The concept was too encompassing for a yes or no. He would let the reassurance of science put a frame around the outlandish moment.

"Tactical," he ordered. "Thirty percent will have to do. Mr. Chekov, if you please."

Chekov slid out of his post and jumped up to the science monitors. Seconds went by like surgical time.

"No wreckage or flotsam . . . No industrial residue . . . No propulsion traces, manufactured surplus, or sensor shadows." Struggling with the idea as much as he struggled with the English language, he turned and added, "No sign of life at all, sir."

Spock sat back in his chair.

"I assume you mean there is no sign of contemporary industrial life, Ensign."

Chekov mentally retreated but seemed strengthened by the demand for accuracy. "Yes, sir."

Spock dug deep within himself for the indifference that sustained him but found it lacking. No one, not even a Vulcan, could gaze upon an emptiness where once there had been teeming intelligent life and roaring progress, the roots of his heritage and the pediments of his civilization, and remain passive. He had no desire to be passive.

But the people glancing at him from all sides expected him to be their logical foundation. He struggled for that and found himself wishing the captain were here.

He pulled his voice up. "Bring us into orbit, Mr. Sulu."

"Bones . . ."

"Right here, Jim. You'll be fine in a minute."

Kirk squeezed his eyes shut hard, then concentrated on opening them. All he saw was a pale gray haze. Maybe blue. Maybe white.

The walls in sickbay.

Mechanical bleeps and whirs—the diagnostic panel. His heart rate was up.

He tried to raise his aching head but succeeded only enough to catch a glimpse at his own body, thick and muscular and lying completely useless on the bed's black cushion.

The mustard-colored uniform shirt and his black trousers beyond; his boots were still on. So it hadn't been long since he collapsed.

He let his head fall back and winced at the memory of folding on the bridge. A captain shouldn't go down that way, slumping in front of his juniors.

How long? An hour? Two? How much could go wrong in that much time?

"Where are you?" he rasped.

A fuzzy blue pillar appeared, and for the life of him Kirk couldn't figure out where from.

"I've got to get up there."

"That's a laugh," the doctor popped back, as though he'd been keeping the response in his pocket for quick use. The slim blue pillar sharpened and became McCoy, regarding him with a scolding wisdom. "Captain, you've been very sick for the past nine hours. You're not out of danger yet."

Kirk thrust himself up on an elbow. For a minute he thought his arm would shatter under the strain. "Was I dead?"

The doctor paused, and blinked. "Well, how much does proximity count?"

"Then I want to be up on the bridge. You get me up there."

"Status?"

"Orbital status at Earth, Captain. Short-range sensors still seventy percent blind."

Spock's voice was subdued, indicative. They instantly understood each other. Trouble. Nothing solved yet. What Kirk had seen before he passed out hadn't been an illusion or a glitch or even a complete crash of their systems. The ship was still in the middle of a great big wrong.

Pulling his arm loose from McCoy's custodial grasp, he cleared himself of the turbolift and made it to the rail. As Spock met him there, he anticipated what he saw in his first officer's expression. "I'm all right. Tell me what we've got."

As the soft orange lights from the low ceiling lay upon his shoulders like warm hands, Spock glanced at the forward screen. "We have no visible signs of current constructed civilization at all. No space docks, cities, or traffic of any kind, nor are we picking up residue from propulsion or other energy emissions. No city lights or other artificial lighting—"

"Power generation?"

"None. This solar system is completely pristine. Void of communication, current or lingering, and all of our colonial installations are absent."

"What about life forms?"

"Tactical sensors are still too weak to break through the atmosphere."

"Then we'll have to go down there for ourselves . . . and look around."

Kirk sensed Spock watching him carefully, as though encroaching on a troubled prayer, waiting to catch the captain's attention. After a minute Kirk couldn't avoid it anymore and looked at him.

"May I suggest," Spock said, "that I lead a science party down, sir, and investigate in some depth."

Anxiety ate at Kirk's stomach as he watched the blue oceans and sienna continents slide by under the white froth of clouds—yes, the atmosphere was still there. Perhaps it was a good sign that it hadn't been ripped away. It was chafing comfort, but at least it was something.

"Organize your landing party, Mr. Spock," he said, "and tell Scotty to come up here and take command. I want to see this for myself."

"Spock, are we in the right place?"

Kirk blinked and shielded his eyes.

A tree bough wagged overhead and cast a sharp movement on the blue uniform tunic as the Vulcan turned away from the eye-level sun and squinted at his tricorder. "Longitude and latitude are exact, I'm afraid, Captain."

Before them, overgrown hills and nestled pockets of grassland rolled five miles out to a blinding blue-gray bay. In the valleys—huge, broad valleys curtained by green crests—entire square miles of open lands were drenched in yellow flowers spotlighted by the setting sun.

McCoy came up beside him. "The transporter officer must have made a mistake."

Favoring his bad foot, Jim Kirk moved to the edge of the bluff. His throat was raw. "You recognize the lay of the land, don't you? We're right where I told you we were going."

McCoy stared at him, then raised his hand and swept it to take in the landscape.

"Then where the devil . . . is San Francisco?"

The great western bay shimmered in the middle distance as the sun sank. No Golden Gate Bridge. No tangled ribbons of municipal streets and skyways. No central metropolis. No polished urban sprawl. No buildings to catch and reflect the buttering sunshine.

And the *no* in those phrases began to knell.

Only the whistle of water birds and the skitter of animals in the darkening bushes—an endless purgatory of pastoral.

"At least the hills are still here," McCoy rasped from beside him.

"It looks exactly as it's supposed to," Kirk said. "All the right trees, grass, a blue sky, the bay . . . just no buildings. No people."

"Feels very void to me."

"To me, too. No one here to appreciate it."

"Jim, do you think—"

McCoy stopped as a crunch of footsteps brought Spock back to them.

Spock came around in front of them despite that it brought him so close to the edge that his boots forced a handful of rocks to drop and rattle down the cliff face. He anchored himself on the captain's gaze.

"Gentlemen, we're standing where the reception solarium of Starfleet Command should be. Admiral Landall's office there, Admirals Oliver and Nogura's offices there, and the VIP sanctum just beyond. On the tip of that hill should be the surgeon general's wing, and in the valley to your left, the physical training ground of Starfleet Academy and the Thomas Jefferson Vintage Rose Garden."

In their minds the recitation went on, places and monuments, trees and bridges they all wanted to be here. But Spock had a point to make and had made it. The three of them stood looking out over the scrubby overgrowth that in their minds was a manicured panorama of old roses whose seeds had been smuggled through wars, hidden in family coffins and ladies' gloves until they could be brought to bloom in the bright new century.

Now there was nothing but overgrown grass and wildflowers, trees rustling in the offshore breeze, sheets upon sheets of yellow blooms waving like fabric as they caught the last strong blaze of sunlight. Not bad, but not roses.

"All right," Kirk groaned. "We'll start from scratch and work our way up. Rundown of crew specialties, please, Mr. Spock."

Spock started pointing at the line of bewildered uniformed personnel, each already swiveling around with ghoulish curiosity. They were an attractive group against the bright daylight, all ages, decked in their bright modern primary reds and blues, edged with black, and the dot of shimmering gold Starfleet delta shield on each breast. Each had a tricorder hanging from a thin black strap over a shoulder, except the four security men who had full phaser weapons and emergency packs. Very competent looking, comforting, crisp against this crackling world that should have been a core of modern development. This was a place where someone would scratch out a campsight, not plan the expansion of a vast and technical civilization through the galaxy.

"Lieutenant Mark Rice, geology and geophysics," Spock began, "Lieutenant Louise LaCerra, paleontology and zoology; Lieutenant Elizabeth Ling, botany and zoology; Lieutenant Dale Bannon, anthropology; his assistant, Ensign Erica Smith; and Chief Chemist Gaston Barnes. Security detail Ensigns Williams and MacGuinness, Yeomen Rhula and Hardy."

"You brought the whole university," Kirk said. He knew their names, except for the newly transferred botanist and one of the Security men, but it helped to be reminded of their departments. "Spread out, teams of two. You know the problem. Let's find the answers."

The murmur of yes-sirs and aye-ayes was unenvigorated. They'd lost San Francisco and had a pretty good idea they weren't going to find it today. He had asked them to come down and confirm that most of their families and certainly all of their heritages were gone.

Even the normally cocky Security types meandered off behind the specialists without even plowing into the lead. In a moment Kirk was alone again with his two partners in command distress, alone in a place that should be home.

"The city wasn't destroyed," he said quietly. He bent with some effort and scooped up a handful of overgrowth. "There's not so much as a broken blade of grass. No signs of annihilation, the atmosphere is still intact . . . Nothing's wrong with the planet, except for the complete absence of San Francisco."

"There are no other cities either, Captain," Spock mentioned. "Despite shortages in tactical sensors, we've been able to verify empty land in place of Los Angeles, New York, Boston, London, and Bangkok. There are no pockets of organized habitation anywhere."

He almost sounded apologetic but checked himself before it overtook his expression. Too late; they'd seen it.

"The climate's the same," Kirk said. "Geography is still here . . . so where in blazes are the people?"

"Something tells me I'd rather be with them than where I am," McCoy murmured thoughtfully. He plucked a bright yellow flower with a distinct black eye and twirled the stem between his fingers as he gazed into the valley. "I used to sit on a lounge right over there and look down on my daughter's house . . ."

The words drifted away on the breeze.

Kirk turned away. "Spock, let's get a wide-range detailed

picture if we can. Can't we bypass the tactical sensor damage somehow?"

"I shall attempt it." Spock pulled out his communicator and flipped open the sensor grid. "Landing party to *Enterprise.*"

"Lieutenant Uhura, sir."

"Tie my tricorder signal directly into the library computer, Lieutenant."

"Aye, sir, one moment."

"Standing by." Spock started to say something else, when the bushes behind him suddenly rattled violently and a red flash burst out of the leaves, smashing into the back of the Vulcan's legs.

He was driven down by a wild ball of red feathers with a long neck and legs. It squawked in terror, veered away from the bluff, and disappeared into a thick stand of bushes about twenty-five yards away.

Before McCoy could react, Kirk was already at Spock's side, hauling his first officer to his feet. "Are you hurt?"

"Not at all, thank you." Spock brushed twigs from his uniform and scowled at the rustling bushes. An instant later, the bushes fell calm as though nothing had happened.

As McCoy hurried to them, Kirk pointed at the bushes. "Bones, did you see that?"

"Did it look like a short ostrich?"

"Yes!"

"Then I saw it."

"That doesn't make sense," Kirk hissed. "There's nothing like that in North America. Spock, did you see it?"

"Only a glimpse, Captain. Can you describe it?"

McCoy pushed between them. "It looked like an ostrich, only the size of a goose and the colors of a Rhode Island Red."

Spock's communicator twittered and he thumbed the exposed controls. "Might it have been a wild turkey? Excuse me—Spock here."

"Could've been," McCoy drawled, "but it wasn't."

"Uhura here, Mr. Spock. You're tied into the main comput-

er system, all memory banks. The tricorder won't be able to store much, but you have full access as long as the channel is open."

"Do I have sensor access as well?"

"Yes, sir, Mr. Scott has tied that in also. Short-range sensors are up to sixty-three percent operational and rising."

"Thank you. Spock out." He adjusted the tricorder and made use of the vast encyclopedic store of information logged in the computer system and the ship's half-blind sensors, which struggled to scan the planet from orbit. "Information is choppy, but coming in, Captain."

Feeling flushed again, Kirk leaned back on a rock in a half-sitting position. "Go ahead, Spock."

Cupping his hands over the tricorder to keep the sun off, Spock paced a few steps while glaring into the tiny screen, then paced back without looking up. "Continental readings show low-lying everglades and deciduous growth in the East and Southeast, prairie and grasslands in the West . . . Mountains north of those. No domesticated crops, however. In the far north there is considerable tundra and barren land toward the Arctic. Abundant sea life . . . Considerable animal life . . . Birds, reptiles, invertebrates—"

"It's the North America we all recognize, is what you're telling me."

Spock's eyes narrowed into black wedges. With a twinge of cautious sorrow, he simply said, "Yes."

From down the hill, somebody called, "Captain?"

Their paleontologist was scratching her way up the hill to their left, dirty up to her elbows. Her knees were caked with mud.

Kirk extended a hand to haul her up over the bluff's edge. He glanced around for Spock, but the Vulcan was striding across the bushy ground toward the other woman on the team, who was signaling that she had something, too.

So he looked down into a pair of bright, troubled eyes and said, "Report, Lieutenant."

"Sir," the small-boned woman said, "Ling, sir, Life Sciences Department. The wild foliage is mostly correct, like the conifer forests north of here, but there's no domesti-cated growth. No cultivation. And something else bothers me, sir, . . . I can't find the redwoods."

With a scowl, Kirk bent toward her. "Explain that."

The woman's delicate face crumpled. "I just can't find any evidence of the major ancient sequoia growth in the whole western coastal region. I checked with the ship, but they couldn't find a single giant redwood tree. Mr. Scott thought it might have something to do with the sensors being partly down, but . . . but I can't find any *evidence* of the redwood forests in recent geology."

"You wouldn't find any," McCoy said. "There are no fossils in the Bay area."

"I know that, sir, but I analyzed a pond floor and I couldn't even find any ancient redwood pollen. At least, nothing over the past ten thousand years. I *should* be able to find something, and I can't." She looked at Kirk. "Sir, why aren't they here?"

Kirk straightened, troubled. "And if they were," he added, "what happened to them?"

She nodded. "There's abundant insect life, but I can't find any of the wildlife that's supposed to be here—no beavers, bears, or even squirrels. There are some large grazing animals registering, but I haven't seen them yet. But a minute ago I was sure I saw a small primate."

"A primate? Here?"

"It just wouldn't make sense, sir! The tricorder's giving me metabolic readings, but I like to see things for myself."

"Smart girl," McCoy dropped in.

"All right," Kirk muttered. "Carry on, Ling. See if you can't pinpoint the large grazers and we'll go have a look."

"Aye, sir."

She seemed relieved to have permission to go after the big targets and made her way down the rock-and-weed slope.

McCoy toed the yellow wildflowers on the cliff's edge. Then he blinked, bent to look at the large blooms, and said, "You know, this looks just like a California poppy."

The captain stretched his sore back. "Is that supposed to mean something?"

"I don't know. Except that poppies should be bright orange. These are banana yellow."

"Mmm."

"Oh—there's a bee." McCoy withdrew his hand from fondling one of the yellow flowers, then on second look bowed lower over the flower, reached down, and carefully snapped the stem. "Jim, . . . look at this."

On the black center of the flower was the bee, industriously plumbing for nectar without giving the men any attention at all.

"So it's a bee," Kirk said.

"Look closer. Look at the colors."

The bee was a bee, perfectly formed for its purpose, big, fat, fuzzy, single-minded, and well armed—and colored bright yellow with white and green stripes.

Kirk tried to concentrate, registered what he was looking at, but had trouble holding the thought. "A green bee. Maybe it came up from Mexico."

McCoy looked up at him, forgot the bee, and dropped the flower. "Feel all right, Jim? You look overheated."

"I am. Why isn't the medication working?"

"It *is* working. If you were in bed, in sickbay, where you belong, you'd be fine. If you keep straining yourself, you're just going to drag out the process of recovery." His expression softened some, and he added, "I don't like my patients making my job harder." McCoy took his arm. "Why don't you sit down?"

"If I sit down, I'll stop thinking."

"Yes, but I might be able to get the fever down."

"Not now—Spock's coming."

Blue on black, recognizable from a mile off, their science officer's slim form was caught by the last shafts of hazy orange sunset as he came toward them, his tricorder in one hand, the other dripping with mud and seaweed. His hair was a dot of stove black against the wild landscape. Without so much as a house or a hut to civilize the background, he looked like a colorful peg driven into the ground by a really big child.

"Geologist LaCerra has made a discovery," he said as he

approached. He had to raise his voice slightly over the miles-wide sizzle of crickets now rising as the darkness settled in.

"What've you got, Spock?"

Spock hesitated—not something that usually happened when he had an answer literally in hand. He paused, shifted from one foot to the other a couple of times, and fixed his eyes on Kirk.

"Ammonites, Captain."

Kirk squinted at him. "What?"

"Ammonites were cephalopods. Shelled sea animals similar to the chambered nautilus. They were bountiful in all bodies of water during the Cretaceous period, roughly seventy million years ago. Beaches were littered with them. There were thousands of species."

"So?"

"With the extinction of the dinosaurs and several other life forms, ammonites ceased to exist almost instantly on the evolutionary time table. There are billions of fossilized impressions of these creatures below the K–T layer, but none above it."

"What's a K–T layer?"

"Pardon me—the Cretaceous–Tertiary layer is the point at which the two geological time periods meet. There are billions of ammonite impressions below this layer—"

"And none above it. So they're extinct. Spock," Kirk interrupted with a telling groan, "tell me *bluntly* what the problem is."

The Vulcan paused, but not because he had been drawn up short. He clamped his lips and simply extended his hand. Embedded in seaweed was a baseball-sized coiled shell, not particularly attractive, but polished and streaked with variegated color and clearly not made of millions of years worth of sediment.

"Captain," Spock said, "this ammonite is alive."

Kirk stepped closer. "Alive? Are you sure what you've got?" He poked at the specimen in Spock's hand.

"Jim," McCoy interrupted, "do you smell something?"

He was squinting through the fresh twilight at the clumps of overgrowth. He stepped toward the bushy tangles. "Manure . . ."

Dread crawled over the captain as he let the little shelled animal fall from his mind and hurried to McCoy. "Phasers. On stun."

"Captain," Spock said, "should we engage our lighting implements?"

"No," Kirk told him. "Let's not disturb the natural goings-on. If we turn lights on, half the wildlife will hide."

Spock offered about a third of a nod. "Logical."

The underbrush caught Kirk's insteps and forced him to work for each step. His arm tingled as he held his phaser above the leaves. The musty smell of manure grew suddenly strong. The crickets had stopped clicking. Silence blanketed the hillside, maybe too much.

"Captain," Spock began, his head tilted slight, "I hear something. Respiration . . . Increasing now."

Between them, McCoy stiffened. "I thought it was the breeze."

Kirk turned to the direction Spock was facing and extended his phaser. "There's no breeze. Spock, back off . . . slowly." When Spock had managed to shift backward a few steps through the tangled bushes, Kirk mouthed, "Tricorder."

The slim dark form of his first officer moved with cautious stealth, lowering the phaser and bringing up his tricorder. A few seconds passed, then Spock clicked the tricorder's power on.

And the tiny mechanical click was all it took. The night cracked open with a single loud shriek. The bushes parted before them.

A wide black mound rose to eye level, bristling in the starlight. It wobbled briefly, then forced itself upward out of the bushes like a seismic eruption, and in seconds it was over their heads. The shriek dropped to a blistering roar and got louder.

McCoy dropped backward and disappeared, but Kirk

never saw what did the pushing. He heard the whine of Spock's phaser and raised his own but was struck in the left shoulder—how could something so big move so fast!

Before the thought set in, he was lying on his right hip with his elbow dug into the underbrush and his good leg pinned under him. Above, against a muted sky and a cloud of flies, rose the outline of a giant head with a five-foot-wide bony frill and a scoop-shaped horn as long as he was tall.

And Spock's phaser whined again through the darkness.

The sound fortified Kirk. He twisted his upper body, brought his arm close to his ear—his own phaser was still somehow in his hand—and he closed his fingers on the firing mechanism.

The night opened up with an electric orange streak that sizzled. The beam struck the giant black shape hovering over them as the animal swung around again and roared.

The sound climbed his bones. Even growing up in the woods and farmlands of rural Iowa, he'd never heard a sound like that before—a cross between the long call of a moose and the shriek of . . . well, a hell of a shriek.

The animal was turning but not toward him. Toward Spock.

Kirk felt its huge feet stomp the ground unevenly, maneuvering to attack the Vulcan, and something inside him snapped.

Forcing himself upward until he could see over the grass, he changed his posture, gripped the phaser with both hands, and aimed where he thought the animal's spine should be.

I'm the captain. If you want meat, come get me.

And he opened fire again.

Chapter Eight

THE MASSIVE ANIMAL'S HOWL was counterplayed by the whine of Starfleet phasers.

Why wasn't it going down? The phaser was designed to neutralize—suddenly the night sky wobbled. The black-on-black mass shuddered, tilted to one side, dropped partially down, then all the way down with a great *humph*. The bushes snapped, and other animals, unseen in the darkness, skittered out of the way.

With a huge breath, the animal gave up the fight and lay heaving in a clearing its own weight had just created. Breath after breath, it huffed the proclamation that it wasn't down for good.

Kirk rolled onto his side, then forced himself up onto his knees, grabbed a handful of branches, and pulled himself up. Fighting to catch his breath, he pushed through the bushes toward where he had last seen McCoy.

"Bones! Spock! Where are you?"

About ten yards away, Spock rose from the overgrowth, dragging McCoy to his feet.

Kirk tried to knee his way through the brush to them. "You all right?"

"Yes, sir," Spock said, but he seemed a little surprised.

"Bones?"

Stumbling to his feet, Leonard McCoy staggered to the stunned creature and circled it, keeping clear of the twitches of sharp cloven hooves. He breathed heavily as he lifted

83

each of his legs high and made a series of little jumps that brought him to the animal that had nearly gored Spock. "Captain, take a look at this!"

The creature was massive—the size of a buffalo. In fact, it had the thick hide and hair of a buffalo, four-toed hooves of a rhino, but also a wide sweeping horn arching out from a faceplate, and a neck crest that must have been five feet across. The creature's tiny eyes rolled, a leg twitched, but otherwise it lay still, heaving.

McCoy reached for the frilled edge of the neck crest and shook it. It barely moved. Just the neck and head were the size of a Starfleet cargo crate. He fingered the animal's hair.

"Look at this—it's hairlike, but it's not hair. It's insulation of some kind . . . probably developed in response to an ice age."

"Most insulation evolved from scales," Spock said. "Some mammallike reptiles developed true hair; some flying reptiles, a hairlike material; and some small meat-eating prehistoric animals may—"

"Look, I *know* there's never been anything like this on Earth!" McCoy wheezed. "Prehistoric or otherwise!"

Without wasting time on pointless agreements, Kirk snapped up his communicator. "Spock, who's the zoologist?"

"Lieutenant La Cerra is senior zoologist and paleontologist, sir, just transferred from the science vessel *John Rockland*. Lieutenant Ling is—"

"Kirk to LaCerra."

The communicator buzzed faintly. When no response came, he switched frequencies. "Kirk to *Enterprise*."

"Lieutenant Dewey here, sir."

"Where's Uhura?"

"Off watch, sir, but she's down in engineering trying to sort out the communications dysfunctions."

He drew a stiff breath. Reassurance washed through him that martial structure was still in play, watches were still being maintained, and all the time-honored, traditional, systematic orderliness that kept a ship's crew from cracking under pressure were still in operation, even in the bowels of catastrophe.

"Dewey, contact Chief Barnes and get me Lieutenant LaCerra. Have her beamed directly here. I've got an animal I want her to look at."

"Aye, sir. Stand by, please."

Keeping his communicator grid open, Kirk fingered the controls of the phaser in his other hand. The smell of the heaving animal at their feet was enough to choke a dead horse. "Both of you, put phasers on kill. Obviously we can't anticipate the usual North American wildlife we've been used to. Either of you have a theory about this thing?"

"It appears to be a slow-moving grazer," Spock said. "Possibly related to the woolly mammoth—"

"Or a rhinoceros," McCoy added. "Or a stegosaurus! Look at this tail!" He reached into the grass and came up with both arms coiled around a shocker of an extra weapon: a tail as big around as a man's rib cage, armed with a single-rowed rack of flesh-colored spikes the size of swords.

"Incredible!" Kirk limped through the grass and put his hand on one of the spikes.

"I'd categorize this creature as ceratopsoid," Spock said. He ran his tricorder over the smelly, fly-clouded mass. "Large bony cranial frill plate protecting heavy neck and shoulders . . . Forward-mounted facial horn . . . Massive low-hanging head, but with a blunt snout, squared off for grazing, though most ceratopsoids had parrotlike beaks."

Making a passing wave at the flies, he knelt beside the animal's huge head. "To my knowledge there has never been a creature like this on the Great Northern Plains, even in prehistory. There are antlered animals here, but none with horns."

"Or there *should* be none. Spock, reanalyze. Have we retreated in time?"

Spock peered through him in the darkness, and his tone was solid. "Absolutely not, Captain."

"All right . . . what took it so long to go down under phaser-stun?"

"Thickness of the hide," McCoy said, "and we might have been hitting that horn or the neck crest. I'd guess it acted as a buffer."

Kirk licked his dry lips. "We're dealing with an Earth whose weather and topography are right, but nothing else. Spock, are you thinking what I'm thinking?"

"I believe so." Spock straightened up.

Limping toward the brink of the cliff, Kirk looked over the open hills, at the empty bay, and listened to the distant whistle of birds that he didn't recognize.

Slowly, he murmured, "Alternative evolution . . ."

"Louise, just back away from it—real slowly."

"Look at its eyes, Dale. That's binocular vision! I just want to get a little closer so my tricorder can pick up the retinal structure. I can't believe what I'm seeing! All the traits of a mammal, but green and yellow abutting scales instead of skin—that's no mammal."

"I'm keeping my phaser trained on it."

"The striped pattern provides camouflage for stalking in tall grass or undergrowth . . . Some large cats developed that kind of pattern—tigers, leopards . . ."

"Louise, I'm not sure of my aim in the dark. At least let's tranquilize it, will ya?"

"Can you believe this? It's stalking me! Just like a mammal . . . Come on, baby, come on . . ."

"Quit that. You're making it follow you. That's it. I'm gonna call Chief Barnes."

"Shh. Don't distract it. Have you got its body temperature? Dale, put the damn communicator down and take some readings! Your tricorder is rigged for microbiology. Mine's not."

"Look, I don't—I don't think . . . All right, but just stay away from it."

"It's nowhere near me. Take the readings. We might not get another chance. Come on, baby . . . Move those pretty yellow legs for Lou—"

"You're backing toward high grass. Don't go in there."

"Shut up, Dale. Look at those wild eyes . . . I can't wait to dissect those—"

"Lou, it's darting! It's running! Lou, run!"

"Take the readings! Take the—"

"Lou, don't go into the grass! Get out of the grass! Oh, God! Look out! Louise, run! Run! Run! Oh, God! Oh, my God! Louise!"

Leonard McCoy squinted as he absorbed what he was seeing. "Yellow poppies . . ."

The three men stood staring heavily at the sulfur curtain draping the moonlit hillsides for miles into the distance.

McCoy's whisper made a terrible din.

Ostriches, primates where they shouldn't be, living shell-fish that should be dead, massive land animals that shouldn't be here in the first place—

Now it had been said. Plagued by the image of McCoy gazing down at his daughter's house, now committed to the veils of memory, Kirk thought of his mother's farm and what Iowa would look like in this condition. He thought of the man-made pond behind the barn that his father had stocked with trout and bass for the Kirk boys to catch.

Nothing but dry grass. Maybe a mud slick at the bottom of that hill.

Funny . . . the hill was probably still there.

A bare hill, no farmhouse, no road leading back to the old settled conclave of Riverside. No thousand memories. No sandy-haired mother in stalwart, eternal mourning for an irascible Starfleet Security man who had gone through the cold window of enemy space and never returned.

A boy without a trout, a hill without a farmhouse. A wild, lonely world.

Jim Kirk endured a moment of random pain and choked his sorrow down. He looked up.

Spock and McCoy were both looking at him.

He started to pace, though it shot his leg and spine with torture every other step. "Whether we like it or not, we have to accept that we've been through some kind of warping effect. It's happened before."

The Vulcan's expression betrayed his racing thoughts. "That forejudgment may be premature, sir."

"May be too obvious, you mean?"

Spock snapped a look at him, gratified. "Yes, sir."

Kirk hobbled toward the huffing animal, his voice hardly more than a choke. "What did we do?"

"Jim," McCoy interrupted, "how do you know we did anything?"

He turned to his doctor. "Because," he said, "we're here."

The statement fell on the shimmering remnants of sunset and was consumed. Spock didn't say anything, but the captain could tell that his intuitive officer found no remedy in that conclusion. Cold with deep mortal panic that somehow he had gummed up the universe by botching one experiment, Kirk felt his throat knot up. Every man at some time in his life wonders if things would be better off without him. As a starship captain, his successes and certainly his blunders had always been magnified. This, though—he could barely grasp the scope.

"If we went back and shot Adam and Eve, it wouldn't affect this much," Kirk pressed. "These bizarre animals can't be just the result of lack of humans. The sky is filled with birds, just as it always has been."

"Evidently," Spock said, "even here they outcompeted the flying reptiles."

"We're not that sure of the science we've been tampering with. Somehow we caused ourselves to jump into a parallel universe or caused our own universe to change." As an embedded chill gripped his spine, he limped between his two officers and looked over the undeveloped landscape. "What if we're not lost . . . but humanity is? It's one thing to accept that we've marooned ourselves interdimensionally, but if we've destroyed the civilization around us . . . I feel damned obliged to fix it."

The statement fell on the broad glazed bay. He started to say something else but chopped his own thoughts away with a motion that whipped his communicator up. It chittered at him. "Kirk here," he barked before the instrument was finished making its sound. "What's the problem with that beam-over?" Frustration rolled through his limbs and tightened them. He determined to win out over the poison in his body if he had to dig for leeches and bleed himself—if there were still leeches. And he would make a decision, no matter how bitter, if he could stitch together a theory. Forward movement of any kind—would he have to strangle a wild guess out of Spock?

"Barnes here, sir . . ."

"Barnes, what's going on with the zoologist?"

"Bannon just came up from the valley floor, sir. Is it possible for you to beam over here?"

"Why?" Kirk demanded.

"Captain," Barnes's voice croaked over the distance between them, *"Lieutenant LaCerra's been killed, sir."*

"We killed about . . . half of them, sir. But they got to LaCerra before we could drive them off. Some of them went that way . . . Sir, if you'd come with me."

Chief Chemist Barnes's uniform had been shredded in several places, leaving ragsicles dripping all over his chest and loose threads clinging like vines around what was left of his trouserlegs. McCoy was eyeing the bloody streaks on the man's arms and chest but didn't try to get between him and the captain yet.

"Anybody else hurt?" Kirk asked.

"Bannon's real shook up, poor kid. This way, sir."

Barnes was in a hurry but moving in a fatalistic way, as though he knew hurrying wouldn't help. He seemed more anxious to hurry himself out of the command ring and get somebody else to take over the situation.

"One of these things started to chase LaCerra," he said, huffing like a racehorse. "She tried to get away from it, but she didn't realize it was deliberately driving her into a pack of others hiding in the tall grass. There must've been eight or ten of them."

On a depressed portion of tall grass, as though fallen asleep on the brink of a pond, lay Lieutenant Louise LaCerra. She could've been dozing in the moonlight, so peaceful was her face. Her body had been slashed open from under one arm to the point of her hip, and from the underside of one breast across and down to the cup of her pelvis. Her uniform had been slit open and the material was curled back, baring the white lips of open wounds cleanly meant to disembowel—not random at all.

McCoy didn't even bother to kneel by the corpse. There just wasn't any point.

And he didn't want to get too close to that thing lying beside her.

Tucked sedately into the warm body was the clawed foot of an animal that lay beside her in a deceptive caress, a creature with skin like a snake and a face like a lizard but eyes wide open that looked like a cat's eyes. Its forepaws were gripping LaCerra's shoulder, dug in to the knuckles. Almost as long from nose to tip of its blunt tail as its prey was tall, the animal had a gaping mouth that showed rows of pointed teeth gleaming in the moonlight. Tiger-striped hide and a bare white belly were like a reptile, but certainly weren't the colors of any known Earth lizard.

And those sure weren't the eyes of a lizard.

"There are six more of those things lying around here, sir," Barnes reported, fighting his emotions down. "I mean, if you want them." He shuffled into the grass and kicked another of those animals, phasered to death, out into the open at the captain's feet. It flopped like a sack of sand. "That one next to her drove her to all these others. Then they were on her like fire ants. She never had a chance."

Kirk moved away from the animal, away from the boiling misery rising in his mind that this girl who had gone into space with spirit and bold initiative, willing to risk her life as far from Earth as a person can get, had died right here, within hiking distance of where she had been educated and trained.

He found something of a betrayal in that. He sidled toward Spock.

"A precise and coordinated attack," Spock commented, keeping his voice low. "A man eater—if you'll pardon the crude colloquialism—must be smarter, faster, and better armed than what it eats. These animals may be the smartest life form on the planet under these conditions. They may be as intelligent as leopards, perhaps even chimpanzees. Driving prey toward an ambush is partly instinctive but definitely partly learned as a hunting technique."

"It's a sprinter," McCoy said. "Look at those long, strong hind legs. And the slashing foreclaws and ripping teeth . . . and what it did to that poor girl. These things know how to disable their targets—"

"While minimizing their own chance of injury," Spock interrupted.

"But it's not a mammal," Kirk said. He pushed down a surge of irritation at Spock for being a little too fascinated and not angry enough. "I don't see anything that's a mammal."

"They may be here," Spock suggested, "but kept in check by the creatures like this." He nodded again to the animals slaughtered in defense of a girl. "It may be interesting to transport to the Amazon region. Arboreal primates may be quite successful under these conditions."

"This isn't a field trip." Kirk spun to the other Starfleet personnel. "The rest of you have anything to put any light on this problem?"

"Yes, sir, I do. Bannon, sir," the red-haired fellow with the buck teeth said. He was trembling. "Anthropology."

"Report, Bannon."

"I've got some data here I'd like Mr. Spock to have a look at."

"Why? Just tell me what you've got."

"Well . . . because I think I've picked up trace evidence of worldwide natural catastrophe." He winced at his own words.

Bannon said "think," but he meant he was damned sure he'd picked that up and he knew he sounded like a lunatic when he reported it.

"You mean there was a civilization here?"

"That's right, sir!" Bannon shook his tricorder. "I've been tied into the ship for a half hour, and all the wide-range readings come up for an organized prehistoric civilization. Then they all . . . just up and died! Or maybe killed each other."

Kirk waved a hand impatiently. "Tell me why you think this. Spock, listen to this."

"The ship's lab is reading several layers of development up to a point," Bannon said, "both manufactured and natural, and then a cutoff, encroachment of nature, then another gradual rising of a civilization, with all the steps we'd expect, then the same cycle of destruction. All the evidence is in the center of the continents, mostly in South America and Africa, and it's several strata down. It's all been covered over, but I had them do some overlays, and we think there's evidence of wooden structures, then later a surge of sophisticated metallurgy. And above those, traces of wide-range warfare."

Kirk tried to hold on to his expression. "War? Are you sure?"

"Yes, sir, real big war. It runs in the same cycle, over and over again."

The anthropologist's ruddy face screwed into a frown. "It doesn't make any sense! There wasn't any industrial life on Earth that long ago. There wasn't even rudimentary tribal life, never mind sophisticated battle capabilities. Seismology indicates deeply embedded geological evidence of destruction on the large scale . . . possibly nuclear!"

"Well," McCoy blurted, "now we know what happened to the redwoods."

Suddenly angry that there wasn't the hum of a city beyond the crackle of crickets and the whistle of birds, Kirk pressed his lips tight. "How old is this evidence of destruction?"

Bannon managed to keep his voice steady. "On the order of ten to twenty million years."

McCoy pushed toward them. "That's ridiculous!"

"Much earlier than tribal hominids," Spock said.

"So it certainly wasn't a human war," Kirk snapped. "Could someone have colonized the planet and made all those wars?" He turned. "Chief Barnes, what do you have to say about the atmospheric chemistry?"

"Not much, sir," the older man said. "It reads just as Earth atmosphere should read under these ... apparent conditions. No trace pollutants from early fossil fuel usage, at least not on the surface, and no artificial sculpting of land masses."

"No evidence of space travel?"

Barnes's reddened eyes widened. "No, sir, nothing like that."

"Doesn't mean it didn't happen ... after ten million years," Kirk said, "anything could clean itself out."

Spock scanned Bannon's tricorder screen. "Preliminary sensor sweeps confirm radiation abnormalities at different places in different strata all over the Earth. We call these 'welded-glass horizons.' The ecology rebounded in every instance, though there were at least four major periods of continentwide obliteration. Given enough time, nature always rebounds. With new forms of life, of course, but it does rebound. Many of these animals may be the result of radiation."

In the deep background, an animal—one that had never lived on this planet before—shrieked at the moon. Alien insects rattled like bacon frying.

He primed his communicator again. "Kirk to *Enterprise*."

"Dewey, sir."

"Launch a lighting flare, five kilometer radius. I want to see this valley floor."

"Aye, sir, one minute."

The sounds of the landscape were damningly familiar. The ratcheting of frogs, the chitter of neocrickets, the soft brush of breeze over long grass that was once the grass of his childhood.

Jimmy, put down that fishing pole and get the lawn tended. You only have one thing to do, so why haven't you done it?

And the smell of it all—the bay, the air, the grass. It played games with his mind as Kirk fought to swallow the reality of what their science told them. He felt as if he were letting go of something he would never retrieve. He'd had this feeling since the *Exeter* and *Farragut* disappeared, and he'd seen it in his crew's faces. The creased eyes, the pursed lips, the guarded fear that something had happened that they couldn't correct, that finally tampering with science on too big a scale had exacted too big a price.

Mankind had run that risk for a long time. Had they gone one step too far? Had he given one order too many?

"There it is, sir!" Barnes shouted, pointing almost directly over his head.

In the slate sky, even smaller than the stars, was a moving pinprick. They watched as it wobbled and spiraled, changing its path with the vagaries of the stratosphere, drifting this way, then that, volleyballed by thermals that argued above the water and land.

Then the flare's altitude trigger kicked in, and it popped —they could almost hear the *crack*—and a sizzling strobelike light burst over the entire valley floor, nearly five miles across. Suddenly the planet was like an old-time movie, cast in gray and opal, and a black wedge of San Francisco Bay anchoring the farthest point.

Startled heads rose over the grass, huge heads with six-foot horns, neck plates, and tiny eyes.

Beyond that, two long-necked relics placidly chewing stalks they had pulled from a tree. They might have been giraffes, except that their heads were smooth and elongated. Their bright white-and-yellow necks arched, long throats constantly working, thick balancing tails lapping slowly from side to side, and spindly legs poised in place. They were patently disinterested in the sudden brightness or the odd little observers way over here. They froze in place and stared but continued to chew.

An ungodly racket far to the left went up like a cannon shot. A pack of LaCerra's new-age banshees were cornering a slothlike animal with a leathery face and a forejaw that lanced downward as a weapon instead of front teeth. It hacked downward again and again now that it could see what was attacking it, then screamed as the relentless predators ganged in on it. Some distracted it while others plunged in and ripped its spine open. Suddenly all Kirk could think of was the girl he'd failed to protect.

Half the banshees kept hacking away with their foreclaws, ignoring the light that had whacked on overhead and was wobbling on the thermals, but the other half were shocked by it and their intelligent minds told them to beat it. Kirk watched them pause, look, squint, try to make the decision between fear and famine. Some even looked at the light, then at the prey, then at the light again.

About a third of those ran away. The rest decided to ignore the hovering white light and feast on that which they had so diligently pursued.

There was the evidence, plain as—day. Creatures swept with instinct, consumed by raw nature, yet smart enough to make a conscious choice. They were on their way to being able to *think*.

Creatures with skin like snakes and minds like leopards.

The flare would have kept lighting the landscape for six or eight more minutes, but a sharp puff of inland wind blasted it out over the water, and the sudden lack of thermals brought it crashing into the bay with an audible *fizzzzz*. The last they saw of it was a thread of smoke twisting toward the moon. Darkness fell in again.

A few feet away, someone sighed heavily. Someone else made a worried *whew*. But no one actually said anything.

James Kirk and his crew stood listening to the snapping of bones and the arguing of smart predators. They might as well be standing on a planet millions of light-years from here.

"All hands," Kirk said, "collect any specimens or information you need right now. We're leaving. You have ten minutes. Stay together."

A cloud of miserable "Aye ayes" rose and dropped away.

The captain moved to the edge of the mesa. He absorbed the slate sky, called with his mind to the empty enameled bay, listened to the shuffles of his command as they gathered what they could.

"This is like a dream inside a nightmare," McCoy sighed. "A pleasant place, decent weather, nice sky . . . on a forgotten planet."

"We haven't forgotten it," Kirk snapped. "Something's wrong. I'll fix it if I can figure out how."

He limped a few feet away to the brink of a hillock and peered through the trees at a sliver of San Francisco Bay. His eyes felt as though they would pop out if he held his breath.

"Earth," he uttered. "The cornerstone of the Federation . . . completely barren of intelligent life."

"This has been the wish of countless human beings for centuries," McCoy said. "A pristine Earth, untouched by the hands of men, free to grow, live at its own pace—"

"Only the wish of those who regard intelligence as a contaminant," Kirk defended. "I don't. This is beautiful, yes, but our Earth was beautiful, too. There are trees and animals by the millions there, too. This . . . it's not all that different from the Earth we know. The same trees, the same grass, the same deserts, not in much different amounts. Mankind isn't a plague on Earth, any more than the Federation is a plague in space. We of all people should be ready to admit we've done some good out there. Humanity is part of nature. Without people, this is an empty, savage, unappreciated place."

Silence coiled around the drained thoughts.

"I agree," Spock said.

McCoy turned to look at him. "You do?"

"Of course."

"I wouldn't have expected that from you, Spock. You're usually so quick to point out humanity's bad judgments— anytime anyone points out to you that you're half human, you feel obliged to be ashamed."

"Bones," Kirk said, "leave him alone."

Everything about Spock was suddenly understated, yet poignant in his alien way. He seemed heavy-laden, deeply disturbed, more than either of his companions would have expected. He specialized in taking even the wildest of occurrences in stride, fielding all the unimaginables of space travel with grace, working by the book, taking things one at a time—well, fifty at a time but in logical order.

Tonight he was different. Finally he visibly let his guard

down a little and blinked into the flames. "A world without intelligence is a primitive place, Doctor, not an enchanted place. Intelligence is part of the advancing scheme of evolution. Without it, nature reaches a plateau very quickly and does not progress beyond raw survival. The full flavor of possibility goes unsavored. And that . . . is a true shame."

McCoy offered a grin. "Well, I'll be."

Beyond the tiny opal solace of the moon was a moist landscape dotted with pockets of fog.

Kirk raised his eyes again to the dark and chirping landscape, and his mind leaped ahead. "I feel like I'm staring at an accident where somebody died. Am I punch-drunk? Am I still in that coma?"

"If you are, Jim," McCoy said, "we're in it with you."

Chapter Nine

"LEAVE THE SOLAR SYSTEM, Mr. Sulu, one-third sublight."

"One-third sublight, aye, sir. Destination, sir?"

"None yet. All right, Dr. McCoy, get to work. Make it fast."

"Yes, Captain. Just stand still and don't breathe too deeply."

"Lieutenant, I want the ship at yellow alert until further notice."

"Yellow alert, sir. Attention all hands, go to yellow alert . . . Repeat, yellow alert."

"Go ahead, Mr. Spock. We're all listening."

The bridge was a buzzing haven, bright and soothing after the pristine world they had just left. This was home now, their only home.

A little more crowded than usual, since Barnes, Bannon, Ling, and the other scientists from the landing party were here, too, dispirited and grim. Ordinarily, this would've been done in the briefing room, but Jim Kirk wasn't about to leave his bridge in what had suddenly become hostile space.

While McCoy applied hypospray after hypospray and fed him little cups of medicated liquid, each of which gave him a new flush or chill, Kirk sat in his command chair and felt his eyes redden. He should be lying down for the treatment, but he refused to have a cot brought to the bridge. His health was at the bottom of his priority list right now.

"Go ahead, Spock," he urged, determined that ship's business come before the hissing and the slurping and the sweating.

Above, on the circular quarterdeck, Spock stood in elegant repose at his station, his shoulders slightly rounded.

"Positions of the continents are unaffected. South America's thorny forests are intact, but there is minimal rain forest. Nearly nine-tenths less than we had, in fact. Africa's grassy savannas, deserts, barren land, and jungles are relatively unaltered. Here is some of the planet's wildlife. Western Ethiopia . . ."

Pictures were popping on and off three science station monitors, high-altitude shots that quickly zeroed in as the ship's tactical sensors picked up life forms right down to heart rates.

"Quite a large population of burrowing and/or colonizing creatures," Spock began, "relatively small primates that are somewhat squirrellike. No rodents, though there are multituberculates with prehensile tails. Billions of insects with appreciable evolutionary changes. In the Orient, Lieutenant Ling has singled out dwarf versions of recognizable sauropods, theropods, and ornithopods. I have yet to find any large roaming predators. There are some sizable grazers, but predation is dominated by small pack-attackers."

"No tyrannosaurs," Kirk muttered, "but there are wolves."

Spock looked down at him. "If you're speaking in the poetic sense, yes." He let the screen continue showing pictures of hippo-sized animals with long necks and heavy tails. "Obviously sauropod descendants. Not as large, but clearly related."

"But no large primates, sir?" Lieutenant Ling broke in from behind the captain's shoulder. There were tears in her eyes. Nobody could blame her. "Nothing that highly evolved?"

Spock shifted his feet. "What is 'highly evolved' depends upon your point of view, Lieutenant. The squirrel-sized early primates are the most advanced we've found so far. And the oceans . . ."

He tapped the controls, and all three screens switched to water shots with creatures shipping through heavy rollers and coasting on crests.

"I don't understand!" Bannon croaked, his voice cracking. "That's a twenty-meter pliosaur! How can that thing possibly be there? How can it be there, sir?"

He turned to Kirk, his face reddened and hot, eyes sorrow-blinded.

Kirk flung a blistering glare at him and dared him to lose control on the bridge. "Control yourself, Lieutenant."

Like a slapped child who was suddenly relieved to know where the boundaries were, Bannon murmured, "Yes, sir."

Spock ticked off ample seconds, then blanketed the bridge with his fluid voice. "We have found large plankton eaters, large-mouthed monosaurs, or rather their descendants, a breed of surface dwellers similar to elasmosaurs . . . billions of Mesozoic shellfish, ammonites, and countless relations on every body of water, including fresh water, and you'll note here some four-meter to eight-meter floating mounds. These are living colonies, probably similar to the Portuguese man-o-war, with sweeping fibrous tendrils as long as fifty meters. There are sharks, also, of course, as they are among the oldest of predatory creatures. Many marine animals are advanced versions of—"

"It's a very nice zoo, Mr. Spock," Kirk bluntly cut in, "but it's not ours. Can you give me a conclusion? Something I can use?"

Spock snapped off the screens and let the void fall. Behind him, the darkened screens were emblematic.

"These animals are unknown, but familiar," he told them, "almost traceable to Earth's Mesozoic background, but clearly they did not exist as they are now on Earth at all, even in prehistoric times. And with the exception of some ocean dwellers, most of these creatures are smaller than their Mesozoic relatives. Our most substantive theory," he finished, "is that they are descendants of an alternative universe . . . one in which the dinosaurs never died out."

The bridge sounds clicked and whirred in purposeful peace, amplifying a human silence after he finished. No one said anything. What could be said to that?

Spock was being charitable by using the word *theory;* it softened the ghastly blow that what they had seen was real, that they had nowhere to go, no Federation to turn to. If he had said *fact* or *conclusion,* he might as well have slapped them each in the face with the nonexistence of their homes and families, their nations, their histories, their homeworld.

"Captain," Sulu said, his voice heavy; "clearing the solar system, sir."

"Ahead standard." Kirk anchored himself to Spock's opiate expression.

"Standard, aye, sir."

Spock came a step or two closer and gazed down at him. "Sir, when the evolution of animals provided no clues, I went to the next most obvious level of analysis: geology. The Earth itself."

Noticing the inflections in his first officer's voice, the glint in his black eyes, Kirk sat forward slightly. "You've got something, haven't you?"

Spock raised a single ink-slash brow. "I've roughly correlated the data we collected on the 'new' Earth and run a comparison with physical conditions of Earth as we know it. Our Earth shows geological evidence of cosmic dust, molten pellets of tectite glass, or shocked quartz, and a thin layer of iridium in the K–T layer of strata. The Earth beneath us now has none of these ballistic details."

"Oh, Jesus," Bannon uttered, and he and the science specialists looked at each other.

Squinting, Kirk asked, "What does that do for us? What happened?"

"What did *not* happen, sir," Spock corrected, plainly hopeful under his mantle of poise, his emphasis nearly poetic. "Iridium is very rare on Earth, but extremely common in asteroids."

"What's that supposed to mean?" Kirk glanced around. Spock and the others seemed to be waiting for him to catch the meaning.

Finally Spock shifted from one foot to the other. "Sir, it is commonly known what killed off the large-bodied animals and much of the sealife of the Cretaceous Earth."

"Well, common it to *me.*"

Everyone around him seemed embarrassed for him, but he didn't care. And what was that look McCoy was giving him? Had he grown horns? What was one asteroid, more or less, to a starship captain?

Flagging his hands in protest, he said, "It's not my venue. So what?"

McCoy gestured at the upper deck. "Come on, Spock, we're playing with *millions* of years here! A million this way or that, ten thousand, a century . . . What are the odds? One asteroid—"

"Gentleman," Kirk said with starch.

They looked at him. Spock nodded heavily. "Roughly sixty to sixty-five million years before now, an asteroid ten to fifteen miles in diameter struck the Earth at a point that is now under water, just off the north coast of the Yucatan Peninsula in Mexico. The crater, known as the Chixilub crater, is nearly one hundred eighty miles in diameter and was hidden under the Gulf waters for millennia. The impact left shocked quartz and tectite glass fragments similar to those in evidence at sites of nuclear detonation and notable iridium in a layer of Earth's strata. When the dust finally settled, the age of dinosaurs was snuffed out. But here, today," he said, nodding at the Earth as it rolled on their forward screen, "there is no notable iridium. There are no fused glass fragments . . . and there is no crater in the Yucatan."

Daring him to be wrong, Kirk scoured him silently. A focal point in time change that was *millions* of years back? How?

"Jim!" McCoy swung around to him. "If that's true, then all of evolution was changed! Mammals never had the chance to evolve on this planet! Humanity never had a chance!"

Chapter Ten

BEING A STARSHIP'S CAPTAIN, one of only twelve such souls in Starfleet, James Kirk absorbed the concept in one hard lump along with all its vast complications. He pushed out of his chair and looked at the undamaged new Earth, the one with no crater below the gleaming blue waters.

"What happened, Spock? What happened to a fifteen-mile-wide ball of rock? Where is it?"

"Unknown, sir," the Vulcan said. The simple words were terrible the way he spoke them.

Irritated, Kirk began to pace, to think. "We know an asteroid hit and most of the dinosaurs went extinct because it did," he thought aloud. "Could we have stopped it from happening? During the warp shield experiment, could we have disrupted the flow of time somehow? Slipped through a crack, even for an instant?"

Burdened with the new question, Spock paused. When he

spoke, his voice was rough, intense, plagued with the problems he saw rising in his captain's eyes. "I have no answer for that theory, sir."

How could evolution itself be changed? This was encompassing, not just the death of a key figure. This was much bigger and much older than that, more astounding in its scope than the effect of a person or even a nation. "What about the civilizations who rose and fell on this Earth?" Kirk asked. "Have you gentlemen confirmed what you found down there? Were they natural to the planet? Or did some alien race colonize this Earth and live and die there?"

Dolefully Bannon sucked a hard breath through his nostrils and glared from under his brows. "If a space-faring race colonized the planet, why are there long periods of preindustrial civilization?"

"Lieutenant," Spock cautioned. When Bannon backed off, he let him off the hook by filling the sudden quiet. "These civilizations rose to industry, flashed into war, destroyed themselves, and fell back into barbarism."

"And finally they're completely gone," Kirk said. "By the time you have the culture to colonize another planet, you've either stopped fighting among yourselves or you've destroyed yourselves. This culture seems to have done the latter . . . on an Earth where mankind never evolved."

He drew away from McCoy and scoured the carpet for answers. He was starting to feel stronger. The hot flash was fading. His uniform felt clammy around his chest and ribs, his shoulders still aching, but it was easier now to hold his head up than it had been twenty minutes ago.

"We've always toyed with the idea of what the galaxy would be like without humans . . . what Earth would be like. Now we know."

So he raised his eyes again to Spock, ignoring the tense blinks from all around. These crewmen had come up through Starfleet and understood how far-reaching a single act could be, how many ripples could go out from a single drop of rain in a pond.

All of humanity was on the *Enterprise.* There weren't any others anywhere.

He pushed himself up from his chair and grasped the rail. "Posts," he said.

The landing party glanced at each other, then Chief Barnes said, "Aye, sir," as though speaking for all of them, and they began to shuffle for the turbolift. In a few moments, the bridge was cleared except for duty personnel, and suddenly it felt as empty as that grass-rimmed bay without a city.

McCoy was packing his medical bags and pretending not to pay attention to him.

Spock was poised over him on the upper deck, arms folded. He also said nothing—verbally.

Jim Kirk scowled at his bridge, at his crew trying to do their jobs in this sudden vacuum, cruising a universe no longer theirs.

"If I wasn't sure before," he said, "I am now. If in fact this ship has done some great wrong with our little swerve into a very big star," he malaised, "then it's my responsibility to put things right."

"Jim, you don't know that!" McCoy plunged around the command chair to face him, cautious not to actually touch the chair when he was challenging the man whose particular privilege it was to sit there. "You could be tampering with something that doesn't involve us at all! There could be millions—billions—of life forms out there, maybe whole civilizations whose history you could wipe out in an instant if we interfere!"

"Ours has been wiped out. I have a responsibility to that and to the civilizations who were *supposed* to be here."

"What about the Prime Directive as it applies to primitive races? Or even advanced races! Doesn't this bother you?"

"It bothers me a lot, Doctor," Kirk cracked, suddenly corrosive. "You'd do well not to say that to me again. As for the Prime Directive, this is why we send people into space instead of rules."

On the bridge of his own ship, Kirk felt as free as any captain to let his provocation show. He turned away from the doctor.

McCoy had the sense to back off, at least his volume—no, there went his attitude too. "Jim, everybody has limits."

"I don't believe in limits. Besides, I'm here. I'm going to interfere. Whatever happened to change the course of time, we're available to put things right. Mr. Spock, assuming you're right about that asteroid . . . that somehow it failed to strike . . . can we take the ship back in time and see that it hits?"

Trouble creased Spock's face. He gazed at the carpet for a moment, then looked up. "Captain, that hypothesis disturbs me. A natural event—one that we *know* happened—cannot simply 'fail' to occur."

"Then something made it fail," Kirk insisted. "I don't have all the answers, but we know the dinosaurs have to die, Mr. Spock. Even if we have to go back and kill them."

Spock dropped to the command deck and came so close to Kirk that their shoulders touched as they looked at the forward screen, showing their departure angle of the unknown Earth.

"Captain, something else. This suggests that we are not in an alternate universe, but that our own universe has been changed around us. To keep a spacial body of such magnitude from striking its assigned target would take sophisticated equipment, great contained energy, and a space-faring science using deliberate and extraordinary effort. If we did not move in time, and I know we did not, then the *Enterprise* could not have been the cause of the change."

"Then what kept us from being changed right along with everything else?" McCoy piped. "How can we still be here?"

Almost breaking his neck, Kirk shot that question right back to Spock. "The accretion disk?"

"Possibly," the Vulcan said, thinking at high speed. "More likely the cosmic string. It may have so warped space around us that time became a meaningless concept. We may have been sheltered from the change by our own experiment at Izell."

Pacing to keep his blood moving, Kirk walked to the other side of the command deck. "You're saying we weren't thrown through a dimensional crack, but instead we're the ones who stayed in our universe while everything else was changed around us?"

"That's a blue giant of a coincidence," McCoy drawled.

"Precisely," Spock said.

Kirk put a hand between them. "Is Izell changed in the previous time line then? Was the cosmic string ever there now?"

McCoy shook his head. "You can't ask for every answer, Jim!"

"Yes, I can. I'm still not sold on the idea that we didn't cause this." He felt the changing light from the forward screen move across his flushed cheeks. "We know how to go back in time. We also know how dangerous time travel is. Touch the wrong thing, cross the wrong street, cause the wrong person to live or die at the wrong time, and all history changes. We can use the slingshot effect around a sun to take the ship back, then use photon torpedoes to duplicate the effects of an asteroid impact or stop the interference from stopping the asteroid, whatever the interference was. That event would have to happen in space, so we'll need the ship."

McCoy shook his head. "The slingshot effect is fine when we're dealing with a century or two, but how will it be with multimillions of years? You don't know what that'll do to us."

"We know a slingshot effect takes us back in time roughly a hundred years to the minute. Spock, run it down for us. Sixty-five million years. Six hundred fifty thousand centuries—"

"Six hundred fifty thousand centuries would take ten thousand eight hundred thirty-three point three hours," Spock said, suddenly monotone as he calculated. "Which would be . . . four hundred fifty-one point three eight eight days."

As his hopes crashed, Kirk felt his shoulders sink. "A year and a half in the dream-stasis of time travel . . . The crew would starve."

"We wouldn't live long enough to starve," McCoy pointed out. "Dehydration would kill us within days. Add to that the

106

fact that you don't even know exactly when this asteroid hit—it could be sixty-two million and twenty years or sixty-eight million and four years. To show up within a thousand years would be fantastically accurate!"

"And the slightest deviance in trajectory," Spock added, gazing at McCoy with surprised appreciation, "movement of the fifth place after the decimal point could put us off the mark by hundreds of years."

Troubled, Kirk looked at them. "And what if we dare take a guess, kill off the dinosaurs, then the asteroid hits anyway? What would two impacts like that do to the Earth? To evolution?"

Plagued, McCoy frowned. "I don't like where this is going, Jim."

"There are even simpler factors, gentlemen," Spock said. "Four hundred fifty point three eight days of gravitational and time-distortion stress on the ship, in her current condition—"

"We'll have to find some other way," Kirk said, sharpening his voice. In as dramatic a gesture as he could make it, he hauled himself to his command chair and slid into it, then faced the helm. "What's your heading, Mr. Sulu?"

"Currently three seven mark one, sir. Straight across the most populated area of . . . well, *our* galaxy."

"Hold your course."

"Aye, sir."

"Forward view."

"Forward view, sir."

The screen abandoned the solar system they knew as the hub of their lives and turned outward the way they were heading, to the unfamiliar galaxy. As the ship wheeled on her way, Kirk gazed at Spock in silence. No one was doing any more analysis of the Earth they were leaving behind. Even Spock had seen enough of it.

A mechanical twitter at his shoulder broke their communication—McCoy's medical scanner.

"Captain," McCoy began, "your temperature is back to normal, for the time being. I'd like you to remain seated as much as possible for the next three hours or so, and even though I might as well be talking to myself, I'd like you to get some sleep."

"Tell yourself you're dreaming. I—"

"Captain!" Sulu sang out. "Long-range scanners hitting us, sir! They tracked us somehow!"

Glowering at the screen, at an enemy he couldn't even see yet, Kirk said, "Shields up."

"Shields, aye."

"There has never been a Romulan this close to Earth!" Chekov spat, his rage stumbling over the English words.

McCoy gathered his med pack under one arm and held tight to the command chair with the other. "Tell them we're parked in a no-Romulan zone."

"Belay that," Kirk snapped. "Sound general quarters."

The klaxon erupted through the ship, the glow of red alert lighting engulfed the bridge, and Uhura's voice announced the incoming danger with a deceptive calmness. The whole ship started to throb with activity.

"Where are they, Mr. Sulu?"

"Ten degrees substarboard abaft the beam, sir . . . bearing three-one . . . range, four point one parsecs and closing. No cloaking device, coming in at high speed."

"Put them on the forward screen, maximum visual."

The screen shifted from what was in front of them to what was coming up on their starboard quarter. Not a full second later, one of the neo-Romulan ships they'd evaded before came plunging down upon them out of deep space.

"Sensors on full capacity. Arm phasers."

"Phasers armed . . . ready—"

"Ready the photon torpedo guidance systems."

"Photons armed . . . Ready, sir."

PART TWO

DAMAGE CONTROL

"Why me? I look around that bridge . . . see the men are waiting for me to make the next move, and, Bones . . . what if I'm wrong?"

—James Kirk,
Balance of Terror

Chapter Eleven

"INTERCEPT COURSE!" Chekov called out.

"Evasive. I don't want to fight here unless I have to. We don't know the politics of this situation—who's right and who's wrong."

From behind him McCoy mumbled, "If it's that simple."

"Evasive, aye," Sulu responded, and the ship plunged away from the enemy. "They're in pursuit, sir."

Kirk didn't look away from the screens but knew Spock had glanced at him. With a grim eye on the forward screen, he leaned on his chair's arm and tapped the comm. "Kirk to Scott."

"Engineering, Scott here, sir."

"Mr. Scott, we're engaging a hostile up here. We've outrun them before and I want to do it again. Power up for high warp."

"No problem, sir, we'll have it."

"Very good. Kirk out."

"Their weapons are armed, sir," Spock said from the upper deck. "They're preparing to fire."

"Mr. Sulu, warp factor six as soon as you can get the power."

"Aye aye, sir . . . warp two . . . three . . . four . . . Captain!"

"Three more ships, sir!" Chekov shouted. "Dead ahead!"

"Belay warp eight—forward visual." Kirk was aware of the eyes flicking at him from different points on the bridge. They were watching him to take their cues from him. Critical, yes, how his enemy perceived him, but also and even more immediate was how his crew perceived him. "Continue evasive." He turned his head slightly to starboard without taking his eyes off the screen and spoke in a manner that would get Spock's attention. "Just like those animals. They led us to the pack."

"Some things," Spock answered quietly, "remain efficient through the eons."

Pressure hit them as Sulu was forced to angle the ship downward and to port to avoid two of the ships, but by the time he did that, the other two ships had closed in on his heading.

"Do what you can, Sulu," he said.

"They're boxing us in, sir," Spock said at the same time, making it clear that he didn't think Sulu could do much by way of maneuvers alone to dodge the big ships.

"We've got the speed, but they're not letting us use it." Kirk gripped his chair's armrest. "All right, if that's the way it is. Come about starboard."

"Coming about. Helm's answering."

"They're firing!" Chekov interrupted. On the auxiliary scanners, ships plunged in and out of frame, circling like vultures. "Incoming salvos!" His eyes were fixed to the screens as a wide arch of coordinated shots from two of the enemy ships crashed toward them.

The starship bucked and whined, then recovered and heaved out of the way of the second wave of shots.

"Incredibly tight movements for big ships, sir," Sulu gasped, all his muscles twitching as he forced the starship to pivot.

"Now I see why they don't have high speed," Kirk said as he and McCoy both clung to the command chair. "They've sacrificed it to close-range maneuverability. Jam their sensors, Mr. Spock. Mr. Chekov, you handle the weapons, multiple targeting . . . Fire at will."

"Aye, sir!"

The young officer climbed up the tilted deck to the weapons subsystems station and plunged into his purpose, playing the four enemy ships like game pieces. Within seconds he was keeping any ship from getting within five thousand miles without paying for it. He managed to detonate a few incoming salvos in time to give *Enterprise* a clear path to fire back before she had to dodge again.

But the starship couldn't get room to gain any way. The four ships had done this before and were good at it. Kirk leered at the forward screen, then at the coordinated monitors. He'd never known Romulans to behave in coordinated attack patterns at all, much less in this persistent pack-dog fashion.

"Photon torpedos, automatic guidance, Mr. Chekov. Wide dispersal. Fire!"

Tense seconds flashed by as Chekov fired four times.

"Two direct hits," Spock droned, his face cast in blue light from the sensor hood as he bent over it, "one glancing blow, one clean miss. Damage uncertain—"

Suddenly the ship heaved to starboard and seemed to grate to a stop—at hyperlight speed!

The vessel around them howled her protest and yanked and chewed at what was holding her.

"Tractors, Captain!" Spock shouted above the mechanical scream.

"Hit them with feedback," Kirk said. "Break those beams."

"Attempting." The Vulcan crossed the bridge to the engineering station and shouldered Nourredine aside. Within moments the ship whined again and scrambled to get her feet under her, but the strain showed itself in the wobbling whine of the mechanics. "Tractors are down forty percent but still affecting a drag on us. May be able to break them down further with maneuvers."

"Do it, Sulu," Kirk said as if the helmsman didn't have enough weighing on him.

"Trying, sir," Sulu choked. He might as well have been pushing the ship with his hands.

Squalls of enemy fire peeled protection off by energy layers the thickness of fingernails. With each hit, the ship was a fraction less protected. With each harsh burst, something was rattled deep inside her, but like a wild horse she held on to freedom and would do it until she went mad.

"Double-load torpedoes. Fire."

Chekov bent over his controls, his young face screwed into a bitter mask. "Double firing mechanism is nonoperational, sir!"

"Then random-fire the single salvos in tight succession. Pick targets on their hull sections and hammer the same place."

"Aye, sir, targeting."

"Don't burn out the firing mechanisms, Ensign. We may need them later."

"Oh—aye, sir."

The bridge became a flurry of bolts, responses, orders, wound shocks, and backhandings as the four heavily armed ships struck and struck again. The black pit in the bottom of Jim Kirk's stomach began to ferment. His ship and crew could beat off the dogs for a long time but not forever. That was the tactic the enemy was using—scratch and fall back, strike and dodge away, until the prey bled to death. Within minutes the ship's power levels would start to slip, her shields to crumble, and all she could hope to do was take one or two of the enemy down with her.

Here there was no one to come to their aid, no chance of calling out into space for reinforcements. Hits on her primary hull wracked the ship as the threat turned into a crisis.

"Sir!" Nourredine called. "Mr. Scott says the magnatomics are taking overflow from the firing chambers!"

"Inform he has permission to lock those down, or we

won't be here very long," Kirk said, soulsick at knowing Scott would have no choice but to deplete the weapons systems long enough to make that repair. Even if it only took thirty seconds, they couldn't afford to cease fire that long. Raw desperation and a dollop of fury came into his mind.

"Mr. Sulu, shields double forward. Pick one of those ships and direct all fire to it. If we disable one of them, maybe we can slip by—if we can manage to keep from getting our stern blown off."

"New contact, Captain!" Spock suddenly announced over the noise. "Arching out of the sun."

"Stand by, Sulu." Kirk cranked around and pulled himself to the ship's rail. "Spock?"

"Unknown construction. I don't recognize the signature. Definitely not another Imperial Guard vessel . . . Much smaller, highly power-packed—fifteen thousand metric tons, all armor and shields . . . Configuration is haphazard, generally cylindrical with a heavily armored nose section . . . probably a one-man ship." He straightened and looked at the forward screen. "Coming in at uncontrolled warp."

"Weapons sequences?" Kirk pulled himself to the front of the helm.

"No reading of that," Spock said.

"Sir, the Romulan ships are backing away!" Chekov called. "They're veering off at high warp!"

"Why would they do that?" Kirk leered at the forward screen on which the four Romulan ships were suddenly gathering into a clutch, wheeling about, and beating for distance.

"Captain, new contact is veering in," Chekov said. "Should I fire?"

They held their breaths and waited for the captain to use the fabulous power of sun and fire under them to slice their way to victory by cutting up everything in sight.

"Hold your fire!" Kirk ordered on an impulse. "Helm, ten degrees port. Move us out of his way."

The ship hummed with effort but arched to port and slightly upward, clearing a path for the unidentified incoming. Abruptly a small flash of light streaked out from the bottom of the forward screen in hot pursuit of the Romulan ships, obviously able to overtake them, without giving the *Enterprise* a pause. But it was like an acorn overtaking a rockslide. What effect could it have on those gargantuans?

"They're firing on it, Captain," Spock went on, squinting again into his sensor hood. "Leaking some atmosphere now . . . Its engines are showing signs of overheating."

The heavy vessels fired wildly, trying to hit the tiny ship racing toward them. Its speed and size made it impossible to hit with aimed shots. Two of the Romulan vessels attempted wide dispersal shots but too late.

Without timidity the little ship rocketed toward its targets and at the last second selected one of the ships to hit. It angled in, plunging headlong at the big ship, and plowed straight up its aft thruster intake chute.

The screen blew white. Volleys of electrical flashes backwashed over the *Enterprise,* blinding the shocked bridge crew and forcing them to shield their eyes.

"One Romulan ship destroyed," Spock said matter-of-factly. Then he hooked his hand over the neck of his sensor hood and squinted. "The others are continuing away at high warp. Reading scattered debris—a life pod, Captain!"

His voice betrayed his shock that anything could have come out of that explosion in less than twenty pieces.

"You're kidding," Kirk muttered, sweating.

"Likely it jettisoned just before impact."

"Prepare for rescue then. Beam any survivors aboard. Send a Security unit to the transporter room. Mr. Sulu, locations of those other three enemy vessels?"

"Out of range, sir. Not even on our monitors anymore."

"One little ship, and they ran like rabbits," Kirk murmured. "I wonder who it is we've got here." He realized his hands were shaking as he grabbed for the comm unit on his chair. "Kirk to transporter room. What's the condition of that beam-in?"

"Transporter Room, Security here. He's coming in now, sir."

"All stop."

"All stop, sir," Sulu sighed.

"Damage control, all decks. Let's do it while we've got the time."

Uhura nodded, then announced that. Her voice throbbing through the ship was a solvent for their tensions.

"Mr. Spock, communicate our circumstances to all department heads and watch leaders."

"Yes, sir."

"Transporter room here, sir. We've got two unconscious rescues, one is pretty bad. Both have superficial burns, some damage to the arms and—"

"Have them taken to sickbay."

"Begging pardon, sir, but I'd like to have them treated in the brig. They're Klingon."

"Repeat that."

"The survivors are both Klingon, sir."

He glanced at Spock. "Acknowledged. Have the prisoners taken to the brig under heavy confinement. Kirk out. Dr. McCoy, get down there."

McCoy looked shaken up but glad to have something to do. "Right away, Captain."

"Secure from battle stations. Go to yellow alert. Let's get out of the vicinity, gentlemen. If they come back, I don't want to be here."

Spock pushed off the console and came down to the command arena, folded his arms, and leaned toward him. "Where will we go, sir?"

As Kirk looked at him, he saw in Spock's inanimate features a thousand expressions, all small. A clutch of sentiment got him by the heart.

"First order of business," he murmured to his first officer, "see to ourselves. We can't put things right until we have a clear barometer of what's wrong. Where's the most logical place to start? The Federation doesn't exist . . . Who can we trust?"

Spock gazed at him with true sympathy, then said, "We know the Klingons and the Romulans still exist."

"Yes, they do," Kirk responded. "And if they're still around, then the Vulcans must be." He looked at Spock. "Will they listen to you?"

Hovering in place, Spock didn't say anything, as though waiting for the captain to answer his own question.

The Vulcans had for decades been the staunchest defenders of Earth and her bombastic people. An unlikely pairing, the same as the bond between the two of them. Nothing anyone expected or would've bet on. The most obvious relationship between the two races would more likely have been constant disapproval, but that wasn't how it had worked out. Humanity had gone flocking into the galaxy, enticing the many inconstant civilizations out there to get together and form a network of commerce and defense, and it had worked. A common theme of decency had risen above the petty differences between people, and those who couldn't get along were beaten back.

And there was Spock, the first Vulcan in Starfleet, standing beside him on their bridge, evidence of it all. The Vulcans had offered a constancy of devotion that was envied and emulated by other alien races, and of everyone in the history of Starfleet, James Kirk had enjoyed that devotion the longest.

Spock. The best of both worlds. The captain gazed at his long-time votary and couldn't help indulge in a tiny grin. The great lie—that Vulcans were without emotion.

Like hell they were.

"We know humanity isn't in the picture," Kirk pushed. "We also know the Romulans and Klingons are here and hostile toward each other. And the chance is good that Vulcan is still here and probably still under the practices of Surak. If so, the Vulcans *should* be willing to accept the evidence of their eyes—a Vulcan/human hybrid." He paused, eyed Spock, and asked, "How did I do?"

Spock offered a composed bauble of those straight black eyebrows. "A reasonably stated argument. Perhaps I should go to sickbay and assist the medical staff."

For anyone else, this was like shouting, "Brilliant!"

"Thank you," Kirk said.

"You're welcome. Development of the Vulcan culture should be relatively unaffected, with the exception of having no Federation to join. The odds of both Earth and Vulcan's being drastically—"

"Not the odds, please."

"However," Spock added with a pause that seemed somehow dangerous, "if the change is limited to Earth and the Vulcans are still following the teachings of Surak, it is unlikely they would cooperate with the Klingons or Romulans. They may have been subjugated . . . or destroyed, sir."

Hope was suddenly creased with rude realism. It was hard to imagine the sober, thoughtful Vulcans successfully beating off the Romulans or the Klingons or both all by themselves.

And apparently they were every bit as alone in the galaxy as the crew of the *Enterprise.*

"Very well," Kirk sighed. "We'll deal with what we find. Like trying to tiptoe in snowboots, but we'll manage. All hands—"

"Captain," Spock said, quieter, "I am obliged to point out whether it is ethical to inform any planet of an alternative existence. The Prime Directive may be in order here."

"The Prime Directive applies to primitive races. This isn't the time to pay homage to a universe that didn't evolve."

"Regulations may require that of us."

"The Prime Directive was never meant to be that specific," the captain said. "We can't call upon any outside morality. As for the Vulcans, they'll just have to buck up and handle it. All hands, secure the ship for silent running. No sense letting ourselves be tracked."

Uhura glanced at him, then tuned herself into the ship's comm system. "This is the bridge. All hands, rig for silent running."

"Shields on standby. Shut down all nonemergency emissions. Long-range sensors only. What would the course be from where we are, Spock?"

"Checking. Four-nine-eight, mark two, sir."

"Mr. Chekov, that's your heading. Mr. Sulu, warp factor six. Let's go to Vulcan."

He gazed at the forward screen, gathered his puckering innards for what was to come, and forced himself not to cry over the biggest puddle of spilled milk in all eternity.

Chapter Twelve

NO CANDLES GLOWING through the dimness. No chanting. But there were lights.

And there was pain, sounding in great horns through his head and parts of his body. Perhaps this was a death dream. Those last few seconds after detonation.

The lights were blurred, cast in blues. He parted his lips, found them cracked, sticky. A tiny bubble of moisture formed between the side of his tongue and his upper teeth. With his tongue he toyed with the bubble, and when it popped, he suddenly realized he was not dreaming. He tried to open his eyes. They fought him. They burned. Acid from the explosion?

Had his Spear detonated? Had he destroyed his target? Where was Zalt? Dead? Probably.

The long tunnel of the enemy thruster shaft flashed in his mind and a sense of victory followed him into it.

His back was the only part of his body that felt complete. His spine and pelvis rested on a cushion, and beneath his head was a small pillow. Who possessed such things?

He concentrated on one hand, then brought the hand upward slowly along his pelvis, his stomach, his ribs. Some of his armor was missing, including the eject harness that should've been across his chest. Bandages in its place . . . His wounds treated . . . His arms and legs without bindings . . . He was being nursed.

Elation poured into his chest. He had been picked up by a home ship! One chance in a thousand, and this had happened to him. His tiny buoy signal had found resonance on a friendly console, and they had come to find him. When he was well, he would tell about his success in destroying an entire enemy ship. He had shaken the enemy all the way to their home planet!

And to have survived . . . to have survived!

Through his aching eyes it suddenly came to him that the color of the walls was wrong. They were pale. No ship of his own people was like this. Nothing around him was Klingon.

His joy sizzled away. Cloying suspicion clunked into place. The enemy had him!

He heard a hum of energy. A barrier field. When he turned his head, he could make out the impeller bands through the haze of his injured vision. Beyond the field, to one side, were the shoulder and elbow of a guard.

Only one guard? Could the enemies be short of forces also?

Fear and desperation balled in his stomach suddenly. Why would they bind his wounds and nurse him? Why hadn't his harness detonator been activated by the enemy ship's transporters? He cursed the mechanism for failing. Klingon scientists had struggled for a decade to isolate that pattern, to allow one particle of matter to be triggered by the enemy transporter, and only that. He might have taken down two ships instead of only one. Any surviving Spear hoped to do that rather than float in space and probably die there.

He moved one leg, then the other. The left was well enough. The right was sore at the knee, but it functioned. His ribs were a source of pain as he moved his legs, forcing him to choke back a gasp. His head hammered as he turned it again.

What was this room? Not any prison cell he had ever encountered. A medical facility? Why would they treat his wounds?

Was he being brought back to health for interrogation? There was nothing he could tell them. He had never been significant, noteworthy in anyway—this one act was his only major contribution, and it was over. They could only be treating his wounds and making him live so they could torture him for information he didn't have.

He was ready to die but not to be tortured. He understood what would happen to him. His people and his enemies were two sides of the same blade. Blood chilled at the unspeakable methods his own kind used.

Had they done this to his eyes to keep him from escaping? He had heard nothing of such practices before. The enemies knew all there was to know about the Klingon warrior habits and all about the machinery and ships, so there was nothing to gain from keeping prisoners. There were no more tactics left to be discovered.

Except for the Spears. They would torture him to find out where the Spears were coming from.

And so they would torture him until he died, because he did not know where the Spears were coming from, and he was a ghastly liar.

He jerked his head up from the bed and refused to let it fall back, no matter the pain in his neck and shoulders. His teeth ground fiercely. He almost slapped himself but knew that would attract the guard. Instead he raised his fists in a gesture of despair and batted the empty air. Think.

He was ready to die, and they had robbed him of this tiny thing.

Zalt was dead already. The chances of two Spears surviving impalement were microscopic. He forced himself to turn onto his side, then lay sucking air from the effort.

No. They would not rob him of this. He would keep the last promise to himself for a violent peace. The first concern would be to break through that barrier and past that guard.

He drew several deep breaths, then parted his lips, and let out a moan that would bend bones.

"Sickbay. McCoy here."

"Doctor, this is Yeoman Chapman, Security. Your patient's making some godawful painful noises in there. He's coming out of it, but he don't sound too good."

McCoy glanced around sickbay at the patients he already had—one case of appendicitis and one savagely broken wrist from a bad fall off one of the engineering walkways—and wondered if he should take up carpentry. He had to get out of this business.

"Probably those eye injuries," he said. "I'll come down with a treatment as soon as I arrange to have a fracture set. Give me fifteen minutes."

"Aye, sir. I'll make sure he's ready for you."

"All right, but take it easy with those manacles, Chapman. No point injuring him any further."

"Oh, aye, sir. Security out."

A way to kill himself quickly. That was a good goal.

Desperation impelled him through bright corridors with lots of room from side to side. Soft places to sit and lay a head down. What kind of place was this?

They had been near no planet, so this must be a ship. That ship he passed by on his way to death. So much open space inside, so much excess of material . . . lightweight supports, open corridors, no guards, no blaster ports, no internal survival pods, good lighting, fresh air, warmth . . .

He had picked up fragmented reports of a ship moving out of enemy space at warp eight point five—was he aboard that ship? Had the enemy built a ship that could outrun even the Spears?

If so, the tide of war would turn away from his people as it had so recently turned toward them. Could they lose the sliver of an edge they had just gained?

His questions pounded him as he hobbled down the corridor, shielding his eyes with one arm and clamping his injured ribs with the other. The fresh air made his head swim.

He had a weapon, taken from the guard whose throat he had squeezed until the man collapsed in his arms, but he wasn't sure how to use it. He had barely been able to see, but a body is a body and he knew where the throat was. The weapon was strange, too.

But it fit his hand, and that was all it had to do.

He could turn it on himself if he could read which of these settings would kill, rather than leave him unconscious to be recaptured.

No—he would have to damage this ship first. No matter the slight odds, he had a chance to strike another blow.

Someone was coming. There were many footsteps on this vessel, and he was quickly learning how to tell where they were and when to hide.

He listened carefully, measuring the shuffle of footfall. He strained his eyes now and hoped the shadow he had ducked into was dark enough. He braced a foot against the wall behind him and stopped breathing.

Visible movement—the footsteps rounded the corner and materialized into a blurred figure moving casually across his shadow.

With a grunt of effort, he launched himself off the wall and attacked.

The starship sailed hot and close-hauled across the black sea with a white wash of a comet's tail as her spinnaker.

As he sat in the command chair behind the helm, James Kirk resented the beauty of space at this aberrant moment. People had compared him to a charioteer with great reins in his hands, and sometimes he felt that way. But there was a definite mudlark humility in captaincy. He hadn't built this ship or even worked on her. She belonged to those who decades ago had envisioned her. No matter how arrogant he tried to act for the benefit of his crew, or himself, or even sometimes to save their lives, there was always a top to his knight attitude, a point at which he became more cow-puncher than chevalier.

He glanced at Spock for security. It helped a little.

Spock had already been here when Kirk came on duty, though "off duty" under these conditions had very little meaning. Kirk almost never stayed in his quarters anyway. Slept there, yes, but stay for nothing? No. He and Spock had developed a watch schedule unlike any other in Starfleet. Or anywhere else, probably.

The Vulcan rested very little, and his private hours were short. He took his double duty as first officer and science officer seriously, doing the work of two men almost every day.

Certainly he was doing that today.

Kirk knew what Spock was up to. Analyzing that cosmic string business that had thrown them here. Trying to figure out a way for them to throw themselves back. He wanted to go over there and stand with Spock and talk to him, but that was too human a need and the disturbance wouldn't do Spock any good.

"Captain!" Uhura belted abruptly. "Security reports the prisoner has broken out of the brig!"

Kirk spun out of his chair and almost made the mistake of putting his weight on his bad leg. "Details," he snapped.

"Security Yeoman Chapman was attacked when he went inside the cell to check on the prisoner's condition. Dr. McCoy was on his way down there to treat the Klingon."

Spock turned. "I shall attempt a physiological track, sir."

Without responding to him, Kirk looked at Uhura again. "Go to shipwide intruder alert. Is Chapman alive?"

"Yes, sir. He's being treated for a crushed esophagus. Attention, Security, all decks . . . Intruder alert . . . Repeat, intruder alert."

With a hard grip on the bridge rail, Kirk narrowed his eyes in empathy. "What about McCoy?"

With his arm tight around his enemy's throat, the Klingon dragged his captive into the shadows. The captive choked and grabbed at the arm around his neck but didn't struggle very much.

A rap on the side of the head sent the captive to the floor, and a point of his own people's weapon apparently made good sense to him. He stayed on the floor. He spoke, but the words were nothing.

Nothing—in a language completely unknown. A new language!

The Klingon stared down. What language could there be that he had never heard before, not even a breath, not a word? There weren't that many languages in the space-faring spectrum.

He reached down for the captive's collar, squinted his damaged eyes to get a good look at what he had. Pale cheeks, a wide face, eyes the color of water and blinking with alarm, expressively set under a casual cap of brown hair.

Suddenly the Klingon drew away. His captive dropped against the wall, choking, and stared at him.

This was no being he recognized. This . . . was *not* his enemy.

He stumbled back, blinking his eyes convulsively, demanding that they operate.

Leonard McCoy glared at the Klingon who had jumped him and knew he was a hostage, but couldn't read that sudden expression on the Klingon's face. His neck pounded from being twisted half off, and his shoulders hurt from being thrown against the wall.

The Klingon had been about to slaughter him, or at least knock him out for easy handling, but had suddenly backed off. Why?

He struggled to one knee, an arm pressed against the bulkhead for support.

"Do you speak English?" he asked.

The Klingon glowered at him in utter perplexity.

"Didn't think you would," McCoy gasped. "Your eyes are hurting, aren't they?" He pointed to his own eyes, then exaggerated a gesture toward the Klingon's. "Eyes," he repeated. "Hurt?" He formed one hand into a claw and made a scratching motion at his own eyes.

His medikit was over there on the floor. He pointed to it. The Klingon looked in that direction, but his burned eyes couldn't see that far.

"Let me help you," McCoy said. He placed his hand gently over his eyes in a comforting manner. *"Help* you, understand? Help?" He put both hands downward in a nonthreatening manner, then put one hand out toward the medikit. "They'll zero in on us, you know," he said just to make himself feel better. "Klingon metabolism—"

"Klingon!" the prisoner gulped suddenly.

McCoy stopped in place. One word in common.

He poked his own chest with a finger. "McCoy," he said broadly. "Mick . . . Coy."

The Klingon shifted his feet—obviously in some pain— and took another gasping, shallow breath.

Then he thumped his own chest. "Roth!"

McCoy straightened up a little. "You're Roth? Well, that's progress." He pointed at the Klingon, then at his own eyes, then at the medikit. "Roth's eyes . . . help?" With both hands he patted the skin under his own eyes. "Yes."

The Klingon sniffed, wiped his nose with the back of his hand, then moved to one side, away from the medikit. Something in his glazed eyes said the right thing.

"You'll get better," McCoy said, hoping his tone of encouragement would carry. Decades as a physician had given him that tone. He moved toward the medikit and picked it up, not taking an eye off Roth. "You're in pretty good hands, as hands go . . ."

The Klingon seemed ready to shoot, ready to trust, alternating by the second.

McCoy forced himself to keep in mind that this Klingon couldn't possibly know English, had never heard it, and wouldn't trust the sound of it. If he could get to the wall comm, he could notify the bridge of their position on deck nine, three corridors port from the brig. But Roth was hurt and confused, unlikely to allow him to get his hands on a comm unit, so he dispatched that plan and resolved to let the bridge find them with the bioscanners and hoped he would live that long.

"Mev! HlghoS!" Roth bellowed just as McCoy's hand caught at the medikit. His sore eyes were watering and he

was wincing every few seconds now. He pushed the phaser out to the end of his reach.

Knowing the phaser could go off at a touch, never mind a good stiff shudder, McCoy knelt to the floor, still gesturing compliance, and pulled the medikit to him. He held up one hand and with the other urged a treatment bottle out of the kit and held it up to show that there was no weapon in there.

Once again he motioned to Roth's eyes and made a motion with the treatment bottle. He closed the steps between them gingerly but now heard the sounds of a half-dozen footsteps pounding down the corridor.

"Oh, fine timing," he moaned. He held a hand out to Roth and said, "Fido, *stay*."

But the Klingon heard the Security detail running toward them. He caught McCoy by the upper arm and dragged him against his own chest, then put the phaser to his captive's cheekbone and waited for the footsteps to round the corner.

Blistering rage and fear for McCoy sent a claw of self-reproach deep into the captain's chest as he and four guards hammered through the corridors of deck nine. He had failed to make his ship safe.

Nowhere the crew could go with their unthinkable power and speed was entirely safe, and all around them, outside the protective walls, lurked the inhospitality of cold space. Of all places, the ship was supposed to be safe, the corridors unbreached. He had failed to keep it that way.

And McCoy in the hands of a foe whose motivations they couldn't measure—Kirk hated that. If he knew something about the Klingons here, he could make a plan in his mind, pick out a half-dozen actions and be ready. But this was impossible to guess ahead no matter how he demanded clairvoyance of himself.

Two of the Security guards skidded around the corner in front of him, but as he caught a glimpse of McCoy held with his shoulderblades rolling against the chest of the Klingon, with a phaser to his cheek, Kirk shouted, "Hold position! Hold your fire!"

Luckily, the men had the sense to realize he was talking to

them and not the Klingon. They braced their legs, aimed their phasers at arms' length, and stayed back.

"No, Jim!" McCoy shouted, half choked. "He had a chance to kill me, but he didn't!"

Kirk held his own phaser down and shifted from run to stalk. His face throbbed with the fever of rushing, of tension, of his fears and furies.

"His name is—" The Klingon's arm tightened. After a breath McCoy coughed out, "R—Roth."

"Roth . . ." Kirk lowered his chin and raised a brow. "Give me my doctor back."

The Klingon spat something back in his own language and shook McCoy in bald threat.

"Security," Kirk said, "one of you contact the bridge. Have Lieutenant Uhura come down here and hang a personal universal translator on him. We can't get anywhere if we can't talk."

"Aye aye, sir!" one of the guards said and ducked back into the main corridor.

"The rest of you," Kirk told them evenly, "back off."

The guards didn't like that order. He felt it in their hesitation but refused to repeat himself. They had their orders.

He had the Klingon's attention. He pushed everything he had ever thought about Klingons, their tactics, their desires, their patterns of loyalty, out through his glare to its target. He needed no commonality of words for what he thought of Klingons. It boiled to the top.

Roth—Kirk knew the Klingon could see the scalding hostility and feared it. He was damned right to fear it. At the moment Kirk could reach out with just his attitude and commit a hanging.

The Klingon blinked at him, and his expression crossed several lines, never quite fixing on one message. Beneath the outer actions was a clear layer of abstract befuddlement. He didn't recognize anything he saw.

A Klingon who didn't know whether or not to hate Terrans.

Kirk tried to do as he had told his Security men, to back

off in his mind and hopefully in his expression, to pocket the feelings brought up by a lifetime of dealing with entirely other Klingons.

Shifting the phaser to his left hand, he kept it down at an angle, ready but down. With his right hand, he reached out and made a beckoning gesture. *Give me my doctor back.*

Roth's watering eyes, skin burned pink all around, blinked as if trying to make sense of what he could see. His arm weakened around McCoy's neck.

Kirk motioned to the Security men. "Phasers down."

"Captain," one of them protested.

"Right now." Slowly he put his own phaser on the deck.

With a sudden shout Roth pushed McCoy forward violently and charged.

Chapter Thirteen

McCoy SLAMMED INTO Kirk's shoulder and spun into the starboard bulkhead, landing a ringing blow to the doctor's collarbone and the side of his head.

The captain writhed to one side, grasped the Klingon's phaser arm by the wrist, and nailed him with a hard right to the ribs.

The injured Klingon gagged and went down, still clinging to the phaser he had hesitated to use.

"Security," Kirk ordered. "Take him to sickbay under triple guard. Have Lieutenant Uhura meet you there with the translator."

"Aye aye, sir," the senior of them said. "Get him up."

As the men crowded in and took charge of the collapsed prisoner and his phaser, Kirk hurried across the corridor to McCoy and pulled the doctor to his feet. "Bones, did he hurt you?"

McCoy hung a hand on that bruised collarbone. "I don't think so, Jim. He seemed more scared than anything else. You and that rabbit punch—he's got fractured ribs, you know."

With a glance to the guards as they hauled the moaning prisoner away, Kirk droned, "Pardon if I knocked him silly. Come over here." He took McCoy by an arm and led him a few steps in the other direction. Desperate prisoners had been known to kick their way clear of guards. "Report. What's your judgment of his condition?"

"His eyes are improving slowly," McCoy said, "but they need treatment. He doesn't speak English, but he does pay close attention to attitude and intent. He's observant, scrupulous, and willing to take each situation moment to moment."

"That's pretty good judging for a hostage."

The doctor rubbed his shoulder and winced. "My job, Captain."

"Anything else?"

"Only that his name or maybe his rank is 'Roth.'"

"Roth . . . Did you notice his clothing? The body-armor design, pads, coils—almost exactly as we know them."

"Not the colors," McCoy commented.

"No, but everything else. The Klingon culture must have been unaffected until the past hundred years."

"When Earth people would have made contact with them."

"Yes." He picked up the medikit, held it briefly, and handed it to the doctor.

"That means evidence is congealing that suggests the original change only affected the evolution of humanity."

Kirk sighed heavily, "And the absence of humanity affected everything else."

McCoy fumbled thoughtfully with the medikit in his hands. "So much for wondering if we'd be missed."

"Or if we've done the right thing by moving out into space," the captain said.

The doctor looked up. "I don't think this is the time for valentines, Jim."

"And I'm not giving one. There are clear rights and wrongs in the universe. With the rights absent, the wrongs flourish. And they're shredding the whole fabric of civilization. If the policemen are gone, the criminals take over."

"How do you know *they're* not the policemen here?" McCoy flared.

"Because it hasn't been long enough for Klingons to be that different. They're still Klingons and we're still the United Federation of Planets. I'm proud of what the Federation has done, or I wouldn't be out here doing it."

McCoy's expression softened. He nodded. "Sorry, Captain. I understand how you feel."

Irritably Kirk clipped, "Good for you."

He spun around and went back to scoop up his discarded phaser. As he straightened up, Spock was there to meet him.

"Security Ensign Beremuk informed me of your location, Captain," the Vulcan said. "I have a report on the fragments of the Klingon vessel . . . Doctor, are you all right?"

"I'm very well, Mr. Spock," McCoy said as he joined them, "give or take the odd contusion. Thank you for asking."

Kirk glowered as if he preferred them to be sniping at each other. "Let's have that report, Spock."

"Yes, sir. The remnants of the small ship are made of a super energy-resistance material, something the Klingon science must have concentrated upon heavily."

"Defense. It's a clue to their priorities."

"Yes. The material is unstable, however. It is breaking down even now and will crumble within days. I would surmise these vessels are built only hours before their actual use and made to be used only once."

"Kamikazes," Kirk said.

"Evidently."

"To sacrifice manpower and resources for the demolition of one enemy post or vessel . . . That's a tactic of desperation. A war between the Klingons and Romulans, relatively equal in technology, going at each other's throats without any interference or referee, no other parties in the settled galaxy able to stand them off . . . both cultures ruled by nothing but shallow parochial honor, but no principles about individual rights . . . How long could it go on before it came down to resources and personnel and one side started whipping the tar out of the other?"

"Do you think that's what's happening, Jim?" McCoy asked. "The Klingons are losing?"

Kirk almost dropped a yes on the floor and kicked it over there, but something made him hesitate. Conclusions too early, believing in what he thought too soon—maybe even wishful thinking—these things could stunt his efficiency.

"We've got to get answers out of that Klingon," he declared.

"Captain," Spock began, "are you intending to explain the situation as we know it to our prisoner? That course may be unwise."

"It's all the wisdom I've got at the moment."

The doctor cocked his head. "Have Spock go up there and explain to him how we were slam-dunked by a ball of thread."

"String, actually," Spock said flatly.

"No need to be so specific, Mr. Spock," McCoy tossed back. "There's nobody around to check up on you. The relentlessly logical culture you're devoted to might not even exist in this time line."

With his hands clasped behind him, Spock pivoted with casual purpose. "We cannot be sure of that, Doctor. And I am not 'devoted' to the Vulcan culture," he added, "or I would be *on* Vulcan."

McCoy looked as if he'd been corked.

Jim Kirk put a hand out between them. With this hour's tumbledown reality chewing at his heels, he felt like a man trying to make a rope of sand.

"All right, as you were," he said. "Let's go talk to him."

"I've got it keyed to translate from Klingon to English on the outgoing speakers and English to Klingon in the earpiece. But he won't let me put it on him, sir. He's afraid of it."

Uhura stood just outside the triage room at sickbay, her even features crimped by frustration.

Kirk frowned and peeked into the treatment area, where the Klingon was sitting in a chair, wrists bound together, flanked by two guards and vultured from behind by one more. All three had phasers drawn, and the clarity of their message shone in the prisoner's bearing as he sat with his arms tight over his ribs.

"Safe distance, all of you." Kirk led the way inside.

The Klingon had heard them, for he was fixed wide-eyed on the entryway as the four came in.

Suddenly his entire body went hard and his reddened eyes stretched wide. He bolted to his feet and charged.

"romuluSngan!" The word was hardly more than a spit. Seeming to realize that, Roth gritted his teeth and hissed again, *"romuluSngan!"*

Reflexively McCoy stumbled back into Uhura, Spock moved to protect them, and Kirk stepped forward to take the brunt of the attack. The two flanking guards hooked Roth by both arms and hauled him back roughly. The third guard flashed around front and took aim with his phaser.

"No, don't stun him!" the captain said.

Roth was pushing at the guard's grips and glaring needles only at Spock.

Reacting to the raw, bald despise in the Klingon's face, Kirk got between him and Spock quickly. "What's *romuluSngan?*"

Spock kept his voice in careful check. "I would surmise that's his word for Romulans."

Hearing that tone, Roth's expression changed. He peered at Spock, took measure of his demeanor, and saw something else. With notable astonishment, he gasped, "Vulcan?"

Spock offered him one confirming nod.

The Klingon stopped pushing at the guards, put his teeth together. "Vulcan!"

But this time, he spat the word.

"Lieutenant Uhura," Kirk summoned, frustrated.

Uhura approached, but Roth jerked back and almost pulled the two guards off their feet.

"Give me the translator," Kirk said, fed up. He attached it to his own collar and indicated to Roth that there was nothing poisonous about it, that it was harmless, then barked at the guards, "Hold him."

The guards put their weight on the Klingon. Kirk stepped in and clipped the translator to the Klingon's shirt collar, glad the heavy harnesses and chest armor had been taken off. Then he put the corresponding ear plug into Roth's right ear.

"How do I engage it?" he asked.

"Tap the earpiece, sir," Uhura said.

The Klingon twisted his face out of the way but didn't fight.

"Jim, wait." McCoy pulled out the little bottle he had tried to use in the corridor. "Hold him down."

All three guards leaned on Roth again, and the doctor stepped in, forced his eyelids up, and put droplets of the treatment into the injured eyes.

"There." McCoy backed off. "If that's not a peace offering, I don't know what is."

Roth blinked, sore eyes set now in a different kind of surprise. His new expression came not from what his eyes were feeling, but from what he had heard.

Kirk watched him. "Do you understand me?"

He waited to see if there was a reaction. He made a gesture that backed the guards off and stepped closer. "Do you understand what I'm saying to you? You might as well answer."

The Klingon blinked his eyes mechanically, but he seemed to see them more clearly—and the shock of whatever had come over that earpiece was working on him.

"What are you?" The facsimile of his voice was so close as to be startling. He flinched at the sound of 'himself' speaking Klingon and getting a strong, blunt echo in a strange language.

Kirk felt a surge of hope. This was the first communication they'd had with this universe that wasn't a yellow poppy or an unknown beast. This was a moment when a wrong turn on his part would mean future or fracture for all involved.

"We are humans," he said deliberately. "I am Captain Kirk. This ship is the *Enterprise,* United Federation of Planets."

"Kirrk?" Roth tipped his head. "It is a Klingon name?"

"No. It's a human name. We're from the planet Earth."

"There is no Earth," Roth said, testing the translator and not entirely trusting it. "Where is Zalt? My commander?"

"Don't tell him," Kirk snapped. He straightened, and they squared off. "Why did you attack my medical officer?"

"I thought I was captive on a *romuluSngan* ship."

"Then why didn't you kill him?"

Roth paused, looked at McCoy. "He is not my enemy."

"Are any of us your enemy?" Kirk gestured at Uhura, the guards. Then he moved to Spock. "Is this your enemy?"

Roth kept tight control over his motions, quite clear on what phasers were meant for, and he stopped short when Kirk put a firm hand on the Klingon's chest and let it be known he'd better state his intentions.

So Roth fixed his sore eyes on Spock and lowered his voice. Even his inflections were brought across effectively by the translator. "Vulcan, why are you here, coward? Animal? Liar? Did you escape?"

Spock hesitated, but when the captain urged him on with a look, he said, "My name is Commander Spock. I am the ship's first officer."

"Impossible! How did you escape?" Roth persisted. The Klingon echo buzzed behind the English words.

"Explain what he escaped from," Kirk urged.

"From the boundary channels!"

At that tone, one of the guards slipped forward a step but didn't encroach on the captain's progress.

"Explain why we aren't your enemy."

"Because I do not *know* you! And the *romuluSpu'* were firing on you."

"The enemy of your enemy . . . is your friend? Is that your belief?"

Reticent to commit himself, the Klingon backed away a pace.

"If we explain our situation to you," Kirk pushed, "will you tell us the nature of yourself and your enemies?"

Roth stared at him, measuring what he saw in Kirk's eyes and the set of his brow, waiting for a flinch or a blink that would give away deception. Kirk had been looked at like that before and refused to do either. He stood his mental ground as much as he stood defense between Roth and Spock, letting the Klingon know he also was not entirely trusted.

Ultimately, the Klingon nodded, once, very bluntly.

"All right," Kirk said, "the rest of you, get out."

"Captain . . ." Spock moved to him, turned a cold shoulder to Roth, and spoke very low. "Respectfully resist your being left alone with him. He is, after all, a Klingon."

Kirk almost smiled. "Prejudice, Spock?

Without offering even a glance at the prisoner, Spock raised a brow. "If necessary, sir."

The captain nodded, warmed that Spock would admit that on his behalf. "Noted. Leave one of the guards here."

The others did as he bade, but McCoy stepped quickly to the captain. "What are you going to do, Jim?"

Kirk felt his eyes tighten at the corners.

"I'm gonna explain it to him."

Chapter Fourteen

ROTH. Once proud, then shamed, now suspicious.

These were the cleverest lies he had ever heard. Such detail. Even on the screen, generated graphics of something the captain called a squeezing disk. Violence and transmutation danced before him on the visual monitor. This, they said, had happened to them.

But it was the pictures . . . the recordings . . . of a civilization unimaginable that shook him. Yes, wars, but the wars were aberrations in a way of life, not themselves a way of life. What kind of minds did these people possess that they could think of life this way?

Pictures of Klingons dealing with these aliens no one had ever seen, of *romuluSngan* and Vulcan interacting on the large scale with these people.

The captain had explained what they thought had happened to them, then turned on the computer, "spacefarer to spacefarer," he said and let the machine take over.

Why would they waste their complex fabrication on a prisoner? Wouldn't they try to find a high council to show it to?

No matter how he wanted to believe, there was that Vulcan who said he was part of the ship's crew. A Vulcan! Who could believe any story now?

Were there Vulcans where these people said they came from? Were they liars and cowards there, too?

His thousand questions twisted with the throbbing of his head. Pictures could be faked.

The captain was watching him. Jamestee Kirrk.

A golden man. Golden hair, golden shirt, gold-and-black shield on his breast. Golden eyes. Hard eyes, this one. Hatred in those eyes.

Spacefarer to spacefarer, yes. But this one didn't like Klingons.

Roth didn't mind being hated. In fact, it was a clue of sorts, coming from this man who said he and his people did not come from this universe at all and sought only mutuality.

"You," he began, "are lost?"

The captain watched him. "Yes. We're lost."

"I don't believe you."

"I know you don't. But I want you to think about all this Somehow I intend to convince you over the next few hours."

"You will fail."

"We'll see about that. Until then, you don't have to say anything. I'll talk. You tell me when I'm wrong. You're the pilot of some kind of suicide vessel. You, and presumably others like you, veer in at high speed and plunge up the thruster ports of those Rom—those *romuluSngan* bulk cruisers. Those are resource-intensive ships. They take time to build and large crews to maintain. To eradicate one is considered a great victory. On the other hand, it only takes a few weeks to put together one of your small attack ships, which are all engine and never meant to come home."

Blinking, Roth felt his jaw grow tighter with every phrase. He set his mouth hard against blurting an accusation of subterfuge against so total a stranger. But how could this man know these things?

"Most pilots of such craft," the captain went on, "expect to die in the explosion, but you didn't. For some reason your people install a life pod in your suicide ships. Why would you do that?"

The captain glared at him so directly that Roth couldn't help but see the petulance. "The Empire is short of men, isn't it? You'll take manpower from anywhere you can get it. You're losing the war, aren't you?"

Roth was forced to break his stoicity with a cough. The captain prowled him.

"Your two empires are nothing but malevolence met with malevolence," the gold man went on. "You've made an evil-fashioned galaxy here, with the two of you pounding each other so relentlessly that you haven't been able to get past the battle to enjoy what you win. Your culture tries to ripen, only to spoil on the ground because you have no time to gather it. All you have to show for years of struggle is the open wound that could've been the Klingon civilization. Now, *you* tell me I'm wrong."

Silence clamped down sharply. The faint twirps of equipment from the lab next door came through. Roth could only offer a corrosive glare through his watering eyes.

139

The captain stopped pacing and faced him down. "When did this war begin?"

Roth released his lip and licked it. "Always."

"Always," Krok said as if the word had a bad taste. "Do you want the war to end?"

In the captain's eyes Roth saw a determination, even a familiarity with war, but there was something about the way he said "end," as if he had seen or made wars end before and calculations were ratcheting up in his mind about how to do it again.

End?

"War does not end," Roth finally pronounced. "Fight enemies, win, then fight friends. Or lose."

"Do you think that's right?"

"Right? What is 'right'? It is what's done."

Kirik seemed to think there was something odd about that perception. "This is a starship of the United Federation of Planets," the man said, his amber eyes angry. "We know what that stands for. War happens for specific reasons. We have no stock in whatever goes on between you and your enemies. I've got a ship and crew to worry about. My first concern is to find a way back. I want you to help me."

Roth pushed his hands to the bench and rose on his hips. "There is no going back for you. If your story is true, you have to live here now."

The words reached out from the mouth of a prisoner and struck his keeper like a slap. Roth felt it ricochet off the walls, swirl around the young guard standing beside the doorway. The captain's own personal dynamism had kept him from believing what he had just been told and for the first time Roth found himself believing a shred of what *he* had been told. More proof than any reams of computer storage, more than any scientific programs, more than seeing it for himself, he saw now in the captain's face. This was a man who had never imagined living out his life in any other than his own universe, where matters were known to him and where he had anchors.

Until now, Jamestee Kirk had never thought of not getting back.

"If you will not be my enemy," Roth began, "whose will you be?"

Kirrik stiffened. "We will be neutral for now."

"There is no neutral."

"There is for us."

"Not here, Captain," Roth said. "For your own lives' sakes, you must join us."

The ship was here, there was no denying that, and it was sophisticated and certainly couldn't have been constructed in any Klingon or *romuluSngan* sphere of patrol without being discovered by one side or other. No one anywhere could build just *one* of such a ship, not without having built many others before it.

They must have come from very far away. Yet they came alone. Why?

Had their people been destroyed? They must be the last to come here like this in the middle of the forever war. And there was that Vulcan. That *Vulcan*.

Doubts crawled in Roth's mind. "You must become part of our fleet," he said bluntly.

"We will not join you. We won't have our ship used for someone else's conquest."

"You will have no choice. The Klingons will be the winners."

This young stick of fire swung around from where he had paced. "Winners who use desperation tactics?"

"The Spears have turned the tide. We were losing, but now the *romuluSnganpu'* run from us. You saw it!"

"Yes, I saw it. And we won't participate in your pattern of conquest, not you or the Romu—*romuluSnganpu'*."

"You have not had hard lives," Roth pushed in, the faint buzz of the translator echoing every syllable. "Your clothing is new. You have resources to devote to that! There's fresh air and laughter on your ship—laughter! But this will all end for you unless you face the truth. How long can you survive in deep space all alone? You must live *here* now and join one side or the other. I want you for mine."

Boiling, the captain glared at him, shoulders racked back. "Not a chance."

"And also no chance of creating this interdimensional distortion more than once. You will never go back. *This* is your life now."

"We aren't that certain of our theory. There are missing elements. And we're not participating in your war. We are absolutely neutral."

Roth widened his eyes. Mick-Coy had given him back his eyes, but they were irritated and tired.

"I do not understand you. There *is* no neutral. None is allowed here. Neutral is . . . water. Nothing else. I don't understand your thinking."

"We are not getting involved in your war of conquest. We will defend ourselves, but that is *absolutely* . . . all."

"You will have no choice, Captain. Word is spreading about you now. You're being pursued without doubt. You must not be captured by the *romuluSngan*. If you have them in your culture, then you know why. If you join my people, you will be brought into our culture and you can gain trust. Your ship will be integrated into our fleet and you may be allowed to continue serving on it. If the *romuluSngan* catch you, your crew will be torched alive until none are left. And you will be last . . . and they will have your ship anyway."

He was making a gamble. He saw in the captain's eyes that the captain knew he wasn't being lied to again.

"In nature," Roth said, "there are two kinds of life. There are the kind who fight and the kind who are food. You are food!"

He lashed out, furious at the idea of keeping this ship out of a conflict whose tide it could turn. "Everyone goes to war with everyone eventually, Captain. No one can resist trying to take what the other has. Sometimes it is done without weapons through the sheer power of authority, but it always happens. You can't stand up to both of us. Eventually we or they will take you, either in battle or when your supplies run low. Join with us while you're strong and can bargain, or fight both my people and the pestilential *romuluSngan* and die. And leave your ship for us."

The captain looked as though his muscles had cured to stone. He looked past Roth to the Security guard, and there was liability for the future burning in his face. The guard was standing too straight, struggling for palace-guard immutability, his eyes turned upward, his face pinched and pale from what he was hearing.

"We're not joining you," the captain said again.

"You will have to!" Roth pushed off his bench and almost fell. He was surprised when the captain reached out and helped him stay on his feet.

The Security guard plunged forward to get between his commander and the Klingon, but the captain pushed him back. "As you were, Ensign."

Putting space between himself and them, Roth forced himself to keep talking. "The *romuluSngan* are toxic people," he gasped. "They will turn your crew into another conquered mass." Roth placed a scratched hand on his chest. "We wouldn't do that. We know the makers of such a ship are worth keeping alive! You are not our enemy yet!"

"I don't intend to be your enemy unless you force me to," the captain said. "Or the *romuluSngan* either."

"Your ship bristles with weapons. Where is the peace in your culture?"

"We keep peace by holding back the violence. We keep it with morality, individualism, and law. Thousands of planets live in prosperity and protection. Even the Klingons are beginning to prosper in spite of their isolationism. You saw the tapes."

"I saw. If it were real, this would be paradise. No one of us has ever—" He clamped his mouth shut. He was talking too much. It was easy to make that mistake with this man and those drilling eyes. This was the kind of man who was hard to lie to.

But he was soft, golden, gentle. The ship was run with too little discipline. It was humiliating to be captive of these softs. They and their fabulous vessel wouldn't survive long if caught between the two sides of the blade.

"There are things you aren't telling me," Roth said. "When I find them out, then I will decide what to believe about your stories. Either you go back where you came from—and you cannot—or ally with my people against the menace we fight."

Korik fixed his eyes on him, moved back, then moved sideways and back, hackles up and prowling. "We aren't going to war with anyone."

Roth didn't even blink this time. "Yes," he said, "you are."

The captain glowered and flexed his hands petulantly. "I liked you better when you wouldn't talk."

"To stand against conquest does not work here," Roth said. "This is where you live from this day on, with me and my people and my enemies. Now . . . will you let me lead you to my fleet's headquarters, Captain Kork?"

There was a bitter cold light in the stranger's eyes. A subdued grin touched his lips—also cold.

"It's Kirk," he said, "and no."

They stared at each other.

Even when the force barrier at the entrance was dropped by the guard as another officer approached from outside, Roth was careful not to look away from the captain. This man would notice any backing down, any at all.

"May I disturb you, Captain?" a baritone voice interrupted.

Kirrk ticked off another two seconds of glare, then broke away. "I'm already disturbed, Mr. Spock. What do you want?"

Through a watery sheen Roth saw the form beside the gold blur of the captain, panels of blue and black.

He pushed to his feet, thrust out one arm before him, the other behind for balance, and plunged forward.

"Coward Vulcan!"

Chapter Fifteen

THE SECURITY GUARD slammed into him, shoulder first, and managed to keep inches between Roth and the Vulcan he was trying to attack. The captain shoved his officer back and came between them.

"Vulcan!" Roth blasted between grinding teeth. "Tell me the truth! I have always dealt fairly with you!"

"Back!" the guard shouted in his ear. "Last chance!"

Beside his face, Roth saw the guard's weapon teeter for aim. For a moment he didn't care, but then he did. He could do nothing unconscious on the deck or dead.

He changed his demeanor, forced himself to gain balance against the guard's grip.

The captain and his officer set each other on their feet and Kirk came toward him. "We've told you the truth."

"There is no truth where a Vulcan walks! This talk of neutrality—it comes from *them.*" Roth looked at the Vulcan and said, "You have broken the treaty. Do you intend to use this ship to go to war with Klingon?"

Slowly the Vulcan shook his head. "I am not at war with Klingon. Nor have I any such plans."

Roth considered spitting on the deck. The guard's arm pressing against his throat wasn't easing up. The weapon's point still picked at his ear.

The captain came closer. "You expect him to recognize you. Why? Will other Vulcans recognize you, too? Can you address them on our behalf? It's your life as much as ours."

"Our lives are over if we go to Vulcan," Roth scorned. "You have nothing in common with them. You are one of us. There is Klingon in you, Captain . . . *Kirk*."

Two futures bawled for attention. Beyond what the captain clearly heard as an ingrained insult blared the hunting horns of a possibility that would not be ignored.

Kirk stared and stared, but the horns wouldn't fade and Roth refused to back down.

"Captain," the Vulcan encouraged, "if you will." He balanced a nod toward the corridor.

"You have no right to comment, coward!" Roth inflamed. "Kirk, the Vulcans will tell you that you can stay neutral— you can't. They say there are always alternatives. There aren't. They tell you the mind can rule the universe . . . It cannot. They say we can all look beyond our differences." He pushed against the guard one final time. "It is a dream."

The captain moved back to the Vulcan's side, summoning a deeper root of the submerged candor. The two were almost opposites in all visible ways, yet there was something solid about their standing together that way.

"Mr. Spock and I look beyond our differences every day," Kirk said. "We're shipmates. And we're friends. And you're wrong."

James Kirk turned away from the Klingon, skin crawling with expectation of a rebuff. He didn't think he'd get the last word. At least his name was finally right.

He stopped in the middle of the corridor, swung around to Spock, and barked, "All right, what've you got?"

Spock's voice was a salve. "Mr. Scott reports the Klingon life pod is made of conventional materials. However, it is a concoction of spare parts of varying ages and stress levels. There's evidence of prior use, some simple age, some violent, including exposure to hard radiation and heavy weapon fire."

"Then I was right. And now that I have him, what do I do with him? Keep him?"

Trying to be tactful, Spock said, "We have no reason to hold him under any articles of war."

"What about other cultures? Governments who were Federation allies in our . . . time."

"Like the Vulcans, we can assume their history did not deviate until recently. They simply have had no Federation to join. Since no one encouraged them to band together, they've been alone against the two most aggressive forces in the settled galaxy. As such, it's likely they've had to subject themselves to harsh compromise."

"Compromise usually means one side giving up a lot," Kirk distilled unhappily.

Spock offered a mild nod. "A war of this magnitude will have taken thousands of planets with it during the fifty to one hundred years during which the Federation would have held the hostile powers apart."

"Then I have to assume the peaceful races have been subjugated?"

"Yes," Spock said.

The simplicity of it was damning. He didn't quote odds or frame his answer in theoreticals. Just yes.

"We know the Vulcans exist," Kirk said when the silence became overbearing. "He's familiar with them, even if he doesn't like them. Can we turn him over to them?"

"A viable solution, unless we consider his knowledge of our ship and situation a risk."

The comm system on the wall clicked on the tail of Spock's words. *"Bridge to Captain Kirk."*

"That damage has been done," Kirk said. "We can't fix it. And I don't want to keep him. We'll turn him over to the Vulcans." He stepped to the wall. "Kirk here."

"Mr. Scott would like to speak to you, sir."

"Put him through."

"He says this might be classified, sir."

"Nothing's classified anymore, Lieutenant."

A pause, then, *"Scott here, sir. We have a new contact. Unfamiliar design, one hundred fifty thousand gross tons, no recognizable signatures. They identify themselves as a Vulcan merchant transport, cargo pharmaceuticals. They'd like to come into beaming range and have a word with you."*

"Understood. All stop. Tell them to stand by."

"Aye aye, sir."

"Spock, take the con. Explain our problem to the Vulcans if you think they should know."

"Yes, sir . . . Captain, where will you be?"

"I'm going to arrange a prisoner transfer," Kirk said. "I'm going to put Roth in the same cell as the other Klingon . . . and let'm work on each other. I might have to live in their universe, but they have to live in mine, too."

Ten minutes later, James Kirk spun out of the turbolift and tilted down the steps toward the lower deck.

To his astonishment, a dozen crudely dressed strangers held his bridge crew at pistol point. All men, the strangers were shaggy haired, robust, rugged, their faces built on angularities that were familiar, and their demonic pointed ears gave them away.

Vulcans, allies otherwise, but not necessarily here.

Every one of these Vulcans held at least one bridge crewman at the point of a weapon. And on the starboard bridge, a shaggy-haired Vulcan in a bulky jacket of olive green, black trousers, and pirate boots, with a gray cowl around his neck, was squared off with Spock, one hand held out at his side, the other hand spread across the side of Spock's face.

Kirk understood that Vulcan telepathic talents could be turned punitive. Mind meld—

The heat dropped out of his body as he absorbed the sight of armed and aggressive Vulcans and what was happening in the only sacred place left to him in the galaxy.

His first officer was under assault. His bridge had been taken.

148

Chapter Sixteen

BETWEEN THE STARSHIP'S CAPTAIN and his first officer, an unfamiliar Vulcan held a weapon on Lieutenant Uhura at the communications station. Only three feet away, this individual made a fair first target.

Blessed with the compact frame of a wrestler and a few bundles of muscle he was proud of, Jim Kirk moved to take his ship back.

He faked a step to port, then dodged to starboard with the point of his elbow plowing his course. As he drove the nearest Vulcan down, Uhura ducked under his arm and out of his way to give him room. Momentum drove the Vulcan aside. Kirk forced himself up with a left hook, and the Vulcan hit the deck.

But these were Vulcans, and he had just played his only surprise card.

There was noise behind him; he hoped it was somebody else in his crew taking advantage of his fake and dodge. The sound of raw resistance pumped him with energy. He launched upward at the other Vulcan with a backhand blow whose impact pried the stranger away from Spock, then punctuated his attack by bringing his right fist around to the stranger's jaw, like a mallet driving a wooden stake into the heart of a demon.

Dazed from the broken telepathic attachment, the stranger staggered back and bumped the bridge rail. Spock fell backward, too, arching over his sensor hood, arms flagging like a rag doll's. Then his ribs tightened, and he found purchase on the science panel and fought for balance.

Kirk grabbed the rail and scanned the deck to size up the situation. Behind him, two engineers had sprung to life. Scott wasn't here—probably headed for the engine room as soon as Spock took the bridge—but Nourredine and an assistant were. The assistant was a big kid who downed the surprised Vulcan who'd been hovering over them, and Nourredine and Chekov were grappling with another one on the lower deck. Three Vulcans down. How many were there?

He fixed on another and braced to get there.

"Captain!" Spock rasped. "Don't."

Kirk almost broke his back grating to a dead halt. Spock would never stop him without a good reason. Better be a hell of one.

The stranger in the olive jacket, now with a swelling lip, snapped something in Vulcan to his own men.

In spite of the fact that they outnumbered the bridge crew, all the Vulcans now lowered their weapons.

Glowering under his brow like a bear just out of a trap, Kirk shoved himself up, pressing the bridge rail so heavily on his right arm that he thought his wrist would snap. He stood straight to deal with the Vulcans. The bridge was his again.

Angling at Uhura, he cracked, "Security."

She touched her board. "Security detail to the bridge—emergency."

On the wide main screen was a thoroughly unfamiliar ship, dull and utilitarian. Kirk skimmed the bulky cargo holds and heavy industrial engines in a mental demand that the ship prove she was what she said she was.

He glanced around. The Vulcans were all crudely and heavily dressed, well fed, and strong, wearing cowls or scarves and heavy boots. Cold over there, apparently.

Fighting a lingering daze, Spock gathered himself. "Captain Kirk . . . may I present Captain Sova, Cargo Vessel *T'Lom,* of the Vulcan Merchant Consortium."

"I don't care who he is. Nobody takes my bridge." Kirk tilted his head toward Uhura without taking his eyes off the Vulcan captain. "Call McCoy to the bridge. Then give me a universal translator bridgewide."

"Aye, sir . . . tied in."

Locked onto Sova's mud-brown eyes, Kirk saw a stability in his expression. If they'd had the room, they would've circled each other.

Before either could speak, the turbolift hissed open and six heavily armed Security guards plunged out and spread across the bridge, scooping up Vulcans as they went.

The lieutenant of the guard glanced around to make sure all was secure, then nodded at Kirk.

Satisfied, Kirk nodded back. Now he could get mad if he wanted to.

He faced Sova again. "You boarded my ship without an invitation. Can you explain that?"

The newcomer offered a blunt, uneasy bow. His voice was gravelly through the translator. "We live on the defensive. We seek the swiftest solutions. This was my way. We have developed a method of matter transport through shields at close range. It costs great power, but I have saved my cargo from pirates many times this way."

"And this looked like a pirate ship to you?"

The Vulcan might have been embarrassed—or was he amused?

"No," he admitted, "it does not. Now I understand and offer greetings, Captain . . . from my universe to yours."

"I don't think much of your manner of greeting," Kirk said roughly. He pivoted to Spock. "You all right?"

"Yes," Spock drawled as he levered to Kirk's side. The glaze of telepathic encroachment was clearing from his eyes, though he still looked as though he'd taken a gut punch.

"Were you under attack?"

Spock eyed the Vulcan commander. "'Interrogation' may be more accurate. Impolite, but efficient."

At first Kirk thought Spock was getting a slap in with that remark, but then he realized that in two words his first officer was giving him critical information—that these Vulcans were different. In their own universe, Vulcans considered such deeply personal intrusion demeaning. Spock was telling him that these people had been through something that changed their attitude about mental manners. Suddenly Jim Kirk was face-to-face with a total stranger who knew a hell of a lot about him and his crew.

The turbolift opened again, and McCoy came out but stopped and gawked at the scene. "What's going on?" he asked.

"You'll know when we do," Kirk told him. "Captain Sova, do you understand what's happened to us?"

Sova moved toward them. "Mr. Spock himself is testimony to your predicament, sir. No native Vulcan—"

"Then you've got the information you need?" Kirk charged. "You know what happened to us?"

"I know what you believe happened, and this ship of yours is evidence that you have not given yourself to fantasy. And it is unlikely that you do."

"Captain—" Chekov cranked around and spoke sharply enough to give away that he'd been waiting for a chance to interrupt. "Long-range sensors tracking two large cruisers, possible three, bearing one-four-nine, extreme distance."

Kirk turned. "Closing?"

"No, sir, traveling laterally across our stern."

"We have screened you," Sova said, "but we can keep doing it only a short time. Keep all your shields up."

"Helm, full shields up." Kirk swung back to Sova. "Can you help us?"

The Vulcan captain shook his head. "I have no authority. But I will let you speak to someone who does."

"Zalt! Alive!"

"Yes, I am alive. I see you are also. It's too bad for you."

"I—made no special attempts to live. You know they found me in the same life pod as you!"

"Still . . . too bad. I offer you my pity."

Zalt was limited to one arm, the other caught up in a traction sling of some kind, and one eye now bore a gory scar, but his face still held that familiar contempt. None of that had gone away after Spear duty, after taking out an entire Ri'ann warship by themselves.

And they had both survived! No medicine Klingon or *romuluSngan* could bring back *two* Spears from a detonation!

The commander was wearing his own leggings and a simple blue shirt from the sickbay. McCoy, then, had been here, too. And so had the captain, for Zalt was wearing one of those translators.

The two of them waited in smoldering silence while the guard outside reestablished the barrier field that would keep them both in here, and its hum covered their voices, at least a little.

"You have been here all the time? In their brig?" Roth asked.

"Yes." Zalt glanced at the two cushioned beds and blankets. "Soft."

"They are soft," Roth agreed. "They asked me questions but without torture. Never even talked about it."

"And what did you tell them without torture?"

"Nothing, I swear."

"What is their heading?"

"I think they go to Vulcan."

"Then you did talk to them!" Zalt erupted.

"No!" Roth gasped. "I told them nothing about me!"

"And when the Vulcans see you, what will they tell these strangers! Fool!"

"I can't stop that . . ." Roth waved despairing hands.

Zalt swung back. "Are they with us or against us?"

"The . . . Vulcan?"

"No! These humans!"

"They say neither."

"That is not an option."

"I told him that."

"I know, Roth, you talk too much. You have always talked and talked. You talked millions of Klingons to their deaths."

Zalt stalked the room but lowered his voice further and eyed the guard outside the cell.

"We must disable this ship while it is still in our space," he said, "or destroy it."

Roth looked up. "Commander, we have no way to confirm their story. We shouldn't destroy them before we know the truth."

"You *talk* too much." Zalt cut him off with a growl. "You show weakness and tiredness to the enemy. I had to tolerate you as my copilot, but the glory is over. You will not question me now. The voice of a humiliated Klingon is not a voice."

Desperation creased Roth's brow. "But I've been a Spear! I've been walking dead! I didn't tell anyone! I've saved my honor!"

"You've saved your *family's* honor. Now they can go on without speaking your name. *You* will never have any honor. Some things cannot be fixed. It's my order that we disregard these people's wild stories and act to cripple this ship. If they are not with us, they are against us."

Roth shuffled backward into the shadow of the two bunks of the wall, put his arms to his sides. "Yes, Commander . . ."

Silence fell, and Roth swore it made a *whack* on the deck. His hands went numb, mind blazing and hopes dashed. He felt filthy.

Zalt wasn't looking at him. It was a shame to look at him.

When the barrier field snapped away, he barely noticed. Only when the guard came in with four other guards did he look up.

"All right, you two," the guard said, "no tricks or we'll shoot you down. Don't make any mistakes about that. Move."

Zalt hesitated two seconds while the translator caught up with the human's fast manner of speech. "Where are you taking us? Are you going to torture us?"

"Yeah, we're going to torture you. How do you feel about eating each other's fingers? Let's go."

Two of the other guards smiled. The first guard waved his weapon and gestured to the open corridor and the red gauntlet of the guards.

Zalt went first and paused as his hands were manacled. "Have we arrived at Vulcan?" he asked while they snapped the cuffs.

"Don't know," the guard said and distributed a square push to the middle of Roth's back. "I said move. Captain wants to see you."

* * *

While the transporter hummed between the two ships, Kirk waved Spock down from the starboard deck. "Come down with me."

Together they dropped to the command deck, the center of the bridge. Kirk had a particular impression he wanted to make.

On the viewscreen was a picture of the Vulcan ship, rough and old, patched together. There was no prosperity, no something-for-something's sake, be it design, art, science, exploration. The boarding party's clothing was basic, with familiar Vulcan stitching, but any jewels, stones, or brooches were conspicuously missing.

Spock landed at his side almost exactly as another Vulcan materialized on the upper bridge, port side. The new Vulcan visitor raised an eyebrow and stepped back when Uhura met him up there and offered him a personal translator.

Uhura arranged the translator on the breast of the Vulcan's bronze tunic—almost the same color as his hair—keyed it to his encephalography, then casually returned to her post.

Crossing the lower deck, Jim Kirk worked to hide his limp. "Welcome to the *Enterprise*. I'm Captain James T. Kirk."

Sova spoke up from the starboard side. "Captain, may I present Secretary Temron of the Vulcan High Council."

The new one looked young for such a heavy title. In fact, they all looked young. Where were all the old Vulcans? Tired? Crippled? Dead from years of fighting? Didn't Vulcans get the chance to grow old in this universe?

Didn't anybody?

Temron looked around, wide-eyed. "Your ship is . . . large. When we heard of an unknown vessel that could outrun the Klingons and Ri'ann, we envisioned a small vessel, powerpacked—but to have such speed in such bulk. You mystify us, Captain T'Kirk."

If he was enthused, it was embalmed in concern and his fascination was muffled. He broke away from scanning the bridge and was now staring at Spock.

Kirk moved back to the command deck's center to stand a little in front of Spock and a little beside him.

"This is Mr. Spock, my first officer."

Now Temron openly stared. He murmured, "Impossible . . ."

Spock mounted the stairs and paused before him on the upper bridge. There was something imposing about the two of them standing there, statuesque and becalmed.

Spock raised his right hand and offered the Vulcan greeting. "Live long and prosper, Temron."

The visitor gazed at him, again mystified and not bothering to hide it. The words meant more than a rote greeting.

Slowly, he raised his own hand. "I wish you peace . . . Spock." With deepening lament he offered the best his own culture had to give, and the poignant disparity between the two greetings seemed to wrack Temron like a blow. His expression did not change, but his despair rang around the bridge.

Temron glanced around, noted that he was slipping, and struggled for impassivity. He *did* look young. But who could really tell with a Vulcan?

Looking at Spock again, Temron lowered his voice. "How can you be here? Were you lost in your youth? Refugeed or castaway? Were your parents killed?"

"My parents are alive," Spock said fluidly. "My father is Vulcan's ambassador to the United Federation of Planets. I believe he is currently on a mission to the planet of Tellar."

"Tellar . . . I know this planet. The civilization there was obliterated by the Klingons when I was a child."

McCoy came forward on the upper aft deck. "What's that supposed to mean? You mean they were killed on purpose?"

"They refused to cooperate," Temron said. "Klingons use it as an example of nonsubmittance." He paused, looked at Kirk, looked at Sova, then back at Spock. "There are none left."

"The population of Tellar," Spock offered solidly, "is six billion as of the last local census."

Temron shook his head. "No."

McCoy came around the rail toward him. "What about the Orions?"

Temron looked at Sova, then at McCoy. "No . . ."

"The Alpha Centauris?"

"I do not know what those are."

Spock supplied, "Their indigenous name is Saroming."

Again Temron shook his head. "There are none of that name surviving here."

"The Tholians?" McCoy pressured.

"They were exterminated long ago."

"The Andorians?"

"Enslaved."

"Melkots?"

"Are being forced to mass-starve."

McCoy's squarish face went chalky. He backed off, as if Temron himself had done the starving and the exterminating.

Spock faced Kirk and lowered his voice. "Captain, if I may suggest— "

The turbolift interrupted him, and there was a commotion on the aft bridge.

Then, Temron spoke suddenly. "Roth! But you are walking dead!"

Chapter Seventeen

AT THE BACK of the bridge, flanked by two guards each, Roth and that other Klingon stood staring at the Vulcan secretary and at Sova.

Kirk narrowed his eyes. "You know each other?"

But it was the other Klingon who spoke up as he put a space between himself and Roth. "We all know him," Zalt said with cold despise. "He was contaminated by *them.*" He wagged his head at Temron.

Kirk puffed up with a warrior's kind of hope. He'd wanted answers and thought there might be clues in throwing these parties up against each other but hardly expected this.

Roth clenched his hands and stepped toward them until one of the guards fish-hooked him. "Vulcans! I knew it! Wish me peace, Temron, so I can wish you *death!*"

Kirk pulled himself to the upper bridge. "Explain that." He turned to Temron. "What's 'walking dead'?"

"He volunteered for Spear duty," the secretary said. "Sacrificed himself for the destruction of an enemy ship. No one comes back from that."

"He did. We rescued him. Now explain how you know him."

Temron suddenly retrieved his Vulcan composure, as though searching for the right words to keep himself dispassionate on a subject that could only be passion.

Below them, Spock connected glances briefly with Sova, then came forward a couple of steps and said, "Roth came to Vulcan as a regional surrogate. It was said that he began to study the teachings of Surak, discover that tolerance could be a tool against contention. He told us . . . told the Vulcans that he believed our way was a better one and that there could be an agreement. He put together a delegation of Klingons and Vulcans on an unauthorized peace mission to the Romulans." Spock paused, looked at Sova, and the Vulcan captain gestured that he continue to spill the beans of their meld. "The Romulans pretended sincere interest, but one of the Vulcans was in fact a Romulan spy. They sent a diplomatic squadron that turned out to be three heavily armed ships and cooperated enough to get inside Klingon space. They obliterated several colonies and almost destroyed a whole continent on the Klingon homeworld. Billions were slaughtered."

Kirk swung around to Roth. "Are you saying that the reason the Klingons are losing . . . is *him?*"

Shame rocketed across Roth's face. Well, there was the answer to that question.

Spock averted his eyes from Roth. "The Klingons turned on the Vulcans in angry retribution, . . . but the Vulcans defended themselves without timidity—"

"Timidity?" Roth gulped. "You came on the attack! There was nothing defensive about it! You cut our fleet down and obliterated the helpless stranded aboard those ships!"

Kirk leveled a finger at him. "Shut up."

Below, Spock sighed. "He is reviled on Klingon as a capitulator who caused the enemy to prevail."

"Because he fell for the Vulcan's methods and tried to make peace?"

Temron drew his hands close to his body. "Roth's efforts were sincere."

"Don't defend me, coward!" Roth shouted. "I volunteered to be a Spear so my reputation would be cleansed!"

"You will never be cleansed," Zalt rumbled from behind. "I was ashamed to have you in my craft. I volunteered for all the right reasons—to harm the enemy."

"And save your culture, isn't that right?" Kirk rounded on him. "You're losing. That's why you've been using this Spear tactic and sacrificing perfectly healthy trained pilots."

Zalt cranked forward against the guard's grip. "But we are winning *now!* Except for *him.*" With a sharp-edged boot he lashed out at Roth.

"Get those two off the bridge," Kirk ordered.

"They're lying to you!" Roth shrieked. "Temron! Tell them the truth! Tell them there is no future for them on Vulcan!"

Kirk snapped his fingers at the Security team. "Off!" As the struggling prisoners receded into the lift and the doors wheezed shut, he turned to the Vulcans. "Is the other Klingon right? Are they winning?"

"It is debatable," Sova said. "They are slowly turning the tide, but they are weak and may not recover. As for Vulcan ... " he added solemnly, then didn't finish his sentence.

Beside Kirk, Temron took on the responsibility that Sova found so uneasy. "We cannot live under the Romulans. They would treat us with murdering revenge. They despise Vulcans."

"I understand," Spock offered, reaching a comforting hand across dimensions.

Temron seemed gratified. "I still do not know how you are here," he said. "Or who you are, or why you know so little of the populated galaxy. Are you from such a distance? Are you a generational ship?"

"Secretary," Sova interrupted, "The details are ... overwhelming, and time is short. I suggest a meld. I will return to the ship and tend the veil."

Sova looked at Temron, Temron looked at Spock, Spock looked at Kirk. The look on McCoy's face wasn't helping much either.

Feeling he could use a breather, Kirk motioned to the turbolift. He thought about suggesting Spock's quarters, but given the decor—musical instruments and sculptures from a whole other Vulcan—might be one too many looking glasses to step Temron through all at once. Maybe later. He said, "The briefing room. We'll give you ten minutes."

Spock wordlessly gestured Temron to the turbolift, and they disappeared on their voyage to the lower decks.

Feeling numb from the hips down, Kirk forced himself around. "Captain Sova, get your boarding part off my ship." It took effort to avoid saying, "the hell off my ship."

Sova motioned his men into a group and touched a mechanism on his belt, and without even contacting their ship, the entire group fizzled into energy and dissolved.

"Security detail dismissed," Kirk said.

The guards flooded into the turbolift—a forest of broad shoulders and biceps that barely fit in there all at once.

McCoy stepped down toward the captain's chair just as Kirk arrived there and slid onto the black leather. His back ached, and his injured foot was on fire again. The leather was cool.

"This is our chance to get someone around here to completely believe us," Kirk said quietly. "I don't think Sova buys the whole story."

"But it was his idea that Temron and Spock do their little brain thing, Jim," the doctor said.

"Sova's a ship's captain in the middle of a war, and it's his business to be suspicious. He wants Temron to shoulder the responsibility."

McCoy sighed. "I don't blame them for being suspicious. Not even the Klingons could swallow that we were slammed through a dimensional crack by one of the rarest phenomena in science."

"I don't know how rare it is. I feel nauseated. Can you do anything about that?"

"I'll try. It's almost time for another treatment."

"Make it now and make it fast. I gave Spock ten minutes. You've got eight."

McCoy looked up at Uhura. "Lieutenant, have one of my interns come up here and bring the captain's prescription, full treatment."

"When's this thing going to get better?" Kirk grilled, shifting his leg to another position.

"It'll get worse before it gets better."

"Worse than this?"

"The toxins have to run their course. It's like a virus. I can't cure it. All I can do is mask the symptoms enough that the symptoms don't kill you."

Rubbing his thigh with the heel of a hand, Kirk slanted his eyes at him. "What a merry profession you have."

He gazed pensively now at the ship off their port bow that was working to keep them screened from the Klingon search pattern. Eventually those screens would break down and they'd have to run again or fight. Or both.

"There are missing pieces to this puzzle, and I'm bound to find all I can before I give up. You've got six minutes left."

* * *

The corridor was slippery with blood. Deck, walls, even the ceiling. Moans of the living and the stench of the dead crawled across the carpet. This human blood . . . it had a smell to it.

Zalt crossed the corridor, snatched Roth by the arm, and hauled him to his feet.

Roth sucked at what air he could get. These human guards, they had put up a demon's fight. Now they lay upon their deck. Were they all dead?

"Get up, Roth," Zalt growled at him. "We have to release ourselves from these manacles."

Wheezing, Roth forced himself to his feet. Struggling, he put his foot down on the slashed body of a guard. Where had the blade come from?

Another guard lay open-eyed and stone dead, throat slashed.

Roth looked up and noted that Zalt was bleeding. A wound from one of the weapons? He hadn't heard one go off. Probably none had, for these people likely had some kind of warning system that would alert them if weapon energy were released. The demon guards must have wounded Zalt with their bare hands.

Such enthusiasm! These guards had celebrated their fight, come in with fire and joy, and gone down with flamboyance. Roth was gratified to have given them this moment.

Zalt paused to adjust something on his hand, and Roth saw what had done the damage. On his hand, the commander wore a steel ring with a symbol upon it that Roth did not recognize. The symbol was flipped up like the top of a box, and the edge of it was a razor-sharp blade. Only an inch long but enough.

Roth looked at the guard with the slit throat.

"Come with me," Zalt said. "We will find the engineering bay and do damage. This ship must not run away."

"Is it better to escape?" Roth said. "To tell our high command that the Vulcans are breaking their agreement?"

"We will do damage!" Zalt roared. "The high command will find out when we drag this hulk to their door. We will do what I say and not you. I would kill you myself if it were not a waste. Find a place to hide these bodies."

"There is blood everywhere. How could we possibly hide this?"

Zalt wasn't paying attention to him, so he started dragging one of the dead guards toward a door.

"I've figured out their truth." Zalt said. "They come from some distant area of the galaxy and were beaten in a war. They're making up their wild story, and now they're conspiring with the Vulcans. *Your* friends."

"The Vulcans are no friends of mine!" Roth rasped. "I hate them. Their nonsense ruined me. I will not consider anything they say."

"Then consider what I say. We will damage this ship."

Jim Kirk and his chief surgeon hurried into the briefing room without announcing their arrival. If the Vulcans hadn't finished their meld yet, too bad.

But they had. In fact, they were on opposite sides of the room.

Temron was sitting in a chair over to the left, his face a pale green. He sat with lips parted, his brows drawn, and his eyes had lost their focus. Whatever Spock had shown him, it had worked.

Who knew what it had been? How compartmentalized could a Vulcan mind be?

Cross sections of human history through the ages, struggle and conquest, intrepid individuals and rugged productivity . . . the U.S. Bill of Rights, the UFP Articles of Federation . . . moments when humans first met Vulcans and the valiant concord that arose to form the core of the United Federation of Planets . . .

Kirk wondered if Temron realized that this mutuality and the stamina it gave to the Federation was due in part to the man who had opened his inner mind to him. The Vulcans had been part of the Federation for a while, yes, but it was Spock's personal defiance of the Vulcan Academy in favor of a Starfleet career that had dissolved the last barriers. As stories filtered back of his stalwart presence on the Federation flagship, the battered beauty that had been through so much, other Vulcans had plunged into the stubborn human dream. The Federation was no longer just the Earth guys' crazy idea.

And when the Klingons and Romulans and other hostile races appeared, the Federation had possessed the soundness to hold them off on a score of fronts.

That hadn't happened here. Kirk saw it in Temron's face.

And he saw the enhanced vision of the blue giant Izell, the accretion disk, the cosmic string—Kirk was sure Spock had handed over the details, even in the blur of a telepathic bond. Even if no one knew what happened, at least the Vulcans could see that the starship had been through something neck breaking. Whether thrown into an alternate universe or somehow altering their own, *something* violent and unthinkable had brought them to this juncture.

There on Temron's face was the crumple in time. And here on this ship, Spock stood with James Kirk.

Logic had its drawbacks.

Temron looked as if he were holding back vomit. Suddenly he didn't know if he, his life, and the universe he knew were the ones that were supposed to be here or not. It was pretty plain that he didn't have any trouble grasping the whole, huge, ugly theory.

Kirk watched in empathy and felt a little guilty. He had no intent to disturb anyone so much. He wanted Temron to believe but not at the price of sanctity, and he saw Temron's peace shredding, file by file. Vulcans just weren't supposed to look that whipped.

In the far corner, his face to the wall, Spock stood with his arms folded tightly over his chest, the muscles of his back and shoulders rigid, pliancy destroyed by whatever the two had shown each other in the open hippodrome of their telepathic minds.

Both were brittle, both changed. One had seen what might have been. The other had seen a fertile galaxy beaten to apathy by contention.

Kirk met eyes with Temron for a long moment, enough to communicate that they now understood each other. The Vulcan secretary was looking at Kirk a whole new way.

Without saying anything, Kirk left McCoy to handle this one and went to the far corner.

"Spock?" he began quietly.

Spock worked valiantly to gather himself but continued to stare at the wall. "Yes, Captain."

"I'm sorry about your having to do this."

This time Spock only nodded.

"You seem to have given our friend a mindfull," Kirk went on, peering across the room. "Tell me."

"The Vulcans here," Spock slowly said, "were spacefarers —explorers and traders—when they first encountered the Klingons, who saw them as an easy prize. But the Vulcans were determined to defend themselves and surprisingly capable of doing so. For many years there were heavy losses on both sides." Spock paused as McCoy approached them. His posture didn't improve, but he turned outward to speak to them both. "Several times the Vulcans defeated the Klingons, but did not pursue and destroy them. Instead, the Vulcans returned home to continue living. The Klingons kept coming back, and each time there was war. Each time great loss, each time the Vulcans beat them away and retired to wait again. After a time, the Klingons grew frustrated and presented the Vulcans with a rather one-sided treaty. With no Federation to join, the Vulcans chose partial subjugation rather than life on the eternal defense."

"I don't blame them," McCoy offered. "At least now they can move through space, live, study—"

"Though always under the watchful eye of the Klingon guard. I don't blame them either, Doctor, but they share their trade with their keepers."

"Extortion," McCoy added.

"Yes. At least they need not participate in the war with the Romulans."

Kirk scowled. "It's the 'leasts' that bother me, Spock. Everyone seems to settle for the least of everything here."

"But the Vulcans have not been only trading and studying, Captain. After fighting the Klingons to a standstill, the Vulcans are surviving day by day, while slowly and methodically working to overthrow the Klingons. Of course, they have to do it in such a way that will not bring the Romulans down upon them. They have been using their 'merchant' status to find budding species and help them hide. They give them their 'veiling' technology and suggest they stay within their own solar systems. Some have been discovered anyway, and others have ignored the warnings and been destroyed. But still others are successfully hidden."

"So the Vulcans are only pretending to cooperate?" McCoy said. "Good for them."

Spock finally turned away from the wall. "Yes, while subtly undermining the Klingons and Romulans. In fact, they've made sure both sides are hammering each other to exhaustion. It was the Vulcans who developed the Spear tactic to keep the Romulans from winning before the Klingons were exhausted."

"Not a bad idea," Kirk said. "What's the catch? I can see it in your face."

"The catch is that there is only an eighteen percent chance of the Klingons and Romulans collapsing before either finds out what the Vulcans are doing and turns on them. The Vulcans are taking that small chance. It's all they have."

"Then what about us?" Kirk pushed off the wall and moved to Temron. He stood over the Vulcan respresentative long enough to get his attention away from the thunder of a million new thoughts. Now what? He couldn't turn the two Klingons over to the Vulcans now. And there was no Starfleet to hand them over to.

Boldly he asked, "Can you help us?"

"No, Captain," Temron said. "There is no assylum for you on Vulcan. Under no condition must you go there."

"Can't you hide us in some way? Where else can we go?"

"Spock has communicated to me a roster of cultures friendly to you in your own time line, and indeed none have gone unsubjugated. Only the Vulcans have managed to strike a treaty, and only because we fought the Klingons to a stalemate. It has been fortunate that we are in Klingon space and not that of the Romulans. Our lost brothers would offer no such judiciousness. They would kill us all."

Temron stood up and paced down the briefing room table, as though putting distance between himself and his problem.

"The Klingons may also conclude that you would come to Vulcan. They will search our planet, scour our atmosphere for hints of your ship. Five hundred of you could never hide for very long. If any traces of you are found, there will be war in Vulcan skies again. The Klingons and Romulans will fight over you, then come down and slaughter us in their search for you. My entire planet would have to go to war again to protect you."

With the admonishment of Starfleet regulations and Federation codes suddenly blistering him, Kirk realized that he and his crew would be driven to self-exile or self-destruction before they could let any of Temron's predictions play out. The *Enterprise* and the humans aboard her—the only humans anywhere in the universe—were only freeloaders now, gate-crashers begging the bonhomie of people who had their hands full just taking care of themselves.

His oath rang in his head, hammering his promise that he would destroy the ship with his own hand before he allowed it to destroy a civilization.

"Do you have a suggestion for me?" he asked.

Empathy shone warmly through Temron's eyes. He understood the heavy menace riding Kirk's shoulders, towing a ship and crew who depended upon him. He scanned the room, the beautiful ship, witness to prosperity, effort, ingenuity, spirit, and a brand of freedom that he had never known. Vulcan or not, there was a shuddering pain behind his face.

"There is virtually no chance of recreating the circumstances that brought you here," he said, speaking with newborn familiarity. He stood beside Spock as if they'd known each other all their lives. In a way, they had. "I know you hope to attempt changing the past . . . to put things . . . right."

The word disturbed him. Sour though his civilization might be, in Temron's eyes Kirk saw the fear of having someone else tamper with his future, his life. Kirk steeled himself to argue his point or at least to try dissolving that fear some, but he never got the chance.

"I laud your valiant attempt," Temron told them. "But even if a cosmic string could be attracted, it wouldn't have the same effect on you as what brought you here. You're brave men to try." He folded his hands and looked at Kirk. "If you do not succeed, I suggest you put your ship to its highest speed, head away from the populated core of the galaxy, and seek out a distant planet upon which you can live out your lives. Settle it, cannibalize the *Enterprise,* then destroy the ship so it can never be found and perverted to another purpose. Begin a new civilization. If you are discovered before then, you must fight to the death and no less. That is your only chance . . . for ours is festered and destined to die."

Chapter Eighteen

"STATUS?"

Kirk dropped into his chair and sat ramrod straight. They were after his ship. It all came down to that.

"Full emergency alert, sir. Two ships, six hundred ninety-two thousand kilometers, warp five and closing." Engineer Scott moved out of the way and eagerly took his station on the port side, talking as he went. "Triple-shielded and powering up their firing sequences, if that alien hardware reads right. They'll have us in weapons' range in roughly ninety seconds."

"Sensors on full capacity."

"Aye, sir."

On the upper bridge, Spock stood with Temron.

They all watched the viewscreen.

The unfamiliar Klingon ships bore down upon them like running dogs, never really looking as though they were moving, yet plowing down on them frame by frame. Nary a swerve, nary a hesitation. There was no canny dance of antagonism or attempt at clever dodging. Just a down and dirty full-out run. They'd found the rabbit and they knew the rabbit was fast, so they were going to run it into the ground.

"We'll beam you back, Mr. Temron," Kirk said, keeping one eye on the screen. "Unfortunately, there's no time for long good-byes. Mr. Sulu, target those vessels' critical points."

"Targeting."

"Scotty, rig a failsafe one-button detonation for the warp core in case we're boarded. We won't have time for codes and countercodes."

Above, Spock moved to the rail. "Captain—"

"We'll take our chances," Kirk said with anticipation, "but I'm not having the Vulcans lose their eighteen percent chance of turning this cesspool around. Rig it, Scott."

Scott glanced at Spock, then headed for the turbolift. "I'll do it myself, sir."

"Kirk to transporter room."

"Transporter room, Simmons."

"Simmons, pinpoint the upper bridge, port side forward. We're going to beam ship-to-ship. Correlate with the Vulcans' bridge."

"Wouldn't you rather do it from the pad down here, sir? It's safer and it doesn't strain the instru—"

"Don't instruct me, Ensign. Set your coordinates."

"Aye, sir. One minute."

"Make it less. Mr. Temron, . . . a short acquaintance, but one we'll all remember for the rest of our lives."

The idea of leaving—forever—this font of the possible struck Temrom hard, and it showed in his eyes. He had just been shown the design for paradise, and now they were locking him behind a glass wall. As long as he lived, he would be able to look but never touch.

"Enemy ships in range, sir," Chekov said.

Spock took Temron's elbow and ushered him to the correct position to be picked up by the transporter sensors when the order was given. Temron allowed himself to be put in place, then turned abruptly and looked at Spock.

"I will teach my people," he pledged, "to live *long* . . . and prosper."

Even beneath the shield of control, Spock appeared complimented, gratified. "You will shear the chains of this circumstance," he sanctioned. "I believe in you."

Heart-stricken and not ashamed to show it, Temron accepted those words with a nod.

Spock stepped back and away.

Ticking off the seconds, Kirk was moved by the intensity of this one moment in all of endless time. What goes on when a person enters another person's mind? When all the memories of childhood and youth, education, and experience are flooded together like two rivers joining?

He didn't envy either of them. Each had sacrificed privacy, one for his ship, the other for his civilization.

Temron took another step backward, a finality of sorts, and looked down. "Thank you, Jim."

"Best luck," Kirk offered. Then suddenly he wished he had come up with more to say. "Kirk to Simmons—energize. Mr. Sulu, prepare to open fire on the Vulcan ship, phasers one-quarter."

"Ready, sir. One-quarter phasers, locked on."

The pillar of lights consumed Temron, and his body was slowly dissembled at the molecular level and sent back to his vessel. The whole process would take eight seconds.

After four, Kirk ordered, "Full about. Fire."

*   *   *

Smoldering with wounds that would later save its life, the Vulcan ship veered off in one direction, and the *Enterprise* in another, with the starship firing as she ran, chasing the echo of her captain's voice.

"Mr. Sulu, warp factor six. Let's outrun them here and now."

"Warp six, aye, sir, . . . warp two . . . three . . ."

The crew held on like bats to a ceiling as the ship hulled over, took a grip on raw space, and sprinted. Enemy fire sliced across her underside and crackled along her shields. Regurgitated energy changed to blinding light and flashed so brightly that they shaded their eyes.

"Sir, they're hailing us," Uhura reported. "They demand we stand down."

"No response," he said, eying the screen.

"Warp four, sir, . . . warp three seven five—sorry, sir—" Sulu was working harder now. He'd had to slow down to angle away from the changing Klingon formation.

The enemy ships weren't giving them time to make high warp without changing course. They weren't like the Klingons Kirk knew. Those wandered around the settled galaxy with a chip on their shoulders, boxed in by stronger powers, and knew very well that they'd better behave. They postured, growled, and threw things, but rarely had they been tested on any scale of battle.

But these Klingons were accustomed to fighting—real fighting. They knew how to do it. Their whole science was devoted to it, everything they could invent, buy, or steal. Working their way in front of a starship, two ships twisted for position while two others circled her abeam, not throttling back because they knew the new ship could outrun them and that they had to change tactics.

It was smart. A sign of experience on the battlefield. They'd learned.

The starship charged through space, but she might as well have been on a leash, stuck at warp four or lower. Vexation poured through Kirk at the prospect of a peaceful galaxy whose chances had been swatted down by these petty contests.

"Never underestimate your enemy," he grumbled. "If we can get clear, we can outrun them. Maybe we can put some strain on them while we do it. Force them to follow us till it hurts."

With his face cast in blue from the sensor hood, Spock nodded once. "We may gain way if we force them to come through heavy fire."

"Noted," Kirk said. "Mr. Chekov, ready full phasers. Photon torpedoes on standby."

"Phasers ready . . . Photons on st—sir!" The navigator's youthful face crumpled. "Firing mechanisms are fused!"

Spock dodged to his side. "Confirmed. Sixty percent shutdown, Captain."

Kirk pounded a comm unit. "Engineering! What's happened to the weapons integrity?"

The line was open, but no one spoke to him. The sounds of shouting and scuffling babbled through as if the engineers had dropped something and were all fighting over it.

Then—

"Intruder alert! Security to main engineering! Intruder alert!"

Chapter Nineteen

"ENGINEERING! Give me a report!"

Jim Kirk grabbed the arm of his command chair and shook it, as if that would help. From the comm unit on the chair's arm, a frantic voice squawked up at him through a haze of static.

"Sir—sir, we're got two Klingons—sit on 'em if you have to, damn it! Henry, aren't you armed?"

Kirk hunched over the comm unit, as if getting closer would do any more good than shaking it. "Anderson, give me a report!"

"We've got intruders, sir; two Klingons are down here. We found 'em in the forward weapons access jacket. I have to assume sabotage."

"You'd better assume it, Lieutenant," Kirk fumed. "Get those two back to the brig and have Security check on the four guards who were supposed to be taking them there."

"Yes, sir."

"All right . . . Mr. Chekov, stand by on that weapons order. We'll have to outmaneuver them. Mr. Sulu, continue evasive."

"Aye, sir."

"Mr. Spock, do you have any way to know what happened to Temron's ship?"

"I noted them engaging warp speed and angling away as the Klingon vessels came upon us," Spock said. "None of the Klingons abandoned pursuit of us to go after them, so I suppose their escape. By the time the Klingons confront them, Temron and his captain will probably have concocted a plausible story for their nearness to us and why we fired on them. I hope their damage will provide a fair substantiation."

"I hope so, too." Kirk suddenly realized he was breathing like a race horse. "When it comes down to it, everybody has to die for himself."

Troubled by that and other things, Spock managed a small nod.

"Let's get out of here," Kirk offered him.

Another small nod, but the eyes changed. "Agreed."

"Mr. Sulu, position of the enemy ships now?"

"Two dead astern, sir, five hundred thousand kilometers . . . one z-minus twenty thousand kilometers . . . One off the starboard beam, thirty-two thousand kilometers. All attempting to close."

"All stop."

The bridge crew stared at him suddenly.

Sulu cranked around. "All stop, sir?"

"Affirmative. All stop—right now."

Parting his lips to argue, Sulu thought better of that and turned to his helm. "Aye, sir. All stop."

He tapped his controls.

With a ghastly squeal the ship folded in on herself and drew up hard, pitching them all forward, even if they were hanging on. The force was enough to pull their skin off.

Kirk managed to stay in his chair and keep his eyes on the screen as his ship and crew buckled around him, hoping that what had worked with the Romulans would work with the Klingons.

Over the whine, Chekov croaked, "Two enemy ships crossing in front of us, sir—overshooting us!"

"Aft ship overtaking us," Spock reported, "coming into collision range with the vessel abeam of us."

On the forward screen, three of the enemy ships plowed past them in different directions at blinding speed, rushing so far into the distance that they were suddenly invisible.

"Full about, Sulu," Kirk barked. "Now's our chance. Warp factor six."

The helmsman didn't respond, but his elbows bent as he tried to work the controls that were buried under his chest.

The ship's squeal fell off, and the engines began to pump again. Warp two . . . three . . . four . . .

"Warp factor five, sir," Sulu heaved. "Warp six, sir."

"Enemy ships coming about, sir," Spock read off his long-range sensors. "Falling far behind." He straightened and turned, offering Kirk the congratulations of his tone. "They were completely surprised."

Kirk nodded but said nothing to him. "Mr. Chekov, maintain surveillance behind us."

"Yes, sir!" The young man stared at the main screen, sweating, but also grinning.

Sulu leered at Chekov—a smile there, too. And Nourredine up at engineering was still hanging on to his chair but grinning.

"Security to bridge, Ensign Meerwald."

"Kirk here. What've you got?"

"Captain, we found the four guards. They were stuffed into an envirosuit locker."

"What's their condition?"

"I'm sorry, sir, but . . . they're all four dead, sir. The bastards killed 'em."

Nausea rushed through Kirk's body and rage through his mind. Losing men made him insane, even though it was part and parcel of the service. Those men hadn't signed up to die at the hands of prisoners who were already arrested and manacled.

He didn't know what happened down there, half a dozen decks below, on the way to the brig. Perhaps those men hadn't been used to this kind of Klingon, the kind who had done more than crow about war, but who instead had waged it all their lives.

Now he would have to write to their families. If . . .

"Acknowledged. Kirk out," he slurred.

For a moment he stared at the carpet. It turned to fuzz before his eyes. A thump on the deck made him look up.

Spock was there, now folding his arms, and regarding his boots briefly before looking up. "Now that we have a clearer picture of the state of affairs . . . where will we go?"

The question was heavy with Spock's perception that Kirk had been thinking about this all along and must, by now, have racked up a possibility or two.

Even for Kirk, this sudden solitary power was a revelation. He'd been independent, yes, almost sovereign, as all captains are once they left the dock, but Starfleet had always been there before. Weeks away, yes. But there.

Now he found himself the true head of all that was left of Starfleet. All that existed of the human race was on this ship, and he was in charge of them.

He sighed and paused to think. "If we manage to correct whatever happened to create this new time line, we won't be destroying any of these species? Am I right?"

Spock offered a not very convincing bob of his brows. "I dare not say."

"Well, I do. My obligation is to see to humanity. We're the only ones who aren't here. Before I give up and resort to colonizing some distant planet to save my crew's life, I want you to tell me there's absolutely no chance of our fixing this or getting back to our own time line."

He was tossing the ball into Spock's court and forcing him to play. Troubled, Spock was suddenly weighted by his role as primary advisor and science answerman.

"I cannot tell you there is *no* chance, Captain," he admitted.

"Then I'm not giving up our millionth of a chance of reversing this. Billions of people who lived and prospered in our universe have died or were never born in this one. Including you and me and everyone we've ever known. I want that back for the sake of the humans, the Klingons, the Romulans, and everyone else."

He gazed past Spock's shoulder at the beautiful empty bowl of velvet stickpinned with diamonds as the ship rushed in controlled high violence through space.

"And, Spock," he added, "I think I know where to start. A way to go back in time that won't take a year and a half."

He was aware of his first officer's unbroken gaze, now complicated with curiosity at the ring in those words. An answer?

Yes, possibly, based as so many of his hunches were on the *Enterprise*'s strange experiences in space where no man had gone before. If he himself couldn't draw on those experiences, who could? If he couldn't exact a profit from his own risks and those of his ship and crew, then who should? He knew firsthand of the quirks of dangerous science. There were things out there akin to magic. If he could pull one more dove out of his hat, move one more mountain . . .

"Secure the ship. Go to yellow alert. Maintain battle stations. Shields on standby. Rig for silent running."

As the drone of repeats and ayes and yes-sirs rumbled about the bridge like a security blanket, he gazed at Spock and made no effort to shield the sting of loss of his four Security men. He knew it showed in his face. Roth and that other one—they'd done what he would have done, and he hated them for it. He'd underestimated his enemy twice in the same hour and now he was jaundiced with rage over it. Mistake, mistakes.

He rammed the point of his elbow back on the chair and clapped his hot hand over his mouth and sat there hating himself.

As the ship hunkered down and waited for her captain's order, Spock quietly prodded, "I inferred that you know what to do next. Where to go."

"I think I know where to go," Kirk ventured, "for our one last chance to fix this. We just have to hope it hasn't already been discovered, Mr. Spock, because these people would destroy it on sight. Mr. Sulu, come about to—where are we? Come to heading four zero five."

"Four zero five, sir."

"Ahead full."

"Ahead full, sir."

"Mr. Chekov, I want you to plot a new course. We're going *very* far away . . . to a place we *have* been before."

PART THREE

DEEP TIME

"Millions and million of lives hanging on what this vessel does next."
"Or what this vessel fails to do, Doctor."

—McCoy and Spock,
Balance of Terror

Chapter Twenty

"THE OVERVIEWS OF HISTORY recorded on our previous mission here are stored in the library computer, sir. I'm having them loaded into this tricorder."

"Fine." The bridge was hot again. "When you're finished, assemble another landing party. Include the two Klingons."

The shadows on the bridge were harsher than yesterday, chiseled out of the colors and shapes of the chairs and consoles. Their edges were cracks on the bridgescape.

"I beg your pardon, sir?"

Jim Kirk blinked once, then screwed his eyes shut again, harder this time. "It may help us if they see whatever happens from now on. When we find out what happened, I want to see the truth in their faces. And bring that kid from before. The anthropologist.

"Lieutenant Bannon, sir."

"Fine. Bring him along."

His spine suddenly compressed. He fell sideways as his bad leg folded under him. His elbow rammed into the science station console beside Spock, and he felt the pointed bone of his hip jar against the housing. His body jackknifed.

Spock caught him by the arm and levered him back onto

his sea legs, but the angular face was turned not to the captain but to the instruments, now whining and beeping for attention.

"Enemy fire?" Kirk gasped, despite the fact that the ship hadn't gone to automatic red alert, despite again the fact that all sensors were on standby.

"No, sir," the Vulcan said, peering into his sensor hood. He studied his sensors' readouts, then turned. His face was animate with victory. "That was a first wave of time displacement, sir. We're in the right place."

Kirk leaned on the science panel and tried to catch his breath. One bump, and he was gasping. The pain in his temples announced itself every few seconds with nerve twinges just under the skin of his forehead.

Time displacement . . . surging outward in the form of raw energy. For the first time in days he felt as if he'd done something right.

"Jim?" On the center deck below them, McCoy came toward the bright red rail. "See you a minute?"

Kirk didn't step down but came to the rail and pressed his hip against it, just in case there was another one of those waves—and there would be. "What is it?"

McCoy's squarish face was blanched. "How are you feeling?"

"Hot, sore, nauseated, foggy-brained, and dizzy. Anything else?"

"You left out irritable."

"Not on purpose. What are you gonna do about it?"

"Well, I can give you another treatment right about now, but you're going to have to understand that part of convalescence is rest. You're not getting any."

"There's nothing I can do about that." Kirk cupped his hand around the back of his neck and let his head hang as the muscles stretched. When he raised his head, his spine cracked like marbles dropping. "Let's get going. Mr. Sulu, hold course into those energy waves. Go to yellow alert. Mr. Spock, you have the con."

McCoy met him on the upper deck and stood between

him and the turbolift. "Jim, there's just one more thing. Bannon doesn't want assignment."

Another energy wave hit, but this time Kirk was ready. It was McCoy who stumbled, then whirled and fought the impact. The ship capered a few yards, bucked, and dropped back into place.

McCoy pulled himself to the rail, knuckled white. "The anthropologist, Jim. He doesn't want an assignment."

"Why not? Was he injured?"

"No, no, that's not it . . . He says he's resigning from Starfleet." The doctor cupped one hand with the other and twisted until the muscles in his bare forearms flexed. His medical smock shimmered in the bridge lights. "I think we might've scared the daylights out of him."

Kirk stepped past him. "I'll take care of it. Give me the treatment right now, then collect whatever you need for this leg and meet us in the transporter room in twenty-five minutes."

"I want you to get off your feet for at least four hours."

"Fine. You can carry me."

"Am I going to have to give you a medical order?"

"If you want to see it stuffed and mounted."

"Now, Jim, you listen to me . . ."

"Bannon?"

"Captain!"

A lieutenant j.g.'s quarters. Nostalgia times ten. Single bunk, dim lighting, plain walls. Head and shower adjoining with the quarters next door. One bed shared on alternative off-watch periods by two crewmen.

"We've almost reached our destination," Kirk said. "Mr. Spock is stuffing a pair of tricorders with historical database and with class-M paleontological and geological databases. We're putting together a landing party. I'd like you to be part of it."

Lanky, red-haired Bannon stared at him without the thinnest idea of what to say. The fact that the captain was here in person proved that Kirk had already heard of

Bannon's plans to abandon his duty, to slide into some nice quiet lab and live out his life not affecting very much at all. After all, anthropologists were pretty much cleanup crew for past and current cultures. It'd been a hell of a long time since a critical bit of research had come off the desk of one of those.

Feeling the pressure of his own responsibility, Kirk paused and raised a brow at him. "Well?"

The boy backed up until his calves butted against the bunk. Couldn't sit down in the captain's presence. "I—I—I—"

Kirk's other brow went up. "You, you, you?"

Bannon rubbed his hands against his thighs. "I don't want to go, sir. I'm thinking of . . ."

A bizarre, heavy silence folded around the little quarters. For James Kirk, the words *leaving* and *Starfleet* didn't go together. As often as he had questioned himself, even wished for respite, the concept of putting his braid on somebody's desk and dropping a "Thanks, bye," beside it was beyond reach.

Nervous, Bannon shifted and twitched. It was one thing to tell a bunkmate that he wanted to quit the Fleet or report it to the watch commander, who then took it to the department head, who reported it to the first officer, who *maybe,* if the situation merited attention, took it to the captain. Maybe. The last person he expected or wanted to spill his guts all over was his commanding officer.

Lowering himself to the desk chair to get weight off his throbbing leg, Kirk asked, "Is this about Lieutenant LaCerra?"

Bannon blinked as if shocked that somebody as up there as the captain had the foggiest intuition about personal things.

"Yes, sir," he finally purged. "Guess it is." He stared at the carpet. "When those animals started to drive her into the high grass, I was taking readings on the biotricorder. I threw it down and grabbed for my phaser." His voice broke as he added, "I got my communicator by mistake."

Out in the corridor, somebody ran by. Then somebody

else. Maybe a couple of engineers. Their footsteps made a hurried *thrum* on the deck under Kirk's feet.

It isn't your fault, Jim.

I'm in command, Bones. It makes it my fault.

Kirk pushed himself to his feet. "I see." Then he half turned. "You're welcome to resign your commission once our problem is resolved, Lieutenant. Until then, we've all got to give a hundred percent. Outfit yourself for a field reconnaissance and be in the transporter room in ten minutes."

Ruins extending to the horizon. An ancient planet, age still in question, despite years of study.

Had it been years already?

Before them at a notable distance, hovering in place as if painted on the sky, tall as two men and wide as four, a circular rock formation stood like a polished slice of a geode on somebody's desk. It seemed inert, but they knew it wasn't.

Muttering like a midshipman, Jim Kirk led the way. He knew the way. He clung to the anchor of his own voice, so he didn't have to listen to the echoes in his head, drumming memories of another voyage to this place, ringing in his head and driving him to distraction.

Hiking over the rocks beside him, Spock had nothing to say. That didn't mean much. Spock, whose compassion had found an unashamed place right behind those black eyes and that satanic mask—amazing just how much could show through that shell. Maybe he just didn't try so hard to hide it anymore.

They'd been here before, done it together, the two of them. Stepped through that glittering donut, arrived in the past, had the future at their fingertips. Fixing the mistake before had meant letting an exceptional woman die under the bumper of a truck, preventing her from actualizing a brilliant future that would have changed history for the much, much worse. Not everything was meant to be.

Now the history of the galaxy rode on Jim Kirk's shoulders.

Did you do something wrong? Whatever it is, let me help.

He stopped between two crops of broken ruin and let his aching arms go limp just for a moment. He'd actually heard her voice.

Spock stood there, chin down, brows up, empathizing for all he was worth. "Captain?"

Kirk looked at him, going over in his mind what they'd been through the last time. Another glitch in history that had to be put right. Here was Spock, wondering where they would find the personal fortitude to go through it again.

And there was McCoy, adding up the billions of innocent lives who never got a chance to live, pained for them every bit as much as if they had died one by one on his surgical table.

"I've felt this way before," Kirk said, "this being alone."

"Intuition, Captain?"

"Not good enough for you?"

They stood together with that thing on their immediate horizon, trying to drum up a little shoulder-to-shoulder knightly spirit to sustain them, then deal with the light-headed thrill of fear, and hope their decisions were crisp.

Kirk knew he was treading thorns, doing double duty as captain and invalid, sweating down the poison in his body and the unholy torment in his soul. He wanted his crew to see him taking it like a man, but his shrinking stomach provided a grisly reminder that his lifted finger could condemn a thousand worlds.

That was what it meant to be out front. This was what it meant to command starships, for himself and his fellow captains, going out there first and bearing the deepest scars—those of their own decisions. After all the braids and decorations, accolades and cocktail parties, only the captains remembered the missions that went wrong. Those memories made all the pats on the back just a little sore, leaving the inner man curdle-blooded and crouching scared.

"Out here in our court dress," he grumbled, "with no castle to come home to."

Spock broke from his scan of the ruins. "Sir?"

"I don't like these things. Of all the good that's come from exploration since human beings crossed the first land bridges onto new continents, there's been no chance to go backward and start over. Usually that's a good thing. As much as we may wish to go back, we're better off slogging forward. It's only recently we've found ways to wedge ourselves into the past, where we don't belong. It's not fair to those who never get a chance to tell us to butt out. I can push forward, take chances, make bets . . . but look backward, and I'm not so sure anymore."

His words dropped upon the rocks, muffled cries for help for which there was no answer.

"Come on, Spock," he resigned. "Let's get this over with."

The ground was littered with crumbled rocks in this area. Huffing with effort of his own, McCoy made a point of getting to Kirk's side. "Captain?"

"Something?"

"Before we get into whatever we're about to get into, I want to suggest sending Bannon back to the ship. My evaluation of his mental state—"

"I've taken care of it."

McCoy glowered. "Did you have a talk with him?"

"I listened."

"You didn't say anything?"

"I told him to report for duty."

"Jim, that boy's in shock. Can't you see it in his face?"

"It takes a good man," Kirk rebuffed, "to think he's wicked because of a fumble. Nothing I've got to say will fix him. That pain of having altered another life . . . There's no bandage for it. It's a power everyone craves but damned few appreciate for the danger it is. He's got to learn some time if he wants to be in Starfleet."

"He says he doesn't."

"He's lying."

"Jim—"

"That's enough. We're almost there."

At the center of the time displacement, the site was completely undisturbed, peaceful as a church. They may as well have been here yesterday, as familiar as it seemed. The sky was gunmetal gray and flat as concrete. This system's sun didn't really want to have much to do with this place.

Spock and a Security guard took Kirk by the arms and hoisted him down from the rocks onto a slab of ground. He came down hard on the heel of his bad leg, pain jarring into his hip. Before he could breathe again he was ready to swear he'd landed on his ear.

McCoy started past him toward the slice of rock sitting up on its edge, with the horizon of this planet showing passively through the middle.

"Bones—" Abruptly Kirk reached out, caught the doctor by his upper arm, and yanked him back. "Don't get too close."

"Place gives me the shivers," McCoy admitted.

"I don't blame you." Pushing McCoy behind him, he threw a collective glance to the rest of the team. "Sensors."

Around him, the landing party brought up their tricorders or phasers respectively and scanned the area. There were seven of them: Kirk, McCoy, Spock, Bannon, two Security guards, and a twenty-three-year-old Tibetan girl who'd begged for a chance as science assistant. Spock, Bannon, and the girl scanned the area electronically while the guards did a cursory walkaround.

"No life forms," Spock said, "no energy output other than the main structure . . . No signs of disturbance."

"Acknowledged," Kirk allowed. "Carry on." He stared up at the huge donut of rock. It wasn't glowing or showing any sign of the energy he knew was there. Yet it raised the hairs on the back of his neck.

A few feet away, a communicator chirped. "Spock to *Enterprise*. The site is secure. Beam down the second landing party now."

Into Kirk's resting mind came the buzz of scrambled energy, the whistle of mechanical effort as a billion molecules were forced through space and reassembled over a matter of seconds.

Before him on the chalk-dry ground stood two more Security guards and the two Klingon prisoners, each manacled at the wrists, both wearing sickbay shirts and their own trousers.

Faces rough as watchdogs', Roth and Zalt glanced around at the forbidding landscape, both probably suspicious that the plan was to abandon them here. Not a bad idea.

"All right," Kirk segued, limping toward the big geode. He started toward it. "Let's see what we've got going for us."

Before him, the two-foot-thick circular frame of what appeared to be solid stone stood in elegant and utterly silent repose.

"Guardian," he began. "Do you hear me?"

The rim of rock accommodated him by lighting up internally, coming alive in response as if excited to have somebody to talk to. A slow, booming voice thrummed across the open landscape.

"I AM THE GUARDIAN OF FOREVER . . . LET ME BE YOUR GATEWAY."

The voice was grand, yet somehow emotional, like a priest coming out of sequester, trying to maintain a lordly distance while desperately wanting to dance at a wedding.

Kirk managed to stifle a pointless nod. "Do you remember us?"

Spock leaned toward him and murmured. "Captain?"

"Maybe it's got memory banks or something."

The lights were already on again. "I AM MACHINE AND BEING . . . BOTH AND NEITHER . . ."

"There, Spock! That's what we asked it when we were here before. It *does* have memory banks. It remembers us."

"Or it may simply have telepathic traits, sir."

A few steps back, without moving his lips, McCoy grumbled, "I'm bet'n on machine myself."

Kirk didn't react. He'd hooked a fish and wanted to reel. "Guardian," he began, "do you know us?"

"YOU ARE FROM BEFORE THE CHANGE," the big voice boomed.

Spock glanced at him again.

"What change," Kirk prodded, "are you referring to?"

"THE CHANGE OF TIME."

Above them, the sky moved a little, smoke grinding against the iron pot of twilight.

"How do you *know* we're from before the change?"

"I AM MY OWN BEGINNING, MY OWN ENDING . . ."

"Yes, we know that."

"Maybe it thinks it's being specific, Jim," McCoy suggested. "You remember how it showed pictures of history before, with sweeping pictures, rushing through centuries in big gulps—"

Kirk narrowed a glance at him. "I'm surprised you remember, considering the condition you were in the last time."

The doctor crimped his mouth into a defensive twinge. "I was overdosed, not unconscious."

"I know you were."

"MANY JOURNEYS ARE POSSIBLE . . ."

Kirk tilted toward Spock. "What do you think we should ask it? How specific should we be?"

"Possibly a general request, while allowing our tricorders to take an overview of whatever it shows us."

"Go ahead."

Spock stepped forward. "Guardian, . . . show us the past."

The center of the ring of rock, empty as a mirror until now, shimmered and took on a milky substance. Inside the milk, images moved, then began to firm up and rush by at uneasy velocity.

"BEHOLD."

There was almost thrill in the big voice. Apparently the Guardian had only two purposes: display history and act as a travel agent to that history. Throughout its existence, however long that was, it had few chances to exercise its purpose. Somebody had put it here a long time ago, then forgotten about it, and here it sat. No matter its lofty talk, it was really here for these visitors and those like them, who wanted to glimpse into history, then maybe take a Sunday stroll there for a while. The chance to do what it was meant to do must be a concert to a starving pianist.

Spock motioned to his assistant, and the young woman turned her tricorder to record what was being shown to them, scenes of history rushing past, focusing briefly on incidents or mass movements, then fading and catching new points of history.

But none of it looked particularly familiar to Kirk. The scenes were strange, alien to him. The costumes, the animals, the plants, the buildings—all strange.

"It's Vulcan history, Captain," Spock said.

Tribal wars, strong and violent, moved in mute testimony across the big screen—mass movements of armies, organized building of settlements, then cities, only to have those cities ripped down building by building under the angry hands of temperament.

Kirk glanced at Spock, who remained sedate and uncomplaining as this shameful portion of the Vulcan past swept by.

Nearby, the two Klingons stood between their guards, staring at what was happening. Zalt's face was a pattern of suspicion, but Roth stared with amazement of a different kind. Every few seconds he glanced at Kirk for a measurement of what was happening.

Noting that, Kirk turned a shoulder to them and didn't look over there anymore. No point giving anything away just yet.

There were fewer fights on the screen now and more funerals. More assemblies, more governing, more freedom. Then the sway into rules, pressures, suppression, order. Too much order.

"Notice, Captain," Spock quietly affirmed. "Vulcan history here is a relative match for Vulcan history as we know it."

"That's one piece of our theory confirmed."

"Yes . . ." Shaded triumph knelled in Spock's tone. He was concentrating hard, glancing from the Guardian to the tricorder and back, but he was deeply satisfied. One step at a time.

Until now, Spock hadn't shown much more than surface distress. Like the captain, though, he'd apparently been riddled with doubt at all these unverified and perilous guesses they'd had to work with. At this moment, the lair opened and Spock's unconcealed relief rushed out of sequester into the light for an occult flap across the open sky.

A smile crept over Kirk's lips. "I wish we'd had more time to talk to Temron and his colleagues. They were spirited people."

Spock canted his head slightly to one side and raised that brow that proved he was intrigued. "What the Vulcans here have learned," he granted earnestly, "is that the principles of peace operate only if all sides abide by them. In our time line, my people had the luxury of never having to learn that."

Mustering a grin, McCoy swaggered in place. "So that's your excuse?"

"Captain," Spock pressed, "the change this entity mentioned—that will be the key."

Kirk steadied himself and nodded. "Guardian," he asked, "can you show us the change?"

The lights pulsed again. "I AM MADE TO DISPLAY THE PAST IN THIS MANNER."

"Then Earth's past, Captain," Spock said, keeping his voice between them. "There has to be some registration of it. Consider the Guardian to be a kind of computer. Ask it to call up specific threads from the tapestry."

Kirk nodded again. "Can you show us," he asked carefully, "the past we have in common?"

A tense moment trundled by, almost as though the Guardian didn't intend to answer this time.

Then the lights came on again and the heavy bass voice boomed.

"FOR THIS . . . I MUST GO FAR BACK."

Glancing at McCoy, Kirk only got a shrug. From his left, Spock's expression was a shrug too, even though he didn't move.

"How far?" Kirk spoke up.

This time the machine didn't answer. Apparently, its idea of an answer for that question was to call up its files and do its job, sifting through the minds—or the physiology?—of the people standing before it, catching the whiff of human evolution and the spice of a half-Vulcan and going deep into its pantry for answers.

The lights on the rim pulsed very dimly, moving almost constantly, not like they did when the entity was talking, but more like a series of rolling electrical surges.

For a moment it seemed the Guardian had blown up. But there was no sound—only a bloom of bright light.

The image zoomed in on a blazing planet being bombarded by meteors, slamming mindlessly into the big hot rock. As the meteor bombardment tapered off, a crust started to form on the planet, rushing along in quicktime on the Guardian's screen, until nature threw it a curve ball—a very big curve ball. A spacial body nearly one-sixth the size of the planet smashed into it, and a moon was born from the splash ejecta.

The infant Earth recovered before them. Most of the crust began to cool. Volcanic centers ran along fractures in its active surface. Huge sheets of the surface were pushed under the edges of other sheets, and new crust was formed. A haze slowly obscured the surface as an atmosphere rich in water vapor began to collect.

"Science department," Kirk blurted, "talk us through it."

After nobody else spoke up, Spock seemed to feel responsible to roll the first ball. "It appears we are witnessing key points in the birth and early history of Earth."

"Where are the continents?" McCoy asked as the cloud cover cleared and a watery planet showed itself to them, interspersed with long volcanic island cones.

Spock didn't take his eyes off the alien screen. "Continents require billions of years of tectonic movement to distill the lighter minerals to the surface. The atmosphere we're seeing is largely CO_2 with some nitrogen and water, much like Venus today. Very dense . . ."

Encouraged by Spock's beginning to explain, Ensign Reenie came forward, then held her tricorder out in front of her. "Life may have appeared, sir, but it's very simple."

"Single celled?" Kirk anticipated.

"Simpler than that, sir . . . bacteria, algae . . . It'll be . . . almost two billion years before DNA gets organized into chromosomes—"

"In an atmosphere devoid of oxygen," McCoy added, "no ozone, high ultraviolet radiation, complex life is impossible at the sea surface."

"Look at the red coloring along the coastlines," Spock said, pointing. "Runoff of metals from the land are forming banded iron deposits as bacterial activity causes the metals to precipitate out. We've seen this before, Captain. The process only occurs during the interval between the origin of life and the time when free oxygen can exist in the atmosphere. The pattern repeats on all planets with carbon-based life."

"Iron," Kirk said, watching the red swirls, "on which to build an early industrial base."

"Look—" McCoy pointed at something else. "There's life! The origins of sex! The whole reason genetic material became organized was so that it could be rearranged. I'd say that puts us at about one and a half billion years. Now things'll start to get interesting!"

Kirk leaned toward him. "Remind me to ask you how you know this."

But the doctor was right. Blue-white jellylike animals began reaching out and capturing other animals and devouring them. In order to do that, they had to push their locomotion to one end of their bodies and the sensory organs to the other end. After all those millions of years, some living things began swimming against the stream. And they liked it.

As if casually photographed by passing divers, elongated wormlike organisms glided over the sediment, multicellular life where moments ago there had been only single cells.

When one of those worms actually burrowed beneath the sediment, McCoy said, "Look, a coelom has developed!"

"A what?" Kirk demanded, irritated that he had to ask.

McCoy moved his hands, trying to explain, "It's a . . .

well, it's a . . . a body cavity. You know, it helps—it's a hydraulic system for the body." When that didn't get a rise out of anyone, he blurted, "It lets an animal push something! It's a major thing!"

When the picture shifted again, Kirk shook his head. "Never mind, Doctor. What's the timetable?"

"Seven hundred million years," Reenie said.

"THIS IS YOUR COMMON PAST," the Guardian boomed as if proud of having found the deep past. "LET ME BE YOUR GATEWAY."

Kirk turned toward Reenie. "Keep going."

"Trilobites, . . . mollusks, echinoderms, arthropods . . . huge numbers of all of these—huge!" Reenie's voice rattled with tension and excitement. "It's the Cambrian explosion, I think . . . Five hundred seventy . . . m-million . . . years, s—"

"Take a deep breath, Ensign."

"Yesssssssir—"

"At least it's familiar," McCoy tossed in, almost a whisper.

Kirk nodded. "The most familiar thing we've seen so far."

Fish now—uncountable billions of them, hundreds of species, as alien as anything the galaxy could cough up. It was an alien world, right there on their home planet, close enough for them to lay out a trolling line.

They watched as the picture focused on a wiggling sack with eyes on the open end and a tail on the other end. A mobile filter feeder of some kind. Ugliest son of a cell Kirk had ever seen, and he'd seen some ugly. Then jawed fish appeared, lungfish, sharks, bony fish. Fish, fish, fish.

"Devonian period," Bannon said, aggravated. "The diversity of life keeps going up and down. The readings of organisms increases, then crashes, then increases, then crashes—"

"Thank you," Kirk interrupted. "Somebody pat that girl on the back before she explodes."

"Captain," Spock spoke up, "life is moving out of the sea. In fact, life has pulled much of the CO_2 out of the atmosphere and buried it on the seafloor in the form of limestone or calcium carbonate. The accumulated remains of billions of shells over hundreds of millions of years."

"Eventually they'll be Earth's great oil and gas reserves," Kirk said appreciatively. He wanted to just lean back and watch the pretty pictures.

"Heavy plant life has released massive quantities of oxygen into the atmosphere," Reenie panted, "countering the high levels of carbon dioxide. Crawling arthropods are colonizing the, um, land masses—"

Bannon interrupted. "They provided a food source for lobe-finned fish and other creatures, so they can come out onto the land."

A series of uglies crawled by, antennae twirling and legs spinning. Giant millipedes were the first big plant eaters. Not quite as beautiful as a moment ago, life went from hiding in a shell in the muck to crawling out on land and sucking at the open air.

"Amphibians," McCoy pointed out, "should be somewhere—there they are."

Suddenly there were almost as many frogs and snakes as fish a few minutes ago. The land was covered with club mosses, horsetails, and tree ferns. A giant dragonfly drifted by. Life started to change very fast as eons were crunched into seconds, a steaming zoo of creatures, flying reptiles, and smooth-skinned predators. A small but angry vulture-sized thing plunged toward them so realistically that Reenie jumped back and McCoy went with her.

"Advanced archosaur," Bannon reported, reading off his own tricorder, the one stuffed with paleontology. "At least, I think it was. Damn! It went by so fast!"

"Jurassic era now," Spock took over. "Humid climate worldwide. Dinosaurs. Large sauropods . . . stegosaurs . . . possibly some small early mammals . . ."

Fabulous numbers of giant herding dinosaurs elegantly led their young across verdant plains, watered themselves in blue green pools, placidly lived and violently died, to be consumed by charging meat eaters. It was raw nature in its chest-thumping glory.

"Lord, I'd love to step through there for just ten minutes," McCoy uttered. "Get my hands on one of those . . ."

"You could," Kirk said.

The doctor huffed. "No, thanks. I wouldn't last the ten."

The dinosaurs went on for a long time. New giants came to replace the old. Whole species died off. Others rose. Spock ticked off the years by tens of millions, but there didn't seem to be any end to it. After a hundred million, ninety, eighty, Kirk found himself numbed to all but the pictures.

Maybe the Guardian wanted them to feel insignificant— or perhaps the opposite, to understand their significance in its reason for showing them all this. If only the damned thing would talk in something other than booming poetry . . .

The Guardian's screen suddenly rippled, went blurry, and winked out. The center of the stone structure was completely empty again.

The starship's crew stared at it. Nothing.

So they stared at the captain.

"What happened?" Kirk looked at Spock. "Why'd it stop?"

Maybe the Guardian had quit because it somehow knew he'd stopped listening and was going into overdrive.

"Nothing we did," Spock offered.

McCoy muttered, "Maybe it's got a short."

Kirk took a step. "Guardian, why did you stop?"

The device flickered. For a moment the lights went out and it seemed the thing had gone dark, shut down.

Then the lights came on again, and the voice drummed, "YOUR COMMON PAST CEASES THERE."

Kirk pushed down a shiver. "Ceases? You mean there's no more history from our planet?"

"THERE IS NO MORE HISTORY THAT IS COMMON BETWEEN YOU."

Feeling as if he'd just been told his parents never got married and his life was all a dream, Kirk backed off a step and kept his voice down. "Spock . . . give me a time frame."

"Roughly fifty to eighty million years ago, Captain."

"Eighty *million* . . ." Aching with pain and frustration, Kirk gritted his teeth. He started looking for a place where the Guardian's rock rim was thin enough to get his hands around it and start choking the answers out. Maybe he could just kick it. Would it understand a phaser?

Give, or I'll blow your inorganic matter out.

"Try something else," he mumbled. "Guardian, . . . can you show me *my* recent past?"

The lights baubled again in that unsure way.

"YOU . . . HAVE NO RECENT PAST."

Feeling like a bouncing ball with a slow leak, Kirk limped forward again. "Can you continue showing us the history of my planet *after* the change in time? Maybe that'll give us something."

The screen popped back on, smoldering oyster gray for a few seconds, before the familiar sun of Earth's star system began to filter through. Dinosaurs again, large ones still flourishing, smaller ones also in greater numbers.

A pretty picture, primitive, elegant, overgreened, years by the thousands scrolling past in seconds, pausing now and then for a steady glimpse at one moment, then moving on.

Then, before the landing party even realized what they were seeing, a bony-skulled, snaggled-toothed dinosaur floated past in a dugout canoe, holding a stick in his paws and propelling himself along through the green water.

"Jim!" McCoy gasped. After that all he could do was point.

Abruptly things on the Guardian's screen stopped looking familiar. The creature on the screen held its leathery head upright but had a tail for counterbalance, narrow but long forearms and fingers capable of gripping the stick and using it as a tool.

An instant later, the creature was gone. In its place were whole tribes of those creatures, building fires, going on hunting parties, gathering into armies, building towns, then cities. Their forearms evolved and became a little shorter, their three-fingered hands better shaped for detailed work, their eyes higher and more forward, their skulls larger and supported by thicker necks. But they still had tails and strong hind legs.

"Spock, are you getting this?" Kirk choked.

The doctor stared but shook his head. "This must be the civilization that destroyed itself over and over!"

"You've never seen anybody like this?" Kirk badgered, forcing the question. "No known aliens?"

"Only the Gorn," McCoy said, "and they've never come near this section of the—"

"Anybody got a time on this? A date?"

"Forty-five million years ago, I think, sir," Reenie spoke up, her voice still too high, "according to this tricorder."

On the big milky screen, the civilization of dinosaur types became more and more advanced, then buckled into massive movements and lots of smoke and fires.

"What's that?" McCoy asked.

Affected, Kirk knotted his fists. "That's a war," he said dismally.

They watched as organized armies of the dinosaur-type creatures flocked past in brilliant organization, step to step, with tails swaying right to left and back with each pace. There was a music about the sight, a pride endemic to celebration and parade. And that meant only one thing. Intelligence.

Technology rushed along next, at a stunning rate. Spock and the Tibetan girl ticked off the years by millions. Still eons before mankind evolved. On the smoky picture before them, a dinosauroid snapped his snaggletoothed jaws at another of his kind, drew blood, lapped it off his scaly cheek, then climbed into his tank and rumbled away.

Suddenly their eyes were crammed shut by a billion-candlepower flash on the huge screen and they all stepped back as if the light were coming through to them.

Pain drumming through his head, Kirk forced his eyes open.

"Nuclear war," Spock uttered. Even he couldn't be impassive.

Unlike the history of Earth that Kirk knew as his own, here there weren't just a couple of detonations. There were dozens. Soon hundreds, flash upon flash, until they had to shield their eyes. Whatever these creatures had managed to develop, they turned it all loose at once. Whoever was mad at whoever else, there was no discretion, no restraint nor sense of future. Only the great Now.

And for this, the thriving civilization on the screen blasted itself back into the muck. In moments, there was nothing left but cinders.

For a few segments, the Earth was barren, smoking, cracked.

Regret chewed at the hearts of the Starfleet crew. Kirk knew they were watching their competitors on the screen, but they were consumed with despair for the life they couldn't help.

Almost instantly the cycle started again. A few survivors of the dinosaur culture struggled to gather into tribal order again, gradually building clan life, civilization, and cities.

This time they got a little farther along in their technology, a little farther into their nuclear age before whim took over.

Then it happened again.

Boom. Whoosh. Gone.

"Oh, God," McCoy murmured, deep in his throat.

Again and again the few remaining members of the funny culture dragged themselves around in huts, then camps, then in tribes. Scenes of history rushed past, but the culture never got beyond the stage at which they could blow themselves to ash. Every time they got the chance, they did it. Every time, the Earth people's stomachs rolled again.

After four times through this ghastly scenario, the creatures were hammering their culture back together yet again, still eating their food raw and snapping at each other in the night. Kirk's communicator sedately beeped.

Now what?

His muscles screamed as he grabbed for the communicator and snapped it up and open.

"Kirk here, what is it?"

"Scott here—Captain, we're under attack. Receiving long-range high-intensity destructive bolts. All I can figure is we've been tracked somehow. Do you want us to lower shields and beam the lot of you back up while y'got the chance, sir? . . . Sir?"

Chapter Twenty-one

HIS SHIP UNDER ATTACK. And the captain off board. Two perilous situations, each demanding his attention. One to save his ship, the other, his civilization.

For a wild instant, the two were equal. Then his oath sank in, his promise to sacrifice one for the other.

"Negative. We're on to something down here. Engage the enemy, Mr. Scott."

"Aye aye, sir. Good luck."

The communicator hovered at Jim Kirk's lips. He couldn't put it down. His eyes went to the sky.

Guilt gnawed at his gut, and he hungered for the option of halfheartedness. Only by mustering his deepest sense of priority could he turn his attention once again to the thing that dubbed itself the Guardian of Forever.

Such a wide term for so many blunt, dangerous seconds.

Something was botched but good. The lives of his crew depended on his next decision. All four hundred thirty-two of them could step through this machine, perhaps into the Vulcan past, and live out their lives, perhaps building their own destiny—the new Adams and Eves of the human race.

The planet moved at his side, the rocks swarmed like water, and somebody took his arm.

"Jim?"

He forced his back straight. "I'm all right."

But with that physician's glower, McCoy frowned at him. "I wish I was half as good a liar as you are. Let me at least have the ship beam down something for you to lean on."

"A cane?"

"Of course, a cane. It'll give you character. After that I'll prescribe five o'clock shadow and a fedora."

Kirk put his hand on McCoy's communicator before the doctor got the grid open. "No. They've got their hands full up there. There'll be time for me later."

In his periphery, a reflection from the screen flashed on his own shoulder, creating a bulb of mustard gold. His uniform . . .

The gravity of his choices weighed him down. He couldn't get away from it anymore than a cat could walk away from its tail.

"Jim." McCoy shook him out of his molasses-covered thoughts. "You're not thinking of going through that thing . . ."

Squeezing his fists, Kirk shuddered out a breath and gazed at the ovoid rock formation. "We might have to," he said.

Even without looking he saw the doctor's face flush white. Not pale, not dusky—absolutely stone white.

Kirk looked at him and suddenly saw only McCoy. Not until now had he realized the villification of the Guardian of Forever in Leonard McCoy's eyes. The thing in front of them had worked a bitter trick on them a long time ago, especially on McCoy. Under the influence of a dangerous drug he had stepped through there and changed history with a sweep of his innocent hand. Mending the slip had nearly torn the innards out of them all and made them sensitive to the tender strands of time.

They'd barely gotten over those terrible hours, and to this day they were still soulsick.

Millions will die who did not die before . . .

"Now wait a minute," McCoy burst in. "Time travel is one thing when it involves a few hundred years. What will the effects be when the expanse is tens of millions of years? How do you know that thing can find us and pull us back over that much time?"

His words frightened them all. Kirk knew he couldn't bat the fear down or kill the rational question with a snap.

He turned to his other side. "Spock? Legitimate concern?"

Glancing at McCoy as though he didn't want to hand over any unconsidered compliments, Spock said, "Of course."

"Can you narrow that risk?"

"The temporal disturbances sent out by this device are strong and radiate outward at unpredictable intervals. I can neither explain nor define their power."

A nonanswer. Kirk hated those. He turned to the source.

"Guardian," he began. "If we go through to a distant past, millions of years, . . . can you return us?"

"TIME IS FLUID. DISTANT HISTORY IS AN OCEAN. NOTHING IS SURE IN AN OCEAN OF TIME."

The sonorous voice shook the rocks around them and made the ground beneath their feet take a shudder. This monster was pretty damned quick to give them a big nothing to work with.

McCoy swung around like an attorney in court. "We could be lost in time!"

"Photon guidance on automatic, Mr. Sulu, long range."

"Ready, sir."

"Leave orbit. Come to course two-four-nine, then hold position. Keep the planet on our stern. That'll offer some protection."

"Course two-four-nine, sir. Helm's answering."

Chief Engineer Montgomery Scott stalked the command chair. He was itching. He could pilot the ship out of the solar system, engage the enemy out there, but before he knew how many ships he would have to face, he was the wiser to huddle here, under the protection of three tightly orbiting planets, whose gravity and proximity would tangle up those husky ships.

"All weapons systems on standby," he said. "Arm every bank. Emergency procedures shipwide. All noncombat posts should be secured and those crewmen leave the outer areas."

He was talking to hear himself talk. What was taking those bastards so long to get here?

If he stayed here, would he be drawing attention to the planet? Did the Romulans or the Klingons here have pinpoint sensors? Would they be able to pick up the heat of living bodies down there?

Or maybe they would think the starship was hunkering down, almost out of fuel, chosing to turn and fight. Let 'em waste time guessing.

The idea of leaving the planet gave him the shakes. If they got too far off and were damaged, could they get back before the landing party died of thirst and starvation down there, unprovisioned? Or would he and the starship have to hang out there, broken, unable to limp into transporter range, while the enemy beamed down and slaughtered the captain and the others?

Options swam before him as he stared at that gem-studded screen like a badger in his hole. In the tumult of these seconds, the awful waiting before a fight, he cursed James Kirk for deciding to stay down there.

But if the galaxy were to be set right, they had to have Kirk and Spock. There wasn't in all the rest of Starfleet a combination like those two.

"Another bolt coming in, sir," Chekov reported from the navigation console. The boy's hands were chalk white.

They had tracked six long-range bolts so far, managed to dodge all but one. That luck wouldn't hold.

"Warp power to the shields, Mr. Chekov," Scott growled.

"Aye, sir . . . adjusting."

The flush of emergency was infectious. Crewmen pounded through the corridors, automatic systems popping on like a cat's claws coming out and back hairs bristling. Red lights flashed, though the alert klaxons had gone silent after five minutes in order to let them do their work and fight their fight without the giant horn in their ears. After five minutes of that honking, anybody who wasn't awake and on station was already dead.

His face felt as red as his shirt. *Below decks, below decks, below decks . . . engine room, engine room . . .*

"Enemy coming into long-range sensor sphere, Mr. Scott." Chekov's voice hiked up a notch.

Scott stepped forward of the command chair. "How many?"

"Two confirmed . . . possibly three, sir."

"Let'm come on up. We'll engage them right here. Inside the solar system they'll have to drop to impulse speed. Those big ships are built for warp speed battle. We'll have a wee advantage. Prepare for tight maneuvers, gentlemen."

"Aye, sir," Sulu said, shoulders hunched.

"Aye, sir," Chekov echoed and keyed his phaser and photon banks for close range. "Sir! Another ship!"

"When'll it get here?"

"Two minutes, sir."

Without turning, Scott said, "Lieutenant Uhura—"

"Sir?"

"Jam all communication frequencies. We've got nobody to talk to and I won't want those buggers talking to each other."

"Here they come, sir!" Chekov's eyes flipped from the screen to his console. "They're dropping to impulse power . . . entering the solar system . . . There they are!"

Two pinpricks flew toward them and swelled into the recognizable Romulan design of this time line—big, thick, tough, angry. The offensive ship swung in at them and without the slightest ceremony opened fire. Impact after impact thrummed against the starship's shields, but she stood her ground. The Romulan ship pounded away at them with some kind of modified laser—might have been phased light weapons, no time to analyze—overshooting the ship by at least thirty percent. Typical Romulans, more concerned about hitting hard than hitting effectively.

"Use your thrusters to dodge those bolts if you can," Scott said. "Make'm slide down our deflector grid. Waste their shots for'm."

"Third ship is now coming into the solar system, Mr. Scott," Chekov reported.

"Let it come. Uhura, keep jamming those signals. Don't let'm coordinate their attack pattern."

"Aye aye, sir. I'm overloading the whole sector."

Suddenly the nearest ship veered into close range, reared up like a snake, and let loose on them.

"Photon torpedo incoming!" Chekov sputtered.

Quickly Scott ordered, "Turn into it, Sulu!"

Sulu leaned into the helm and the great ship took a strong diving turn to starboard just as the enemy salvo met her deflectors and scattered along the rim of her primary hull. At the angle it hit, the photon grazed the ship's edge, then flickered off into space, scorching their deflectors as it ran.

Beside them, the Romulan vessel teetered suddenly, its tail section dropped, and it went up on its backside as if kicked under the chin before the people inside got control again.

Scott glared at the screen. "Nourredine! What did that to 'em?"

On the upper deck the young engineer was beginning to grow gray hairs. "I think they were rattled by the backwash from that photon when it came off our shields and detonated. We're only a hundred forty thousand kilometers apart."

Scott squinted fiercely at the ship on the screen. "No proximity safeties. Those salvos must be fully prearmed! Chekov, target their photon tubes and fire just as the torpedo comes out of the tube!"

Chekov's brow crumpled. *"Before* it leaves their shield sphere?"

"That's right, lad. Do it, do it."

"But, sir, our phasers can't get through their shields—"

"If I figure right, you won't have to. There's one warming up! Take aim! Fire on it!"

Chekov aimed at the oval red glow inside the enemy ship's photon tube. It turned white as the photon was propelled out. He hit his controls. A phaser launched from the *Enterprise* and struck the enemy's shields almost at the point at which the photon was coming through the shields. The phaser fire crackled in a dozen directions along the energy wall surrounding that ship, dissipating without rupturing the shields. The photon bolt hit the disruption and exploded into a white blast.

"Brace yourselves!" Sulu shouted. "Shock waves!"

The proximity detonation grabbed the Romulan ship's left fin and tore it clean off, and the ship's own propulsion took over from there. Moving just enough to kill itself, the ship folded almost in half, hulls crumpling as artificial gravity went wild. Finally the warp core ruptured, and the ship blew into a huge ball of sparks and blinding light.

The *Enterprise* bucked and shuddered under wave after wave of convulsive energy being released over there. Sulu's shoulders worked as he fought to keep the ship nose forward into the waves, or she'd be sent spinning and crammed into that planet.

"Mr. Scott, I don't understand!" Chekov squawked, throat dry.

"We detonated their photon inside their shield sphere," Scott said. "They've got no safeties that prevent those things from going off too close to their own ships. Where're the other two?"

"Maneuvering to come about, sir," Sulu reported. "One above us, four hundred sixty thousand kilometers . . . The other on our port flank, five hundred thousand kilometers."

"Ready phasers," Scott ordered. "Target their main structural braces and their engine room."

"Phasers on target, sir."

"Attack maneuvers, Mr. Sulu. Prepare to veer away from the planet. Let's see if they can run an obstacle course. Mr. Chekov, open fire."

Out into the tight solar system the starship zagged, leading the two remaining Romulan vessels in a tantalizing ballet. Scott tempted the enemy ships into firing over and over. The Romulans were missing a lot. *Enterprise*'s hits weren't so strong, but all were striking the marks. The starship had a certain agility that he could use to their advantage. Cause the enemy to drain their weapons, then duck back close to the planet and scoop up the landing party. Then hand the battle over to the captain where it belonged, and go back to the engine room.

Where I belong.

He leaned forward over the helm unit, between Sulu and Chekov. "Selective targeting. Don't hurry, lads. We'll draw'm away, then veer back in, drop our screens, pick up the captain, and go. Aft visual."

Evidently the Romulans in this time line didn't have much experience with scrupulous fighting or espionage or the concept of being tricked. Here, the Klingons and Romulans just pounded each other from day to day, and whoever was still standing at the end of the day got to do the first pounding tomorrow. Sad.

With stoic nobility his bridge crew made the starship whip around the planets at tight angles, forcing the Romulan ships to take wider sweeps. With every turn, the *Enterprise* gained a few thousand kilometers.

"Head toward open space," Scott said. "Let them think we're making a run for it."

"Aye, sir." Sulu sounded grim but satisfied.

"They're firing again, sir," Chekov announced.

His words were drowned by hits on the hull. Scott could tell by the intensity of throbs coming up from below decks and from the aft end of the primary hull where the hits were striking.

"Reinforce aft shields," he said.

On the upper deck Nourredine hammered the engineering console and bellowed, "Sensor shutdown! Overload! Overload!"

Scott whirled toward him, saw him for an instant hunched over those panels, then the ship went dark. *Dark.* Blackout swept through the vessel. Sounds spiraled down to silence deep as the grave, lights winked to memory.

For a ghastly instant there was utter quiet, even from the crew. Nobody moved.

Scott made a gravelly sound in the back of his throat, then growled, "Report, let's have it."

"Sensors are down shipwide, Mr. Scott," Nourredine reported.

"Full about, Mr. Sulu. Get us back to the planet."

"I can only guess," Sulu said.

Scott swung at him in the dark. "Then guess!"

The blackness was maddening. Scott clenched his fists to hold back from clawing at the ceiling. He wanted desperately to dig into the repair trunks, start fixing what was wrong, pull and hammer and twist until there was once again light and power, sensors—he wanted to *mend*.

"Where are the emergency bloody lights?" he grumbled. "I'll have somebody's skull on my desk if I don't get lights on my feet in a minute."

"Working, sir," Nourredine's shaky voice came through the darkness. "Engineering says they've got lights down there and they're looking for the damage."

"Tell 'em it's up here," Scott uttered.

Inexactness ate at him. Where there were no numbers, no measurements, no fittings, he was uneasy. He didn't care for the chancy nature of command, where monumental decisions were usually forerun by precarious doubt.

Relief poured over them as tiny blue walkway lights came on along the floor. Not much, but at least they could see the forms of each other now, cast in indigo. All the screens remained dark, all sensors still down. The ship was not only blind, but her hands were tied, and there was no way to tell how closely they were being followed. Had the Romulans been outmaneuvered? Were they making cumbersome turns in space, trying to thread their way back between the crowded planets and moons?

He hoped so. If he was any judge of those big, wide-set ships, then he might have bought himself and the captain a precious two or three minutes. If only he could see.

"Mr. Scott, I think we're approaching the planet," Sulu said, hunched over his console, groping along with his fingers, using only his memory of how the approach had measured before. "Coming into transporter range . . . I hope."

"All stop."

"All stop, sir."

"Open communication to the planet."

"Yes, sir, go ahead—"

"Scott to Captain! Do you read? Lieutenant, shields down. Ready transporter. Captain, . . . Scott here. Come in!"

"Kirk here. Report, Scotty."

"We've dropped our shields to beam you up, sir. We've only got a two-minute—"

"Sensors coming on!" Nourredine's announcement was shot with victory. Everybody looked up, every back aching now.

"Forward visual," Scott ordered.

Around the bridge, small monitors flooded with spackling lights, shimmered, then solidified. Above the consoles were a dozen beautiful pictures of readouts from inner systems references, schematics of damage, flight operations, cross-checks, ship's attitude, all pretty as holiday lights.

And the dominant main viewing screen flooded the bridge with presence. Lights, space, stars, planets, and the glow of an oblivious foreign sun.

They weren't blind anymore, and they weren't alone anymore.

There, in space, with sunlight glowing upon brushed gunmetal hulls, no less than seven enemy ships stood before them against the black bowl of space. Four, six, seven. Yes.

"Scotty! . . . Give me a report. What's the matter?"

Photon portals began to glow. Three. Seven. Twelve bright blisters about to erupt.

Montgomery Scott stared at the screen. His mouth went dry. Fourteen.

The crew stood in bewilderment and denial, not really comprehending what they saw. The photons blasting toward their unshielded ship, floating toward them in appalling slow motion.

The screen raged white.

Scott parted his lips and pushed out one more breath. He wouldn't get another. "I'm sorry, sir."

Chapter Twenty-two

"I'M SORRY, SIR . . ."

As Chief Engineer Scott's voice rumbled through empty space from the ship to the landing party, Jim Kirk parted his lips to speak but never got the chance. What could he say? He was here, not on the bridge, and didn't know the details, didn't know what the ship faced up there.

Couldn't stop what was about to happen any more than he could stop his own heartbeat.

Something in Scott's voice turned him to ice. He looked up.

Across the periwinkle sky, a bright amber streak creased the atmosphere, arching from the dim upper regions of thin space to the heavy horizon, spitting fire all the way.

There was no mistaking the pumping white light streaking into the atmosphere. They'd seen it a hundred times in training tapes, warning memos, and their own minds. It was the magnificent release of matter and antimatter coming together in mutual annihilation, so bright they could see it from ten thousand miles away like the birth of a new star.

Beautiful, in its way. A beautiful horror. Destruction of the keystone of their lives. The death of a ship of the line.

McCoy whispered, "Oh, Jim . . ."

Desire embedded itself to catch this moment, freeze it, abey it until they could fix what went wrong, but before anyone could move so much as a finger or an eye, the broad amber brushstroke blew into bright yellow, then white—and finally fell dark. Never even made it to the horizon.

Off to the back someplace, Lieutenant Bannon whispered, "Sir . . . was that . . ."

Disaster. Disaster.

James Kirk stared and stared into the empty sky. Why hadn't he been up there?

Captain must go down with his ship . . .

Reality lanced his mind and he came awake, as if his body were suddenly shot with the sheer power of his starship. It wasn't gone, it was in here, in his chest, his legs, his heart, and it screamed for implementation.

"Phasers out!" he ordered. "Take cover!"

The guards pulled their weapons, then yanked their prisoners down beside a rock, not sure what to aim at. Kirk seized his own phaser with one hand and McCoy's arm with the other and whirled toward a nearby set of fallen pillars.

"Cover?" McCoy reacted. "Cover from what?"

"No questions," Kirk preempted and shoved the doctor down. He almost stumbled himself but caught his elbow on a rock—a damned sharp rock—and forced himself around. "Spock! Get those people down!"

Spock reached for Reenie and Bannon and funneled them through confusion toward another clutch of ancient pillars. They made it only halfway there.

Between them and the rocks they were heading for, six streaks of transporter beams shimmered out of empty air and grew thicker and thicker. Spock shoved Bannon to one side and Reenie to the other and stood his ground with his phaser drawn, his narrow lips bracketed by two stern creases, chin down and eyes harsh.

Kirk shouted, "Spock, get down!"

Dodging a dozen columns of crackling energy, Spock tried to step to the side as the transporter beams drew tight and formed into recognizable figures wearing unfamiliar costumes. They might have been Vulcans, though more severe, more threatening. These seemed to have worked on that image.

The Romulans came out of the matter streams already firing their disruptors, skimming an area that they couldn't possibly see yet. Their weapons might have been preprogrammed. Whatever they had, it worked. Energy beams sliced along the ground and etched their initials into nearby rock and ruins that had probably lay undisturbed for ten thousand years.

Spock plunged for the sandy ground. Disruptor beams skimmed over him, raising the black hair on the back on his head and causing his blue uniform tunic to smoke. In the seconds between the first volley and the Romulans' gathering of their senses, he rolled over, fired, reduced one of the enemy to a puff, and crawled behind a square stone.

One of the Security boys popped up from behind the fallen pillars, lay his arms across the rock with his phaser in both hands, and opened fire with continuous volley, narrow beam.

Kirk squinted in that direction. Were the prisoners going to cause trouble? But Roth and the other one were huddled behind a square thing that might have once been an altar. Apparently they had no desire to turn themselves over to the Romulans.

Dispersing in prearranged patterns, the Romulans bloomed outward, spreading across the area and taking cover. Spock took one down, the second Security guard another before the enemy soldiers found cover.

Would there be more? How many could they hold off before their phasers were drained?

Down with the ship, down with the ship, sunk without a trace . . .

"Guardian!" Kirk squirmed around to the upended ring of stone. "Show us our common history again! Begin with the large-bodied land animals, approximately—Spock!"

"One hundred million years ago!" Spock shouted over the whine of phaser fire.

Without bothering to use its "voice," the Guardian of Forever conjured up pictures they'd seen only a few minutes ago. Again the spooky images of prehistoric Earth rumbled by like a grade school simulation. Oblivious to the phaser fire grazing its rim and sparking off its pedestal, the Guardian calmly did its job.

"Spock, tell me when!"

Phaser fire ceased from Spock's corner, and Kirk knew his science officer was nose down to the tricorder, ticking off centuries in gulps.

"Thirty seconds, Captain!"

"All hands!" Kirk shouted, "Follow me!"

The wide phaser beam blanketed the area with crackling energy and forced the Romulans to cease fire and huddle.

Follow me—two words that made history. Once upon a time these had been two grunts, two waves of the paw, the claw, the hand, the club, the spear, two flashes of the eye. *Follow me.* The quintessence of leadership, boxed up and shipped.

Starfleet personnel vaulted out of the ruins and ran toward him. Kirk led them to the enormous slice of rock that had a voice and gestured them all between it and him, then turned and fired the wide beam again.

Romulans ducked out of sight and their disruptors stayed quiet for a delicious second more.

The Starfleet crew came tight to Kirk's side. Spock gathered the group snugly together on the narrow pedestal. They huddled like fools on a ledge, between death and suicide.

"Nine seconds, Captain," Spock said. "Seven . . . six . . . five . . . four . . ."

"All at once!" Kirk ordered.

McCoy shied from the smoking chasm of the Guardian's portal. "Jim, you've got to be kidding!"

Kirk blistered the area with another blanket shot, then grabbed McCoy on one side, Bannon and Reenie on the other, glanced at Spock, who had corralled the two guards and the two Klingons.

"Two . . . one . . . now, Captain!"

"Go!" Kirk shouted. "Go! Go!"

Chapter Twenty-three

HEAD DOWN into the storm they went, pressing barehanded to their chests an unshielded sense of peril. Hardly more than a blink, a taste of vapor, and they were here. As if stepping through a door they came into another room, and the door disappeared behind them.

Captain of nothing, representative of no one. But still leader of this wayward group. He had said follow, and they had.

Now they were in wonderland.

The first and most abruptly obvious difference was the smell of the place. Rotten eggs. Swamp gas. And a touch of salt . . . saline seas. But how near? Hothouse conditions raised the scent of a constant stir-fry, suddenly moist on their cheeks, uncomfortable inside their collars and sleeves.

Starfleet tunics were made of special fibers meant to shed sweat in hot climates and insulate in cold, and maybe it was working, but in his poisoned condition, Kirk couldn't tell. He glanced around. Except for Spock, who wouldn't sweat on the Amazon, everyone's face was glazed with perspiration.

Bedewed ferns beckoned lazily above a carpet of pulpy undergrowth. Heavy mist veiled the sun, diffusing its light through vaulting branches of trees whose wide trunks were shamrock green from sky to roots with velvet moss and lichen. Palmettos, prickly growth, palms. Stumpy cylindrical trees were armored with overlapping scales the size of a man's hand, and from the tops sprouted fans of lacy fronds that seemed too small for the trunks. Some plants had stout trunks shaped like globes, and others like cones. Trumpet-shaped florets hung from stalks and trees. Ficus, magnolia, catkins.

"Looks like Florida," somebody said. It was Security Ensign Emmendorf.

Through the tips of the conifers shone the purple summits of mountains laced in mist. Paradise, but deceptive. Kirk didn't feel at all as if he belonged here. But it was Earth . . .

He pivoted around for a quick head count. All here. Even the Klingons, one of whom appeared shocked and amazed, the other shocked and suspicious. The two Security guards held their prisoners as if the Klingons had done this somehow. Good boys.

Thick as a grown man's thigh, a snake moved in a gnarled tree. Looked like a boa. Its peacock-marked back glinted in the diffused sunlight as it paused and turned its perfume-bottle head to them, then lost interest and went slowly on its way.

Something shrieked across the sky, but they never saw it. It was over them and gone in seconds. One of the Security men drew a phaser, but there was nothing to shoot at.

McCoy was the first to speak, his human voice out of place here. "What if they follow us through?"

The crickets' rattle dropped off by half. A creature in a tree plunged away through the jungle's encroaching growth. Spock turned but not fast enough to see what it was.

"They'll have to figure out the Guardian," Kirk said. "Anyway, it'll probably take them ten or twenty million years. Mr. Spock, I'd ask where we are, but I think I'd better ask *when* are we? Did you understand what I was yelling for back there?"

"The moment of the change in history," Spock said, brushing a gauzy web from his arm. He looked up. "I assumed."

Kirk nodded. There were advantages to working so closely together for so long. "I hope this is right. Otherwise, it's going to be a hell of a long camping trip. Do you have a rough estimate of the date?"

Spock adjusted his tricorder and peered into the tiny screen. "Sixty-four million twenty thousand four hundred ten years."

Kirk blinked at him. "That's . . . pretty good for rough. I want you to designate duties. Set one of the Security guards to inventing and making weapons out of indigenous materials. We have no way of knowing how many months or years we'll be stuck here. I want the phasers conserved at all cost. See if you can locate fresh water. And put McCoy and Ensign Reenie on deciding what we can eat and what we can't. I don't want anyone swallowing any toxic berries. Have Bannon see what he can do about shelter. It won't snow here, but I'll bet it rains like wildcats."

"Very well, sir." Spock moved off a few paces to talk to Bannon, and McCoy moved into his place beside Kirk, obviously uneasy.

"We've been on some alien worlds," he said, "some exotic, some horrifying, but I don't think any are so alien as our own world this far in the past. And what good does it do? We might be ten years off. Come to think of it, how do we know we're not ten years too late?"

Turning to them, overhearing as was his sacred duty, Spock said, "The captain and I formed a theory about the Guardian, that time travel flows like a river, with currents that carry us along certain patterns and spirals toward critical points. I hope that's what has happened here."

"There's also the possibility that the Guardian is more than just an elevator up and down through time," Kirk carried on. "I'm betting it knows what happened and it's sent us to the right time and place."

"That's a whopping hope," McCoy agreed gutturally. "And which place? Where are we? Looks like Hawaii or the Congo."

"Sixty-four million years?" Bannon tossed in from across

their clearing. "Could be downtown Chicago for all we know."

"See if you can figure it out. This is one of those situations where you find you don't have any control, and all you can do is the best you can. Spock, I'd like as full a report on our surroundings as possible in thirty minutes."

As his crew wandered away, taking their first cautious steps through bug-heavy leaves that rattled in their ears with the tatter of crickets, Kirk limped to the Security guards, who parted for him and let him through to Roth and Zalt.

"Let's understand each other," he said. "I hate you and you hate me. We don't have to be soul mates. All I want is a devil's bargain. We'll keep you alive. You cooperate."

Zalt's eyes squeezed down to slits and the translator buzzed. "I do not cooperate with you."

"Fine," Kirk said. "When we run out of food, we'll know where to turn. You're just another animal to us."

He swung around, a little too fast, but managed to keep his balance. He didn't care how the Klingons reacted.

How much of his humanity showed in his face?

And what was his mission? Stop whatever had happened to make this change. It had something to do with San Francisco, didn't it? San Francisco . . .

I am pleased and proud to confer upon you, James T. Kirk, the rank of starship captain, Starfleet, United Federation of Planets, with all the rights, privileges and responsibilities appertaining thereto. Congratulations, Captain Kirk . . .

Aren't you taking leave in Iowa this year for Christmas, Jim? Captain April's going to be there, visiting your parents. I think you'd better take it as a direct order to attend . . .

Jimmy, when is it going to dawn on you that rules exist for a reason? . . .

"Captain, sit down for a minute. Jim. Jim, right here."

For long, dragged seconds he could see only leaves and brown mush. Then his eyes focused on his boots.

What was he sitting on? Whatever it was, it was soggy.

A hiss at his shoulder made him flinch and inhale sharply. This was great, just great. Deliver a threat, then fog out while the enemy's watching.

His head started to clear some. McCoy had put him down on a moss-draped tree trunk.

"Jim, listen to me. Listen to me. Look at me."

"I'm looking. Keep your voice down." He blinked hard, irritated at having to be told what to do. His joints, inflamed with infection, speared him with sharp pain as he arranged his legs. Around him, the jungle whistled and reeked. "Just do your medicine. The rest is my business."

"That's the problem," McCoy said. "You have to understand. I only have enough medicine for a few days. This toxin that's got you, it's like diabetes once was. Perfectly manageable with medication and finally curable through treatment. It's no problem in our time, but back here . . . I can relieve the symptoms to some degree, but the cure is back on the *Enterprise.*"

Under the gassy pall of thinly overcast skies, crickets rattled with unremittance and purpose, and creatures undescribed bellowed in the distance. Jim Kirk stared into his friend's eyes and found so little hope there that the noise of insects began to close in. Here he was, socked in beside an ironbound coast to which he had relentlessly steered.

"Some of us might survive, Jim," McCoy finished, "but you certainly won't."

Chapter Twenty-four

"ALL RIGHT, SPOCK, let's have it."

Spock drew up a patch of ground beside where Kirk was sitting with his back against a rock and his bad leg raised on a mossy mound.

"Massive life forms, Captain," he said simply. "Astonishing numbers. Vast herds of creatures, five to seven tons each."

"How close?"

"Within five miles. We've compiled a cursory analysis of our immediate surroundings and overlaid it against information in the tricorders about this time period," the Vulcan said, his cheeks flushed copper with intensity. "According to growth lines in fossil corals and highly refined atomic and crystal clocks, we know that the ocean tides are slowing the Earth's rotation by friction of the ocean against the sea floor and continents. The Cretaceous day is twenty-one minutes, twenty seconds shorter than our day, the moon is eighteen hundred miles closer. The month is seven hours, ten minutes, forty seconds shorter, and there are approximately three hundred seventy days in the Cretaceous year."

"Spock . . ."

"Because of continental drift, the poles of rotation are different, the North Pole being approximately halfway between the Bering Strait and where it—"

"I don't want to know this."

Spock dropped his shoulders. "I beg your pardon?"

"Tell me something I can use."

Dashed, Spock glowered thoughtfully. "We *have* used this information, sir."

"How?"

"We've used it to ascertain our specific location.

"Then tell me where we are."

"We're are on the eastern North American continent. Though this appears to be Florida or the Caribbean, we are actually in a location that will be southern Georgia, a few degrees north of the Florida line. I believe we're on a large thumb of land, a peninsula raised by the rugged southern spine of the Appalachians—those mountains. To the far north, a sea extends from Hudson Bay across the high plains of Canada, to cover North Dakota. To the south the Mississippi embayment extends inland to western Tennessee."

"That's a lot of water."

"Yes, it is. By the way, there are no ice caps yet on either pole." Spock spoke quickly again, as if wanting to stick that detail in before he was told not to.

"Eastern and western North America are two separate continents right now?"

"They are *acting* as two separate continents. However, they're part of the same tectonic plate and will not separate. Sea levels seem to be on the rise again, which contradicts what we thought about the Upper Cretaceous period. Most studies concluded that the sea level was at its lowest point, but that is evidently wrong."

"I'll bet a lot is going to contradict what we thought about this place."

"Mmm," Spock murmured, not exactly an agreement. "Eventually the inland sea will separate and the transcontinental arch will be revealed and become the Great Plains. It may have already happened, but I cannot tell without a satellite connection."

Kirk had heard the last few sentences, but the words drummed with meaningless order for him. Iowa . . . maybe under water, drowned, struggling to form itself into the place where someday he and his brother would be born. The big glaciers weren't even here yet, the ones that would carve out the Great Lakes and the Saginaw Valley, cutting out the fingers and thumb of Michigan and leaving the state half pine-studded dunes and half sandy basin.

So many centuries, eons, and the little decades of their lives began to dribble and shrink.

"So Florida's still under water," he managed, trying to draw a map in his mind.

Sensing Kirk's conflict, Spock raised his inflections to a more scholarly tenor. "And much of eastern Mexico. West of us, the Central Rockies are probably rising. When dealing on a scale of millions of years, there is enough time to raise a mountain range over a mile above sea level, then wear it back down to sea level again. Everything here is a theoretical conclusion based on knowledge that is rebelliously sweeping, sir."

That was his way of apologizing for not being more sure.

Kirk felt his lips curl up at one corner in a pathetic grin. "Deep time," he murmured.

Spock paused and questioned with his eyes.

Kirk plucked at a fern just within reach. "As with deep space, Mr. Spock, there seems to be deep time."

Caught by the concept, Spock gazed at him. Nothing else.

"Spock," Kirk began again quietly, "back on the ship, just after this happened, I wasn't in a fever-induced fog when I heard you say we hadn't made any jumps in time, correct?"

"Correct. According to the locations of stars, we were steady to the month, and the planets of the Izell system gave us accuracy down to the minute. We had not shifted at all in time."

"Of course," Kirk pressed, "I could still be in the midst of being crushed to death by that cosmic string and ripped apart by time distortions. This could be the last imaginings of a dying mind. What do you say to that?"

"Captain . . . I . . . see *no* evidence for that line of thinking at all . . ."

"Well, you wouldn't, since I'm inventing you."

Spock opened his mouth again, but nothing came out. He was probably plotting to have McCoy check the captain's medication and find it was being mixed too rich.

Kirk's naughty-boy grin gave him away as he left Spock on the hook, but he didn't care. "It's a damned shame. To rise to intelligence, then completely disappear, and for that to happen time after time, failure after failure."

"Extinction *is* part of the normal scheme of nature, Captain. Even mass extinction . . ."

"Not for intelligent creatures who can design their own future. Who were they, Spock? And what were they doing here? They're not from here, so who are they?"

Discontent limned Spock's sharp features. Trouble stressed his posture, and sympathy, his eyes. "Perhaps," he attempted, "I could find you a drink of fresh water, sir."

"I'm sorry," Kirk said. "I'm fine. Go on with your geography."

"Paleogeography, sir," Spock corrected. "According to our recorded data, India is an island now, much like Australia in our time. Australia is still linked to the Antarctic and South America. Transylvania, Italy, and Romania are slowly colliding with Europe. The hot climate is due to increased CO_2 levels. We're reading a great amount of vulcanism and mountain building. Much of the equator is enveloped in a supertropic. At this latitude, we're in a full-blown tropical climate. The water we're reading in the distance to the east and south is hypersaline and warm, resulting in a sluggish ocean, which carries much less oxygen. There is no cold, dense, oxygen-rich water sinking and propelling circulation. Less nutrients come back to the surface."

"Spock, not so much monumental analysis, please. I don't want to build any mountains. Give me some functional details."

"Very well. The most profound difference in flora from our own time would be the complete absence of grasses. Other than the herds of large-bodied animals we're picking up on our tricorders, we're also reading millions of small-bodied animals, primarily small mammals, lizards, salamanders, and frogs."

"So even if I'm not in Florida, I'm still in Florida."

"Essentially so. Although perhaps a bit more like the Amazon."

"And these large animals . . . they're dinosaurs?"

"Yes, though Ensign Emmendorf captured a mouse-sized creature which is vaguely squirrellike, which Mr. Bannon and I suspect is the earliest known primate. A stunning find, in paleontological terms."

"Not here. Did he kill it?"

"Accidentally."

"Too bad. It was probably my great-great-great-grandad and I already don't exist anymore. Go on."

Seeming to accept that as perfectly plausible logic, Spock said, "We have not yet ascertained which animals and plants are poisonous, therefore we must assume they all are. As for

223

the creatures we saw on the Guardian's screen, after cursory tricorder analysis I do have a theory."

"Let's hear it."

"They may have evolved on Earth."

"Intelligent?"

"Potentially intelligent."

"What's the theory?"

"Island locales are often sights of rapid evolution. If they lived on islands and were a fisher–hunter culture in the dugout canoes we saw, they may have fallen victim to tidal waves or other conditions of maritime life. The fossil record may have been wiped out by violent conditions."

"Wait a minute, wait . . . aren't you jumping to the conclusions? Those animals appeared after the change, whatever the change was."

"In higher intelligence, yes, but nothing begins in a vacuum. If they are of Earth, then their ancestors are here now. Relatively immediate ancestors, I would think, given the time spans we recorded."

"I don't believe that, Spock. Earth's labs are gushing with fossils. We've got so many we haven't had enough room to store them for three hundred years. My roommate at the Academy used to complain about that. Is it logical that our fossil record is overflowing and complete, except for one particular brand of intelligent dinosaur?"

Bothered by that, Spock rolled his shoulders. "Not logical, but possible. In fact, we have copious fossils of a creature the tricorder brought up when we requested a comparison. It is the Troodon and other related troodontids. This is the classification for a large group of theropods, sickle-clawed, blade-toothed, very fast bipedal dinosaurs. Troodon possessed a large brain case for its body weight, roughly the size of a cat's. It had a snout that was receding to facilitate better vision, flexible fingers and wrist bones." He glanced at the landscape. "They're here somewhere . . . We think they attacked in coordinated groups and possibly even cared for their young."

"How big?"

"Not large. Roughly thirty kilograms."

Kirk eyed him. "Doesn't sound like a crash course to me, exactly. I didn't know you knew all this."

Spock paused as if not sure whether to take that as a compliment or not but knew he was being put on somehow.

"This is not my theory," he smoothly evaded. "There has been speculation for two centuries that Troodon might have evolved to intelligent biped status, given the chance. Of all Earth's dinosaur population, this was the strain that possessed qualifications for ultimate tool use, though their 'fingers' never became as specialized as those of primates."

"What happened to them?"

Spock shrugged with his eyebrows. "Extinction."

An exasperating answer. Kirk eyed him cannily. "You know more about this than you implied."

"I have always harbored an interest in Earth's history."

"I know you have. Do you know why?"

"Do I . . ."

"Because it's your Earth, too, that's why."

They looked at each other.

Kirk refused to back down, staring in mild challenge, feeling a touch of bemusement rise in his eyes. "You could go off with the Vulcans and probably live a perfectly contented life. But you don't want to live your life out there anymore than I do, do you?"

Spock shifted his weight casually. "My mother impressed her background upon me with only cautious restraint. She knew I would be shunned among the young Vulcans and wanted me to feel fully Vulcan . . . Yet, curiosity about her background, my human ancestry . . . intrigued me." He plucked a small branch from the ground and began folding it in half, in quarters, in eighths. "She was my only representation of Earth. She was wise and yet self-questioning at times. I grew up among her possessions. Antique furniture, her piano . . . an environment less austere, if less efficient, than most Vulcans preferred. Earth was an exotic legend to me."

Kirk grinned. "Did we disappoint you?"

"I tried to be disappointed, as my father preferred." Spock tossed the branch away after reducing it to an accordion. "But some truths were pervasive. Most planets boast only one or two races, because they exterminated all others during their planetary development. Though they've come out into space, they have failed at diversity. Even the Vulcans, who claim diversity as a founding principle. Earth made a success of diversity by protecting the individual over the group."

Kirk beamed. "I used to wonder how long it would take before you admitted that you're really just one of us."

Though complacent, Spock seemed saddened and stared into the moss. "It is easy to speak of diversity when all are the same."

"Mmm," Kirk muttered, thinking about what Roth had said before. "Have I mentioned lately that I appreciate you, Mr. Spock?"

The tacit smile came up behind Spock's eyes. "Yes, you have."

"Well . . . good. Get me up. I've got to move around, let the blood into my backside. My legs are going numb."

Plagued by much of what he'd just heard, Kirk batted irrational thoughts against the thready lights of what made sense.

"Spock . . ."

"Sir?"

He started to turn, but his toe caught on a thin spiraling ground vine that had done a pretty good job of its own evolution. He put a hand out to check his fall, but the tree he aimed for was too far away.

Plunging in, Spock caught him, then held him until he got both feet squared under his weight.

"Thanks," Kirk grunted. He was pouring sweat. Damn, it was uncomfortable here.

He pressed a hand to Spock's arm and levered himself straight. His heart was pounding in his chest. "These Troodons . . . they went extinct because of the asteroid?"

"Yes, sir. If they had not—"

"Then they might have become the animals we saw on the new Earth. The ones that killed LaCerra."

"Or the ones we saw on the Guardian's screen," Spock said. "The ones who killed themselves cycle after cycle. We may have simply been witness to the cycle's beginning again."

"Yes, life gave them a chance again and again, and every time . . ."

"Every time," Spock nodded, "they threw it away."

"I want to change that," Kirk sighed, "but here, without the ship . . . how can I change something that's happening thousands of miles out in space?"

"What the hell is that *noise?*"

Lieutenant Bannon swiveled his head among the thick-trunked trees and bushy cycads.

The jungle was thick up to about twenty feet, then spindled with tree trunks and heavy tangled vines, then canopied about forty feet up by top growth. Visibility of the sky was cut off, but there wasn't much to see. Haze, mostly, and a hot sun beyond.

An inconstant hooting sound permeated the heavy air, like concert tubas tuning in an empty hall but never playing.

Nobody tried to answer Bannon's complaint. Nobody had an answer yet.

The Tibetan girl's butterfly eyes were shadowed as she approached the place where her captain leaned on a fallen log as wide in diameter as he was tall. In her posture was the clear message that she felt uneasy bothering her commander. "Sir? I'm getting some over-the-top readings, sir, and . . . I just don't understand what it's giving me."

Uncomforted by the dark shade from the thick-canopied trees, Kirk settled gratefully onto the fork of a fallen conifer branch. "Over what top?"

"Just . . . big," she said. "Metabolic readings on a scale that's confusing the tricorder. I think it might be overloading."

"Dinosaurs. Mr. Spock says they're all around here, in the thousands."

She raised her round face. Nearby, dozens of birds picked at insects and flew from tree trunk to tree trunk. "Then where are they?"

With a surfeiting nod, Kirk said, "Don't go looking for trouble, Ensign."

She shrugged. "Aye, sir."

From where he sat Kirk could see most of his crew picking about among the various tree trunks, testing what they found, feeding information into their tricorders and analyzing the landscape as if on some foreign world.

But it was a complicated place, jumping with more kinds of life than most planets could even begin to cough up. How many barren rocks had they explored in the course of the starship's mission? Most planets could barely get beyond the single-celled stage, while rugged old Earth effused like hot buttered popcorn.

Hundreds of birds scrabbling through the fringes of palm leaves suddenly bolted in a great explosion. The low tuba hoot in the sky was abruptly overlaid by the snare-drum rattle of a thousand wings. These birds were like pigeons in a city park—uninterested and unfrightened by the people who had come among them.

He glanced around. Some of his crew ducked, the Klingons swatted at birds, and Security Ensign Vernon fell down, but nobody panicked. Fifty feet through the foliage, Spock was visible from the waist up, tricorder raised as he tried to suck all these species into a catalog, where he preferred everything be but scowled at what he saw. Didn't like the readings he was getting.

"Captain . . ." Spock held his tricorder out again, running it up and down a thirty-inch-diameter tree trunk, still unhappy with the readings.

"Coming," Kirk wheezed. The fifty feet between them looked like a football field.

Spock lowered the tricorder and touched the tree. "This is not . . ."

That was a signal to hurry. Spock didn't usually express half a thought.

All at once one of the Klingons dropped backward against a bush and started to yell.

Kirk swung around. The Klingon—not Roth, the other

one—was staring up into the trees, bellowing as loud as he could with every breath he could get.

Swinging around, Kirk saw no sense to it. Nothing had changed, except the birds.

Suddenly the tree trunk beside Spock shuddered, flexed, raised itself into the air, and put itself down six feet away with a kettledrum thud, grazing the Vulcan with a giant blunt claw. Spock squirmed to one side, then stumbled.

Swiveling his sore neck, Kirk looked up. His mouth dried up.

"Spock, get out of there! Everybody back—back—back . . . slowly! Security formation—"

The two Security men responded as he hoped they would, stumbling around behind the Klingons and pulling them backward. One of them had the sense to give the squalling Klingon a hard slap and stop the noise.

Over their heads a giant crane swiveled over the tops of the trees forty feet in the air. More birds flushed, rattling violently between what were no longer tree trunks, but the thick gray brown legs of beasts the size of barns. One . . . two, three . . . four horse-shaped heads swept across the sky.

More of the tree-trunk-sized legs moved among stationary conifer trunks. One of the animals turned its big head downward casually, parted its wide snout, and made its noise—the hooting tuba sound rolled through the valley, frightening now that they realized how close it was. The animal pivoted its entire body twenty feet or so, forcing Spock and Vernon to duck as the thick forelegs came down with a *whump*. Two-thirds of the animal's weight rested on those hindquarters, on legs so big that they had seemed to be only shadows in the wide open forest's undergrowth.

Hollow chested, Kirk fought down the shock of what he was seeing and tried to rationally count how many of the huge animals were around them as the yard-wide legs began to move and which direction to retreat. He angled toward Spock.

"Move out of the trees." Kirk gestured toward an area

that looked as though it might have a stream running through it. He wanted his people away from anything that might step on them.

Evidently unhurt by the graze of a big claw, Spock had come up out of the bushes and was making his way toward the clearing. The crew stumbled in the right direction, their heads back, mouths hanging open like baby birds staring up at a parent's gullet.

"Brontosaurs?" Emmendorf choked on his own saliva.

"Brachiosaurs," Reenie said.

McCoy shook his head as he gaped upward. "Not big enough."

"Apatosaurus," Bannon said. "Maybe—but this is the Cretaceous, not the Jurassic . . ."

"Spock," Kirk called, controlling how his voice carried. "Species identification?"

"Checking," Spock responded through the squeal of another flush of birds.

The birds were everywhere now, alighting upon the barn-roof backs of the huge dinosaurs, picking off parasites. Over there, angling like a bridge through the trees, was one of their tails.

"Some conflicting evidence." Spock moved ever backward. "Alamosaurus is the closest cataloging. Sauropods, common everywhere, average thirty tons, seventy-five feet in length—"

"All hands, move out quickly," Kirk interrupted. "Let's get away from them before somebody gets kicked."

As they came out of the thick trees they got a good look at what they had seen only at kneecap level until now. Peaceful in their enormity, the towering beasts looked down at them and blinked but continued grazing at the tips of the trees. Some were bigger than others, and there were only eight or ten of them. Thirty-foot tails swung placidly.

"Probably a family group," McCoy offered as they hopped over the small trickle of a stream and put some space between themselves and the chance of being squashed.

"I thought sauropods were extinct in North America by now," Bannon said.

"These must be titanosaurs," Spock went on. "According to these records, they may have migrated here when the Cuban land bridge connected North America to South America during the late Cretaceous. They have been found as far north as southern Wyoming."

"Cuban land bridge?" McCoy pestered, then winced, as if realizing he'd given Spock a reason to continue.

"What we know as Central America was a string of large islands," Spock said. "And I think you'll agree these animals did not swim here."

A dozen titanosaurs were visible now, as two more rose among the trees. The two largest began leading the others along the stream, with the other ten following in elephantine peace.

Now one of the largest of them paused, reached for the leafy tip of a tree, pulled the top growth off, and swung its cranelike neck around to give the branch to one of those following.

The other of the larger animals simply pushed over another tree with a satisfying crack and moved aside while a half dozen of the smaller giants came in to feed on the supple branches.

"They're feeding their babies!" McCoy said.

"Babies?" Kirk looked at the barn-sized hides. "They're twenty feet long!"

"Rapid growth is a defense mechanism in wild species, Jim. An ostrich grows from a chick to six feet tall in no time. Horses and cattle, too. Foals and calves are born with legs almost two-thirds the length of their mothers' legs in order to keep up with the herd. These might be yearlings . . . but the big ones are definitely showing them what to eat."

"I've seen birds do that," Reenie offered.

"Come this way a few more feet, Ensign," Kirk said, herding them up a scruffy branch-littered slope.

McCoy continued watching the behavior of the sky-filling dinosaurs. "I don't think they're interested in us, Jim."

"Fine, but I don't want anybody crushed by their passive disinterest. Mr. Vernon, get those Klingons up there."

"Aye, sir."

They grew calm in the pressing heat and were drawn by the scene that a fluke of high science had privileged them to witness. The vast-bodied titanosaurs were eminently at home here, huge heads waving into the sky-high mist. Their hides were subtly variegated, an illusion of stripes that served to let their bulks be disguised in the trees. White and gray birds of different sizes fluttered from titanosaur to titanosaur, lighting on the broad backs, clinging to the long necks, dodging between the thick legs, and picking in the ground stirred up by the sauropods' shipping-crate feet.

"Hey, look!" Bannon went up on his toes and pointed. "Look over there. Look at that!"

"Triceratops! Wow!" Reenie bubbled, jumping up.

"Two of them!" Bannon exuded.

A pair of tank-sized beasts wandered toward them along the creek, ignoring the titanosaurs who returned the ignore. Each had a horn over each eye and one on the nose and a flaring scalloped neck frill. Grazing in a manner hauntingly cowlike, they rooted at the edges of the stream, pushing their sharp beaks into the mud and pulling up hidden roots. As they grazed, two convex oval-shaped areas of the wide frills expanded and contracted. Jaw muscles—all the way up into those neck frills.

"Triceratops!" Reenie twittered, her voice high. "I always wanted one for a pet!"

"Who didn't?" Bannon grumbled from beside her.

Kirk motioned to Spock. "Well?"

Unhappy again as he tried to focus his tricorder on the two new animals, Spock said, "Not Triceratops, but the same family. Either Torosaurus . . . or Pentaceratops. Probably the former. Torosaurus was large as Triceratops, but much more rare, possibly traveled alone rather than in large herds as Triceratops probably did. Small extended beak . . . nasal and brow horns . . . twenty-one to twenty-five feet long . . . generally believed to have populated Wyoming, South Dakota, Montana, Saskatchewan—"

"I thought we were in southern Georgia," Bannon interrupted, skewering Spock with an improper look.

The Vulcan met the look with one of his own, masterfully cold. "The fact that we haven't *found* them here, Lieutenant, does not preclude the possibility of their having *been* here. In fact, there is virtually no terrestrial fossil record in Georgia at all. It was all eroded into the sea."

"Good Lord," McCoy exclaimed as the pair of animals drew nearer, "just the skulls must be ten feet long!"

"Average of eight point five feet, with the crest accounting for half the skull area."

The doctor twisted a lip. "That's it, ruin it for me."

Spock gave him almost as much attention as the titanosaurs were giving the approaching torosaurs. "This animal's skull was the largest of any land animal ever known." He turned to Kirk. "If these *are* torosaurs, Captain, this is a remarkable cataloging opportunity. I would like to attempt to get closer."

Torn between scrambling for safety and allowing his crew to do their jobs, Kirk looked at the unshrouded curiosity in his first officer's face. "Spock, I don't know . . ."

Spock stepped closer. "Captain, if I could get—"

A bellowing roar cut him off, at first sounding like another tuba howl, but this had a guttural severity that failed to echo. Kirk pressed Spock aside in time to see a massive angled form charge out of the trees on giant turkey legs ten feet long each. With brutal singularity of purpose, five tons of force propelled a huge mouth gaping with pointed teeth the length of bananas, plowing full bore into the side of one of the sauropods.

"Aw!" Emmendorf bellowed in empathy.

There was no question about what they were watching, no need to consult a tricorder. Every schoolchild recognized the great North American Tyrannosaurus rex, everybody's favorite bad guy, the one animal of Earth history that everyone wanted to watch in action but nobody wanted to meet.

Well, there it was, pounding its torpedo of a face into the shocked sixty-foot titanosaur and knocking both of them to their knees. Propelled by the force of the charge, the two dinosaurs skidded together into the creek and out of that trickle of water somehow made an enormous splash.

In a cloud of maddened birds, the other sauropods swung full about and stampeded stiff-legged down the creek and out of sight in astonishing speed, leaving their wounded family member and the tyrannosaur to deal with each other. As they stampeded through the maddened birds, they stumbled into the pair of torosaurs, who were turned and driven before them in a panic.

The titanosaur was the first to get to its feet. It swung around on its hind legs to face the tyrannosaur and reared upward. As blood poured down its hindquarters from the wounds on its hip, the animal swiveled and began dropping its full weight toward the tyrannosaur, which was struggling to get both massive legs out of the water and back underneath. Squirming as the titanosaur came down, the big T bellowed an enduring sound like metal scraping against metal. The titanosaur's foot came down on its attacker's tail, and there was another ghastly bellow, this time more of pain than rage.

The thunder lizard twisted its thick, strong neck and bit into the titanosaur's shoulder, shoving its toothy face through hide, muscle, and bone in one snap with sheer force. Shaking its head, it ripped out a mouthful and bolted it down like a crocodile bolts down a calf.

"What are the chances he'll come over here?" Kirk asked, cautious of his volume.

"He probably won't notice us," McCoy said.

"Everybody get down anyway. Stay near the ground."

While they all huddled near the ground or hid behind broken tree branches, Bannon murmured, "What a sight!"

Before them on the creek bed, the titanosaur slid down onto one knee but was able to wheel around again on those tree-thick hind legs. Coming down with a bass drum *boom*, it slammed that immense tail into the tyrannosaur's side, knocking the predator over.

The movements were shocking and fast, much more supple than Kirk ever would have imagined creatures of such bulk could move. At a circus he'd seen a female African elephant driven into a rage. Before its trainers or anyone could react, it attacked and killed two workers, then thundered into the bleachers and drove its wide head through a wall. But that was on Rigel Four . . .

With another metal-scraping scream, the tyrannosaur rolled over onto its pointy spine and came crashing down on its other side, legs thrashing and small arms pushing at the ground.

While it thrashed, the titanosaur turned and charged across the creek toward Kirk and the others. *Boom, boom, boom, boom.*

He heard McCoy. "Uh-oh—"

Spewing blood, the titanosaur pounded past them and smashed straight through the trees, not bothering to look for a better way out. With a ghastly crackle the dense trees were driven down, making a path wide enough to fly a shuttlecraft through.

All at once, the titanosaur was gone.

Boom, boom, boom . . . the sound faded away.

"Down! Now!" Kirk gasped, pushing McCoy and Emmendorf down, hoping the others would have the chance to drop, too.

The tyrannosaur scratched to its feet, extended its neck, and roared in frustration. Snapping its maw twice—*crack, crack*—it sniffed at the air. Could it smell them? Were foreign scents clinging to them that would bring that beast over here?

Limping, the tyrannosaur sniffed again—the air, the ground, the trail of blood—and pounded deliberately toward them, each step a drum beat.

"Nobody . . . move," Kirk murmured, barely audible. This would be a prefect time for the Klingons to attempt an escape.

Yellow eyes like needlepoints within skeletal sockets, the animal lowered its head, stretched out its neck, and screamed again, long and hard. Then it put its snout to the dirt and deliberately tracked the smashed trail left by the titanosaur, hammering its fifty-foot body and tail past Kirk and his party without a glance. Apparently it knew what it could have with a little perseverance.

They watched, hearts pounding, as the most renowned killer of all time drummed into the dense woods. At the edge of the woods, it paused, turned toward them again, lowered its giant skull and screamed one more time, waited until the echo fell, then also disappeared into the wilds.

"Wow . . . " Reenie breathed.

"He's a walking nose with teeth," McCoy said softly. "Did you notice that he didn't fight except when he was pinned down? He smashed open that animal's rib cage, then pulled back to let nature take its course. I bet he'll track the titanosaur for miles if he has to. Even a minor bite will kill it before long. Those animals' mouths must be havens for bacteria."

"I can't believe we saw that!" Bannon pushed to his feet.

"On the contrary," Spock said, "with the sheer numbers of those varieties of creatures on this continent at this time, it would be surprising if we did *not* encounter them."

Kirk put an elbow out and let Emmendorf hoist him up. "Let's move on. I don't want to be here if—"

"Jim!" McCoy's arm shot out in a point. "Look!"

Scanning the landscape, Kirk drew a breath and snapped, "Down!"

On the creek bed, sniffing at the ground, were two more tyrannosaurs. One was two-thirds the size of the first they'd seen, thirty feet or so, and the other was only about fifteen feet long.

"It's a baby!" Ensign Reenie panted.

"A baby that could eat a Clydesdale," McCoy drawled, appreciating the young T's ottoman-sized head. "The scale is incredible!"

Baby or not, there wasn't much cute about this thing. In every way a duplicate of its elders, the little T stuffed its horny snout into the mud, scooped up a bloody chunk of muscle torn from the sauropod, and greedily coughed it down, mud and all.

"Is the other one its mother?" Emmendorf asked.

"No way to tell," McCoy said, squinting.

Now the larger of the two caught the scent of the trail and roared. Tails whipping, they trundled past the Starfleet crew toward the path of crushed trees, sniffing at the bloody rubble as they stomped through.

Shaken and stunned, Kirk and his party cautiously got to their feet. Face-to-face with the big ones, that was what Starfleet had promised—a life of adventure and exploration.

Well, they'd just come face-to-face with the biggest big ones of all.

Now they had to learn how to hide from them.

"Jim, we found some food. Or at least, we *think* it's food."

As McCoy picked his way across the clearing, and with every one of his steps, Kirk realized with one more pang how hungry he had become. His body was fighting off the toxins, dealing with the medication, struggling for clarity of mind, and all this took a vat of energy.

"Y'know," McCoy rambled, "it's a jungle out there. I've never seen so many funny-looking animals. You can't take ten steps out there, but some nest of big lizards jumps up and scatters. It's bad for the heart."

With his body rewarding him for his diligence with well-timed twinges, Kirk bent over McCoy's bundle of unfamiliar fruits. A few were round, fuzzy, and brown, some meaty and yellow green and scored with cut marks, some nuts still in the shells. He pushed at the soft brown round ones with his finger.

"What are those?"

"Some kind of fig," McCoy said. "And these are palm hearts. Over here might be a version of raspberry. Now, don't hold me to that—"

"Have you tasted it yet?"

"I've been too busy stanching the wounds on the backs of my hands. It had three-inch thorns."

"You set me up for that question, didn't you?

237

"Look at this one. Pick it up."

Kirk plucked up a pickle-shaped green vegetable a little over an inch long, rolled it between his fingers, and pinched it. It grated between his thumb and forefinger. "Full of seeds. You want us to eat seeds?"

"No, I don't think they're edible. You know what I think it is?"

"In a minute I'm not gonna care."

"I think that's a protobanana."

"You mean, it'll be a banana in a few million years?"

"Incredible, isn't it?"

"Do we have enough to survive on?"

"No. Well, it's not *my* fault. It took us four hours to get just this many. Most of the large growth here are conifers and there's not much edible about them. There's an understory of stunted plants that might be on their way to extinction. Bannon says they're being replaced by an explosion of angiosperms, which will be most of the flowers and plants we know from our time. Other than evergreens, he says. But there's a cypress swamp about two miles away, and where there's water, there's food. One thing we know about Cretaceous fauna is that there were enough fish to carpet every starbase in the Federation."

"That's a lot of fish. Let's go."

"Go? Aren't you going to eat?"

"Later." He dug for his communicator and flipped up the grid. "Kirk to Bannon."

"Jim," McCoy urged, "at least eat one of these. Medical order." He scooped up the palm hearts and held them out.

"Bring them along. Kirk to Bannon, respond."

Seconds ticked by, during which he and McCoy gazed at each other with that mutual sinking feeling—not sinking . . . draining. As if they were spiraling down some terrible drain with no fingerholds, thrashing their hands in futile search for a grip—

"Bannon here."

"We're going to gather some food, Lieutenant, or we won't have the energy to accomplish our mission. Assemble your team and meet us at the base of the mountains to our immediate east. We'll meet you there. Your mission is to catch fish."

"Acknowledged."

"Kirk out. Bones, let's go down to the fishing hole."

"If you say so, Captain, but I've got a feeling it's not going to be your average Georgia day off."

"Gars, bowfins, sturgeon, . . . something that looks like a herring. Take my tricorder and hand me that net."

Lieutenant Dale Bannon tossed his tricorder to Security Ensign Emmendorf and Ensign Reenie, who crouched on the bank of this slow-moving marshy river.

And Bannon was up to his belt line in the warm, mucky water. It had started with just his boots, but he'd gotten carried away. In this moist air, he'd probably never be dry again. He caught the monkey's attempt at macramé they'd fashioned out of vines and tried to arrange it in a manner that might in his wildest dreams catch a fish. How'd he gotten into this? What was that hole the captain had pushed them through?

"Why don't you just use the phaser?" Emmendorf said. "Hey, look at that needle-nosed sucker!"

Reenie glanced up. "Captain doesn't want us to waste phaser energy."

"Well, the captain would sure know."

"That was a pike!" Emmendorf pointed at a swish in the water. "I swear that was a pike."

"It's too early for pikes," Bannon argued.

"Not necessarily," Reenie said.

"Catch it, sir," Emmendorf said. "Pike make good eatin'. You know what we can do? We can wrap it in one of them big leafs right over there, and we smoke it up. Git the capt'n back on his feet."

"Why don't you come in here and catch it yourself, Emmendorf? Just stick your mouth in the water. The fish'll swim right in."

"Can't swim, sir."

"It's only waist high, you landlubber."

"Well, sir, you're already so wet'n all."

"This is what I joined up for," Bannon muttered. "Up to my armpits in swamp muck, grabbing for Devonian prototrash with my bare hands . . ."

Flashing in his periphery, a large flat-bodied form thrust from the water, flapped once in open air, then crashed beneath the surface again.

Sending swirls through the water, Bannon spun around. "What was that!"

"It's a ray!" Reenie said and pointed at the moving shadow.

"It can't be!"

"I know a ray when I see one, Bannon," the girl said. "That's fantastic! I've never seen one that color before!"

"Rays are saltwater fish. This stream's very low saline. It's got to be mostly mountain fed."

"Rays aren't just saltwater fish. Got'em in the Amazon."

"Okay, okay."

"The captain's coming," Reenie said. "I see him and Dr. McCoy coming down the ridge."

"That's all I need."

She shook her head and in her tiny voice asked, "What's your problem, Dale?"

"I don't have any problems."

"Sure act like it," Emmendorf muttered.

Bannon stabbed a finger toward him. "You mind your mouth, mister! Or I'll use your face as bait!"

Emmendorf glanced at Reenie. "Sorry, sir. My fault, sir."

Enraged by the glance, Bannon bit into his own lower lip to get control. "Sure as hell was. Now, help me spot a fish for the son of a bitch."

He glanced up and craned his neck to see how close the captain and the doctor were getting, irritated that the senior officers weren't satisfied to leave him alone to do what they'd sent him out to do. Get food and analyze the landscape were practically the same thing. All right, so he was doing both. Lieutenants were the hands, feet, eyes, and ears of Starfleet. They should just leave him alone.

Something grated against his leg, caressing, as if to measure his stability in the muck. He turned, tried to look.

The water swirled, peacock green with algae, its surface dyed and oily with natural ejecta. A form cut the twisting brilliantines and ghosted under as quickly. The surface closed in around it, leaving an incision as if cut by a knife.

On the bank, Reenie and Emmendorf stared into the water, both rising off their haunches and standing like gunfighters, unsure of what they had just seen. The water salved like lanolin in the gauzy sunlight. The form reappeared and skimmed past Bannon's legs again, this time between him and the shore. The sun made an illusion of something four or five feet long, but it was only the elongated shadow cast on the rocky bottom.

Emmendorf crouched and squinted, sinking his palm into the soft bank. Reenie came up on her toes, moving her head like a cobra as she tried to find a way to see through the demulcent surface.

Suddenly Reenie gasped, "Bannon, get out!"

Bannon looked up. "Why? So it's a big pike. So what?"

"Come on out, sir!" Emmendorf stood up and reached for him, coming into the water up to his ankles.

"There it is!" Reenie grabbed for her phaser but not fast enough.

Bannon took a breath to order her to back off and get a grip on herself, but he felt something slice across his left calf. The skin popped. Then a swirling motion—and something clamped down on his leg.

His knee buckled, and he staggered, twisting wildly to get a look at what had hold of him. Turning did more harm than good. He reeled back, wrenching away from the force that had his leg and contributed to the ripping of his own ligaments. Plumes of blood burst into the greens of the water and quickly turned everything purple. The creature took a swipe of its long tail and turned on its side for a firmer bite.

Bannon cried out and pulled away harder, but his leg was caught as if he'd stepped into a bear trap.

Then he saw what had him. Its button black eye peered up at him, seeing everything while appearing to see nothing, its skin beautifully striped like wallpaper in a foreign embassy, and its pectoral fin wobbling as the animal twisted against its own bite.

Reenie grabbed for her phaser again, and her cry filled the great primordial outdoors and echoed against the mountain.

"Shark! It's a shark! A shark!"

Chapter Twenty-five

"No PHASERS! No phasers! Get him out!"

Jim Kirk skidded down the last quarter of the ridge, shouting as he hit the bottom. He wrenched his hips around in the lucky direction and managed to land on his good leg.

"Pull him out of there!"

He plunged past Reenie and Emmendorf, crashed into the water, and sent green spray fanning in every direction. He grabbed for Bannon, who was batting frantically at the water with his bare hands as if to take karate chops at the frothy surface.

The water was too warm, unnatural and invisible on the body. Kirk had braced himself for a chill, but it never came and for an instant he thought he was losing the feeling in his legs. He got his hands around Bannon's arm, pulled hard, and kicked viciously at the gaudy spear that had its teeth sunk into his crewman.

McCoy came crashing into the water past the two stunned crewmen and somehow this shook the two out of their terrorized stupor and they followed him in. Of course, nobody was more terrorized than the bunch of four-foot crocodiles on the opposite bank, who jolted and suddenly scattered.

The creature in the water, shark or not, had no spine for combat. It was a scavenger, and easier food would present itself in due time. It disengaged from Bannon's calf, and like a wizard into a puff of smoke made two swipes of its tail and disappeared, to forget in moments where it had just been.

Kirk stuffed Bannon into Emmendorf's thick short arms and snapped an order to get ashore before those crocodiles wised up. He struggled to get out of the sucking grit that held his boots underwater. There was a lot of heart thump in the vulgar fear of being eaten. Bannon was chalk white as they dropped him on the shore, and McCoy fell to his side, a hand already clamped to the artery in the young man's calf.

"Did anybody see what it was?" the doctor asked.

"I did," Reenie said. "It was sort of a shark, but the slash in his leg came from its dorsal fin. It was kind of . . . serrated. Then it turned around and bit him."

"There's a bite here. Not bad. The fin did a lot more damage."

Bannon swore and gasped but didn't make much sense. Reenie held his head and stuffed back tears, but Emmendorf's wide young face was drenched with tear tracks cutting through the slime that had splashed on his cheeks, and he evidently didn't care who saw him cry.

Kirk felt his heart quit drumming and start cracking at the sight of them crumpled there on the shore at his feet. He'd failed to protect them. His hands were both clenched in their raw-nerve imaginations twisting the spine out of that fish. "Bones?"

"Checking." The doctor didn't look up.

Bannon choked and tried to sit up. "I'm gonna lose my leg—"

"No, you're not," Kirk stated bluntly with deliberate force.

McCoy's ice blue eyes snapped up to him. He glared at the captain.

With his posture and his own glaring eyes, Kirk communicated a silent order. *Anything you have to do.*

McCoy looked down again. "No," he said. "You're not

going to lose it. Tissue damage, torn muscle. I don't think it got through to the bone."

"Let's get him back up the ridge," Kirk ordered. "There are clouds moving in and I want to find shelter."

"Let's find higher ground. Maybe we can find *drier* ground."

Kirk was choked with frustration. And sweat, there was always that. The temperature slogged between 105 and 110 degrees.

"I hear something," McCoy said. "Does anybody hear that? Like a foghorn or a . . . lot of foghorns."

McCoy tipped his head and listened, but he was the only one paying much attention to the distant woofing and hooting.

"Sir!" Emmendorf called from the brink of what looked like a game trail, a flatlands scraped out of the landscape. "Captain, it looks like there might be some caves up there, sir, you know, up in those crags?"

"We'll go up," Kirk agreed, glancing at the unhappy sky.

He glanced behind, where Vernon and Spock were struggling along with the injured Bannon, still in a drug-induced haze.

Emmendorf's round face gleamed with sweat. "Right this way, sir. We gotta cross the flats."

"I just felt the ground move," McCoy said and stopped picking his way through the heavy bushes. "Did anybody else feel that?"

"Big animals," Reenie said, pausing to read off her tricorder. "Those are your foghorns."

"Do you know what kind of dinosaur makes that sound?"

"Nobody really knows what dinosaurs sounded like, sir." She shrugged, and her small eyes crinkled. "Sorry . . ."

"You're doing fine," McCoy said, but his look of encouragement only lasted a moment.

"Let's get across those flats quickly," Kirk said, shooing them on. "I don't want to be out in the open any longer than we have to be. Mr. Emmendorf, come back here and spell Mr. Spock with Lieutenant Bannon. Spock, take the—"

A scream tore between them, and the crew scattered. Reenie bolted backward and struck Emmendorf. Both of them toppled, pulled Bannon and Vernon down, and Reenie scrambled toward Kirk like a cat with all claws out. The Klingons, shackled to each other and grim as rocks, stumbled but managed to stay on their feet. McCoy kept his wits and turned a phaser on them.

Kirk snatched Reenie before she had a chance to scream again, dragged her back, and clapped a hand over her open mouth. "It's all right—it's all right! Freeze!"

Before them, standing like startled deer in a bright light were four bizarre animals with long necks and long pointed tails, tiny forearms, and hollow rectangular faces with plant-eating beaks. Their yellowish skin blended with the variegated foliage.

"Spock," Kirk whispered.

"Checking," came the quiet response.

The animals blinked at them without the inclination to run. They'd never seen anything like humans before, and odds were good they hadn't seen Klingons either. At ten or more feet from tip to tip, they weren't so different in size from the people who had startled them.

Nearby, Spock's voice was low. "Thescelosaurus. Adult length, twelve feet, body weight of—"

"Shhh."

Through the buzzing foliage before them four, then five, then more heads rose from the leaves. Dozens of gawking, blinking faces came out of the bushes to stare at them, like flower stalks suddenly coming to sprout. Some of them kept chewing, nostrils passively flexing and puffing. One of the animals opened its goatish mouth and bawled at them.

More faces popped up, large, small, all different ages of the same species, until the jungle before them was prickled with hundreds of long skinny necks, knobby heads, and blinking eyes.

It was one thing to spook a rabbit and have it sprint, but to bump something the size of themselves—as Kirk stared at these animals and they stared back, he began to comprehend what he was looking at. This multitude of hidden, dull grazers were the deer of this age. Quiet, shy, and not very bright, these were the prey of the Cretaceous.

Somehow he couldn't imagine mounting one of those heads over a mantle.

Reenie panted and let go of his thick arm. "I think I . . . I think . . . I think I . . . stepped on it . . ."

"It's all right. They're not going to hurt us," he murmured. "Let's go."

They broke out of the bushes and onto a flatlands that appeared to once have been a riverbed. Stretched around the base of the mountain in both directions, it had been trampled time and again. There wasn't so much as a sapling growing across the two-hundred-foot expanse, but there were hundreds of footprints the size of basketballs.

"Natural migration trail." Spock blinked in the hazy sunlight. "Captain, I feel some vibrations also."

"Let's hurry up then." Kirk stood twenty feet out from the tree line and turned to Vernon and Emmendorf as they pulled Bannon toward the flats, with McCoy and Reenie herding the Klingons after them. "Gentlemen, hurry along."

"Coming, sir!" Vernon called, hoisting Bannon over a clutch of ferns. "Don't worry, sir!"

Kirk glanced at McCoy. "Well, if I can't have answers, at least I've got enthusiasm."

McCoy couldn't muster a grin. "Jim, I'm telling you, the ground is rumbling. Is it rumbling where you are?"

"I'm only twenty feet from you."

"Well, is it?"

"Spock, scan this area. What do you pick up?"

Pausing thirty feet out, Spock adjusted his already overloaded tricorder. He turned in place, then paused.

"Captain . . . I suggest we retreat." He slung the tricorder strap over his shoulder, hurried back to Kirk, and took his arm. "Quickly."

Kirk took the cue for what it was. "Fall back!"

The ground *was* rumbling. And that honking was closer, a

lot closer. His chest throbbed as he hurried back toward the brush line, relieved to see that his crew made it, but he couldn't make himself go all the way into the bushes without seeing what they were running from.

Foolish—what if it wanted to eat them?

"Captain, this way," Spock encouraged.

"Just a minute. I want to see them." Crouching at the edge of the thick growth, Kirk was gratified when Spock came to wait with him instead of trying to convince him to back away. The honking was very close now, echoing on the mountain in front of them.

"There they are!" Emmendorf shouted, standing on a stump and pointing wildly north.

Spock shot to a standing position and actually forgot to raise his tricorder.

"Spock!" Kirk snapped. "Record!"

The Vulcan blinked, then fumbled for his tricorder. "Yes—"

"Back up, everybody back up. Back up!"

The rumbling of the ground became a solid drumbeat, and a wall of animals that looked like plucked ostriches came hammering through the open flatlands. Within seconds, dozens swarmed into hundreds.

"Everybody stay back," Kirk mumbled as much to himself as his crew. The urge to step out and stare was overwhelming. He'd never seen so many animals in one place before, not on any planet.

"Hadrosaurs, Captain," Spock said. "Anatotitan, specifically. Thirty feet long on average . . . herbivores. Apparently ninety percent of dinosaur species were plant eaters."

"I'm glad. Unless, of course, they step on you." Kirk glanced back at his people, nervous and custodial.

He pressed his hands on a stump and pushed up for a better view. The adult hadrosaurs were massive animals, with flattened duck-billed faces, probably for foraging in mud—comic, except that the average of these beasts was about seven tons each and Kirk wasn't about to call them names. As the hadrosaurs thudded by on their thick hind legs, it was like watching old films of elephant herds pushing through the Congo.

"They probably do not live in these forests," Spock said. "Likely this is a game trail. Natural migration or a route to water."

"Numbers, Spock. How many are there?"

"Off the scale, Captain."

Kirk strained to see where the pounding herd was coming from, but there was no way to see so far around the mountain bend.

"If they're plant eaters, they'll leave us alone," Kirk said.

"They will," McCoy put in, "but doesn't it make you wonder what eats all those animals?"

Kirk shot him a shut-up look. "All we have to do is hold position and let them pass. Then we'll move on. Emmendorf, Vernon, put Bannon down and let him rest. We'll wait. It can't take them more than a half hour to clear out."

Six hours.

Hour after hour of honking, snorting duckbills, a hundred fifty thick, thousands long, moving like bison across the plains.

It was a sight. During the third hour of this honking, smelly, muddy expedition, Kirk had to make Spock stop recording. By the time the last hundred hadrosaurs lumped by, sloughing through the dung of the thousands who had come before, he'd have been happy never to see another dinosaur for the rest of his life.

When he was finally able to order his crew across the flats, it was an expedition through a sewer.

Caked with manure, they hauled up the mountain and found their way into the lush foliage of the mountainside.

By nightfall the younger members of the crew found sustaining victories in fashioning crude shelter at the mouth of a shallow cave, more a spoon-shaped hack out of the side of a ridge. They built a rooflike structure that drove the rain outward, back into the jungle.

They'd found out they had to. That or drown. It had started to rain.

Rain pounded at the cave mouth as if it understood the reason why. The ground was reduced to a muddy carpet, pocked incessantly by lashing spray. Behind the sound of the rain was the erratic, nearly subsonic rumbling and bellowing of the hadrosaurs. The sound traveled for miles, and there were thousands of them honking into the deep night. At first it had been eerie, then exotic, and now it was just plain annoying.

Kirk sat at one of four small fires they'd tried to keep going. Behind him, in the edge of darkness, Bannon was still sedated.

In Kirk's periphery on the far side of the cave, the two Klingons were shackled to stakes driven into the ground. This freed the two guards to participate in gathering or capturing food and building the shelter and weapons.

Now what? What was he supposed to do with those two? Turn them loose here, then look over his shoulder for the rest of his life?

Aggravated, he stared into the fire. He was irritable, twitching, fixated on the one chance he insisted they still had.

McCoy had thinned out the medication and the schedule of applying it to make it last as long as possible. That meant about a week. And it would be a feverish, painful week, because the rationed dose was only a stopgap, barely enough to keep the toxin from overcoming him. This was the long way around.

After that week, if the poison hadn't been sufficiently evicted from his body, the captain, the man everyone was counting on for their survival, would be the first to die.

He had to keep alive. He had to keep his landing party alive, every one of them, *every* one. The stoic nobility of his crew wouldn't be compromised. As he sat here, he swore in his mind that he would fire all kilns, set all headsails, deny all denials, never miss a beat, and he would keep them alive, every one.

All this would be easier if only those blasted animals would stop hooting at the moon.

"Seafood is really ugly when it's alive, id'n it? Maybe that's what helps us eat it. We figure we're doing it a favor."

"If you had to breathe through your neck, you'd be ugly, too."

Irritated by the conversation that Reenie, Emmendorf, and McCoy were having behind him at another fire, Kirk stared at the rain with pent-up contempt. The curtain of silvery slashing water stood between him and his needs. He hated it.

Plucking another slab of cooked fish off the scorching rocks in the fire, he found it ironic that this fresh-caught slop would be precious findings in a fossil dig a few million years from now.

Come to think of it, so would he.

Imagine the face of some dried-up, windblown, socially stunted hermit of a paleontologist, with a two-foot beard and a dirty hat, brushing off the skeleton of a human male from sixty million years too early. That'd be a mysterious case of cardiac arrest on the plateau for sure.

But then he remembered. There wouldn't be anybody to dig him up. There wouldn't *be* anybody at all.

To get that thought out of his head, he turned to Spock, who had been sitting beside him in prudent silence for nearly an hour.

"How much do you know about this time period?" Kirk asked, just to make noise.

"A cursory appreciation within the general venue of my science studies," Spock admitted, his voice raspy with fatigue and probably the same frustration Kirk was feeling. "We have the data chips in two of the tricorders loaded with Earth paleontology and paleogeology. Your order to bring along the download about Earth's past was prime foresight."

"Thank you," Kirk muttered. "Let's hope it's not the last thing I do right. Spock . . ."

"Sir?"

"Something wrong?"

Caught, Spock let his eyes fall into a shadow, his face grooved with cracks of firelight. He looked into the fire. "I've been thinking about Temron."

Kirk nodded. "Vulcans with no Federation to join. I feel as if I've let them down somehow."

Looking up, Spock said, "I had not intended to imply that."

"We're both orphans, Mr. Spock. Orphaned and lost in time. We'll keep focused. Continue our mission until we succeed or discover it can't be done."

"The situation may be out of our hands," Spock said quietly. "At this moment, an asteroid is plummeting toward us. Whatever happens to stop it is going to happen thousands of miles out in space."

"And I can't will myself out there from down here," Kirk agreed, with a sour frown.

Making a little grunt of what might have been agreement, Spock shifted the way his legs were folded and fingered the cluster of vegetarian edibles Bannon and McCoy had plucked out of the hostile growth for him. "Your mind," he said, "your pattern of thinking has always been broader than mine. You are capable of creative leaps. I have come to have confidence in them."

Kirk knew it was as much statement as compliment, but he felt warmed just the same. "I find you very creative, Mr. Spock. In a logical manner."

"Thank you, Captain."

"You're welcome. Eat your twigs. You'll need all your stamina if that blasted rain ever—"

"Captain! Captain! Found something!"

Kirk straightened his back quickly and reached for Spock to haul him to his feet. "Who's that? Who's yelling?"

"Ensign Vernon, sir."

Vernon was a twenty-three-year-old six-foot-two Security grunt who loved muscling prisoners around, took standing guard as seriously as Spock took science, and went after any other assignment with equal relish. He was a simple fellow who wanted nothing more in life than to tackle one-dimensional tasks. As such, he found magnificent satisfaction every ten minutes or so and was one of the happiest crewmen Kirk had ever known.

"Captain, sir, sir! I found something," the big kid panted. "Out there, 'bout half a mile! You gotta see it!"

Chapter Twenty-six

"WE HAVE TRAVELED TIME!"

Reflecting the impossible, Zalt's cheeks were russet with the fury of science, of magic, of the astounded, the angry who had been left out of a secret. How many of their own scientists knew about this machine and had not told?

Roth felt the same betrayal. Had Klingon preoccupation with killing the romuluSnganpu' and taking their possessions left his people dry of discovery? Had his civilization forgotten how to explore? While he and his fellow soldiers were fighting, was nothing else being pursued?

Yes, nothing. Scientific advancement had grated to a stop in all but space vehicle design and propulsion and weaponry. Even that had been relatively static for years.

"Time!" Zalt hissed again, staring at the empty place where the starship captain and his officer had sat moments ago, then suddenly twisted around to look at the sleeping man at the far back of their shallow cave. "Unconscious," he rumbled. "Good."

"Why have they left us unguarded?" Roth tugged at the shackles that pinned him to the ground. "Are they so sure of this?"

Zalt craned his neck toward the jungle. "Listen to me. We are back in time. They have brought us here for a reason. They are trying to change what must happen."

"How can they?" Roth dared to sound sarcastic. "Time is time. Their story is insane."

"You're not a thinker. You can't see in your mind what could come to pass. They could end everything we know. Cause us not to exist anymore! And the Vulcans are mixed up in this somehow . . ."

"Then you believe what they told us on their ship?" Roth stared into the little fire the Starfleet men had made for him and Zalt. A fire for the enemies to warm themselves by. Comfort of the enemy . . . it would never have occurred to him. What kind of men were these?

Zalt suddenly lurched to his feet, braced hard against the ground, and began pulling with set-jawed effort at the stake that held them to the ground. "Help me!" he growled through his teeth.

Surprised, Roth bolted up, raised his hands until the tether stopped them, and also began to pull.

The stake was made of hard wood, cut out of a tree by their captors, a long spear driven deeply into the stony ground.

Zalt's face turned purple as he strained. Roth tried to match the effort, but his own personal drive to break free couldn't match Zalt's.

The long stake came up a hand's width, filling Zalt with a rage of determination. He roared and slammed Roth aside so hard that Roth fell to the ground on his side, then rearranged his stance directly over the stake, coiled his shackled arms against his chest, and put all his physical power into a great upward thrust.

The spear of wood began to cry out, scratching against the stone-riddled earth into which it had been driven. Finally the earth itself parted and released the shaft of wood. Zalt staggered back, lungs heaving.

"Free!" he gasped. "Now, now we can fight them!"

Roth scratched to his feet. "Fight how? We don't know if

they were telling the truth. Do we dare tamper with time? We could be ruining our own eternity!"

"Or saving it!" Zalt's voice was bitter and vicious, loaded with dare. "Close your teeth and listen. These are your orders. You're going to make friends with these people. Swear on your honor that you will not interfere with what they are doing. Then interfere greatly."

"On my honor? I cannot!"

"You will. You have no honor left upon which to swear, so you can swear all you like. Do it."

Roth sank back against the moist rock, as Zalt shook the tethers from his wrists and threw the useless stake to the ground.

"Follow me," Zalt said.

Shuddering like a wounded dog, Jim Kirk followed his excited young Security man through the rain's consistent assault. By the time they reached a bluff in the middle of the low-slung mountain, all were whipped and panting. Reenie and the other Security man, Vernon, went ahead and took readings and made sure the environment was relatively secure.

They were all soaked, but now the rain was stopping, or they were climbing out of it. The veiled sun had westered and slid behind the mountain, and the sky was getting dark. Kirk looked down into the valley from which they had just come. A cottony fog rested in the valley like soup in a bowl. Here it was nearly dry, moistened only by the heat and thready fog from that cloud down there. Above them, the star-shingled night was black and beckoning.

He squinted down at his boots in the fading light and at the ground beneath them. Dry. His sopping uniform shirt clung to his chest, arms, and back. They were on an incline, a natural pathway that spiraled up this mountain. The pathway beneath his feet was hard rock coated with a layer of gritty soil and a tenacious moss, leaving this convenient indentation in the mountainside. Still an uphill climb but walkable.

"Here, Captain," McCoy said and handed him a stick he'd ripped out of a fallen tree. It was four feet long and almost two inches thick, not quite straight, but straight enough. "In England they call it 'fellwalking.' Now you can tell people you've done it. Just say it was in Georgia."

Kirk glared at him but took the stick. Something to lean on.

Vernon's tall, shoulderwide form appeared at the crest, where this incline curved along the body of the mountain. "Right up here, sir! You're not gonna believe it!"

"Bet I will," Kirk grumbled.

The doctor stayed a pace or two behind him, which irritated him because Kirk knew McCoy was anticipating having to catch him if he fell. He didn't want to be caught or picked up or even empathized with.

He staggered as his stick slipped on a mossy place but beat off McCoy's attempt to help him with only a well-aimed glare. Before them, Spock turned in concern but had the sense to wait until they caught up rather than coming back to help.

He knows me too blasted well, Kirk thought as he glared forward at the Vulcan.

Spock stood against the incongruous junglescape, a blue and black pillar of high civilization, and waited as his captain approached. "One hundred yards, sir. Emmendorf and Reenie are setting up lighting implements."

"Good. I'm getting a feeling we shouldn't have come here until morning. We'll get what we can, then go back to the cave."

"Agreed," Spock said. "Jungle settings are generally more dangerous during the night hours."

Kirk nodded automatically. "Let's go."

One hundred yards farther along, and twenty feet below them on a lush plateau, lay one of the strangest sights Kirk had ever encountered. Ten or so large-bodied animals lay slaughtered, peppered with the bodies of smaller animals. The ferns and groundcover all around were blood-spackled in the portable daylight the junior officers had set up. Insects swarmed in the unnatural lights, eerily silent, feasting on the corpses.

A sight of prehistoric slaughter? So what?

Spock and McCoy plunged past him, and Kirk found himself inadequate in the light of their professional curiosity. He wanted to throw up but not with his junior officers watching. Or senior officers either, for that matter. A captain's dilemma: couldn't throw up in front of anybody.

Withered intestines hung like holiday decorations all over the green growth and ferns, some still linked to the open guts of the animals from which they came. The larger animals were a good ten feet from head to tail and on those thick hind legs could rear back almost as tall as he was. Their gaping mouths were snaggled with bloody teeth. Their eyes stared, even more terrible because these were large brown eyes, like the eyes of an owl, not like a crocodile. He couldn't feel for a crocodile, but this . . .

"All right, Mr. Vernon," he started bluntly, "what's the attraction? We've got a bunch of dead animals. What did you want us to see that couldn't wait?"

The tall Security man pointed. "The faces of the big ones, sir—look at their faces!"

Kirk moved forward glaring through a band of artificial light. "Is that paint?"

Spock drew his fingers along the yellow and purple designs on the animal's long skull. "Paint, Captain . . . acrylic pigment. Synthetic, not natural." His voice dropped away and he murmured, "Amazing! Meant for visibility . . . or possibly to frighten an enemy."

"Somebody else must have painted these creature's faces to throw us off."

"Somebody else?" McCoy looked up. "What makes you think that, Captain?"

"If we can travel time, so can someone else."

"Only the big ones have paint on them," Reenie said.

"Maybe these little ones are the babies of the big ones," Vernon wondered.

"No," Reenie said. "The small ones have their claws between the ribs of the big ones. They were attacking."

"A coordinated attack, also," Spock noted, fascination rising again in his voice. "Note the angles from which the smaller ones approached . . . nearly all the same."

McCoy got down on both knees and put his hands into the laid-open animal. "Warm blood."

Kirk leaned hard on his stick. "How long have these animals been dead?"

"Minutes. Maybe an hour. But some of the bodies are still warmer than others. They may have lay here dying for a while. But not very long. Trauma like this doesn't let an animal hang on for long."

"We may have frightened off the victors," Spock said.

"Which means whatever did this is probably still nearby." Kirk motioned to Emmendorf, Vernon, and Reenie. "Stay on your toes, people."

"Jim, do you have the time for me to dissect one of these?" McCoy asked.

"We've got sixty million years. Help yourself. But we'll do it back at the campsite. Mr. Emmendorf, come down here and assist Dr. McCoy. Mr. Spock, secure the area while you have the chance, please."

"Yes, sir."

Spock stood up, his gaze lingering on the face of the sad creature lying at his feet, its painted face calling to his scientific mind with contradiction after contradiction. Kirk empathized with him, but there wasn't time to indulge. They needed something more concrete, something the tricorder would recognize and say, "Got it!"

They needed that thing, that one hint to drive away their doubts. To Jim Kirk, that was the perfect world—one with no doubts. The hard decisions weren't really the worst part of command. It was the doubting he hated.

Command . . . the ship . . . the beautiful *Enterprise* . . . a ghost of it blew past him in the dark sky overhead, so real he almost looked up and waved. They had counted on him. They hadn't doubted him.

I'm sorry, sir . . . I'm sorry, sir . . ."

"Not your fault, Scotty . . ."

His own voice startled him. He glanced around, self-aware, wondering if anyone else had heard him.

No one was looking. McCoy was elbow-deep in slaughtered dinosaur, giving orders to a nauseated Emmendorf, and Spock was up on the incline, intently scanning.

Kirk knew he was better at the art of roughing it than Spock, but for how long? His medication had been thinned until he barely felt it working. The fever was back, his legs hurt, his thoughts wandered, and he had to pull them back every few minutes. How long could he hold on? Would they find him dead in his sleep a few days from now and be forced to go on without him?

He looked up the incline at Spock. He knew Spock's sterling loyalty and cautious foresight wouldn't serve long or well in this place. Eventually one of the young officers would be killed by this nightmare environment, and Spock would have to live with that. Spock always pretended to take those things in his logical stride, but Kirk knew it was fake. He'd seen the change in Spock's behavior, watched him grow more mellow as he paid the toll of being a first officer, of having a subordinate's life slip through his fingers from time to time. It soured an officer's iron-willed confidence.

Doubt. It was the demon on a leader's shoulder. The one Kirk had never gotten used to.

Spock looked up from the tricorder, and for an instant Kirk was afraid he'd been thinking too loudly. "Something here, Captain."

"Coming."

Climbing was torture. Kirk dug his fingers into the stubby overgrowth, took each step one at a time. He couldn't let them see him fall.

A hand caught him under the upper arm and gave him support. One more hitch upward, and Spock had him. Kirk sat on the edge of the stony embankment. His face was clammy, his breath rattling in his chest, and he gripped the edge of the ridge with both hands. Spock knelt to hold the tricorder in front of him.

"Traces of refined metal." There was victory in the Vulcan's voice.

Invigorated, Kirk cranked to look directly at him. "Spock, are you sure?"

"Very faint traces on the limestone below this soil." He scooted back a few inches to gesture up the incline. "Note a pattern scraped into the soil . . . something has been dragged along here, possibly some form of travoy. It carved grooves into the ground, and where it struck stone we have these traces. Definitely high-grade steel composite."

It didn't show in his voice, but it did in his eyes—he was thrilled. Probably relieved. *Steel* . . .

"Then there *is* more going on than we've seen so far," Kirk said. "Somebody else has been here and has been tampering with these animals."

Spock lowered his tricorder. "Yes."

They looked at each other.

Somewhere an animal shrieked, its cry carried to them on a gust of moist wind. Their brief visit to the modern age was cut off by the sound of primitive hunt.

"Spock, go back over the the readings you took from the Guardian. See if you can find something there . . . or *not* there. Not just the animals, but something else."

"I understand," the Vulcan condensed.

"And analyze these metal traces—"

"Captain!" Ensign Reenie was craning her neck over a crest of bushes, her slick hair, somehow blacker than Spock's, waving as she shifted from toe to toe. "Something's happening down there."

"Ensign!" Kirk snapped. Shaking out of Spock's grasp, he slid down the incline and shambled through the litter of bodies and entrails to Reenie's side, where he caught her elbow and pulled her back, putting himself in her place.

He looked over the bushes but saw only glimpses of movement on a lower level. There was noise, huffing of effort, grunts and howls, now getting louder. Something solid arched into the air—a tail. Big. With a knot on the end.

"Let's have a look. Heads down."

He led the way through gaudy flora and spiked plants twice his height, cautiously pointing out those large webs that no one wanted to disturb and murmuring every few steps, "Look out for this . . . Don't touch that . . . Duck under this . . ."

Suddenly before them was the edge of this stand of bushes. Kirk almost stumbled out into the open before realizing how close he was to the activity out there.

"Down, everyone," he whispered. "Spock?"

"Here." Spock shuffled through as Reenie made way for him. He held his tricorder before him, but the scene upon which they had stumbled was too astounding for analysis yet.

Before them was the savage waltz of a hunt. On an open plateau, where lush vegetation had attracted creatures to come and graze, was a sight of the most horrible and inspiring kind. For decades, paintings and animations had been done of such things, but this was real and they were here to see it.

"Recording," Spock murmured automatically.

Kirk didn't care. He was engrossed in fantasy.

In the plateau's center, nearly two dozen creatures huddled in a curious circle. Down on all fours like grizzly bears were stocky armored animals with noses like camels, the adults more than twenty feet long. On their backs, rows of curved plates tapered down to the long tails, each row of plates knobby all the way across like a dog's collar, mounted with protrusions on which moss had settled as if on the shingles of an Irish church roof. Each had a heavy-looking armored skull, bony eyelids, a toothless beak, large flat feet with heavy toenails, and a no-kidding knot of embedded bone fused into two lobes mounted side to side on the end of the tail.

Mixed in with them were a few bipeds, brightly colored, with their dome heads rising above the knobby backs of the armored animals, their small paws sometimes resting on those knobs.

"They've formed a defensive circle," Kirk uttered appreciatively. "Look at the outer perimeter."

A pack of more than fifty much smaller creatures were moving in, walking on two legs, using a border collie method of corralling the armored animals and the dome-heads hiding among them.

"The four-legged animals may be Ankylosaurus," Spock responded, squinting into the tricorder screen. "Order Ornithichia . . . heavily armored, roughly seven meters in length, possessing a bony club on the tail. I may be incorrect about the species. This readout has ankylosaurs as upland dinosaurs, characteristic of drier environments."

"Then what are they doing here?" Kirk asked.

"Unknown. With the draining of the seaways, they may be expanding to new habitats. The bipeds among them are . . . I believe, pachycephalosaurs. Interesting, Captain, how the prey are banding together. It's extraordinary behavior—"

"Sir, if I had those things stalking me," Reenie said, "I'd make a deal with the devil."

"What are those?" Kirk pointed at the dozens of prowling creatures on two legs.

Spock lowered meaningfully. "Raptors, sir. Generally accepted as the most viciously efficient of prehistoric hunters on land. I'm reading over a hundred of them."

"I only see fifty . . . sixty . . ."

"Others are waiting in the brush." Spock raised his tricorder slightly. "According to this, the varieties known range from the twenty-foot Utahraptor to the ten-foot deinonychus to the six-foot light-weight velociraptors. Strangely, the larger ones occur earlier than the smaller ones. It's possible they were responsible for the extinction of sauropods in North America—the large long-necked dinosaurs—which would have caused the raptors to become smaller and hunt smaller prey in larger numbers."

Kirk peered through thick elephant-ear leaves. "Those are, I'd say, four feet."

Spock looked up. "Captain . . . I believe these are troodontids."

"You mean—"

"Yes, exactly. Very successful predators. Bladed teeth . . . expanded braincase, dexterous hands . . . sizable thumb claw, blunt snout, forward-directed eyes—odd, the tricorder is reading out these creatures with longer snouts than what we are observing—"

Kirk glanced at him. "You don't have time, Mr. Spock."

"I beg your pardon?" He looked up.

"You don't have time to get a degree in paleobiology. Don't fret over it."

Spock's brow crinkled. "I had not noted fretting, sir, . . . simply an attempt to narrow the facts—"

"And be accurate, of course. Well, there are times when accuracy isn't everything. Just make sure we understand what we need to understand."

After a valiant effort to pretend insult, Spock gave up and said, "Always, sir."

The dozens of troodonts had their hands full—claws full. If surprise had been part of their strategy, they'd failed. Or if they had meant to get at the young, they'd also failed. The adult ankylosaurs presented their knobby armored backs and wielded the bony clubs at the ends of their tails in purposeful warning sweeps. Not even a tyrannosaurus would bother trying to bite through that armor.

No chance for surprise, no cornering a loner . . . Some days, nothing goes right. Kirk found himself empathizing with the troodonts. After all, everybody has to eat.

A gurgling whistle broke his thoughts. To the left of where he peered through the leaves, one medium-sized troodont stood a few feet back from the ones who were closing in. This one extended its snout and made a low-pitched cooing sound. Neither impressive in size nor color, this troodont had signs of wear and tear—scars on its elongated face, scars on its tail, and a healed break that left its right arm bent noticeably outward.

In responses eerily matched, half of the approaching troodonts closed in, crowing and snapping at each other, while the other half lingered back. And Spock said there were plenty more in the bushes.

At first the stalkers moved slowly, unruffled by the honks of the dome-headed pachys. Kirk found himself watching that leader as its growls and whines made the others move in certain ways, rank by rank. Finally the troodont with the crooked arm made one long-winded sound, like metal scraping against metal. Dozens of troodonts made a barn-yard scream and plunged in.

Almost too fast to watch, the first rank flew to their prey on long, muscular legs, tails whipping and foreclaws grasping the knobby backs of the ankylosaurs.

They didn't even bother attacking the adult ankylosaurs. They leaped over and attached themselves to the bare throats and shoulders of the pachys and went to work with those sickle claws. Fans of blood blew into the breeze as if to proclaim that the dome-heads didn't stand a chance. Kirk felt his skin shrink with empathy and a certain unexpected guilt as he realized that he might have to do the same thing, possibly to the same creatures, if his landing party were to survive.

The ankylosaurs raised their tails, lowered their heads, and swung inward at the troodonts who had broken their circle. Clubbed tails cracked hideously against the spines of several troodonts, folding the attackers backward in agony, to be dragged through the stomping feet of the encircled victims. But it wasn't enough.

The broken-armed troodont barked again. Now the second rank of troodonts streaked in, charging not the impregnable armor of the ankyosaurs, but the ankylosaurs' naked young hiding among their legs. The leader made his grating scream again, louder now.

Suddenly the bushes rattled. Another fifty or more troodonts flew out of the fronds and rushed the scene.

"Spock, are you seeing this?" Kirk was barely able to keep to a whisper. "That's a coordinated attack. There's a command structure! That one over there—it's giving orders!"

"Even more, Captain," Spock appraised. "There's rudimentary language at work."

"Are you serious?"

"I've distinguished roughly ten sounds that elicit specific actions, all being delivered to one attacking rank at a time. Until you pointed it out, I had not noted all were coming from a specific individual."

"I guess it takes a captain to know one."

Instincts whistled at him, warnings as clear as the ship's red alert klaxon. Before them, the ground grew saturated with blood churned to soup by stomping feet and the slash and thump of those clubbed tails.

The defensive circle cracked. The ankylosaurs broke and ran for the horizon, followed by their young and the panicked pachycephalosaurs. They stumbled over each other and the coughing bodies of their dying fellows and made a run for it.

Only a few of the troodonts had been killed. Only three or four out of a hundred. Most of the prey who escaped made it to the open plateau, though some were wounded and would fall eventually, if only to die elsewhere and float down some waterway and clog up a stream and become feast or fossil later on.

It was hard to think of that; to imagine millions of years in any direction was daunting. Kirk knew this was why he wasn't a historian. He was too much a man of the moment. He felt too much for those animals out there, understood too much being predator and prey.

"Captain . . ." Reenie pointed through the leaves.

There was his friend, the barking, yipping leader of the troodont vanguard, the scruffy face and crooked right paw now held absolutely still. Even the tail was poised, countering the raised head, and did not move. It was looking right at them.

"Nobody move," Kirk whispered.

The other troodonts plunged into a meal, ripping into the bodies of animals both dead and dying. Except for this one.

And now it was peering right into Jim Kirk's eyes.

Chapter Twenty-seven

"PHASERS."

The captain drew his weapon, keeping the muzzle up. They had to conserve phaser power, but here, in the ferns and cycads, they could be ambushed.

"Ensign Reenie . . . warn and assist Dr. McCoy. Clear the area."

Orders bolted from Kirk's throat like photons firing, so blunt that his guts hurt and his throat scratched.

The girl bent low and disappeared, faintly rustling the bushes. Kirk saw Spock narrow his eyes in a kind of wince, and that made him look out at the troodont.

Enlighteningly catlike, the animal lowered its head without ever taking its eyes from them. Kirk's nerves shriveled as the troodont opened its snaggled mouth, drew its lips back from those mythological teeth, and made a noise that somehow sounded familiar, purposeful.

The other troodonts suddenly raised their heads in a thing so near unison as to be beautiful. Not one of them failed to look up at the call of its leader. They began a deliberate chirping, several of the sounds recognizably the same. Spock was right—rudimentary language.

"Higher intelligence," the captain whispered. "It's outlandish. So far above what we've always concluded about this era . . ."

"There have been theories," Spock said, "but not so early."

Kirk drew his head down another inch. The desire to run

crashed through him, but he had to stay here, keep those creatures staring, long enough for McCoy and the others to clear out of the other killing ground.

In the distance the large dinosaurs pounded off into the trees, a sorry few collapsing before reaching safety, drained of blood by their gory wounds. Before they even had a chance to be prey, they would be carrion.

A whistling shriek in the sky overhead made Kirk look up—a mistake—to creatures circling in the sky that were certainly not birds. Recognizable from his earliest childhood, from kids' stories and animations, animals soared overhead who were not birds, occasionally taking a pelicanlike single flap of their twenty-five-foot spans of skin stretched over bone, with skeletal arms and fingers visible through wing membranes, gracefully flexing with the thermals overhead.

Spock scanned the sky "Pterosaurs . . ."

The flying creatures cruised in and out of the artificial light, their heads shaped like a pair of Scotty's isomagnetic pliers. Their elongated pelicanlike beaks were toothless and looked heavy, off balance with their scrawny extended necks, but their flight was fluid and easy. Among them were smaller birds. Probably waiting for the pickin's.

"I thought they were extinct by now," Spock rasped.

Kirk glanced up. "Do they lay eggs?"

"I believe so . . . Why?"

"I'm hungry."

Two of the pterosaurs swooped low to have a look at the carnage, spiraling out of the sky so suddenly that Kirk broke his concentration and ducked. Perspective failed him, they were almost to the ground before he realized it. They were huge! One was ten feet in wingspan, the other over thirty feet. As their long beaks scooped at the ferns, the artificial lights startled them and they panicked. They made three or four great flaps, found a thermal, and rose again into the darkened sky.

Spock slowly brought his tricorder up. "Stunning, Captain, if we could capture one—"

"We'd eat it. Let's get out of here."

Usually Spock went about business with simple circumspection, but today his smoothness was marred by pauses and glances of concern—the worst kind. Concern about Kirk, about whether the captain would be able to go on commanding, about the pain he was forced to endure, and even about whether he would live. In spite of his own blurred senses, Kirk saw those glances and felt that concern and knew there was nothing either of them could do but slog, hack, carve their way through the unforeseeable and try to bend the situation to their needs.

He wanted to tell Spock there was no cause for worry. He couldn't.

He offered a reassuring pat on the arm and a not so polite push. "Go on, go."

Bringing up the rear made him feel better, even though he had to lean on a stick. He didn't dare try to predict what curious creatures would do and didn't want to be here when they did it.

"Rusa . . . Rusa! Look!"

"Look at what? Weeds and blood. Keep moving."

"Below us . . . someone else is here!"

"You're in the way, technicist. Let the spikers pass."

Tons of equipment had been a constant burden, much more taxing now that their number was halved. In order to make room for all the hardware, they had been forced to leave several of the antigravs behind in the future and use the spikers to haul harnessed rigs, but now there were fewer spikers and not enough antigravs to make up for them, and they grumbled by the minute for those forsaken antigravs.

So much for the joy of the innocent hunt. Healthy spikers slaughtered. Like simple animals.

"Rusa, that light is mechanical. Look down. See what I see."

Rusa was still angry about losing the other spikers, and if Oya wasn't cautious, she would be the target of that anger.

She said nothing but pointed in the correct direction and handed the magnifier to Rusa, who placed the magnifier over her eyes and waited for the automatic focus.

Holding her breath, Oya imagined what her leader was seeing. Artificial lighting implements casting a blue silver glow on the night-shaded plateau far below them, where not long ago they had paused for entertainment and ended up expending their weapons and sacrificing so many of their team.

"Terrans. Starfleet!" Rusa swung to Oya. "Did *you* give away our plans?"

Blinking, Oya looked up squarely. "Of course not."

Deprived of an argument, Rusa moved her head from side to side, searching out a better view. "The same animals that attacked our spikers are stalking them. They'll be killed, too."

"No, it won't be enough," Oya insisted. "Terrans have phasers. These have Starfleet issue. No animals can stand against that. They must be here to follow us—stop us . . . but how can they have followed? And to be here so fast, they must have come back in time *before* we did! But how could they *know* to follow?"

Her thoughts grew frantic as one piled upon the next, each with a new question attached.

"When did they come through?" She let the others shuffle past her and gazed down the slope. "The moment we went through the time device, we either succeed or fail. If we are successful, there would be no humans to follow us through. So how are the humans here? Do we fail? If we fail, no one would bother to follow us! *Why* are they here? *How* are they?"

"You think too much," Rusa grieved, glowering down the hillside at the dome of cold blue white light. "We have to send a team to kill them. Don't interrupt me again."

She swung around, away from Oya, and the colors on her painted face winked in the starlight in three panels.

Oya's questions were like flies buzzing. She was just annoying them with her struggle to understand the paradox.

The Clan had developed thought as a necessary evil, like passing waste. It had to be done, but it wasn't very satisfying. Full belly, empty mind, and not much drive beyond that.

But for the few thinkers among her people, even their simple space travel would never have been acquired, and what they had of that they had borrowed from other races. Instinct versus intelligence.

One of the other females had joined Rusa at the edge of the incline. "If they have phasers, they can destroy our machine. We have to kill them first. Send a team."

"I will," Rusa said. "Two spikers . . . and Oya goes."

Oya shoved up on her heavy hind legs. "I have to assemble the launcher!"

"These spikers can assemble it."

"Not well!"

"As long as it works. Aur and I and the other females are needed here to control the spikers. You're lame and no good to lead or carry. You'll be the leader of the attack on the Terrans."

"I'm a technicist!"

"You're a thinker. So think."

Rusa spat the word with contempt. Thinker. To sit and think. And Oya had committed the ultimate shame: she had enjoyed it. The *process* of thinking, element to element, evidence to conclusion, to extrapolation. And she had been good at it.

Rusa, Aur, and the other females didn't wait for her to choose her team. They took the packs from two spikers, argued briefly among themselves, and snapped their teeth at the spikers to make them obey this bizarre twist of plans. Now it would be only herself and two young spikers in an environment that was perfect for them.

Her desires tore in half—she watched as the females trundled off with the other spikers and their crates of precious technology. She wanted to go with them and build her machine and watch as she commited one single act that would give her civilization prominence.

Far down the hill slopes, the artificial lights were winking out. The Starfleet team was moving again.

Excitement surged through her. She was going to have the chance to hunt the most dangerous animals in the galaxy.

* * *

"This isn't a tropical holiday. We're in enemy territory. We have to act like it."

It was well after midnight as Kirk and Spock saw the soft yellow glow of the fires inside their camp. Those gentle lights looked as inviting, as civilized as the gentle lights and shadows of the *Enterprise*'s bridge.

Smoke skeined along the ceiling of their shelter, blunting against the awning of fronds they had built. McCoy, Vernon, Emmendorf, and Reenie had gone before them to the cave and had been here doing their work while Kirk and Spock gathered up their lighting implements and did a lame man's version of hurrying after.

"Captain! Here, sir!"

They angled toward Vernon's voice. Why wasn't he in the cave?

Vernon stumbled out of the tangled overgrowth.

"What's the noise for?" Kirk asked. "Give me a report."

"Aye, sir—I've been searching about fifteen minutes. No sign of 'em."

"Of who?"

"The two Klingons, sir. They pulled themselves loose and they're gone. I'm sorry, sir. I couldn't track them in this stuff." Furious, he kicked at the heavy greenery.

"Gone," Kirk impugned and glanced at Spock. "Fine Starfleet contingent. Can't even hold on to two Klingons. All right, terminate the search. Continue to fabricate weapons."

"Aye, sir! Sorry again, sir!"

"I don't want to hear it."

"Yes, sir!"

"Captain—" Spock pulled up close. "Lieutenant Bannon was in the cave with the Klingons."

"Let's go." Kirk plunged past him.

As he led Spock inside the wide opening, he was struck with a gout of scents, some from the fire over to their left, where Vernon and Reenie were cooking fish. To his right, McCoy was already elbow deep in autopsy on the slaughtered animal he'd taken a fancy to. The spilled intestines, spools of scalpeled muscle and visible white bone glistening in the firelight made the food roasting at the other fire about as appetizing as ear wax.

And at the far back of the cave, Lieutenant Bannon lay on his back, apparently conscious.

McCoy looked up from the corpse. "Jim! We were getting worried about you two. You both all right?"

Without answering, Kirk stepped to where Bannon lay.

"Lieutenant?" He thought about kneeling, but he probably wouldn't be able to get up again. "Did the Klingons hurt you?"

"I'm here, aren't I?"

"How did they get away?"

"Don't know. I was unconscious. Pulled out the stake, I guess. Lucky they didn't brain me with it."

The young man's face was pallid, his tone sandy, he wouldn't meet Kirk's eyes, and he hadn't said *sir* once.

Kirk straightened. Not exactly teatime. He motioned to Spock to come with him. They crossed to McCoy.

"Report on Bannon."

McCoy glanced up. "It was a clean wound. I cauterized it. He'll be walking by tomorrow noon."

"Doesn't sound that way."

"Well, I didn't say he was happy about it."

"What're you doing?"

"Postmortem. I'm finding some surprises, too." The doctor motioned to his medical tricorder, which was lying propped against the cave wall, clicking placidly. "I did DNA testing, but it fouled up somehow. I got ridiculous results."

"Run it again."

"Already doing that, Captain. Are you ready for the shock of your life?"

"Too late." Kirk took Spock's arm and levered himself to the ground, then motioned for Spock to sit beside him. "All right, Doctor. Make me understand."

McCoy moved his hands over the laid-open corpse of the dinosaur as a pianist caresses the white keys. "Does this animal remind you of anything, Jim?"

"Reminds me remind me of a lizard. So what?"

"It's not a lizard. Look. These are abutting scales, not overlapping ones. It's primitive skin. Primitive to us, I

271

mean. We're not looking at a crocodile here. And it's not a dinosaur either."

"Then what is it?"

"It's a dinosauroid. That's not saying it's a dinosaur. It does have a tail, but it's still bipedal." The doctor pointed at a bundle of muscles at the place where the creature's tail was attached to its spinal column. "When mammals evolved, the caudofemoralis muscles—here, the ones anchoring the tail—were replaced as the pelvis rotated. But in this animal the caudofemoralis muscle group is anchored by the tail and is used to pull the leg back in the power stroke of the running stride. What we end up with is a very powerful stride. Something similar happens in birds as a weight-saving measure. The most similar stride to us would be that of an ostrich. And look here—a four-chambered heart."

"Like a bird's," Spock put in, not hiding his infatuation.

"A bird," McCoy confirmed, engulfed in the ballad of anatomy. "And it has an air sack system on the vertebral column. This is why it doesn't sweat. This system is involved with the braincase and the vertebrae, and it's hooked into the lungs. This happens in birds, too. The arm folds like an accordion. Upper arm back, forearm forward, hand back. The legs do the same. And this large bone here, forward pointing, shaped like a pendulum . . . that's the pubis bone. But it's not set back toward the tail like a crawling animal's. It's set forward. I'd say this creature settles at rest the way a bird does."

"Doctor," Kirk bristled, "are you telling me I'm looking at a twelve-foot-long bird?"

"I'm telling you you're looking at something disturbingly similar to a cross between *yourself* and a bird. But my friend here has a tail. That means, even though it's a two-legged animal, it never had a knuckle-walking ancestor. They're not fully upright, because their 'hands' were already free to begin with. They never went through that series of evolutionary steps." He sounded delighted in a schoolroom way, at all these things he could share with a captive audience.

Kirk peered at him. "Just how do you know all this?"

McCoy spread his bloody hands. "I'm a doctor! Do you think I sent in for a mail-order certificate?"

"Sorry."

Dismissing him with a blink, McCoy swung around on his knees to lift the heavy tail. "The tail isn't just a balancing device. The whole center of gravity is right here, over the hind legs. That's for power at a full run. They're faster than we are. After all, you have to be faster than your food."

"Or have a phaser."

"Bear with me, Jim, I'm getting to something. This creature has a bulky body, which developed to support a heavy head, which supports a large brain. The neck is S shaped and maneuverable but has to be thick enough to support that head with its large brain—"

"Wait a minute," Kirk interrupted. "What's a large head got to do with a large brain? A horse has a large head, but the brain is only the size of a lemon. How do you know this thing has a big brain?"

"I looked."

"Oh."

"Look at the fingers."

"Three."

"Two," McCoy corrected, "with an opposable thumb. That thumb is *it*." He maneuvered the precious digits like a puppeteer making a marionette's joints. *"This* is what lets us develop tools, Jim. This is what built every useful commodity in history, culturally and technically, since the first deliberately lit campfire. Without this, we could have a brain the size of a basketball and not be able to make use of it."

Kirk forced himself not to press for a point. He knew one was coming. Ordinarily all this would've held his attention, but here in a sweltering cave, sick and overburdened, he found concentrating an effort. Beside him, Spock was utterly rapt by what McCoy was saying, and that was a clue to shut up and pay attention.

McCoy inched forward on his mud-caked knees to turn the animal's face toward Kirk and Spock. "The brow ridge is more typical of primitive evolution. Most intelligent races eventually lose the bone crest over the eyes because we don't need protection from our friend's tails while we go after prey."

Kirk pointed at the animal's aft end. "But this still has a tail."

"Exactly."

"Most upright hominids bear the lingering traits of devolved tails, specifically a tail bone," Spock assisted. "Humans, Klingons, Rigelians—"

"And Vulcans," McCoy added joyously. The doctor lifted the animal's beautiful but mutilated head, its broken skull and snaggle-toothed mouth resting pliantly in his hands. "The muzzle is pushed downward slightly," he said as he ran a finger down his own nose. "Like ours. That indicates priority to the vision. And the brain sits back, also like ours, to allow for better positioning of the eyes. Jim, this is binocular vision. This is a highly evolved element! It suggests that vision is more important to them than olfactory ability. And the bright skin colors back that up. It suggests they're visually oriented, like birds and primates."

"Then we can sneak up on them," Kirk concluded.

McCoy wagged his free hand in frustration. "That's not my point, Captain!"

"Then what is!"

"All right, all right . . ." Hesitation clouded McCoy's response. His eyes grew troubled, his mouth pressed and drawn, but finally he folded his arms, ignoring the messy stuff on his hands while professionally managing to keep most of it off his shirt. "Jim, all this adds up to something that doesn't make sense. They're so much like us . . . the right eyes, the right thumb, the right evolutionary priorities."

Kirk gazed at one of the few people in the galaxy he trusted as much as he trusted himself, and his brow furrowed. "Go ahead, Bones. Say what you think."

Struggle showed in McCoy's eyes. "If I wasn't in this place," he said slowly, "in this time, I'd have to conclude that I'm looking at an advanced being, with culture, with communication, and with science. Nobody painted this animal's face. It painted itself."

Chapter Twenty-eight

"ARE YOU TRYING to tell me," Kirk incited, "that on a planet stuffed to the gun'ls with dinosaurs, you've found an *advanced* being?"

"Well, *we're* here, aren't we?" McCoy twisted the statement with irony.

"We don't look like the other dinosaurs, Doctor. This thing does. Are you trying to kill me just so I can turn over in my grave?"

McCoy shook his head at the argumentative truth but refused to apologize. "Jim, it's about the size we are, five to seven feet tall, a hundred eighty pounds or so. I'd say that's the physiological average. Think about it, gentlemen . . . the right size for space travel. Large enough to mine and manipulate ore, yet small enough to fit in a spacecraft that can break out of gravitational pull."

Kirk felt the tight rack of his brow. He turned to Spock. "So why didn't you think of this?"

The Vulcan actually broke into an expression of surprise. "Why didn't I—?"

"Follow that line of logic and see what you get. What about the trace of refined metal you found? And the acrylic pigment on their faces? Are these better clues than we think?"

"If we follow this line of logic," Spock picked up, "binocular vision would provide them with greater depth perception. Therefore they can be more proficient in tool use. It also suggests that technology is more critical to their civilization now than hunting, despite their savage appearance."

"Right," McCoy said.

Kirk leaned forward. "You think this animal could actually come from somewhere else? Another planet?"

Here, McCoy stopped having the answers. His brow furrowed, his folded his arms again and sat back on his knees, gazing down at the sliced-up creature that was starting to smell up their cave. "I don't *think* so . . ."

"Why not?"

"Because of the DNA of this thing."

"You're running the analysis again—you said it fouled up."

"Yes . . . and I'll give you my report as soon as I can."

"Make it sooner than that."

Noticing Spock and McCoy glancing at each other with those looks of concern that he appreciated but really didn't like, Kirk rolled onto one knee, put his hand out for them to help him to his feet, and when he was up withdrew his hand as if to claim independence.

"Get back to work. Food, weapons, and answers. That's what we need, gentlemen. And at this point, I'd be hard pressed to tell you which we need most."

Spock nodded. "Yes, sir."

"I'm getting some fresh air." Kirk stepped past them without giving anyone a chance to ask if he should be going outside alone.

The night was tar black. Usually, he enjoyed the black sky, the stars. Some had accused him of going to space so he could see the stars all the time. Well, there were stars. Lots of them.

The sky. The empty sky. Before him, the jungle was midnight green, sizzling with insects.

And there was something moving out there.

"Spock . . ."

Holding himself stock still, leaning on his stick, Kirk waited until he felt a living warmth brush against his arm, then raised that arm sharply to stop Spock and hold him against the false protection of the rock wall.

Knotted, Kirk nodded significantly out into the jungle foliage to their middle left. Staying still, Spock didn't need to look very long.

"Followed us," Kirk very quietly observed.

"Tenacity," Spock commented. "Could be a sign of intelligence. Most predators are frugal. They give up and pursue easier prey before their energies are exhausted."

Kirk shook his head. "There's more. They made a significant kill today. Enough to feed ten times their number for days. So why are they stalking us?"

"I don't know . . . prudence, possibly?"

"Instinct isn't prudent, Mr. Spock, it acts on the moment. There's more going on here than survival."

"What do you think it is, Captain?"

"I think . . . curiosity." He buried a shiver.

Spock took his arm, firmly drawing him inside toward the fire. "Would be well to avoid them in any case, Captain. If you will please sit down . . ."

"Have Vernon stand guard at the entrance."

"Mr. Vernon," Spock summoned.

"Sir!" The tall kid unfolded himself from his sitting position and bolted to attention. "Yes, sir!"

"As you were. Stand guard outside the entrance. Notify us if you see anything moving in the foliage—anything at all. Take nothing for granted. Do not fire your phaser unless your life is threatened. Is that clear?"

"Aye aye, sir!"

"Dismissed."

Vernon dashed outside, so fast he probably scared off the things they'd sent him out there to guard against.

Inside, the cave had become a department store. In one section, Bannon was recuperating, sitting up now, staring at the jungle. In another, Reenie was trying to rig a crude slingshot. On the mezzanine, Emmendorf was scaling a big sturgeon. On the fire near him, some kind of acorns or nuts were merrily roasting on a flat rock in the middle of the flames, and a sizable chunk of animal meat—Kirk had no idea what kind—was cooking on a spit rigged between two Y-shaped sticks in the ground. Well, they wouldn't starve.

He made his way to the girl, reached down, and scooped up one of the slingshots. Ignoring the grating of his joints, he swung the sling in his hand, testing the weight.

"Balance is off," he said.

Reenie looked up as if she'd just been told her newborn infant was ugly. "Oh, I'm sorry, sir."

"I didn't say it wouldn't work. But this piece of wood is too short. Whoever fires this will have to know how to compensate."

"I'll start over, sir."

"Good. What else have we got?"

"Oh—um . . . we got some primitive high-glucose grain and we're mashing it . . . Over here is a yeasty organism, and Dr. McCoy had an accelerant we can use to distill it. We're boiling out the alcohol. With some hollowed-out pieces of wood, we can make little Molotov cocktails. Mr. Spock got an idea to dissolve some silver in nitric acid—"

"Precipitate it as silver chloride," Kirk said. "Any source of salt will work. But it'll have to be done in the dark or it'll reduce back to silver. Then you add ammonia—"

"Dr. McCoy had some of that, too. We can make silver amiochloride and dry it."

"Yes, it dries to silver azide. Remember it's a contact explosive. Scratch it, and it blows. Don't let anyone touch it without being very careful. Where'd you get the silver?"

She wagged her bare fingers. "My wedding ring, sir."

Sadly, Kirk grinned at her. "That's valiant, Ensign."

"Captain?" It was McCoy, holding his medical tricorder in both hands. "If you have a moment, I've got the confirmed DNA results."

Kirk looked down at Reenie. "Continue what you're doing, Ensign."

He hated being responsible for a woman in this uncivilized place, especially one so young, who should have a future. He shouldn't have brought her. He hated to see women die.

He shuffled to McCoy. "Go ahead, Bones. Spock, over here."

"Don't you want to sit down?" McCoy asked, stalling.

"No. Go ahead."

"Well . . . I don't know how explain this. This flies in the face of everything I said before. I don't know what to do."

"Tell me. I'll do something about it."

"Jim . . . the . . ." He pointed to the dead dinosauroid on their camp floor. "The DNA of this animal points conclusively to Earth roots. Despite all the anatomical evidence I gave you before, this creature's ancestry is from this planet."

"How do you know?"

"There are certain key indicators," McCoy said, sparing the jargon. "I can take your DNA and the DNA of a porcupine and find out that neither of you is a Klingon. If I have the planet's microbiology, I can tell you which planet you're from. Just don't give me Spock's—"

"Are you that sure?"

"I'd like to say I'm *not* sure, but I'm standing in the middle of about eighty billion gross tons of DNA that exactly matches this animal's." He gestured to the great outdoors, then back at the corpse on their floor. "This thing is from Earth."

The cave was heavy with smoke from the cooking fires and thick with the stench of the dead dinosauroid sprawled across a quarter of the floor space. The revelation they'd just had did nothing to perfume the bizarre.

Spock's face was troubled. "I must disagree, Doctor. I accept your autopsy results. There can't possibly be so large a gap in the fossil record as to allow for this creature's existence here and now. This animal cannot possibly be from Earth sixty million years ago. It has highly advanced traits that simply cannot have developed here yet."

McCoy angled at him. "And the moon has a man's face, Spock. Given millions of monkeys, nature will eventually invent a typewriter."

"Captain," Spock persisted, "there is a third possibility, which I find galling."

Defiantly the doctor stepped closer. "Which is?"

"That we're a million years too late, that's what," Kirk interrupted. "We just watched thousands of animals like these go by on the Guardian's screen *after* the change. If we're late, we're sunk."

Petulance came off in his tone, but he didn't try to stop it. If he was staring at an ugly truth, then the others would have to look at it, too. He limped across the cave, casting a grudgeful glance from wall to wall.

"Jim." Spock followed him and came around in front of him, not grim, but earnest. "You're right, of course. However, we have dealt with the Guardian before. It tends to send travelers on the same currents and eddies. Chances are fair that we've been deposited in the correct area as the situation demands."

Kirk looked at him and snapped, "A guess, Mr. Spock." He heard the harshness in his words. "But I'll take your 'fair chance' over anybody else's sure thing," he added. "Could that be it, Spock? Could we be too late?"

Deep trouble grooved Spock's face. "If I could set up two correspondant tricorders to—"

"Captain! Sir!" Vernon surged back inside with his phaser drawn. "Something's coming through the trees, sir! Right toward us!"

Without giving him acknowledgment, Kirk swung around.

"Ensign Reenie, let's have those weapons. Quickly, quickly. Attention, everyone. All hands . . . battle stations!"

Chapter Twenty-nine

MOVEMENT IN THE jungle gallery, thunder in the wings. Every tiny sound, insect, footfall, was deafening, enormous.

Crunching through a carpet of deadwood, cycads pricking their thighs, they went into the deep gray shadows with shoulders hunched and phaser hands leading. Flanked by Spock and Vernon, Kirk struggled to stay a step or two ahead of them. Reenie was right behind them.

He thrust his phaser outward. "Hold it!"

Behind, his crew stopped and held position. Laughing too hard to move probably. He'd just told a dinosaur to hold it.

His reputation was saved when a rough voice came out of the midnight jungle. "I have no weapon."

Well, at least the dinosaur was cooperating. In English?

Vernon plunged forward two steps, straddled a fern with both legs flexed, thrust his own phaser out with both fists and shouted, "Starfleet Security! Get your hands up!"

"My hands are up."

"Come forward! No tricks!"

"I possess no tricks . . ."

Not English. A translator's echo—Klingon with an English echo.

Kirk moved to his right, toward Spock, and let the Security man do what he did best. Vernon ticked off a few seconds, then plunged into the ferns and came out with a rumpled but recognizable character.

"Roth," Kirk prompted. "Welcome back. Ensign Reenie,

take charge of the prisoner. Mr. Spock, Mr. Vernon, secure the area for the other Klingon. Be careful and stay together."

"Very well, sir," Spock said, and both were suddenly gone.

Even in the dimness Roth's face was scored with scratches from plants and thorns. His chin was lowered, but he gazed up at Kirk with a roguish languor.

The captain peered back. "So you missed us. Where's your friend?"

"He was never my friend. He was my commander. I was compelled to serve with him."

"Where is he now?"

"Killed by an animal. Out there."

"What kind of animal?"

"A terrible one."

Suddenly Roth stopped walking and turned sharply to him. "Kirk—"

"Move along!" The girl held her phaser to the Klingon's cheek, but he ignored her.

"At ease, Ensign," Kirk allowed.

Roth pushed toward him a step. "Kirk, you understand me. We have spoken honestly to each other. I have realized I can't survive in this world. I do not know how you brought me here or why, but I do not wish to spend my life out there alone. If I swear not to act against you, . . . will you promise not to stake me down again?"

Beneath the sense of bluff and tactical suspicions charged between them was an undeniable quiver of truth. Kirk caught it, just a glimpse, like a tiny red lizard ducking under a leaf. But there had been a falter in Roth's voice, a hesitation that may have been deceit.

Kirk tapped his instincts, experience, his own talent as a rascal wire-puller to interpret what he was seeing and hearing. If there was a scheme here, it was deep laid and subtle. He couldn't read Roth like other Klingons he'd known. This wasn't the kind of Klingon he was used to, but a whole new batch. A Klingon who differentiated between enemies, allies, and *non*enemies. *You are not my enemy.*

"I won't stake you down," Kirk said. "But I want your

promise as a soldier. You and I both know how important that is to men like us."

"One more thing . . ."

"Yes?"

Letting his head sag, Roth sighed, "Have you got any food? I have found nothing I dare eat. Nothing but animals that spit and trees with needles growing from them and plants that swallow whole insects! What kind of planet is this? I know how to survive in open space, but not on . . . parasitical shrubbery!"

"Yes, we have food," Kirk said. "In fact, you may find you've never eaten better in your life."

Spock and Vernon appeared as Kirk drew his prisoner out from the fronds.

"Area's secure, sir," Vernon reported. "No sign of the other one."

"Very good. Carry on."

"Captain," Spock began, staying far enough from the Klingon, "my science tricorder holds a base encyclopedia of information on general Earth prehistory and history from the Office of the Federation Direction of Archives . . . physics, biology, paleogeology, as you requested. With your permission I'll attempt to merge information in this unit with that history that we recorded passing on the screen of the Guardian."

"Yes, Spock. More than anything we have to find out who changed history, and how they did it."

Spock lowered the tricorder and fell into a more relaxed pose. "Perhaps this would be an opportune time for you to rest. Perhaps eat."

"I will. Don't worry. Go on."

But Spock was worried. It showed on his face without rein. As Reenie and Vernon ushered the prisoner to one side of the shelter, drawing him along despite his horror at the shriven corpse on the floor, Spock ushered Kirk inside so McCoy could take over. The one subject upon which Spock and McCoy trusted each other was Jim Kirk, and he knew that. Spock couldn't give him orders but knew McCoy could. It made Kirk angry at his condition, belligerent against treatment, as if that would help. The weakness was harder this afternoon to will against than it had been this morning. He was in almost constant discomfort now that McCoy couldn't afford to be free with the painkillers.

Inside, the aromas were thick, the fires still crackling, and that corpse beginning to fester. He thought about telling McCoy to get rid of it but knew the doctor would've done that already if he were finished with the thing. Apparently McCoy still wasn't happy with that DNA conclusion.

The doctor showed up immediately to take Kirk from Spock, and the two of them looked at each other with that plying worry that made him feel too far out of the picture.

"All right, gentlemen, as you were," he rumbled, pushing them both back a step, and they broke it up.

As Spock turned away, McCoy handed Kirk a ground-out rock with a heavy glazed liquid in the middle.

"Boiled-down tree sap," the doctor said. "Sugar content. Eat it."

Kirk took the rock and sniffed at the concoction. "What do I do—pour it on the roasted acorns?"

"If you want to define those as acorns, be my guest. It's not bad on the pond-lily roots either."

"All right, I'll go over here."

The Klingon was picking at a fish tail. Out of the whole sturgeon, he wanted the tail? He looked up as Kirk sat down.

"So," Roth said. "Do you dine with enemies?"

"What we are to each other," Kirk told him, "time will tell. But we're not enemies. You said it yourself."

"Then why do you run with a Vulcan?"

Kirk remained passive. "He's my friend."

Roth paused. "The Vulcan way is childish. They fought the Empire and won but retreated instead of pursuing. Retreated! They didn't win. They only made sure we didn't win! Is that any way to fight a war? I do not respect them."

"You did once. Enough to try to get the Klingons and the Romulans talking. Maybe it failed, but your idea was on the right track. The Vulcans are united, adaptable, and in spite of their claims of total peace, they're good fighters. They stood up for themselves, and your empire couldn't fight a two-front war."

"Their only wrong tactic was failure to press advantage," Roth said. "After each attack, instead of striking the weak spot, they simply sat back and waited for the next attack."

Putting his "plate" down on his swollen knee, Kirk leaned forward. "It was a Romulan—*romuluSngan*—spy who betrayed you, not the Vulcans."

Roth stopped eating also and shook his head. "I don't like you, Captain. I don't like you at all."

"Then tell me, how does a pilot become a Spear?"

The Klingon paused again but seemed relieved that the subject of the personal had been forgiven for a moment.

"There are no ceremonies, no rituals, no good-bye . . . The greatest honor is to tell no one. The honor is depleted by letting anyone know you are walking dead."

"Why wouldn't you want your family's support?"

"It is a shame to tell. We can't give it away—"

"Because morale is crucial to your people. Isn't that right?"

Roth peered at him, then shrugged. "I really don't like you."

Kirk deliberately didn't say anything, letting the silence pressure the Klingon.

"We are a society that survives," Roth said. "That is all we do. It is how we raise our children, how we use our resources, everything. There is nothing left except the necessities of survival." He looked out at the sky, remembering. "The dying was not so hard, but to remain silent was harder than I expected. To know I was seeing each of my family for the last time . . . but I couldn't give it away, or my family would remember me that way and my act would be a selfish one."

"But *why* did you volunteer?" Kirk pressed. "You're healthy, strong, young enough. Why sacrifice yourself?"

For a moment Kirk thought the Klingon was choking on his roots and fishtails, but that wasn't it. Roth had stopped dead in his confessions and couldn't seem to go on.

Kirk simply gazed at him as if they'd known each other twenty years. He could get Spock to open up this way, too, if his timing were right. Just that stare. Nose down a little, lips pursed, brows up, eyes just right.

Roth sighed. The anger flushed from his face. "War is the only way. Fight enemies, then fight friends. Someone will always want what another has. The teachings of Surak only function if all agree. The only place where all agree," he said, "is *on* Vulcan."

His mouth turned hard. He stared at the ground between his feet, raised the fish tail to his teeth and ripped it in half.

"Excuse me, Captain." McCoy stepped in. "Eat this, please."

He handed Kirk a weed.

Kirk looked at it without taking it. "What's that?"

"Few million years from now, I think it'll be a foxglove."

"Why am I eating it?"

"My medical tricorder indicates this contains digitalis and I want you to have a dose. It'll serve as a facsimile for some more refined medication. Now, be careful and only eat what I give you. Too much of it would be poisonous, and you're poisoned enough."

"We couldn't skip this step?"

"No."

Without waiting to be dismissed, McCoy dismissed himself.

Roth watched him go. "Being wounded," he said, "is inconvenient."

Biting off a leaf, Kirk chewed it like tobacco. "Don't change the subject."

"We are enemies in your time," Roth said abruptly. "I have seen it in your eyes from the start. You are like us, yet you hate us. What are my people to you, Captain?"

"In our 'time,' your people and mine have struck an agreement. Because of that, the Klingons have prospered despite being hemmed in."

"You hemmed them in?"

"Yes, we did. They're combative and imperialistic. The cooperative nations of the Federation had to establish a neutral zone as a buffer and allow the Klingons to prosper as long as they don't encroach upon the rights of anybody else. There's even an element of commerce. I showed you the pictures."

Roth huffed at him. "Healthy Klingons, many children, clothing like yours . . . big ships with light in the corridors —it is a fantasy."

"It's no fantasy. It's my reality. My Klingons have a martial culture, but there's peace for everyone through our strength. Gradually they're doing business outside their culture, and it works for everybody. You see life as punishment—that's what constant war has done to your civilization. There's been nothing to hold back your butchery of each other. I'd become a Spear, too, if that was all I had to live for."

He shoved the rock off his knee. Melted tree sap oozed into the sand.

"If you don't believe me," he insisted, "tell me why I would bother to fake all this instead of just killing you?"

They stared at each other.

Slowly the animosity flowed out of Roth's eyes. His shoulders settled. Leaning over, he scooped up the rock with Kirk's tree sap trickling out and ran a finger along the edge to stop the spilling, then handed the questionable delicacy back to him.

"It is a good question," he said.

Kirk took the rock. "Is the answer any good?"

Roth picked at his fish, took a bite, chewed, spat out about half of it. "On Vulcan I was a treaty monitor. I came to respect them before I discovered the truth. Before they lied to me. Their talk of peace showed itself in battle. They cut our fleet down without second thought."

Pushing, Kirk undergirded, "But . . ."

Roth twitched. "But they . . . Vulcans have families. They don't die young, they have other interests . . . They live for more than just survival. They talked to me about diversity and pacifism. I believed them. I tried to change the Klingon pattern. It came to disaster when my truce was betrayed. My leaders said contamination was too strong in me. They took me away from Vulcan, lowered my position. They turned on the Vulcans, and the Vulcans hammered them back."

"You were drummed out?"

"What?"

"Stripped of rank, kicked out."

"A trained pilot? Never. I could disembowel the emperor and I would still fly. I was . . . disgraced. My family was in shame. No one would speak to them."

"Why should you pay so much for a good effort?" Kirk said with a shrug. "Intermediaries have been trying and failing throughout history."

Suddenly Roth's eyes flared and he looked up. *"Your* history, not mine! The Vulcans are liars! They kept me from the most important factor—that their ways are planetbound and cannot survive in diversity! Pacifism works only if all are the *same!"*

He cranked around and fiercely glared across the cave at Spock, who was working with the two tricorders.

Spock stopped in place, poised in case the Klingon turned that expression into an attack.

There was caution but not revelation in Spock's face. Kirk knew these things weren't a surprise to his first officer. The preachings of the long-dead pacifist philosopher Surak hadn't pulled Spock away from Kirk's side nor from Christopher Pike's before him.

Kirk seized Roth's meaty upper arm and dug his fingers in. "Leave him alone," he ordered. With the grip he forced the Klingon to break off his sizzling accusations across the cave.

Roth hunched his shoulders and he turned his back on Spock.

Keenly, Spock met Kirk's eyes with bottled thanks, then made a point of attending to his tricorders.

"My people did not stop fighting among themselves until we found someone else to fight," Roth said, caustic now. "If the Spear tactic works and we defeat the *romuluSngan,* we will turn on the Vulcans. When they are gone, we will turn on each other. If the *romuluSngan* defeat us, then they will be the ones who doom the Vulcans. What difference does it make? Already *romuluSngan* ships fire on others of their own kind, scrabbling like animals over scraps. And when the scraps begin to disappear, each will fight harder to be the one who brings in the last scrap. Like us, Captain, the war is all that holds them together. When it goes, they will murder each other out of habit. And in their death throes they will slaughter all who are enslaved until not a living thing breathes. I became a Spear to reclaim what shred of dignity was left to me. I wanted to find a way to kill myself by hurting my enemy, to die with respect. But I did not die. When I tried to escape, I was going to find a way to kill myself, because I wanted to die."

Looking up at Kirk now, Roth no longer hesitated to meet the captain's trenchant eyes. He bent forward until his elbows rested upon his knees, and he clasped his hands.

"I would slit a thousand throats," he said, "for one day of peace."

"All hands, front and center."

The crew was nervous beneath their fatigue. Sweltering heat sapped their energy, yet they were jumpy. They'd done a bellywhop into the past and now all their muscles hurt and their minds were working like sailors on the zero-four-hundred bow watch—nothing to stare but eternity stretched out before them and no way to rest.

Blanketed by the rising stench of the wood fires and the dead dinorsauroid, they gathered around the log where their captain was sitting.

"Mr. Spock, go ahead."

Spock stood beside him. His voice filled the cave. "We have a working, incomplete theory regarding our situation: we are on Earth, sixty to seventy million years before our own time. Fauna is consistent with the summer months of the Cretaceous era, southeastern North America, in the vicinity of southern Georgia along the spine of what will eventually become the Appalachian Mountain chain. All is as it should be," he said and paced to the corpse on the floor, "except for this animal. Despite appearances, this animal is not consistent with biped development in this era, but is several million years beyond that. The pigment on the creature's face is acrylic paint, certainly not available in the late Cretaceous. These inconsistencies give us reason to suspect contamination by other advanced beings than ourselves. Confirmation of that is our new objective."

"Thank you," Kirk said. "Strange as it may seem, this is *good* news. We've been looking for a focal point in time and we guessed it was the asteroid, but we weren't sure. Now we've found advanced beings who don't belong here any more than we do. That means they're here for a specific purpose. It also means we still have a chance to stop them. But keep in mind, if there are other advanced beings out there, then we're a target. Any questions?"

He hoped there would be a few. For some reason the silence was nettlesome.

"When dawn comes, we'll fan out. Work in pairs. Mr. Emmendorf, take the first guard watch outside. Don't stray far."

"Aye aye, sir."

Pushing to his feet and leaning on his stick, Kirk hobbled around the dead animal, glancing at McCoy and implying with his eyes that it was really time to get rid of this thing. He made his way to where Bannon sat huddled at a fire. "Mr. Bannon, do you consider yourself fit for duty?" Kirk handed a communicator down to him.

But the lieutenant didn't take the communicator. Didn't even look at it. "Who cares?"

Bannon's hair was matted with sweat, soggy red spikes clawing at his eyes. Firelight glinted off the white of his cheeks. His shoulders were hunched forward.

"Lieutenant," Kirk said, "you will address me as 'sir.'"

Bannon's sweat-stung eyes flipped up. "Go to hell."

The air in the cave electrified. Kirk felt the prickle of the crew's eyes. And the Klingon was watching, too. Insubordination was a nasty thing. It made him itch.

He stepped back a pace. "Get on your feet, Lieutenant."

The focus of all the others was on him. He didn't care. His only attention was on the discipline drying to dust before him.

Favoring his injured thigh with considered drama, the unshaven lieutenant slowly got up. Every movement rotting with melancholia, Bannon wagged his arms at his sides in one bitter, languorous shrug.

"So I'm on my feet. What do you want?"

For the first time Kirk noticed that Bannon was a good ten inches taller than he was. But he wasn't ten inches madder.

"I want you to obey the Starfleet Code of Conduct as applying to officers," Kirk said.

"Who cares?" Bannon said. "We're going to die in this moldy sewer. You can't get us back and Starfleet's not coming to rescue us."

Jim Kirk met his young officer's melted mood fiber by fiber with his own doggedness. He had no old-world recourse of lashings or keelhauling. Usually there was no trouble keeping the devotion of a starship crew, who considered service as much privilege as duty. If insubordination appeared, it was on a much lower level than the starship's bridge, shown to officers of the deck, bosuns, watch leaders, or even bunkmates. The crew themselves kept each other in line before irritation could siphon all the way to the bridge.

"Lieutenant," he said, "we *are* Starfleet."

Bannon's right eye flinched, and he blinked. His hands flexed, but there was no other movement.

Kirk squared off and braced both legs. His cane pirouetted and hit the dirt.

"All right," he said. "I'm lame, I'm feverish, weak, drugged, and overworked. If you think you can take me, mister . . . there's no better time."

Jim Kirk said his piece and stood waiting, muscular arms slightly flexed, chin up a little, ready to take the punch he'd dared be thrown.

Bannon swallowed hard, then again and again, until he seemed to be sucking on rocks. Everything was finished for him. He had achieved a scientist's paradise and hated it. The massiveness of the past was overwhelming him. And now he had insulted and threatened a senior officer. It didn't get any worse than that.

So he dumped his commission on the cave floor and pitched a roundhouse right at his captain.

He'd as well have launched a paper plane. The punch he threw was predictable, sketched on page one of every boxing manual in the UFP, and the easiest to dodge.

The boy's height betrayed him. Kirk's compact stature along with his brawler's scrapbook of lower-deck vendettas let him recoil just right. He slid under Bannon's twenty-foot arm, rabbit-punched him in the ribs, concentrating the power of his whole weight into the five-inch square of his fist. Then he pulled back to see the effect.

Bannon's eyeballs were halfway across the cave, his face purple as a grape. He staggered back two steps, one elbow drawn inward to his ribs, hands knotted. There would be no second swing. Bannon was done with defiance.

"Captain, we're being attacked!"

Ah, beautiful distraction.

Emmendorf stumbled toward them, one finger wagging at the midnight jungle. "Sir—sir! Like Mr. Spock said!"

The stocky Security man swallowed and pointed, but that was all he could get out that made any sense.

Outside there were sounds of phaser fire.

"Acknowledged. Go on," he said to Emmendorf. As the Security man charged back outside, Kirk turned back to Bannon. "I'll give you two seconds to decide whether you want to be in my crew anymore. Either take another swing at me or get out there and do your job."

Ignoring the humming crackle of shots in the jungle, Kirk refused to dismiss one emergency for another.

Bannon shivered, his tongue pressed up against his teeth, both elbows tight to his hammered body now.

Scooping up an armload of their contrived weapons, Kirk shoved them into Bannon's arms. "You're on report. Get moving. Roth, stay here. McCoy, make sure he does."

As Kirk veered away, Spock shoved the cane into his

hand, and they both plunged for the cave mouth, toward phaser shots whistling through the magnolias.

In the rush of battle Kirk forgot his enfeeblement and drove himself into fighting posture, head low, eyes searching for his crew as they defended themselves with their phasers.

Green lances spewed through the foliage, casting a green flickering light on wide dark leaves, set fire to the fronds, and turned ferns into smoking flakes.

Something was wrong about this. The neon green streaks fell quiet, then started up again. A lot of energy . . . Whoever was shooting didn't care about using up their weapons.

"Spock!"

"Yes, Captain, I see."

"Answers our question, doesn't it?"

"Yes, it does."

They crouched together briefly. Starfleet issue weapons emitted a red-orange lance of phased light, different from any others, from Klingon, Romulan, or any other known destructive handheld energy emitters. But these streaks were neon green, right off a peacock's tail.

He leaned toward Spock. "Numbers?"

"Shots are coming from two distinct directions, sir. Possibly three. Firing seems arbitrary . . . possibly an attempt to frighten us."

"Let them think it's working. Take the left flank."

They melted away from each other into the scaly bushes.

"Vernon!" Kirk called. "Have you got the alcohol grenades?"

"Got'm, sir!"

"No better time than now. Let's introduce ballistic chemistry to the Cretaceous era. Commence firing, Mr. Vernon."

Vernon bent down. Before him lay a wooden catapult about the size of a man's folded leg, and beside it eight plant stalks sliced into cylinders and standing like a little brown infantry. Each wore a tufted hat of dried moss. Not very big, but they didn't have to be.

Setting the miniature catapult, Vernon fitted one of the plant stalks into the launcher, then clumsily tried to ignite the dried moss with the tip of his hand phaser's boost injector. The phaser clicked but didn't spark the moss. Self-conscious, Vernon hunched his shoulders and kept trying.

"What setting have you got it on?" Kirk asked, empathizing with the nervous young man.

"Stun select, sir," Vernon squawked.

"Go to disrupt select. Keep your face away."

"Oh—yes, sir."

He flinched when the phaser sparked. The moss caught fire and burned enthusiastically.

"Get rid of it," Kirk urged.

For a horrible second Vernon fumbled with the catapult, then found the catch and tripped it. The rubber thong holding the flexed branch that would do the shooting, in real life a tourniquet from McCoy's all-knowing medikit, did its job as if preordained. The catapult jumped, the thong flipped, and the flaming stalk soared through the foliage to unfortunately smash into one of the twenty-foot palmetto trunks. The stalk busted into shards, the hastily distilled alcohol inside ignited, and the tree was set on fire.

The flash illuminated a dinosauroid face. Yellow and red paint flickered and the shapes of the elongated face and bladelike teeth glittered.

"Adjust your aim," Kirk snapped. "Two degrees higher."

The second volley flew through the leaves in a bright arch through the darkness, seemed for an instant to disappear, then flashed near the ground. Their reward was an agonized howl.

"Got'm!" Vernon chirped.

"Keep firing. Drive them back."

"Aye, sir."

Together they tracked sounds, motion, and those green lancets.

When they were down to two cocktails, Kirk motioned Vernon to cease fire. "Good shots. Move in."

Vernon grabbed a four-foot javelin and scratched into a run, parting a stand of shrubby preoaks with the bulbs of his shoulders. Like an offensive lineman the Security man dodged stumpy ten-foot plant trunks that would've cheerfully taken his skin off and charged one of the big attackers with a fervor that made his captain proud.

Kirk shuddered at the sight. Vernon was unprotected from the whipping tail and crescent-shaped hacking claws, going after that huge animal with nothing but a four-foot javelin.

Vernon swung at the beast's head, made contact, and put a five-inch furrow in the animal's neck with the javelin blade. Blood sheeted down the animal's long neck to its shoulder.

Starfleet's Security team was the best trained in the settled galaxy, capable of wrestling down any other humanoid. But they weren't bullfighters. They weren't trained for this. Vernon went after the animal's eyes and was knocked back by a whip-crack of the thick tail. He staggered up and braced the javelin above his head in both hands. He charged, made a jump, and forced the javelin sideways into the dinosauroid's mouth. Digging his toes into the dusty slab, Vernon crammed forward, a hand on either side of the creature's enormous snaggled mouth, pushing angrily on the two ends of the javelin.

The dinosauroid gargled and twisted against the pressure Vernon put on its mouth. Bringing its long hands forward, it gripped Vernon around the body as if dancing. If it dug those claws in or punctured his lungs with those opposable thumbs—

"Vernon, use your phaser!" Kirk shouted.

Vernon grimaced in the middle of the hand-to-hand fighting. "Don't worry, sir, I won't use it!"

Kirk took a breath to shout again, but there was no chance. The dinosauroid cranked its neck hard to one side, tipping Vernon almost completely over on his head. The javelin fell from its mouth, and Vernon hit the ground and rolled, still clinging to the wooden shaft.

Kirk whipped his own phaser up, but there was too much movement for a narrow phaser beam. If he switched to wider beam, he'd take out his own man. The Security guard was already back on his feet, viciously slashing his short spear, whipping it in both hands like a club, not knowing how to make the sharpened point work in his favor against an animal whose head and teeth reached out farther than its hands. The dinosauroid moved in on him, caught the javelin in its teeth, and snapped the wood to splinters.

"Vernon!" Kirk called again. "Use your phaser!"

"Yes, sir!" the man called, but he kept slashing with the frayed end of the stick.

"Get out of the way!" Kirk attempted, trying again to get a clear shot, but Vernon parried and jumped between him and the dinosauroid. "Vernon! Down! Down!"

Where was Spock? Any tree trunk could've been a crouching man or another of those animals waiting to attack.

He moved his bad leg under him but didn't dare stand up. He couldn't move fast enough in this condition to duck a shot or defend his crewmen. Vernon was down, a lifeless rag on the slab, with the dinosauroid's wide foot pressing him to the hard ground. As the animal aimed its toothy snout and began a move that would've ripped Vernon's head off, three arrows thunked into its thick neck just below its jaw.

It roared and shook its head, raising both arms to pull at the thick stalks embedded in its neck.

Kirk craned to see where the arrows had come from—that's where Spock would be, with Emmendorf and Reenie. Where Bannon was, he had no idea, and the thought flickered that the humiliated lieutenant might have run away.

Bringing up his phaser again, Kirk took aim through the trees at the dinosauroid. The head was coming up and down, in and out of the shadow as the creature dug at the short arrows in its throat and screamed in frustration. He held his fire.

"Move, move," he muttered, holding the phaser in both hands, waiting for a clear shot. If the animal were in physical contact with Vernon, a phaser hit could suck the downed man away, too. He couldn't risk that.

"Left flank!" he shouted. "Charge!"

As he came into the open, flanked by two fern-topped

trunks as thick around as he was, a bright green flash blinded him.

Everything around him exploded. His body was throttled by flying tree scales that tore at his arms and face. The earth turned drunkenly, trees danced, and the ground came up to meet him.

Chapter Thirty

"DON'T FIRE! Don't fire! Hold your fire! Idiots!" Oya shrieked at the spikers, but they weren't listening. The two males had come barreling out of the bushes toward the enemy outpost, drawn by the scent of smoke, cooking fish, and dead flesh. If they weren't held back, the smell of blood would drive them wild and she would have no hope at all of controlling them.

The spikers were lathered, moving on the imperative with princelike unrestraint, jumping beautifully, ducking, charging, making perfect targets. Children! Males!

They had never fought against Starfleet before. They would give away in seconds that there were only the three of them. Their attack would dissolve against opponents of this caliber.

The air detonated a few strides from her, a barbaric flash that frightened her into falling back. Paces away, one of the spikers fell back, too, blinking and desperately scraping hot sparks from his face. Cautiously lifting her head, Oya sniffed at the air. Alcohol. Where in this jungle had the Starfleet people found alcohol? While Rusa and those other fools had been playing games with local animals and being slaughtered for it, the Starfleeters had scraped an explosive out of the past!

Clang—a stone-bladed weapon fell against the barrel of an energy pistol, and Oya turned in time to see one of the humans charge a spiker with some sort of spear. The spiker's energy pistol flew out of his grip and skidded into the moss. The other humans were shouting, driving the spiker back. He had allowed himself to be pressed up against the opening of the humans' camp, and now he was paying for it in having no room to maneuver.

Leveling her own weapon, Oya selected a target: the Vulcan among them. He was an officer, a commander, and his loss would debilitate them.

All at once, across the breadth of the cavern mouth, she saw a glint of amber gold illuminated by the flash of another alcohol bomb. Oya scoured her memory for Starfleet color codes. Amber—

Their captain! If she could cut his legs off, slice him in half, the enemy team would be crushed. Humans were nothing without their leaders, without ancestors and histories on which to stack their confidence. She pivoted to change her aim.

She shook her head. How often her culture talked about killing, crowed about strength, about massacres, about conquest—but it was all talk, all howling in the night! The Clan would have to possess more than talk if the future were to be taken.

Bracing her good leg on a mass of roots, she narrowed one eye for focus and settled lightly on her resting bone. She tilted her bulky hindquarters toward the braced leg, angled her shoulders, lay her head back on her curved neck, held her breath, and fired.

Chemical green energy broke from the muzzle of her pistol and split the hanging moss bundles directly in front of her, not random and slanted like the spikers' careless shots, but level with the ground. Moss and snaggled fronds burst into flame. She was blinded by the brightness of her own weapon.

Instantly there was a bitter crack somewhere in the

bushes. Had she killed the leader? Was he cut in half by the cauterizing beam?

As she forced her eyes open, she imagined the tattered Starfleet team, stunned and frazzled by what she had done, decapitated, confused, too frightened to carry on. And in their frazzle they could be easily cut down. Now the spikers would pay attention to her. Rusa would pay attention. Aur and the other females would listen.

She couldn't see their captain anymore. Where he had stood there was now a shattered and burning stump.

Suddenly she wished she had talked to him before she had slashed him down. Why had he come here? How had he known to come?

In a flurry of movement to her right, the trapped spiker now had shafts of wood stuck in his neck. He pounded the ground to threaten two more Starfleet men who had cornered him and plunged into the foliage to get room to maneuver. The bushes rustled, and he plunged back toward the Starfleet team, but they didn't disperse. They stood their ground and hammered the spiker with well-planned shots of weapons they had built from these rocks and sticks, and two more of them now were dragging their collapsed teammate off the slab of rock while the others held the furious spiker back.

A shriek at her side rattled her mind and made her stumble. A force struck her in the neck, snapping her head back and knocking her onto her resting bone. Pain shot across her shoulder. Blood squirted at the side of her face. She knew her shoulder had been laid open in a long slash.

Tucking her tail, she swung around with her claws flashing out at the height of a Terran. The scent of blood, even her own, made her suddenly wild. But it wasn't a Terran who had attacked her. There was something on her back now, but she spun so fast that she threw the weight off.

A long gray form tumbled into the leaves, raking down shreds of hanging moss. Horror swelled as Oya saw what had attacked her. Not Starfleet—she wished it had been.

Her torn body bled freely as she raised her weapon again and tried to aim. Out of the daze came a terrible mutation of her own face, mouth parted in a shriek, tongue twisting, lips peeled back, eyes yellow and dilated for night attack, plunging toward her.

She counted off terrible seconds until the animal was nearly on her again, then opened fire. Green light broke into the leaves and burned the open mouth of the animal charging her. It choked as though trying to swallow the concentrated energy, its eyes flaring, then the ghastly stink of burning flesh rose in a puff, and the animal broke into pieces, and each piece sizzled away like ashes cooling.

There were more coming—she could smell them!

She had to protect herself, find out if the other spikers were still alive, order them to fall back, and let the ancient predators kill the humans. She lowered her head and tail and began to back away when a voice behind her made her spin around, crushing the leaves as she turned—

A Starfleet phaser hovered between her eyes, just out of arm's sweep.

Oya closed her eyes and prepared to burn.

Out of a green shabby nowhere Spock appeared and put his shoulder to the shattered stump beside Kirk, ducking from the hot shards. His voice was a baritone shock of reassurance in the panic erupting around them.

"Jim, are you all right?"

"What's left of me is," Kirk coughed from under a palmetto. His face was spackled with bits of the blown-up tree trunk, his uniform shirt pocked with ash, and he came out on his hands and knees, but he was still alive. "How many of those things are there?"

Spock pulled him to a better position. "At least ten. These are the troodonts you noted were stalking us."

"Vernon was following my order to hold back use of the phasers." Kirk's words were bitter, his eyes narrow and angry. "I didn't intend that he should sacrifice himself instead."

"I underst—"

"Spock!" An unkind elbow in the chest crushed him aside as Kirk fired past him into a lizardish face that charged them

300

out of the fanning leaves. In an instant the face, its glare recoiled in shock, blew into hot colors, and were erased by the bright civility of a phaser strike. And what a stink it left behind.

"Thank you," Spock rasped as he levered himself up. The side of his face was bleeding now, laid open by the hand-sized overlapping scales on the remains of the trunk.

"Did you get Vernon out of there?" Kirk asked.

"Yes, sir. Roth is defending the cave mouth."

"Willingly?"

"Quite willingly. He has no more desire to face these individuals than we do."

"You gave him a phaser?"

Spock looked insulted. "He's using a spear and a knife."

"Where are the other two dinosauroids?"

"Unknown. When we killed the one that attacked Vernon, the others ceased fire. They may have fallen back, but it's more likely they're also under attack by the troodonts. There—and there."

"Communicate to all hands to use phasers until we drive the little ones back," Kirk said. "I don't want to lose anybody else."

"Very well." Spock scanned the shuddering, noisy jungle, then turned and spoke as if they were back on the ship's bridge, safe. "Are you sure you're all right?"

Kirk frowned but realized he must really look a wreck for Spock to ask twice. Probably had plant sap in his hair and wood flakes all over his face. He turned the frown into a shrug that gave the Vulcan his answer, along with a companionable shove. "So I'll impress the girls with my bruises. Go on."

Spock hesitated but ultimately knew he would have to leave his debilitated captain whether he liked it or not. Kirk silently appreciated the concern but didn't like it. He was glad when Spock filtered away into the bushes.

"Be careful," he called quietly after him.

The situation scalded him. The native assailants were a hell of a lot more dangerous than intelligent aliens with modern weapons that were at least a known quantity and something the Starfleeters were accustomed to. These smart primitives, though . . . they knew the savage arts.

Shrieks in the foliage shook him out of his huddle.

He recognized that noise—a whine with a whip at the end. Yes, he'd heard that before, while he and Spock were watching the troodonts attacking the other dinosaur. An order.

As the foliage broke with activity and six or eight troodonts surged out onto the slab, screaming at the cave mouth, he realized he was right. That was the first rank, ordered to attack by his smart little friend out there.

Roth plunged out of the cave mouth, fanning a torch in one hand and a spear in the other, whipping the torch in great half circles that drove the troodonts leaping backward. It wouldn't work for long. They weren't running away. Any second, Roth would swing one way and the troodonts on the other side would plunge in. They were working together—it was obvious.

Kirk fired his phaser and took out one of the raptors closest to him, then swung around to face the dark open jungle. There would be a second flank, and he didn't want to have his back to it. He fell back against the sheer rock and opened fire with a wide burst.

Four troodonts were burned out of existence in front of him. The others at the cave mouth whirled in shock, then two of them charged him. He dodged, and their own body weight carried them past him. They snapped at him as he squirmed between them but couldn't get him.

Spinning around on his good leg, he was now in the middle of the rock slab, right in the line of fire.

So he dropped flat and shouted, "Spock! Wheel right! Fire!"

At his order, Spock, Emmendorf, and Reenie came out of the jungle, firing in bursts all at once. Over the space between them Kirk could see Spock's lips moving in the order to fire, cannily using as little phaser power as possible but staggering the shocked attackers with every burst. Several of the animals were handily killed, the rest terrified into falling back.

At the cave mouth, Roth had fallen back, out of the way. One troodont squirmed on the rock slab, a spear crammed up its throat and out the back of its head.

As he lay on the slab, Kirk forced up the details McCoy had talked about when he examined the dinosauroid corpse, and he tried to apply them to the dying troodont ten feet from him. No opposable thumb . . . The four-foot animal had three long fingers, almost the same length. Binocular vision . . . This animal's nose was not as down-turned as the dinosauroid, but the beginnings of the change were there. It still had pronounced eye-protection plates to protect it from its friends' tails during feeding frenzies. The dinosauroid's brow plates were smaller, smoother. Devolving. Not needed in a civilized society—

A thud on the ground beside him shook him hard. He rolled over, phaser up, and held his breath for one heartbeat to make sure he wasn't about to fire into the face of one of his own people.

Bad breath hit him in the face, pushed by a blustering scream, and he was looking down a nasty red throat rimmed with two-inch-long teeth, so close he could see the serrations.

He brought his knees up and let out a blunt kick. His foot bolted into the troodont's underside and knocked it back a step.

That was all Kirk needed. He clutched his phaser in both hands and fired. In a puff, the troodont separated into a dozen burning blobs and melted away, right in the middle of a good long scream.

The foliage was rustling wildly, like maracas rattling in his ears. Gasping, Kirk pushed himself up on his elbows, rolled over, and struggled to his knees. Around him, the rock slab was bloody but clear. The troodonts had retreated into the jungle, their number cut in half.

The dead dinosauroid and the dead troodont lay inches from each other, gaudy wounds oozing the same red blood. They looked like each other, but he knew they weren't alike. It would be as if a human saw a chimpanzee and thought it was the same because it had two eyes, two legs, two arms, and a mouth. These animals were millions of years apart. Now they were here, dying together.

He made it to one knee, then stopped and gasped for air. His throat was dry, caked with dust. Someone grasped his arm and hoisted him to his feet.

"Captain?" Spock held him up with both hands. That meant he'd holstered his phaser. *That* meant he thought he didn't need it anymore.

Good. They had control of the moment. Kirk nodded at his logic. "I'm fine," he choked. All he wanted was a drink of water. "Situation?"

"The troodonts have retreated. There is no sign of the dinosauroids. Evidently there were only three of them."

Kirk nodded again. "Not a bad day's work . . . Doesn't give us any answers though . . ."

"Captain!" Dale Bannon stood at the edge of the stone slab, holding his phaser at arm's length. In front of him he ushered one of the oddest creatures Kirk had ever seen.

With its arms folded back at rest against a decorated leather harness, the dinosauroid gazed at him—not at anyone else, but at Kirk specifically. It knew he was the captain. That meant it was familiar with Starfleet color coding.

Its face was painted, but with more colors than the other ones. Red, yellow, bronze, in a zigzag design across the elegant, primitive face. Its brown eyes were particularly intelligent, even over the decidedly hideous rows of snaggled teeth.

"Prisoner, sir," Bannon said.

Inside the cave, James Kirk limped to the back, where his ship's surgeon was trying to hold the tenuous threads of life still pulsing in Ensign Vernon. Condemning himself for his prudence in saving phaser energy, he boiled at the sight of his downed Security man.

"How bad?" he asked.

"I don't know yet, Captain," McCoy said.

To their right, on the other side of the cave, the prisoner narrowed its eyes at Emmendorf and Bannon, flexed its long-boned hands with their notable claws, but clearly had no desire to take on the humans as long as they held those phasers. Every time it flexed a claw at him, Emmendorf teased with his weapon and the animal backed off.

"Well," Kirk muttered, "it knows what a phaser is. And it's just like that one. The same face painting, same size, same features, energy weapons . . . You were right, Bones. It's an advanced being."

"She's a she." McCoy said casually, glancing up from his bloody patient to the new prisoner. "Female."

Kirk shifted only his eyes. "How do you know?"

The doctor looked up with a devilish flicker in his eye. "Trust me. And as long as we're on the subject, she was in charge. The other ones were acting on her gestures."

"How do you know *that?*"

"Just happened to notice. While I was trying to keep my throat from getting slashed, that is. And notice, Captain, she's slightly larger than the males. That might be normal in her culture. It's very common in the wild, anywhere you look."

A female. A great thick-legged, smooth-scaled, snaggle-toothed, yellow-eyed girl with a beautiful tail sweeping the air placidly behind her, watching him with an expression decidedly intelligent. Waiting for him to take the next step.

Not an it, nor even a he, but a she.

McCoy suddenly stood up, wiping his hands. "I've done all I can for him, Captain," he said, looking down at Vernon. "His ribcage is partially crushed, and I've set and bound it. He doesn't have many open wounds. We all have our own personal rate of recuperation. We just have to wait." He sighed and turned to the dinosauroid prisoner, and his blue eyes flared with interest. "Now . . . I'm going to treat *her.*"

He stooped, picked up his medical implements, and straightened again. In those seconds, something changed.

As he stepped past Kirk, the captain snatched him by the arm and held him back. "No. Don't treat her."

McCoy stared at him. "She's got slashes from her spine to her underside! Her shoulder's laid open! I've got a duty to that!"

"My duty comes first," Kirk said. "I have to find answers. Her discomfort might encourage her to talk."

"Jim, that's barbaric!"

"That's right."

"Jim, she doesn't belong here! She's an advanced being! She's just like that animal over there!" The doctor swung an arm and pointed at the creature he had autopsied. "Neither one of these are from sixty-five million years ago on Earth. Spock's right—there *can't* be that big a gap in the fossil record!"

"What about the DNA results? You said the dead one is absolutely from Earth. Didn't you say that?"

As if he'd forgotten, McCoy withdrew his accusing finger. "I don't know . . . I don't understand that part."

"Then get your equipment out and take a DNA sample from her! I'm going to get to the bottom of this if I have to have my own leg cut off and dissected!"

Overwhelmed, McCoy mumbled, "We'll probably find out you're a dinosaur, too."

He sighed and moved toward the fourteen-foot-long dinosauroid who sat in sedate, civilized repose, watching them.

She drew back her head from the doctor as he approached, but when Emmendorf put his phaser into her prehistoric face, she knew exactly what that meant.

McCoy glanced at Kirk, then drew a sample of her blood for his test and withdrew as quickly as he could.

Kirk paced toward the prisoner. She never took her eyes off him. She didn't belong here any more than the *Enterprise* crew did. He tried to think like a paleontologist: to ignore the obvious and look for subtle differences. At first glance, she was just a large version of those troodonts who had attacked them, but that's not what she was. He noticed that she held her body, her posture, more upright than the troodonts. Her claws were smaller in relation to her size than theirs. She held her head higher. Her hands were more free to maneuver, her arms longer, her thumb more opposable.

No, she didn't belong here. So why was she here?

Ready to prosecute somebody for stealing his planet out from under his aching feet, Kirk snapped his fingers into the hot air over one of the fires. "Where's that translator we had on the other Klingon? Did he take it?"

"Right here, sir."

"Hand it over, Ensign."

He snatched it from Reenie, fumbled briefly with it, then at Emmendorf's phaser point slipped it over the large, elegant head of the prisoner.

Then he stepped back.

"Do you understand what I'm saying to you?"

The dinosauroid didn't respond. But her expression, the creases of her shimmering boalike skin, and the way she drew her nose downward gave her away.

He squared his shoulders, his instincts on to something.

"I'm Captain James T. Kirk of the *U.S.S. Enterprise* and you know damned well what I'm doing here, don't you?"

Again she said nothing, but her head shrank back on that long curved neck and her face turned a little to the side as if she had been slapped. Her dark eyes widened, then abruptly narrowed.

Yes, she knew.

He bent forward, crushing down the instinctive revulsion of staring into a long, slim gray face of scales, leering eyes, and two-inch-long serrated teeth.

"That equipment your people are hauling," he drummed, and he was unremitting. "It's an asteroid deflector, isn't it?"

The dinosauroid's eyes widened. She drew her head farther back in subtle response.

Kirk leaned forward to match her backing away, and he gave her his catlike glare.

"Who are you?" he demanded. "And what are you doing in my past?"

Chapter Thirty-one

THE PRISONER blinked at him, enthralling and savage in her saurian way. Her tail moved slowly one way, then the other, clawed fingers hanging down.

"Oya." The translator seemed to have an easier time with her vocal inflections than it had with the Klingons', which, given the shape of her mouth, didn't make any sense at all. "I am a scientist. No soldier."

Kirk almost jumped into her lap, so relieved was he to hear a real language. Not just paint on a face or a harness or energy weapons, but the most critical trait of the civilized: communication.

"Oya . . ." He glanced at McCoy. "Is that a greeting?"

Before the doctor had a chance to postulate, the dinosauroid rippled, "It is my name."

Kirk licked his lips. "What are you doing here?"

"Research."

"Why did you choose this planet?"

"A good jungle."

Straightening, Kirk backed off a step as he felt his legs going numb. He didn't want to fall on a prisoner. Wouldn't look right.

"Captain, talk to you a minute?" McCoy came out of Kirk's periphery, clearly troubled, holding his medical tricorder with both hands. "I have a partial result here . . . enough to risk a conclusion."

"Over here. Spock, you too." Dragging a menacing pall like a security blanket, Kirk led the way aside. "Go."

McCoy didn't like what he had to say. "Well, the medical tricorder hasn't got the capacity of the ship's computer, that's why running these sequences are taking so long, but the DNA sample from the . . . from her . . . It's just like the other one."

Kirk popped an eyebrow at him. "From Earth?"

Like a guilty man, McCoy nodded. "Unless I've made a grievous error."

"Have you?"

"No, I haven't."

Beside him, Spock was a pillar of sobriety, and that was damned annoying right now. "Captain, this is a disturbing incongruity."

"Thank you, I thought of that. What are we going to do about it?"

"Further tests?"

"We don't have time for that. We either have a million years or ten minutes, and we don't know which. There she sits, an advanced being with weapons like ours and a language and the whole bucket of brass, as out of place as we are. She's our answer, gentlemen. We just don't have the right questions yet."

"Perhaps we do, sir." Spock folded his arms and lowered his voice, his tone grimly hopeful. "We have encountered races in parts of the galaxy where logically they cannot have evolved, on planets where they live out of context with the indigenous life. I submit that Oya may not be quite the incongruity we believe she is."

He looked at Kirk with that brow up and those eyes sparkling, and though he said nothing more, he was still talking.

Kirk kept looking at him, just to make sure they were thinking the same thing.

He swung around. Well, he clunked around. "Analysis, Bones. Do you have a record of this species anywhere in our known galaxy?"

Feeling left out, the doctor raised despairing hands. "I'm telling you, Jim, like it or not, she's from Earth!"

"I don't accept that. Give me a new analysis or I'll order you to grow a mustache so I can pull it out."

"Well, there's a command you don't hear every day. I'll do my best, Captain."

Kirk circled the dinosauroid prisoner, scanning her harness and her reposing form, avoiding her resting tail. She followed him with her eyes, her large head turning almost completely around on that long neck to look straight behind her. As he continued pacing, she whipped the head back around to catch him on the other side.

He had a specific question to ask, but it would get him either the truth or a lie, and he wouldn't be able to tell the difference. He had to be smarter than that.

"Starfleet has been watching you," he handily lied. "We followed you through the Guardian of Forever."

Except for a flicker of recognition, the lady didn't react. She wasn't curious or surprised, and Kirk grabbed that as a clue. She knew what the Guardian was and what it did. Somehow, she and her team had found it. Maybe through spies, maybe by following a trail of folklore.

Damned few knew about that place, classified since Kirk and his crew had discovered it. Starfleet maintained an outpost there, but the machine's existence was kept secret as a potentially dangerous mechanism.

Now he understood even more than he had the time before, when tampering with history had almost destroyed everything they knew.

That time, it had been an accident. It had seemed complicated then, but suddenly he realized how much harder the fix would be now, to alter not an accident, but a deliberate sabotage of time.

He hated this. He hated playing with time.

"Who are you that you want to inflict so much damage on everything you've ever known?"

She didn't respond. Those big brown eyes blinked at him, incongruous with her bony face and yet somehow beautiful there, like a set of onyx stones set in snakeskin.

"I know who it is."

They turned.

Bannon stood at the back of the cave, his face pasty, revealing an unmistakable flicker of giving a damn.

Kirk took a pace toward him. "Well?"

"I think I know . . . I did a paper . . . junior year . . ."

"Snap out of it, Lieutenant. What's the bottom line?"

Bannon's chin tucked and his eyes were still heavy with turmoil. "I think she's one of the Clan Ru."

"Clan Ru," Spock repeated as he turned and looked at Oya. "Yes . . . possibly . . ."

"Clan who?" McCoy asked.

"I've never heard of them," Kirk said, insisting with his tone that he shouldn't have to ask. He looked at Oya and got at least a partial answer when she glared at Bannon with those wide yellow eyes as if he'd opened her safe. "Spock?" he urged.

Gazing at Oya, Spock came toward them. "Translated originally, Ru simply means 'all.' The Clan of All. Their culture is like Orion sects and some original American Indian tribes who consider their own tribe to be the only life with a soul."

"In other words, if you're not the chosen 'oids,' then you don't exist morally. Laws and rights and any supernatural consideration don't extend beyond their own species?"

"Correct."

"So they wouldn't lose any sleep over eradicating the rest of us."

Bannon took a few steps forward. "They never wanted to participate in the Federation, even though they're well inside our space. They've gotten most of the benefits of membership anyway. Protection, emergency supplies, technology . . ."

"The Federation had to make an unfortunate choice," Spock said. "The Ru planet was so deeply embedded inside UFP space that we had to surround them. They were offered membership and could have claimed it at any time. Still they refused to participate. They have been left alone but have never mixed with us."

In a sideward gaze riddled with anger, Kirk watched Oya's face. "Well?" he prodded.

The female turned her ovoid head slightly to one side, and suddenly it was as if the two of them had known each other for years. Millions of years. After all, they had been playing a bizarre game of tag for many dangerous hours now, and each knew only half of the rules.

He paced in front of her, then stopped. "Are you going to talk to me?"

"Our place in the galaxy is providential," Oya said, her long lips moving against the grain of the sounds that came out of the translator, and there was a coo and hiss behind the words. "We were thriving before humanoids came. Nature wanted us. Predators are critical to natural health. You have seen on your own planet what happens when only the prey flourishes. You . . . held us down."

"You're talking about primitive existence," Kirk punctuated. "We've not only beaten down the blatant predator, but the shivering of the prey. This way, intelligence flourishes in both. That's what you're trying to destroy, don't you understand?"

Provoked, he pressed closer, his eyes intense.

"We didn't hold you down in order to hold you back. The Clan was welcome to flourish with the Federation. Exclusion has been your own choice. Only the lazy blame someone else for their inferiority."

"Lazy!" the Ru scientist flared, tail and all, and the stripe of color down her back surged reddish brown. "Is that what you think of us?"

"Maybe." Kirk refused to flinch. "And what do you think of us?"

She looked at him, then scanned Spock, McCoy, the Klingon.

Finally she looked back at Kirk. "You are meat," she said.

He had his answers. He even had some of the questions.

An asteroid deflector dragged into the deep past to murder the greatest murderer of all time, the mindless rock that had changed the history of the galaxy. The realization was galling that someone with a plot and purpose had changed the past deliberately.

Most planets had their upheavals and cataclysms, but seldom was there one remarkable event to which the development of a whole new set of species could cling. The dinosaurs rumbled over Earth for hundreds of millions of years to be snuffed in a relatively short passage by the smothering dust of a once-in-a-billion-years event: the impact of an asteroid that swung too close and was sucked in by the planet's own gravity.

Space was big, too big for things like that to happen very often. Entire galaxies had been cataloged passing through each other, virtually without impact.

Yet there had been impact here, right here. And now there was tampering.

A race that wanted to change everything, botch up the future so they could take charge of it. Bloodcurdled and feeling discarded, James Kirk leaned on his cane and absorbed the incomprehensible.

"They want a future without humanity," he said, "because humanity started the Federation."

Spock nodded. "Her attitude explains why the Clan has resisted contact."

"Yes, it does," McCoy agreed. "Would you want to have to make small talk with your lunch? Jim, what if we try negotiating with her landing party? Maybe they want to live through this as much as we do."

Kirk scowled at Oya. "They want possession of something that isn't theirs. They want supremacy that they don't deserve. I won't negotiate on those terms."

"Then tell me this," the doctor challenged. "If the Guardian shows the native past of whoever is looking at it . . . I mean, if the Klingons would see the past of their planet, and the Argelians would see the past of theirs, then how did the Clan Ru landing party jump through into Earth's past instead of their own planet's?"

"Good question." His mouth screwing up with frustration, Kirk glowered at him. "I hate good questions. All hands, prepare to break camp."

"Where are we going?"

The captain gazed north into the gauze of dawn.

"Up the mountain. We're going to knock out that launcher before it knocks out humanity."

Chapter Thirty-two

"TRACKING THE MICROSCOPIC RESIDUE of complex metals, Captain. This is the correct path."

The killing ground lay beneath them on the plateau, nearly saturated into the landscape now. Large pterosaurs and small ones, as well as scavengers of other types, and even a few of the troodonts who had done the killing were clustered around the much-decimated corpses of the animals now known as Oya's Clan Ru conspirators in the sabotage of time.

Behind him, Emmendorf and Roth brought the unconscious Vernon along on a makeshift stretcher, while Bannon held a phaser on Roth, just in case.

Oya slogged up the path under Reenie's phaser but did not look down to the plateau. Another clue. Or at least a kind of confirmation.

Treading the soft ground of a haywire universe, Kirk was thinking about ways to get information out of Oya when he went down on one knee for the fifth time in twenty minutes.

Emmendorf plunged in to catch him. "I'll help you, sir!"

"Ensign," Spock said smoothly and managed to tactfully take over. "Scan the peak of this incline for metallic residue."

"Oh," Emmendorf said, backing off and taking Spock's tricorder. "Aye, sir."

Kirk leaned into Spock's support and levered himself to his feet, but he could barely fill his lungs. Maybe it was the altitude. Before he could take a step, his insides convulsed. He locked his knees, but the pain crushed his eyes closed and he wouldn't get far that way.

"Take it easy, Jim. Let us sit you down." That was McCoy on the other side from Spock.

Kirk didn't want to sit down, not in front of two potential enemies. That could work to the wrong advantage, and right now he needed all the advantages to himself.

He forced his eyes open a fraction, saw brown dirt, and spore-matted stones below. Were his legs moving at least? He didn't want to be carried.

The movement stopped. The angle of his spine changed, the balance of his heavy head also. Two Spocks, two McCoys. Double vision? Great. Two wrecked universes.

He leaned back a little and found support. They'd put him down on a rock or something and he leaned back against the mountain.

Good thing it was there, sea levels rising and all.

McCoy, you've got to do something about this.

A hypo hissed in the hollow of his shoulder, and with a jolt his head began to clear. He dared open his eyes. One Spock, standing beside him, holding him up . . . one McCoy in front of him, holding a hypo and waiting.

One haywire universe. Fine. He could handle one.

He pressed a hot hand to his forehead, then pressed his hair out of his eyes. "Better," he said. "Take over the scan, Spock. I'll be all right."

Spock looked at McCoy, who nodded and waved him away.

Vernon's stretcher was on the ground. Reenie and Bannon held Roth and Oya under guard a few yards away. Emmendorf was looking over the incline, fascinated with the scene of day-old mutilation down there.

On the upper end of the incline, Spock fanned his

tricorder across the ground. "We should be able to track them, assuming they do not raise this equipment off the ground or veer into the deep jungle."

"I will not help you," Oya said when Kirk looked at her.

"I don't need your help," he said.

It was all he could do to push out the statement without giving away that he was on the edge of collapse. He had been slogging along in the middle of his team, careful to keep away from the prisoners, because an injured captain could very easily become a helpless hostage and his crewmen didn't need any more problems than they already had.

"Jim." McCoy crouched beside him with that goshdarnit concern on his face that he reserved for moments when he had some data but didn't believe it.

Softened somewhat by the humanizing sight of a bit of moss clinging to McCoy's dusty brown hair, Kirk asked, "Something?"

Disarmed, McCoy's animated features accepted the damnable. He patted the medical tricorder. "It's confirmed. I've been through the DNA sequences three times, I've run the paleoanatomical data up against the information I have about the Ru from our own time. It doesn't make any sense, but the apparently alien species calling themselves Clan Ru are almost assuredly an Earthborn race. I don't know how they got to where they ended up, Captain . . . but they started right here." The doctor pointed at the ground beneath them like a farmer poking a cow to get into the barn.

"If this is true," Kirk said, "then what we were looking at down the mountain . . . Those were intelligent, advanced, scientific individuals being slaughtered by—"

"By their own prehistoric ancestors," McCoy confirmed. "Direct evolutionary line. I'll bet I could trace it as completely as we've traced the evolution of the modern horse."

Under the flurry of new thoughts, Kirk mumbled, "I like horses . . ." Hearing himself, he gripped his cane with both hands and pushed to his feet.

With McCoy's steadying hand on his elbow, he limped

between Reenie and Bannon to where the prisoners were being held.

He forced himself to stand there, immutable, as Spock came down the incline to his side. Little glances were worth a good strong yell anytime.

With his two most trusted companions at his sides, he squarely faced the Ru scientist and steeled himself to do the best he could at the strangest story ever told.

"Oya," he began, "listen to me. I don't know how, I don't know when, but some time in the past many millions of years, there was a . . . crossover between your past and mine. You are Clan Ru, I know, with your own past. But in the deep beginning, Clan Ru was spawned not on your own planet . . . but on Earth."

The female dinosauroid blinked at him again in that way she had. Her head moved backward on that long neck.

Kirk drew a breath to keep going and held out an imploring hand.

"After the time changes you made," he continued, "the Clan began on Earth and this time continued on Earth. The transplantation that we believe happened, this time never occurred. The Clan evolved here and went on here, cycle after cycle. But there was never unity. Your people fought among yourselves eon after eon . . . to utter obliteration. By changing evolution," he said, "you made yourselves extinct millions of years before any of us would have been born."

With a flash of panic in her eyes and attitude, the Ru scientist looked from Kirk to Spock and back. In the silence the jungle began to sizzle with insect noises in the extended silence.

Oya was thinking about what had just been said, combing the conclusions, the basic premises, walking backward step by step through the logic, weighing the elements that took blind trust and could never be proven. They could tell she did not want to believe what she had been heard, but this was a creature who had stepped through the Guardian of Forever to do something that was also beyond credibility.

She knew the impossible did exist. She was here to do it.

"If I am of Earth," she reckoned slowly, "how can I have my own planet? My own history? If I am dead forty million years before you, then how am I alive?"

Kirk stepped back and waved at the empty space between them. "Mr. Spock . . . one scientist to another, would you address the lady, please?"

Spock stepped forward, gazing at the ground, steadied himself and his theories with a pause of effort, then looked up. He spoke slowly.

"Federation scientists have logged evidence of the seeding of some species from one planet to another by beings in our distant past. Some have taken to referring to the source of this seeding as done by an intelligent interference by 'the Preservers.' I find the phrase somewhat poetic. Federation research has suggested that there has been conscious intent to rescue certain cultural and genetic pools and transplant them to planets where they had a chance to survive. This theory fits the case of the Clan Ru. Can you tell me whether there is any genetic link between your species and the planet on which you live?"

"There is none," Oya said bluntly, "because we were placed there by choice of providence. We were meant to survive and control those around us."

"Mmm," Spock noted grimly. "As a scientist, you know that such an explanation is mythological and incomplete. What we do know for certain is that your DNA sequences are undeniably tied to Earth's biosystem. Yet in the normal scheme of evolution you did not evolve here beyond the strike of the asteroid. Though we cannot conclude the method, we know your ancestral line was somehow tagged as ultimately intelligent, then rescued and transplanted from this planet to your planet. According to the accepted scientific evidence, the conclusion is . . . quite credible."

There was something about Spock, his simple poise and understated delivery. His hair was still in place despite what they'd been through, his tidy blue uniform only had one stain on it, and he still had good posture. He could be reciting flapdoodle and it would sound completely plausible.

Oya was staring at him, running over it and over it.

318

Reeled with respect for her that she didn't flare out with disbelief at them, Kirk was suddenly flushed with how silly all that really did sound. Leap after leap, based on things they'd seen or that had been recorded by people they trusted, but that she hadn't and didn't. But she wasn't dismissing what they had said. She was considering it. Truly advanced . . .

He had to choke up something, and it had to be fast.

"Doctor," Kirk said, "give her the medical tricorder. She's a scientist—let her see the DNA results. Let her look at the comparisons we've made between her and the animals here. Let her see for herself . . . just who she is. And give her Spock's tricorder as well. Show her what kind of Earth her actions will create."

McCoy handed Oya the tricorder. As she held it in her graceful prehistoric fingers, he tapped the display, then stood back to let the magic box work.

History spun by on the tiny screen. No one could see it but the prisoner and, a few feet behind her, Roth.

Kirk held still and watched them, gripping his cane with both hands until his knuckles went numb. How many times in his career had he cajoled, coaxed, begged, taunted someone to cross over to his way of thinking for the sake of whatever was on the line at the time? And when in his career had so much been on the line?

Words weren't enough anymore. He'd used all he had. Now there would be only the raw candor of faith in himself and in unimpeachable science, in Spock, McCoy, and in all the probity they could get across with the moral strength of their actions. He hoped the integrity of everything he stood for showed in his face. Sometimes it just came down to that.

Some latent magnetism fixed him not to Oya as the tiny lights plastered across the pain on her face, but to Roth as he watched from behind. A Klingon. Hostile, angry, suspicious. Did he believe?

No way to know. A guess could be fatal in a very large sense. But all Jim Kirk felt he had right now was a sack of guesses and a couple of seeds of hope.

Suddenly, before anyone expected, Oya looked up from

the tricorder. She looked at Spock, then at McCoy, and finally Kirk. When she parted her lips to speak, the interpretation coming from the translator was hauntingly different from any sound she had made before.

She blinked her eyes. "We have destroyed ourselves."

PART FOUR

FORK IN THE FUTURE

"Out here we're the only policemen around. And a crime has been committed. Do I make myself clear?"

—James Kirk,
Arena

Chapter Thirty-three

"YOU DID THIS!"

From a good twelve feet away, Roth launched into the air and delivered a club kick to the side of Oya's face. The stubby brow plate above her left eye took the impact and protected her eye, but her head was knocked aside and her neck whiplashed.

She rocked up onto her massive legs, drew up the tail that was as thick around as Roth's thigh, and swung around purposefully. The tail caught Roth flush across the chest. The blow sent him panting but otherwise only made him angry. He gathered to leap again.

"Security!" Kirk shouted.

Emmendorf throttled Roth once on the soft back of the neck with his phaser handle, then dragged him away.

"*You* did this to us!" the Klingon roared. "We could have had life! All we have now is slow death!"

The massive dinosauroid raised herself high on those thick legs, lowered her head—her tail went down, too—and spread her long grayish arms. The translator hummed and hissed.

"The universe could have been our hunting ground," Oya said, unshaken, "a thousand planets our arenas. The flowering of power and portion, we felt at the tip of our claw. Instead we were locked down, beaten back, held from our great probability. The aggression given to us by providence has been wasted. We were made to lick the dust. The festering wound of being overridden has been a day-to-day irritant. We never hold our necks high anymore."

She drew her head up as though to illustrate. Her pointed teeth glistened and her eyes widened.

"Once there were banners on every tail," she went on. "But I have not seen a tail banner for nine generations. We were a whipped race . . . brought to the knee before our blossoming."

"Fools! Thoughtless fools!" Grinding his teeth, Roth threw his weight backward and to one side, at once pulling out of Emmendorf's grip while burying an elbow in Bannon's gut and laying him to the ground. Suddenly free, he bolted toward Oya.

Kirk vaulted to his feet but wobbled, bumped McCoy, and threw them both sprawling. He rolled over and saw Roth's thick legs above him as the Klingon jumped clear of him and nearly made it to Oya, so close that she drew her huge head back and tried to turn it away. Roth's kick could knock that eye right out.

All at once Spock moved in. He got between Roth and Oya and almost took the kick himself, managing instead to squirm south of it and seize Roth by the upper arms. Wresting him off balance, Spock recklessly pushed the Klingon out of the other men's grips, went right between them, and rammed Roth back against the sheer rib of the mountain. There, he clamped him hard in place.

"Listen to me," Spock demanded, barely inches between his face and Roth's. "You, the Romulans, the Clan—you are all acting on instinct, and that's why all of you are on the brink of destroying yourselves. To be anything but rational is to ultimately destroy yourselves. The cultures of the United Federation of Planets have adopted the basic philosophy of Vulcan, but they have made it work for everyone— laws and cooperation rather than the anarchy of emotion and envy."

Roth squirmed for release, but Spock wrestled briefly with the strong soldier-pilot and managed to hold him against the rocks. As bits of stone and moss rained onto them from the mountain wall, Spock pressed in even harder and met Roth's anger with his own.

"You were right in what you attempted to do for your people," he ratified fiercely. "Rationality *does* work. You were *right!*"

A hand of wind came down across them and ruffled the jungle fronds. Tropical flora genuflected around them as if agreeing.

The unminced moral strength put a shiver down every spine. Whether they had enjoyed it all their lives, rejected it, or simply savored it, they knew what he was talking about, so pure was the forthrightness in Spock's eyes and voice. Kirk found himself warm with pride. Even in the midst of all this he couldn't help it. This might be the last flush of satisfaction he would ever feel, and he was glad to be feeling it about Spock.

Invigorated, he pushed to his feet without anyone's help and stepped around McCoy. He looked at Roth, then Oya, and swung an accusatory finger between them.

"You did this to yourselves. No one forced you to go to war with your neighbors, no one forced you to go to war with each other . . . All this, you did to yourselves, while claiming to be someone else's victim." He turned and pointed at Roth. "You're using the Vulcans' success as an excuse for your own failures. Fact is, you and your people are responsible for yourselves. If someone leaves their door open, you don't blame them when you get caught stealing their things. Because of her action, you've had the *opportunity* for chaos, but that didn't mean you had to accept delivery. I think that's what you really hate about her and about the Vulcans, too."

Pausing, he held Roth's attention and let his words ring. Roth stared at him and didn't move as Spock backed away from him.

Dismissing him, Kirk shuffled around to peer now into

the embodiment of the deepest past. Oya blinked the eye that Roth had kicked and tucked her large face downward.

"And you," Kirk scolded, "you're blaming everyone else for your condition. But how many times has the Federation asked you to join in?"

Impulsively he snatched up one of the tricorders from Ensign Reenie—it didn't matter which one—and shook it in her face.

"Now what are your people going to do when the galaxy evolves without humans? What you did here on Earth? Slaughter after war after conquest until there's nothing but ashes, millions of years before the first man walked here? Are you going to blame me for that, too?"

Everyone listened. All were embarrassed. Not just for Oya and Roth, who from their expressions admitted guilt to these things, but for themselves in some small ways, because everyone had at some time in his or her life done this.

"Let's move," he said. "We've got a job to do, we're going to do it no matter how we feel about each other. Because I don't want to die in this place."

All the way up the mountain Oya talked. She heard her own voice but felt detached from it. She told them about her culture, about the harsh planetary life, how the males hunted and the females had control over mating and guarded the eggs. How they had wet-nurse farms, where they placed their eggs in the nests of other creatures, and when the young hatched, they killed and ate the young of the others, still tended by the mothers of the animals they ate, until finally one of them was large enough to kill her, too.

Describing the everyday life on her planet, Oya saw the looks in the humans' eyes, the contempt and disbelief. Perhaps, she thought, our ways are not the best, even for ourselves.

Their captain came up with a plan to break the spikers' line and gain access to the launcher. Under the nagging sense of doubt, Oya found herself trusting him. Right or wrong, he believed in what he was doing. If what she had seen on the tricorder screen was a fantasy, then someone had fooled the captain, too.

And both he and she were limping. Oya found some bemusement there. At least they had something physical in common.

Something physical . . . They had the entire Earth in common.

Rusa's face, Aur's—what would it be like to see them when they realized she had thrown in with the Starfleets? There wouldn't be time to explain, to slap the spikers aside and sit the female leaders down for a lesson in the past and future. They would fight, and whoever died, even herself, would die believing Oya was a traitor.

There it was . . . The tip of the launcher showing through the scrubby bushes that would someday be towering trees.

"Captain," she gargled, drawing herself downward into the ferns. He made his way to her, favoring one of his legs, though she wasn't familiar enough with the way humans moved to know which leg. "They will smell you," she said. "Let me go first."

"No," he said bluntly. "I don't know you well enough to lay the future of the Federation on your actions. Just explain to me what I'm looking at."

"I will," she agreed. He had eyes like a predator. "There is a platform of cast rhodinium, six meters square. Upon it is an antigravity launcher, and within the launcher is a matter/antimatter warhead with a blunt-strike detonator. Over the bushes I can see the nose of the detonator. They must be nearly finished in their construction. We must move quickly."

"I intend to."

"Remember, Captain . . . do not stand your ground before the spikers. They're too aggressive once battle starts and will win if you try to face them down. They'll be confused if you hit, then fall back, then hit again. Keep backing off, and the spikers' instincts will take over. They'll be confused, and the female leaders will lose control of them. We must win quickly enough to stop the launch."

327

"And we're not going to do that sitting here," Kirk said to her. "Emmendorf, Bannon, take the left flank. Spock, Reenie, the right. McCoy, stay behind with Vernon. Hold the middle ground. Roth—make your decision here and now. There won't be any other time."

"There will be no other time for any of us, Captain," Oya admitted. "If they succeed in launching the deflector, then you and I and all we have known . . . we will be all done."

"Right flank, move! Distract them, Spock!"

Watching every rustle of every leaf in the mountainous terrain before him, Jim Kirk shouted at the top of his lungs over the spewing whine of phasers and the crack Ru energy weapons.

He had the advantage. The Ru didn't understand what he was saying. Their leaders were whistling and neighing, too, but if what Oya had told him was right, their leaders would have less control over the spikers than he had over his people. He could use that.

There were eight spikers that he could see, at least six of which were moving through the jungle, leaping like gazelles toward the advancing Starfleet team in urgent counterattack. Oya had told him there would be twelve. Kirk couldn't guess whether she was just wrong or spikers had been killed on the hard climb, or if they were just off on some other mission somewhere, collecting food or something. Eight was what he had to deal with. If others showed up, fine.

The spikers were closing the distance between themselves and the humans who were scattered on the lower ground. They wore harnesses like Oya's, but not all the same. Some had leg greaves on their knees and splatterguards on their heads, others had leather and brass bandoliers, gauntlets on their wrists or quilled neck decorations, probably something that evolved from fighting with their own kind or whatever prey existed on their home planet.

Their home planet . . . Kirk shook away the complications of that thought and forced himself to concentrate on the fight erupting around him. His people knew what they were doing this time, understood what they were fighting.

Barely able to keep on his feet, medicated up to the eyeballs, dragging one foot and sheeted with sweat, Kirk limped over the rocks, advancing toward the biggest one. He had her right square in front of him now.

Rusa. The leader, Oya had said. There she was.

Yes, this one was big and influential. She stood on a level plateau with the launch platform, defending it while the spikers took on the Starfleet offensive. Rusa's tricolor-painted face, her weapon halter decorated with enameled inlay, the bright red shell belt around her tail, and her gray-brown stucco skin provided an image of the particularly savage. She was watching the spikers and the Starfleet team divide below her, and from time to time she crowed furiously, and something about the fight would change.

Below Rusa by about ten feet was another spiker, wearing an eye-plated hood. Maybe this was her personal guard. The spiker waved his weapon back and forth and drummed his great legs on the ground, near enough for Kirk to pick up the tremors.

He held himself low behind the ten-foot-tall stump of a broken conifer.

Thirty feet across from him on his right, Spock moved in with Reenie, taking short but deliberate phaser shots at two spikers they'd managed to attract. To his left, Bannon and Emmendorf teased the spikers away from the launcher, using as little phaser power as possible.

Above him, Rusa crowed suddenly, very loudly. The spikers surged toward the Starfleet people on an open physical attack at Rusa's order. They weren't using their energy weapons this time, but charging with their claws open and the crescent-shaped claws on their feet flexed upward, ready to hack.

For an instant he was tempted to pause, appreciate the beautiful things he was seeing, things others would give their careers to see, these strange gifts of fate's quirks.

He ticked off ten seconds and cupped his hand at his mouth. "Fall back!"

Instantly the Starfleet team dropped out of target range and melted into the bushes. The lathered spikers pulled up their charge, heated, bristle crested, and confused. The female leaders screamed at them but without effect.

Above him, Rusa stomped the plateau, watching the spikers stumble like a gaggle of geese, their charge interrupted. They'd expected hand-to-hand fighting, and instead the enemy had dropped away. Now, hotheaded and frenzied, the spikers couldn't think clearly enough to know who to follow.

"Perfect," Kirk muttered. He pulled out his communicator. "Kirk to Spock . . ."

"Spock here."

"I don't want to shout—tip them off that something's happening." Kirk dipped to get another look at Rusa. "Now that you've attracted them in two different directions, move our two teams together into the middle, then draw the spikers' attention again. I want you to let them flank us."

"Sir?"

"We're quicker than they are. Let's use that. Let them get on either side of us."

"Kirk!"

A shudder rushed down Kirk's arms. "Roth, how did you get Spock's communicator?"

"I took the doctor's. You'll let them flank us? We can't fight them on two sides!"

"We're not going to fight. We're going to run. Everybody get ready."

"Run!"

"I said get ready. Kirk out."

He ducked back into the bushes and tried to measure the breeze to see if he was downwind. Around him, the bushes were unmoved, the moist air hot and cloying. No way to tell about scent.

No reason to wait. He brought his communicator to his lips. "Go, Spock."

The cycads and magnolias thirty yards away on either side began to rustle. While the spikers were still confused, raising their heads high over the foliage and trying to see, the Starfleet team moved underneath the leaves and over the roots of ancient plants.

He wanted the leaders. Rusa and three others, Oya had said, but Kirk saw only one other, so that was what he would deal with for the moment. Had the other two been killed? This environment could do that. He'd keep his eyes open, but those were his targets.

As he glanced to one side, he couldn't see Oya. The ferns and prickly bushes were adversarial here, where there was more sunlight directly on the mountainside to nurture them. The Appalachians someday.

On the plateau above them, trying to see what was going on, Rusa howled. Kirk tried to get a phaser shot clear, but she was from the future, like him, and understood that she had to keep low behind the conifer trunks and the rocks.

He brought the communicator up again. "Center."

Spread out after chasing his crew in four or five directions, the spikers were still confused, expecting the Starfleet people to stay on the perimeters. When he saw Spock directly in front of him, Kirk moved.

He grabbed for the rocky ground and climbed. Bristly undergrowth scored his hands and pulled at his hair as he pushed through it. An insect web creased his face and clogged his vision, forcing him to give up one hand to pull it away, and he lost a couple of precious seconds.

Damn this weakness! His muscles felt like thread snapping. On board the ship he would've been cured by now, back on duty.

But for soldiers, sailors, that has always been the call of duty. To work not at one's best, but at one's worst to save the ship, to save the day.

He reached the middle point between the confused spikers and bumped into Emmendorf. It was like hitting a sandbag.

"Sorry, sir," the Security man grunted.

"Move aside, Ensign. Spock?"

"Here, sir."

"Take the rear. All hands . . . advance!"

He gathered his last shards of strength and charged between his crewmen and went for the spiker below Rusa. His phaser sang, and the spiker dissolved into tortured spasms and fizzled away, its screech echoing against the landscape.

Kirk looked up as his shoulder struck the sheer wall under the launching plateau. Above him, he saw the muzzle of an energy weapon swing into aim, certainly sighting down one of his crew. He had fooled the spikers into splitting up and made a mad dash right down the middle.

Now he grabbed his cane with both hands and swung it in a long arch upward. The wood rang against metal, and the connection felt solid. The weapon whined into open air, and with a final shove he managed to dislodge it from Rusa's hand and fling it into the bushes.

The female leader shrieked. Foreign language or not, other species or not, there was no mistaking that noise. She was mad.

Kirk put his shoulder to the rock wall just as a massive shape blocked out the light. A flash of teeth startled him as instinct took over whether he liked it or not. He knew he didn't dare let her get in position with one of those claws on her feet. Taking hold of his cane like a baseball bat, he pushed off the rocks and came out slashing. The cane caught Rusa across the muzzle and sent her reeling backward. She shook her head and roared at him, drawing a knife from a holster on her stone-studded harness.

If she got that knife in place, he'd never be able to fight her off. He plunged forward, hoping only to close the space between them and take the advantage of his smaller size and quicker movements. Before she could bring her knife around, Kirk shoved the cane into Rusa's enormous mouth and braced it like handlebars, just as he had seen Vernon do to the spiker. Digging his toes into the soft ground, he pushed the cane all the way into Rusa's mouth to the soft flanges of skin at the back, making it impossible for her to close those massive snaggletoothed jaws. Any second he would get that knife in the back. Or one of those crescent-shaped foot claws in the guts. His muscles shriveled in expectation of the shock. He didn't want to die here. He'd steeled himself for death in a hundred places, but a prehistoric jungle wasn't one of them. Most of them were on the ship.

Until this moment he'd shielded himself from his chances of saving the ship by saving the correct time line. Right now the most important thing was to keep from getting his head bitten off, and he was staring into a maw of serrated teeth that would just about fit his head perfectly.

He pushed for all he was worth upward against the soft sides of Rusa's mouth, glad she didn't have the sense to take a step back, for that would've thrown him off. The only thing between the bitten-off head and him was this shabby wooden cane. His palms were scored and his arms locked, shoulders screaming.

Rusa's massive body was a terrific barrier between him and what he wanted. He kept thinking of her that way, and second to second he kept pushing. Willing all his strength to his left arm, he pressed the cane into her mouth and let go with his right hand, knotted that fist, and cudgeled her in the eye a couple times.

He felt the tremor of pain go through her thick neck. Only then did he realized the mistake he'd made.

Until now Rusa had been pushing foolishly forward, so annoyed to have something jammed in her mouth that she forgot about the knife in her claws. But the pain in her eye made her shake her head, and that shook Kirk off balance.

He lost his grip on the cane and was swiped to the ground, landing hard on his back. Rusa raised her huge head, jangled a screech of rage, got the cane forward between her teeth, and bit it in half.

Half of it fell across Kirk's heaving chest. The other half impaled a mossy mound beside him. He rolled onto his side and scrambled for the phaser he'd hung back on his belt. He had a clear shot—

The phaser was gone. Knocked off.

Rusa stomped over him, so close now that his shipmates probably wouldn't dare a phaser shot, whinnying at him like a stallion kicking. He knew that sound. The sound that meant get away or die and I'll be happy if you die.

He tried to roll away, but the ground lay against him. Rocks on one side, the impaled mossy mound on the other.

Rusa's foot clipped his shoulder as she took another step closer, and her posture changed. Her tail went down, her neck muscles tightened. She lowered her painted face.

Kirk raised his feet. He basted her nostrils with his bootheels, setting her back an inch or two, but it was obvious her bony face was meant by nature to take the swats and kicks of wounded animals many times his weight with armor of their own.

But in that extra second Kirk rolled to his side and snatched the longer half of the broken cane out of the moss. Scraps of moss blew into his face as the jagged edge tore out and he swept it upward. Rusa took a cleansing suck of air through her battered nostrils, then plunged. Kirk curved his spine and thrust the pointed end of the broken cane into the soft flesh under Rusa's V-shaped lower jaw. He felt the tough skin pop away, then a grating of bone, and Rusa choked.

Saliva and blood poured between her pointed teeth. She gobbled in pain and grabbed for the stick impaling her throat. Pink foam bubbled through the teeth.

Suddenly she threw her head back, and her great tail swept upward as if her spine were convulsing. Blood poured from her mouth, and she let go of the stick. Her head rocked back wildly. Kirk dodged away from her feet as they gnashed the ground, the two huge crescent claws flexing and tearing up the soil just centimeters from his legs. He couldn't run. All he could do was scramble inch by inch away from those drumming legs and clacking claws.

With a howl of fury, Rusa collapsed as her legs folded under her like a swan's legs folding out of the way. As she fell, Kirk saw a saddle of blood across her back and caught a swatch of blue among the stalks and scaly trunks around them.

The ground shuddered. Plants cracked as Rusa's whole weight crashed and dissolved into tortured spasms. She pushed upward with her arms, but the weight of her head was too much and it too slammed to the ground, driving the impaled cane all the way into her skull.

As he crouched inches away, Kirk saw the light fall out of her eyes. Her last breath heaved across his legs.

Stuck there on one knee, he gathered enough strength to look up. Impaled in Rusa's spine was one of their home-made javelins, blood pumping from the wound every couple of seconds. So her great heart was still forcing blood through her veins. He looked at her face. Someday she'd make a hell of a fossil.

Heaving like a set of bellows, Kirk put a hand on Rusa's dying body for support. The patch of blue materialized beside him.

"Thanks," Kirk coughed, looking at Spock's blood-splattered tunic. "I didn't . . . think you'd let her . . . get me."

"You're welcome. We have the high ground," Spock said, and even he was trying to catch breath. He took Kirk's arm with both hands. "Can you walk?"

"I'll walk. We did it—we stopped it, Spock."

"Yes." Spock glanced up at the plateau. Above them, the launcher and its missile looked like an elongated kid's toy. Bare alloys and heavy plastics. No colors. No numbers.

Abruptly Kirk's pleasure dropped away. "Then why hasn't the Guardian pulled us back? If we really changed things—"

Troubled by that, Spock looked up at the missile, brows drawn. "I don't know."

"Then we have to take the next step. We have to dismantle that launcher and destroy the warhead. Let's take a look at that launcher."

"Captain—"

"Just get me up there, Spock."

Some notable agony later, Kirk stood beside the crude platform and the missile with the warhead that would have changed history.

Below, the spikers hissed and crowed at the Starfleet team that held them at phaser point. Beside him, Spock and Oya were checking the trigger mechanism, a relatively simply on–off box mounted to the platform at eye level. Dino-sauroid eye level.

"Simple orbiter," Spock said, screwing the long cylindrical missile with a scientist's glare. "With a crude but efficient tracking mechanism and a . . ."

"It is ready to launch," Oya told them. "I believe they were waiting for a clear sky. Without me, they did not know it could be launched in any weather."

"Very dangerous," Spock said. "A hair-trigger mechanism. Even a strong blast of wind may have set it off."

"Everything is sensitive," Oya confirmed. "We meant it to launch quickly, without complication, then detonate its warhead at the first contact with the asteroid."

"Scares the hell out of me," Kirk admitted. "Let's get it out of commission."

Spock circled the six-meter-square platform. "We'll have to be careful, Captain."

"Then be careful. Just get it done."

"Yes, sir."

"Captain Kirk, let me look at it." Below, near the still corpse of Rusa, Roth gazed up at them with his hands on the edge of the plateau. "I know something about launchers and detonators."

Kirk looked down at him and managed a grin. "Not a chance."

Roth's face bled with fresh scratches. "Even after I have fought at your side?"

"I like you, but I don't trust you. Not you nor anybody else is getting within spitting distance of this thing until it's nonfunctional."

"Captain." Spock was standing away from the platform now, looking into the sky just northeast of them. "Look."

Kirk straightened and was suddenly hit with a burst of pain. He hadn't realized he'd been slouching. As he winced through it, he limped to Spock and looked into the sky. "I don't see—"

Then he did see. In the misty sky, a long way from where the sun should be, there was a glowing dot barely showing through the milky atmosphere.

"Is that it?"

"Yes."

Their universe's savior. And their death sentence if they were wrong about why they hadn't been pulled back. If the Guardian couldn't get them back, they were looking up at the club that would smash them all to bits. They couldn't run fast enough or dig deep enough to protect themselves from the impact of a ball of rock that big caught in Earth's gravitational pull.

"How big did you say it was?" he murmured.

"Ten miles," Spock concurred, "in accordance with the one-hundred-eighty-five-mile-diameter crater that was discovered in the Gulf of Mexico."

"Imagine walking ten miles, Spock. That's . . . what? About sixty starships straight through the middle?"

"A long walk, sir."

Squinting, Kirk let out a little moan of appreciation. "What's its mass? Do we know?"

"According to the information on my tricorder, it was calculated to weigh five point three times ten to the twelfth power metric tons."

"What's that in English?"

"Five trillion tons. In the mid-1990s, someone calculated its being the weight equal to fifty-three million aircraft carriers."

Kirk looked at him. "My father took me to see the nuclear carrier *George Washington* in museum dock in Norfolk. It had crew of four or five thousand, I think. Fifty-three *million* of those would make . . . a hell of a hole."

"It will have the force of two hundred million hydrogen bombs, Jim. All going off at the same time, in the same spot."

The thing in the sky was a soft glow, deceptive and distant. The power to wipe out two hundred million cities, all rolled up into a ball and heading right toward them. Kirk shook his head and felt weak.

"Funny, but I find myself wishing I could protect Earth from that much damage."

Spock spared him the comment about how illogical that was. "It will set fire to over a quarter of the Earth's biomass.

Earthquakes, volcanoes . . . a violent day that we were not meant to see."

"A murderous tragedy if it happened to a populated planet."

They'd gone out of their way more than once to blow asteroids off track that were headed toward inhabited planets. But for this one, they were clearing the way. In fact, they were *in* the way.

They started to turn, but a sudden furious shout broke between them.

"Get out of the way! Get out of the way!"

Something struck Kirk hard in the upper left arm and knocked him over. In his periphery he saw Spock reel away.

Roth!

The Klingon had climbed up behind them and now was shouting wildly, so fast that the translator was only picking up parts of what he shouted or sending it through too late.

"Get away!—*jIyajchu'*—*qalehgh!* I see you! We all see it—*ghobe'*—*ghobe'*—*vaj batlh Daqawlu jiH! Mev! Mev!*"

"Spock, stop him!" Kirk rolled toward Roth's legs as they hammered past him and grabbed viciously but missed by a mile. "Oya, look out!"

A day ago she had been his enemy. Today, they were partners in impending disaster. Roth knocked Spock away as the Vulcan charged him and pounded toward the launcher.

Panicked, Kirk stumbled to his feet, but he was far behind. His phaser—where was his phaser? He'd forgotten to look for it!

Oya spun around and looked at him in confusion, then at Roth who was barreling at her, but too late. He dodged her well out of reach of tail or teeth, skidding around the corner of the launch platform. If he reached the control panel—

Then, he saw Roth angle away from the platform, and the Klingon was shouting again. Another form vaulted out of the lush bushes. The other Klingon!

Roth took a flying dive and caught Zalt around the hips, but Zalt was rested and ready. He cracked Roth on the back of the skull with his bare knuckles, and Roth went down.

Five steps, and Zalt was at the control box. He burrowed one glare of dazzling hatred at Kirk, then put his shoulder into throwing the switch.

Chemical smoke blew furiously from the missile's propellants as its version of engines fired. Ignition was hot and violent, a great hand knocking them all over and pressing them to the ground.

Kirk was instantly blinded by the light and buried his head under his arms while the raw force washed over him and the sound deafened him and the heat scalded his bare hands. The ground on which he lay shook and pounded, rattling his bones.

With a shriek too much like Rusa's enraged bawl, the missile rumbled off its platform and shuddered into the sky, trailing bright light and a moustache of smoke.

Kirk rolled over, shielding his eyes with one arm.

Above him in the air, the missile made a white fire as it slowly arched to its programmed trajectory.

He dragged himself up, stumbled to Spock, and they stood together, flushed, astonished, and watched the thing that would kill their universe go soaring into the innocent midday sky.

Chapter Thirty-four

THERE IT WENT.

What could stop it now?

Nothing. No phaser could reach out there, no will, no determination, no command. It was off and flying on the way to its appointment with the dot in the sky.

From behind, Oya came to stand on the other side of Spock, gazing with surprising expression into the sky. Her arms hung limp. Her tail was down.

The smoke of blastoff stung Kirk's eyes and scorched his lungs. Helplessness washed through him.

On the other side of the platform, Zalt pulled himself to his feet. His face was seared, his skull ridge bleeding, his hair wild, but he had succeeded.

With a glance at Kirk and Spock and one final, "Hah!" of victory, he angled into the jungle and disappeared at a dead run.

Spock tensed to give chase, but Kirk grasped his first officer's wrist. "Don't bother," he said.

The platform was bare now, scorched and littered with support struts broken during the launch, now lying blackened and smoldering. From somewhere in the smoke, Roth came staggering toward them, his face a mask of bitter anger.

"Give me a weapon," he demanded.

Kirk managed to straighten a little but didn't say anything.

Roth glared at him and Spock, then shouted, "Give me a weapon!"

When none of them moved, and Spock certainly wasn't going to hand over his phaser, Roth dodged toward them and yanked a serrated knife from Oya's harness.

Kirk had returned Oya's weapon when he released her. Now, that seemed to have been a mistake.

Now Roth had the knife. He waved it before them and blasted, "I will make one more emotional act!"

He turned, picked his way past the launcher through the smoke, then jumped down a slope and charged into the jungle in the direction Zalt had taken.

"I'm sorry, Captain," Spock rasped, his words laden with emotion he would otherwise have denied. He was watching the sky again. He didn't care about the Klingons.

Kirk didn't either. Failure, failure.

The biggest failure of all time. Suddenly all the successes of his career were canceled out. Nothing mattered.

Bitterly, he moved away from Spock, away from Oya. He kept his back to the lower area where his crewmen were holding the spikers. He didn't want to look at McCoy. But he had to turn when a flurry erupted down there. He looked without really turning all the way around.

The spikers were breaking up, rushing past Bannon and the others, who weren't sure whether or not to shoot them now. Bannon fired and stunned one spiker, but the others disappeared into the jungle.

Why not? Their mission was completed. All they had to do was melt into this environment and survive as long as they could in a place that was ideal for them.

Gritting his teeth to keep from bellowing, he stared into the sky at the fizzling spot that was the deflector rocket, now very small, off to orbit the Earth and wait until the asteroid attracted it. They'd probably see the impact from here.

"Damn," he murmured. "Oh, damn."

Nearby, Oya also stared. There didn't seem to be much else to do now.

"Captain," she buzzed, "I have never been so ashamed."

His jaw working to hold in the rage, Kirk stared another two seconds, then stepped away. "You should be."

It was a simple device according to Oya. It would orbit the Earth placidly until the asteroid came close, then the tiny matter/antimatter container inside the warhead would split the asteroid into millions of harmless chunks. They would be witness to one of the prettiest meteor showers of all time, but that would be all.

She explained how she had asked the "Forever Machine" to show her and her team pictures of Earth's history, and of course it had given them those pictures, because in the distant past they were from Earth. They had used their version of tricorders to slow the pictures, then jumped through at the right moment. Now the asteroid was less than two days away.

The Clan team had cut it close to make sure nothing could go wrong.

Kirk brooded like a charcoal fire. No matter how he combed the problem, there was nothing he could do. They had hand phasers and a few Ru energy weapons, but there wasn't enough power there to hit the asteroid from the surface or even hit the deflector in geosynchronous orbit, twenty-three thousand miles up.

They were sunk without a trace.

Spock appeared and sat beside him on the bump of snarled roots he was using as a command chair.

"Oya says the orbiter has no receivers of any kind, no internal command devices other than its basic control computer, which cannot receive an incoming signal of any sort. There's no way to tamper with it or alter its instructions from here."

"Not even something as simple as changing its orbit?" Kirk asked. "Maybe we can make it go to the other side of the planet when the asteroid comes."

"Even from the other side of the planet, it has sufficient time to find the asteroid, sir."

Kirk picked up a stick and cracked it in half, then in fourths. "There's got to be something we can do, Spock . . . something we're not thinking of. If only my head would clear up—"

"My head is clear," Spock said quickly, resisting the twang of guilt in Kirk's voice. "And I can think of nothing that will reach twenty-three thousand miles from here."

The sticks cracked in Kirk's hands. His knuckles were swollen. His own breath roared in his ears. Twenty-three thousand miles. Twenty-three thousand . . .

"Wait a minute—" He raised his head suddenly. "Did you ask her whether or not that thing's in geosynchronous orbit?"

Spock blinked.

"Oya! Oya, come here!" Kirk hobbled toward the sad dinosauroid who had been crouching near the useless platform since the thing blasted off. "How far above us is your detonator in orbit? Is it in synchronous orbit around the equator? Twenty-three thousand miles up?"

Oya glanced at Spock, then back, and waited for the translator to come through with those numbers in her own language.

"No . . . it has a small thruster system. We did not want to take the chance of wide orbit. It orbits only two hundred miles above us."

"Hell!" Kirk swung toward Spock. "We can practically touch it from here!" He rounded on Oya again. "Did you bring any spare launching equipment? Backups? You must have assumed something could go wrong!"

"Yes, we have a crude backup launch system, but it is meant to be used with the deton—"

"Spock! Gather up every scrap of extra equipment they have, everything we have, and calculate all the energy left in our phasers and the Ru weapons combined. Organize all hands and have them pick up the scattered pieces of the platform and those antigravs over there and the tools down the slope. We're gonna shoot that popgun down!"

Chapter Thirty-five

"ANIMAL! How long will you run? Come and face me, you low thing! I can go forever! Do you know how long forever will be today? Step out of the weeds! I will find a way back, do you hear me? Somehow I'll go back and tell everyone what you are! If I have to come back as the spirit of their own disappointment, I'll do it! I'll tell them all about you, coward!"

He had been running, pushing, rattling, through the

prehistoric understory of plants and weeds for a long time. He had no idea how long. His throat was raw, that was how long. Shouting insults was a lot of work.

Above him towered silent conifers, standing as they had for decades, and now as they would for decades more.

No, Kirk would find some way. He was that kind of man. Somehow there was an answer, another chance, an alternative, and that man would find it. He wouldn't give up.

And so Roth refused to give up, pushing unremittingly through the bushes, wild eyed, shouting anything he could think that might tease Zalt from hiding.

Just when he thought he could conjure up no worse words than he already had, he would cough up something else. There was a lot to say about Zalt.

So far he had cursed Zalt, Klingons, the Klingon home planets, their moons, several ships and their crews, Zalt again, and when he fell and bruised his skull, he cursed the rock that had tripped him.

As he scrambled to his feet again, caked with spores and wet soil and the defecation of some animal—large—he stumbled out onto an angled flat slab of ground where the surface had been worn away and only stone was left. There was much of that in these mountains, strata heaved up at vaulting angles as the mountains were pushed up from underneath. Something about a midocean fault and planetary surface plates crumpling this part of the continent. He had heard Kirk and the Vulcan talking about it. Until now, he hadn't cared.

"You smell like a barn."

Roth spun around. Zalt stood a few paces away, face flushed purple with anger.

Roth stalked toward his commander, his leader, his better, his tormenter. "I am ashamed to be Klingon, and before I die I'm going to do one decent thing. I'm going to kill you."

Zalt smiled. "You're going to kill me with that little blade?"

"You are the attitude that has wrecked us," Roth said. "Refusal to question what you see, refusal to question what you want. If you want to kill, then kill. If you want something someone else has, then get it. If someone is in your way, enslave them or kill them. That's all we are! It's not the Vulcans who embarrass me! It's *you!*"

He flung the knife over the embankment stretching out to one side of them and listened to it clatter.

Without glancing as the knife went clicking down the embankment, Zalt let his grin fall away. "These humans . . . they are more our enemy than the *romuluSngan* ever were. All these turtledoves who say they will not fight, yet in their 'universe' they have imprisoned the Klingons in their own space."

"Where they come from, everyone lives better because men like him insist that everyone behave."

"And you will do what *he* says? I'm not surprised, Roth. You're just angry because you're going to die a bad Klingon."

Roth didn't plunge, didn't run or jump forward, but walked to Zalt and took him by the collar in a manner so mellow that Zalt didn't resist or grasp at Roth's hands.

"We are all bad Klingons," Roth said. "Kill, eat, and be eaten. So go. Be with your own kind."

With a sudden surge of power, unexpected and unbalanced, he pushed Zalt sideways onto one foot and continued pushing. When Zalt realized this was all the fight would be, it was too late.

Roth cupped the side of Zalt's head and pushed hard.

Zalt spun off the side of the embankment and rolled roughly down, tumbling with his legs bent and his arms flung out.

At the bottom of the embankment, caught softly by a bundle of ragged pollen-bearing catkins, Zalt bumped to a stop. Dirty and bruised, he fumbled to his feet and glowered up at Roth, who was watching without expression.

Zalt raised his fists to emphasize his anger, but movement at his sides distracted him. He looked.

Open mouths rowed with serrated teeth snapped at the air nearby. Five . . . seven . . . ten . . . yellow eyes narrowed. Long-tailed bodies drew downward in attack stance. Crescent claws clicked on the rocks.

From above, just as the slashing began, he heard one last insult from Roth as a scream bolted from his own throat.

"Cry, victim."

The launcher was crude. No, it was worse.

Hardly more than a black tin box six meters square, a metal hut cannibalized from one of the spikers' cargo carriers, with eight antigravs strapped, glued, or fused to it. Four Starfleet tricorders inside to read four Clan tricorders mounted outside. There were even two long skinny "windows" made out of sheets of transparent flex-aluminum that Oya's team had brought with them in rolls.

The weapons had provided fuel for the launch, antigravs would keep them two hundred miles up, and the thrusters would hold them in place while waiting for the detonator to swing around the Earth. Then, one phaser would be enough.

And all the while they were cannibalizing the old launcher and fitting in standby equipment to do things beyond intent, the glow in the sky got bigger and brighter. Overnight, it had set like the sun as the Earth turned, and this morning it had risen, closer now.

Twenty-nine hours later, the thing in the sky was bigger than the moon, glowing and oblong. As if packed with purpose instead of iron, it was racing toward the Earth at fifty thousand miles per hour. When it hit—if it did—it would bore sixty miles into the planet's mantle.

Strange . . . to be sitting here, wishing with all his heart for that to happen.

As Spock circled the strange contraption they'd built, Kirk watched him and measured off their chances of success by the look in the Vulcan's face.

Well, maybe that wasn't the best idea.

They hadn't let him do much work, and he was in bad enough shape not to argue. They worked fast, but that didn't ease his frustrations. He was their captain and he should be working at their sides.

Oya interrupted his plagued thoughts when she came to settle beside him like a big chicken on a nest.

"We are nearly finished," she said. "We have fueled the launcher with several phasers and all of the spikers' pistols. After the launcher gives initial thrust, the antigravs will take the box up. Then the combined thrusters and antigravs will steer. At first we thought it would fail, but Mr. Spock devised a method of combining them. The tricorders on the outside will serve as sensors and aiming devices to be read off by someone inside. There is no navigation equipment, but there are the eight antigravs and seven of you. Mr. Spock will work two of them, but it will take all of you to keep the platform from spinning out of control. I am sorry there is no way for your crew to be safe. Even if you manage to shoot the deflector down, there will be no way to come back or land lightly if you do come down by mistake somehow."

"On the surface or in orbit," Kirk said, "I don't think it much matters. I could let your machine crack up the asteroid and we'd all have a savage life of raw survival here, or we can go up there and probably die, but I'm not giving up this chance for our handful of lives. That's not why any of us joined Starfleet."

"You are a brave man."

"I'm a desperate man. They're often the same. After all, you were willing to give up your life when you thought it would bring your people something better. You just turned out to be wrong."

"Most wrong." She lowered her monstrous head, her eyes surprisingly human.

"How much air will there be left in that thing?"

"Perhaps two hours, three—"

"Did you say seven of *us*? You're not going with us?"

She turned her large toothy head and seemed very civilized. "I cannot go. There is no room for me."

"We'll make room."

"No, Captain. It is an old story with my people. We have

347

the wrong body for space. Small ships, corridors, companionways—these are hard for us. Those of us who have taken to space for a profession, many have their tails amputated to make them more like humanoids. Besides, as you say, on the surface or not, it doesn't matter after tomorrow."

Sympathizing, Kirk fell silent. There were reasons for some races' success in space. He couldn't deny it.

"If you come back with us," he said, "assuming we make it back, you could talk to your people. Explain all this. Show them what we've recorded on the tricorders . . ."

"I am a scientist," she told him. "I am the lowest caste. They would not believe me."

Fighting tunnel vision, Kirk fanned his hot face with a leaf. "Why did you become a scientist then?"

"I was injured while in spiker leader training. While resting, I discovered that I enjoyed reading and studying. Eventually there was nothing else for me to do but follow my true interest. It was the only way I could be worth anything. You see . . . I have a crippled leg."

She moved, raised her body enough to show him her bent limb.

"So do I," Kirk said.

The two of them weren't worth much at this point. Spock knew more about propulsion than Oya did, so once the launcher was explained to him, even she wasn't much good over there. Just hoisting and bolting, phaser fusing and air tightening.

Oya's muzzle bumped up against his arm, and he flinched.

"Sorry," he said. "Did I hit you?"

"No," she answered. "I was . . . smelling you."

"Smelling me? What for?"

"You smell *good* to us." Was she smiling? Her eyes certainly were.

A shiver ran through him. He got her meaning. Not "good" as in nice, pleasant. But good as in *tasty*.

Suddenly he could empathize with her people. Mammals probably smelled like a hot dinner to the Ru. He tried to imagine humans negotiating with or even taking seriously people who smelled like warm baking bread.

How crushing would it be to be constantly saddled by instinct? Some things nature just insists we do. Nature had taken leisurely millions of years to establish some things, to make men attracted to women, women in love with their babies, and make some animals constantly hungry for others.

He inched a little to his left and really wanted to take a shower and smell like soap.

In the sky, the glowing oblong shape seemed larger than it had been an hour ago.

"Come on, Spock," he muttered. "How much longer can this take?" He looked up at the oblong shape in the sky. "I've only got fifty-three million aircraft carriers to go . . ."

Chapter Thirty-six

"HE'S DEAD."

"Are you sure this time?"

"I have no proof but the satisfaction in my eye, Captain Kirk. I give you that. I watched him die. They ripped him and ate him, and it is no less that the Klingon deserves."

Blunt silence fell between them. Roth looked satisfied and somehow humble. Kirk studied him, looking for those hints of vulnerability that he looked for in enemies and sometimes in friends, but he couldn't read Roth's face.

Roth had described Zalt as "the Klingon." So something had changed.

"We're ready to lift off," he said simply. "We're going to put ourselves between the asteroid and the warhead and blow the warhead."

"Risky," Roth said. "I like it." He looked at the tin box, about the size of a spare parts shed. "All of us in there?"

"All but Oya. She's staying behind."

"Staying behind . . . And what happens to this wild land when the asteroid comes?"

Kirk glanced across the plateau to where Oya was working with Spock and the others. "Nothing very nice," he admitted.

"So you and your Vulcan have talked about it. And he has told you what such a rock does."

"Yes. The numbers are mindboggling."

"The strike itself will boggle a few things too, I think." Roth was in the fulfilled mood of a man condemned who had first condemned his rival. "How are you powering this?"

"We've drained most of the phasers and all of the Ru weapons for initial liftoff. Then the antigravs take over. Spock's phaser and Ensign Emmendorf's are still operational," Kirk added, "in case you get any ideas."

"I have no ideas." Roth chuckled. "I believe what you— Captain!"

Kirk tried to sidestep, but Roth was faster. He slammed into Kirk and knocked him to the ground.

Tumbling once, then rolling once, Kirk fought to come up on his elbows, and looked up in time to see Roth take a hard attack from one of the troodonts. It came out of nowhere without ruffling a single bush until this instant, and suddenly there were attacking troodonts everywhere.

He saw Roth roll backward to the ground, holding off the snapping teeth of one of these small, smart things and kicking at the hinds legs to keep those hacking claws from ripping into his body.

"Spock, trouble!" Kirk pushed off the ground and tackled the troodont. He and the animal and Roth tumbled like dancers, rolling down a slight incline to be blessedly stopped by a palmetto. Tightening his arms around the animal's neck from behind, Kirk dragged it off Roth, held its spine against his chest with its tail slashing at his legs, and dared not let go. He pitched backward, with an armload of wild kicking dinosaur.

Its spine scratched his face as the troodont threw its head from side to side, yanking Kirk along the ground on his back. The tail bruised his legs, and just as he thought he couldn't hold on anymore, Roth was on them. The Klingon got his big hands around the troodont's muzzle, forcing the animal to scream through its nostrils like a kidnap victim. He leaned forward so hard that Kirk's shoulder was pinned against a scaly trunk without chance of squirming free.

Roth leaned harder, and—*crack, crack, crack*—the troodont's neck vertebrae snapped. The animal fell limp on top of Kirk. He kicked it off and rolled over. "Spock! Fire it up!"

There were phaser shots up there. He struggled back up the incline, with Roth shoving him from behind.

His friend was back. That rugged troodont with the crooked arm, chirping orders to his pack. First flank, rushing in. Second rank, waiting in the wings.

Kirk paused to look at the leader. How long had this tricky animal stalked them? Tenacity—a sign of intelligence.

As Spock's phaser crackled through the hot air, taking out two of the charging troodonts, Emmendorf took out another one before he was charged from behind and knocked to the ground. Before the troodont standing on him could rake a furrow in his spine with one of those claws, Bannon tackled the animal bare-handed, wrestling it to the side. It took the two of them to pummel the beast to unconsciousness. Emmendorf came up bloody, glancing around for another troodont to defend against.

They were everywhere.

"Get in the vehicle!" Kirk shouted. "Let's go!"

"I'll stay here, sir!" Bannon called, scooping up a discarded piece of metal. "I'll hold them off!"

Though his first reaction was to order everyone inside, Kirk realized that Bannon was right. The troodonts were closing in, sacrificing a few first charges in order to weaken them, so the second and third ranks could overwhelm them. It would work, too. There were dozens of yellow-eyed pouncers all around them, smacking their chops, clicking their sickle-claws, and waiting for the order to charge.

Suddenly Roth shoved Bannon toward the tin-box vehicle and snatched the shaft of metal out of the boy's hand. "Go!" he shouted. "I will stay!"

His mouth gaping, Bannon looked at his empty hand, then at Roth.

Roth shoved him viciously toward the tin box, then swung around to where Kirk and Spock were standing off a flank of troodonts while the others hobbled toward the vehicle.

"Give me a phaser! I will hold them off!" When he saw their hesitation, he shouted, "Kirk! I was willing to risk my life for one more day's existence for my people! I will do it for you! Give me a phaser! Let me be the ultimate Spear!" He kicked an approaching troodont square in the nose and waved sharply at Kirk. "I'll stay and save you," he said. "You go and save us all."

Caught by those words, Kirk fixed a truth-serum glare on him. The decision was his and he knew it.

"Spock," he said, "give him a phaser. Roth, you know what to do with the antigravs—"

"I will do everything!"

From the far side, another proclamation came. The buzz of Oya's translator. When Kirk turned, she was there. "We will do it, Captain," she said. "Go. And save us all."

Emmendorf fired again, blowing away two more troodonts and somehow encouraging the others to come forward out of the bushes. They understood sacrifice.

Kirk peered at Roth and Oya.

"All hands," he called, "on board!"

* * *

"We have ignition, sir."

Kirk clung to the steadiness of Spock's acknowledgment as the tin box jolted and began to quiver.

Through the eight-inch-wide, twenty-inch-long "window" in front of him, he saw Roth swatting and kicking the troodonts two at a time, while Oya hurried around the vehicle, firing the antigravs manually.

The troodonts seemed confused, probably because they weren't used to jumping onto a humanoid and didn't know how to do it. Many of the troodonts he kicked away were heading toward Oya—a familiar body shape.

"Everyone stay coordinated," he said, keeping his tone calm. "Hold balance while we lift off."

The squarish vehicle shuddered beneath them. Phaser and pistol power that had been funneled into the launch mechanism fired, and suddenly the platform puffed upward and became airborne, wobbling as they struggled for control.

The last thing Kirk saw on the planet's surface was the top of Roth's head. Then there was jungle, then mountain.

There was no gravitational compensation, and as the craft accelerated, Kirk felt his body suddenly grow heavy, crushed to the bench seats they'd hastily built. He heard his crew moan with strain and wished he could help them.

On the right-angled wall beside him, Spock had one inside tricorder mounted where he could see it and opposite him the medical tricorder mounted where Bannon and Vernon could see it. In front of Kirk was a third tricorder, and on the far side, where Reenie and Emmendorf worked their antigravs, the fourth tricorder. Each was tied into one of the four Clan Ru tricorders scavenged from the leftover deflector camp, mounted in protective shells on the outside, which would act as sensors.

For a quick build, it wasn't a bad little craft. Simple, but serviceable. So far, so good.

"Antigravs taking over liftoff," Spock reported, his tone professional. "One hundred meters . . . one hundred fifty . . . two hundred . . . Exhaust equalizing . . . Motive power levels rough but stabilizing."

"All hands, concentrate, maintain balance," Kirk encouraged. "Mr. Spock and I will steer with the thrusters."

"Jim, how are you going to find the warhead?" McCoy asked.

"Oya gave us calculations of its orbit. We'll have to get between the warhead and the asteroid as they approach each other."

"We'll do it, sir," Emmendorf piped up.

"Yes, sir," Reenie echoed.

The Earth peeled away beneath them, a lovely and savage planet, stuffed with life. From the sky as they gained altitude, Kirk could see herds of dinosaurs, a dozen shapes, a hundred colors. Some he recognized—ceratopians, torosaurs, alamosauruses, simple beasts, dumb as dirt, following instinct through the eons.

The pressure of his own weight went away as they came higher and higher, closer to the top levels of the atmosphere, closer to weightlessness. They were strapped in, but not very tightly. They had to hang on.

A cloud cleared away, and there was a bizarre map below, deep greens threaded with browns and other greens as they went high into the atmosphere, wobbling and straining for control.

"Cartography on automatic," he ordered.

The planet below looked foreign—the continents were completely wrong, unfamiliar land masses overrun with oceans. If he looked carefully and used his imagination, he could make out North America, much smaller than he was used to, with strange shorelines. There was a lot of water.

"Tracking the warhead, Captain," Spock reported. "Relatively simple . . . It is changing course slightly. Adjusting trajectory to compensate. Velocity peak stabilizing."

"Intercept course."

"Captain . . ." Reenie began.

Aggravated, Kirk turned.

The girl had her cheek pressed up against the window slit, eyes straining outward toward space.

"I can see it," she said, her voice catching in her throat. "Oh, my God, I can *see* it . . ."

354

She wasn't talking about the warhead. That was coming from the other direction.

"Ensign," Kirk snapped. "Mind your post. Mr. Spock, bring us around to firing position. I don't want to be late coming about."

"Aye, sir. Coming about."

"Heading?"

"Heading is south by southwest. We took off slightly earlier than I had calculated. I'm attempting a geostationary orbit and to hold position and wait for the warhead to orbit toward us."

"That won't do any good if it leaves orbit to intercept the asteroid. Sacrifice whatever power you need to get between them."

"Acknowledged. Of course," Spock added quietly, "that will also sacrifice our ability to land safely."

Kirk glanced at him. "Doesn't matter, Mr. Spock."

Returning the glance, Spock paused. "Understood, sir."

"Prepare to fire phasers."

"Phasers ready."

The drone of order and response was reassuring. The practicality of military redundance—it had a purpose. It kept them calm. One step at a time. Each moment became a progressive victory. Habit set fear to second place, and protocol took over. That which had brought men through uncounted battles in the midst of choking smoke and mind-numbing terror now would serve to propel them through this last circus hoop.

As they left the lower atmosphere, the warmth of the supertropics fell away, and Kirk felt his sweat turn clammy and his body go completely weightless. It was dizzying. His hands stiffened on the crude controls. Frost started to form on the insides of the walls, and their breath began to steam.

"Captain, I've got the deflector warhead on screen." Reenie put her nose to the tiny screen. "Unless it's one of those forty-foot pterosaurs—"

"Negative," Spock said. "Warhead confirmed. It's leaving orbit, zeroing in on the asteroid. Coming into phaser range . . ."

"I want point blank range, Spock. We won't get a second chance. The warhead's moving faster than we are. If we miss, we'll never catch it."

He kept one hand on his thruster controls and with the other he tried to focus his tricorder as the screen rippled. The tie-in to the Ru tricorders outside was tenuous and incompatible. He wished he'd put one of their own tricorders on the exterior. Too late now.

"Reading the asteroid now, Captain." Spock's eyes were fixed on the tiny tricorder screen. "Slightly larger in diameter than we had thought . . . however, less dense. Possibly due to some ice content. Current trajectory will take it to the expected impact point, lower Gulf of Mexico. Speed is . . . forty-seven thousand six hundred miles per hour, increasing steadily as Earth's gravity affects it."

"Captain!" Bannon flinched suddenly at Kirk's right. "The warhead—I think I'm reading it! Coming from the west—it's angling out of orbit!"

"Hold your course, Mr. Bannon," Kirk said. "Mr. Spock, can you zero in on that thing?"

"Zeroing in," Spock responded. "Targeting phasers."

"Hold course, everyone. I'll do the shooting."

He tried to take his own advice and keep his eyes on the tricorder screen, which struggled to register the tiny blip that was the angling deflector warhead.

Another dumb bullet. All it had to do was go to the right place and hit. No sense of consequence.

"Clearer readings on the asteroid now, sir," Reenie reported, her tiny voice like a shiver.

"Confirmed," Spock said. "Asteroid is a typical bolide . . . irregular spheroid with several broken edges . . . Content, primarily iron, nickel, iridium . . . carbon . . . ice . . . various common ores. Density, roughly twenty-six thousand kilograms per cubic meter."

Typical. Common. The words pounded in Kirk's head. In the twists of nature's wind tunnel, an average space rock with no chance for success had become evolution's hatchet man.

"Detonator at one hundred kilometers and closing,"

Spock read off. "Ninety . . . eighty . . . seventy . . . sixty . . . fifty—"

"Firing phasers."

Eyes tight and legs tense, Kirk thumbed the firing mechanism that was tied into the hand phasers mounted on the vehicle's exterior. A hand phaser was a mighty child, a power-packed minireactor that could tear down half a city. Training for hand phaser handling alone was nearly a full year's course at Starfleet Training Grounds, required for everyone who wore the uniform.

He looked up from the tricorder and out the skinny window and pressed the firing mechanism.

A thin thread of phaser fire spewed from the vehicle's cold hull beneath him and spindled across the outer rim of the Earth's hazy atmosphere, a red line dividing the white atmosphere from the darkness of space.

"Slight thermal drift," Spock said quickly.

"Compensate. Maintaining fire."

"Compensating."

Kirk held his thumb on the firing tie-in, his mind already tangled with alternatives to try if he was making a clean miss. There had to be something he could—

"There it goes!" Bannon had apparently looked up.

The line between Earth and space suddenly blew wide with yellow light and a plume of silver smoke. Kirk recognized the chemical reaction and suddenly felt tied to his own time.

His mind went numb, filled with a crackling noise. The crew was cheering behind him. That was the crackle.

He pressed forward on the slanted wall, fighting to stay upright, staring out at the gas jet cashiering across the rim of the atmosphere and its long blue tail.

Strange how small the detonation seemed against the canvas of Earth's curvature and the depths of space beyond. A few moments later, that strike would have split the asteroid, blown it into splinters, causing the debris to spiral away from Earth, and the the future would be consumed.

"Warhead is destroyed, Captain," Spock quietly reported.

They shared one of those almost-smiles reserved for

moments when the relief was almost too much to bear. Kirk's hands were shaking, and the quiver of his muscles ran all the way from his wrists up his arms and through his shoulders. His midsection cramped and his legs throbbed.

"Jim—Jim!" Hiked around on his bench, McCoy was staring at him.

"What?"

"That was it, wasn't it? That was the thing that changed history?"

"Yes, of course."

Cheeks pale and eyes strained, McCoy turned more toward him and held out an imploring hand.

"Then why are we still here?"

Chapter Thirty-seven

THE CAPTAIN was supposed to have all the answers.

Jim Kirk looked at the doctor with pain in his silence. Finally, as he always did, he turned to his left.

"Spock?"

The Vulcan was gazing at them both, troubled and overloaded, as if he had forgotten about that, too.

"I don't know," he said, mild with thought. "We should be pulled back through the Guardian's portal upon successfully correcting the error in the flow of time. The deflector is destroyed . . . The asteroid *must* strike the Earth now. Logically, time should be repaired."

He stopped. They ticked off another five seconds.

Still here.

"Could it be," McCoy pressed, "we've come back too far?

Maybe the Guardian can't handle years by the tens of millions. Maybe it just can't find us!"

Across the cramped cabin, Vernon whimpered, "Oh, Jesus . . ."

His face clammy, Kirk drew his brows tight. "Then we'll have to give it time to find us."

"Are you kidding?" McCoy prattled and pointed out the window. "Have you seen the size of that rock?"

"That's enough, Doctor." Kirk gripped his controls and shuddered down the weakness in his body. He summoned his last reserves. A few more minutes, that was all he needed. "Spock, where's the safest place to be when this thing hits?"

"The safest place to be at the moment of impact would be at the antipode, on the opposite side of the planet, at least for several hours, until the shock waves encircle the planet—"

"We can't get there in time. Where's the second safest place?"

"The second safest place is inside the cone of ejecta, beside the asteroid as it hits, but not directly above it."

"Explain that."

Spock swiveled toward him. "When a marble is dropped into a pool of water, it creates two immediate reactions. One is a cone of water that is spewed upward around it in the shape of a paper cup, and the other is a tower that sprays directly up the way the marble came. Between those two reactions, there is an area of relative calm."

"Like the eye of a hurricane."

"Exactly."

"Then that's where we've got to be."

Bannon's eyes were hollow as he gaped at them. "I don't want to be there."

"That's where we're going to be," Kirk sizzled, and everybody turned back to their jobs. "Spock, calculate trajectory. Get me a course. Dr. McCoy, record the patterns of atmospheric turbulence. Miss Reenie, focus on the aster-oid and impact shrapnel."

"Ejecta, sir," Spock said.

"You call it what you want; I'll call it what I want."

"Yes, sir."

"Mr. Bannon, you record geophysics and—"

"Why?" Shaking like a wet lamb, Bannon was nearly in tears. "Why bother?"

"Because we're explorers and scientists. People have died willingly for much lesser sights than we're about to witness. We're going to do our jobs until the last possible second. Is that understood?"

Part of McCoy's mouth twisted up in a sorry grin. The Security men shared a glance and Emmendorf gave up a silent thumbs-up.

Spock was looking at him, too.

Bannon's narrow face lost its panicked expression. Somehow the younger man screwed up his resolve as he gazed at his captain. His voice cracked. "Aye aye, sir," he said.

Like survivors in a life craft on a wide empty sea, feet soaked, lips parched, they steeled themselves to get through the next minute, then the minute after that.

"Jim." Spock's face was occult with shadows. "It's coming."

He wasn't looking at his tricorder anymore. He was looking out the window of the tilted craft as it struggled to hold itself in place over the gulf of what someday would be Mexico.

Kirk felt his chest tighten and his feet get suddenly colder. He had to look, too, to see eternity's superstar with his own eyes.

Back on the planet's surface, seen through the atmosphere, the asteroid had been a glowing orb in the sky. That was what Roth and Oya were seeing now if they were still alive.

From here, above most of the atmosphere, it was a dull spacial body glittering on one side from the sun's reflection. It seemed not to be moving at all.

But it was. It sang through space toward them at forty-thousand-plus miles per hour, accelerating every second. Femme fatale Earth had whispered into the night with the perfume of her gravity and caught the unsuspecting passerby cantering by without a thought. Now this crude peddler, insignificant dot in the mob of space debris, would have its chance to swashbuckle. Its incendiary kiss would pivot history. This was its day.

Kirk squinted out the narrow window. "Spock, do you know what month this is?"

"It's early June, sir."

"What day is it?"

Spock looked at him. "I don't know."

"All right. You know, I wish that thing could understand what it's about to do. I resent its ignorance somehow."

"That . . . makes no sense at all, sir. The asteroid is nothing more than an amalgam of silica."

"I don't care. Everyday I have the power of that thing in my hands and I keep control over it. What's the depth of the ocean at the point of impact?"

"Zero to two hundred feet, sir. On its current trajectory, it will hit the continental shelf."

"Will this thing go through the Earth's mantle?"

"It's believed to have cracked the mantle to a depth of roughly fifty miles but did not penetrate to create a volcanic site."

Roaring in at hypersonic speed, the oblong ball seemed to be swelling a little each second, as if they were watching any other space vehicle come toward them—no sense of the actual speed. It was a piece of some other cataclysm, a lackluster stone determined to make something of itself. The big bang had come and gone, the crash that had made the moon was long forgotten, the birth of life a past accomplishment. Now this chunk of dirt wanted to dwarf the fame of those and give itself primacy. And the plan would work. The Federation and all its member worlds, the Klingons, the Romulans, the Orions, the Tholians, the Clan—they were all wrapped up in that rock.

"Captain—" Reenie gulped. "It's—it's—"

"Understood, Ensign. Spock, altitude, we need altitude."

"Thrust at maximum, Captain."

"We have to be inside that cone. This thing's gonna rattle us . . ."

Bannon pulled out of his straps, jerked away from his seat, and stumbled to the window on the other side of Spock. "Here it comes!"

"Lieutenant, get back in your seat!" Kirk broiled. "All hands, secure for collision!"

Chapter Thirty-eight

"HERE IT COMES!"

In a blur as big as Manhattan Island, the asteroid shot past them at 138.8888 miles per second, slightly over a hundred miles to the west of them, pulled in by the beckoning Earth. What they saw then was a forbidden sight wisely done in the shadows of deep time, so violent that mass spectrometers had been needed to discover the secret that it had happened at all. In his fever and the terror he couldn't push away, James Kirk fought himself through the temptation to put his thumb to his phaser and keep that kill-crazy stone from erasing billions of years of life.

Earth had called out for this, as if saying this was the time to smash the canvas and start again. He had stewardship over the future. He had prevented cataclysms—today he needed one.

His hand quivered as he drew it toward his chest and held it against his ribs. A few more seconds . . .

In extravagance that only bold, brainless nature could manage, the asteroid blew past them, causing only a moment's shadow to fall inside the baubling little vehicle.

He pushed up against his restraints, nauseated by weightlessness, put his face to the window, and looked down at the Earth.

He'd seen stars explode. But those were only stars.

Below their little vehicle, bucking in the swarming upper atmosphere, the asteroid spun in at hypersonic speed, too fast for the atmosphere to blow out of the way.

Kirk watched, mind numbed, as the kinetic explosion opened up beneath them. For an instant there was a flash of heat energy being released, a wall of brightness reaching all the way down and all the way up as high as the atmosphere. A trumpet-bell plume of white-bright fire vomited back upward past them and back over their heads, expanding into a vacuum that couldn't stop it, a violent seismic upheaval of molten rock, shock-modified minerals, and fine hot dust.

In fifteen years in space he had voyaged countless light-years through the galaxy, yet he had to come home to witness the most spectacular event of his career. As the force equal to two hundred million hydrogen bombs went off under them, the vapor cloud impelled upward toward them like the head of a rising jellyfish.

"Shield your eyes! Cover your eyes!" McCoy's shouts were drowned by the concussion from all around them.

Kirk managed to bury his face in the crook of his elbow as the white-hot fireball of vaporized matter shot back out into space in the biggest mushroom cloud any tyrant could dream of on any drunken night.

He'd seen death coming before but never with ballistics on this scale. He held the thruster lever and hoped the vehicle didn't go into a spin. If Spock could hold his steady—

"The asteroid vaporized!" Reenie sobbed. "It's a fire-ball!"

The curtain of blistering molten rock and pulverized planet shot back upward past them, some moving fast enough to reach escape velocity and rocket out into space, never to return.

"Hold on!" It might have been Bannon. "Shock waves!"

The vehicle spun like Dorothy's house in the twister. Much of the ejecta curtain was curling into orbit in what would become the smothering ashfall of days to come. The sun would be blocked out. Asteroid winter would chill the planet.

Chunks of molten matter pummeled the vehicle. Precision was thrown to the wind as the giant blowtorch shot by on one side and the ghastly wreckage on the other.

Kirk wanted to look at his crew, give them his last glance of inspiration, smooth out the malignant eruption with his confidence, see their sober faces as they gave each other the final gift of noble silence.

But his arms, his neck, his chest, were frozen still. His eyes fixed on the mushroom tower of fire retching into space, and his eyes burned.

With his last thought he wondered about the tricky troodont with the crooked arm. Was it intelligent enough to be afraid as the sheer mile-high wall of displaced water and the incandescent curtain of debris as high as the atmosphere expanded out of the Gulf and swallowed part of North America? Did it have its last thought for its young?

And Oya . . . Roth. He'd left them behind at ground zero. Someday he would find a Klingon and tell him who he owed his existence to.

The tin box around them began to crack.

Beneath them, he saw Earth begin all over again.

Chapter Thirty-nine

"I'M SORRY, SIR . . ."

Montgomery Scott sank into the sounds of the bridge for one last moment, those peaceful twitters and beeps that in a second would be ripped out of his head, buried in explosions of machinery and the cracking of the ship's heavy hull.

He'd put his life into this one ship, out of all the others, and never looked back. His heartbeat and this ship's were the same. Had been for years. Some ships could do that to a person.

"Sorry, lass," he murmured.

"Mr. Scott, the incoming has disappeared!" Sulu's voice had a squawk of disbelief.

"Mr. Scott!" Chekov choked at the navigation station. "No sign of hostile vessels! They're gone, sir! They disappeared!"

Scott blinked and held his breath. No hit. No savaging of his lady. The viewscreen was free of all but stars and Earth's moon as it came lazily around them.

"The captain!" he rasped. "Have y'got contact with the planet's surface?" He swung around to Uhura and gripped the red rail. "Lieutenant?"

The tin box around them was gone.

Had it been shattered by the plume of ejecta? Was this the split second between destruction and death?

Everybody said that second was there, but how could anyone really know?

Jim Kirk stared into the white heat of the vampire fireball. It was as if he had poured pepper into his eyes and put his hands on a pilot light. His body was blistered, his mind bedlam.

Hard ground came up under his feet, and he staggered. He wished he hadn't looked out the little window, but some sights really were worth dying for.

We were there on the day a cold rock became a star. One tree, one frog, enough will live now to start over. Incorrigible nature—

"Captain . . . Captain. We are being signaled. Your communicator . . ."

That was Spock's voice. Were the two of them in hell together? It figured.

In hell with a communicator?

Blinking his eyes as they watered and stung, Kirk shook his head and let out a small cough. "That was . . . some ride."

He shook off the frigidity of orbit and tried to set aside the tantalizing blowtorch he'd just witness.

"Sixty-four million years," McCoy grumbled beside him. "Jim, the ship—the *ship!*"

They were standing on stone, not metal. Kirk looked down. Rocks. His feet were braced on pebbles.

But not Earth. He blinked up at dusty ruins and a glum pastel sky, then at the doctor beside him and realized the buzzing in his head was the communicator on his belt. He pawed for it, failing, until McCoy got it and placed it in his hand.

The ship!

He raised the communicator. "Kirk here . . ."

"Captain! You did it, sir!"

"Scotty?"

"You must've done it, sir!"

Well, at least Scotty had a grasp on what had happened. Yes, the ship's engineer had been here the last time. He understood this place, this smart-aleck monument over Kirk's shoulder.

Turning to look at the Guardian of Forever—he'd always thought there should be a really bad poem under that title—he took a shuddering breath. "It got us back . . . all the way from there." Suddenly he turned and started counting heads. "Did we *all* get back? Is everyone here?"

"All accounted for, sir." Spock appeared at his side, his tone much less severe than the words. He gazed at Kirk with undisguised sympathy.

"The tricorders—"

"All four of ours came through with us." The Vulcan held one of them up for him to see. Near him, their rattled crew picked at the other three, clinging to them as if clinging to the past. Now they had more than fossils and shocked quartz to use as a peek into the past. Now they had the past recorded.

And the *Enterprise* was up there, orbiting this forsaken grotto. She was back, she was back.

Kirk sought for his voice again. "Status, Scotty."

"We were under attack by a bundle'a Romulan bastards when all at once they just vanished! They were about to melt us alive!"

"I'm glad this machine has its timing right. We were pretty melted ourselves. Either a hell of a coincidence, or this thing knows what it's doing. Secure all decks and stand by, Scotty."

"Standing by, sir."

Hoisting his shuddering body around, he scanned his landing party. They were shaken, doubtful of their surroundings, as if coming out of a long dream. McCoy and Reenie each had a grip on Vernon, who had an arm wrapped around his crushed ribs.

So it *had* happened.

He sighed. "Well, I'd say that was a big splash."

The crew rewarded him with a couple of smiles and a few huffs of relief. That was all he wanted.

"Let's get a grip on ourselves. Mr. Emmendorf, Mr. Bannon, secure the area. Be back here in five minutes. Doctor, make your patient comfortable. We'll beam up as soon as we're stable."

"Aye aye, sir," Emmendorf said.

Bannon said nothing but hurried after the Security man. Both were pale with shock and seemed relieved to have something concrete to do. Being sucked back through the Guardian's portal had left them all in a protective state of disbelief.

Now he would have to see if they were back in the *correct* time. No Romulan ships up there. He clung to that clue. He cleared his throat and uttered, "Spock . . ."

Spock came to his side. "How are you?" he asked.

"Rattled. What's your evaluation?"

"If our experience with the Guardian is accurate, and our suppositions about Oya's race correct—that her race actually began on Earth millions of years before us—then all should be in order. We did see the asteroid hit, after all."

"We did, but that's a lot of ifs."

"I would surmise the key to the change was the impact itself, not simply our destruction of the warhead. The Guardian had waited until the asteroid actually struck the Earth. Until then, the extinction of the dinosaurs was not guaranteed."

Kirk nodded. "Had me scared for a minute."

"More than a minute," McCoy grumbled from behind them.

Relieved to hear the smart-ass crack, Kirk nodded at him but turned to Spock again. "What do you think happened to Oya?"

"Unknown. Certainly anyone in the lower North American area would have been killed by tidal waves crashing across that area. I am sure," Spock added gently, "they did not suffer long."

Realizing he was giving too much away—as if he could hide his crushing sense of injustice from Spock—Kirk fought for control.

"The mass extinction by asteroid impact," Spock said, "is no longer a conclusion based upon bits of evidence. We have just proven it. And we have a recording of the actual impact. So successful a species as the dinosaurs, a two-hundred-million-year species . . . destroyed in a matter of months."

Kirk stepped past him. "Species go extinct all the time, Mr. Spock. Extinction is part of the game. Just goes to show you how tough life is once it gets started." He snapped up his communicator. "Kirk to Bannon, report."

"Bannon here, sir. You'd better come this way. We've got something here."

"All right, stay where you are. We'll triangulate on your communicator."

"Yes, sir."

The kid didn't sound too good. Kirk turned to McCoy. "The rest of you stay here. Mr. Spock, with me."

Not far, as the pterosaur flies, but every step was agony for a man who'd left his cane stuck in a dinosauroid sixty-odd million years back. By the time they found Emmendorf waving at them to go toward him, Kirk was sweat-drenched. He followed Spock over the crunchy ground and around an upright slab of ruin.

There, they found the bodies. Starfleet bodies.

These people had put up a fight and lost. And for their loss they were ripped into parts and horridly mutilated. A Starfleet research team, who never intended to fight, who wanted only to do quiet work here, maybe shed some light on these ruins. Only tacitly were they meant to guard the Guardian.

"Captain," Spock addressed, not loud, "these people were killed, then eaten. And there is one of the spikers' wrist launchers. Several footprints also."

Numb beyond shock, Kirk nodded. He thought about setting his crew to burying the dead here, but his people were exhausted and, truth be told, there wasn't much left here to bury. These bodies were rended to bits and already sinking back into the dust. They were burying themselves.

"Emmendorf, Bannon," he spoke up, "go back with the others."

The two young men glanced at him as though entranced, then Emmendorf said, "Yes, sir . . ."

And they went away. Nothing to be done here.

"We wanted proof, Mr. Spock," he said sadly, "proof that it all happened. I guess we've got that now."

Silent, Spock watched him.

"Oya believed in this mission," Kirk went on. "I'd have done the same thing. Let's go."

Spock reached for him to help him over a boulder, but the communicator chirped and stopped them.

"Kirk here."

"Scott, sir. We've got three ships approaching, no identity yet."

"Red alert. Beam us up immediately, these coordinates. And pick up the others at our previous location."

Spock's expression was heavy with concern as Kirk

watched his first officer's face begin to sparkle with the transporter effect.

Then his mind went numb for the few seconds the transporter needed to draw him back . . . back to his ship.

And his heart began to pound.

"This is the Starship Exeter—*Newman here. Jim, are you and your crew all right? I've never heard of any force that could throw a ship this far!"*

Jim Kirk settled into his command chair, legs aching and spine screaming for rest. On the forward screen, Doug Newman's face was better than a star on a Christmas tree.

The starship inhaled around him, as vibrant a thing as any, cupped his aching body in this old chair, gathered her wings and shook the droplets of turmoil from them once again, just because he asked her to. Together they had survived.

"We didn't exactly get thrown. How did you find us?"

"We thought you were crushed by the accretion disk that appeared in that blue giant. Then these other people showed up and they said they knew where you were. We took a chance, and here you are. They want to talk to you."

Off the *Enterprise*'s gleaming white port bow, three ships hovered, basking in the light of this system's thrifty sun. The *Starship Exeter,* the *Farragut,* and another ship, a squatty, squarish vessel only a few decks thick, with warp nacelles mounts on the sides that looked like old wares cannibalized from former Starfleet designs.

The forward screen fizzled, then cleared. Kirk stared into the faces of six dinosauroids.

Well, well.

"Clan Ru," he said. "Welcome out of your cave. I wish I could say I'm surprised, but I don't think I am."

"Captain Kirk," the brown one in the middle said. A heavy female with four colors painted on her face. Probably the captain. *"I am Ozur. We come to talk. She here will talk for us."*

Ozur unceremoniously moved aside, and the screen filled again, this time with a stunning grayish face.

Kirk's snideness dropped away. "Oya! You made it back!"

"Several days ago, somehow," she buzzed through the ship's translator. Her voice was a little different, coming through Uhura's system instead of the portable translator. A little higher. *"The science of the Guardian is unclear. Somehow I was returned to the Guardian planet only seconds after I first entered."*

"Yes, we know," Kirk said. "And since we entered several days later than you did, we only just returned a few minutes ago."

"I have been back for many days," Oya said, *"and I haven't been idle. Captain Kirk, I went to my leaders. I told them about your pictures and what I saw on the young Earth. We have always known we did not come from our planet. We assumed everything there was meant to be food for us and that we were the chosen of providence, held back by the Federation. Now I believe as you, and I have told my people. Someone had respect for our species, enough to move us and save us. We never had respect for others. Now we do. Earth is a charmed place to give birth to two intelligent species while so many planets are barren. We understand now, Captain Kirk, and we want to join."*

Swallowing past the lump in his throat, Kirk managed a smile. He shifted his hips a couple of times, trying to think. He gazed at his tidbit of profit from this huge stumble. Some good was going to come of this after all. They hadn't just managed to put things right but to put things better.

"We welcome you," he said finally, simply. "If you'll follow us to Starbase 10, we'll introduce you to our fleet commander and arrange for an exchange of ambassadors."

"Our thanks to you. We will come happily."

"I'm looking forward to hearing your account of the impact from the planet's surface."

"I have it recorded. It is a revelation for science."

"I'll bet it is. Oya . . ."

"Yes?"

Pressing his hands to the command chair, the vital core of his universe, past and future, Jim Kirk leaned forward as if the two of them were having a private conversation. "I thought you said they wouldn't believe you."

Oya moved her lips around those massive teeth, and her eyes grew narrow and gleamed.

"They did."

PART FIVE

WELCOME ABOARD

*A pennon whimpers—the breeze has found
  us—
A headsail jumps through the thinning haze.
The whole hull follows, till—broad around
  us—
The clean-swept ocean says: "Go your ways!"*

—Rudyard Kipling

Chapter Forty

A STARSHIP's auxiliary monitor is a high-resolution contraption, darned good at doing what it was designed to do.

The screen was small, but it communicated the enormity of the impact with a valiance that made Jim Kirk proud and humble. He lay in his diagnostic bed in sickbay, head resting back and medication pumping through his shell-shocked body. Tricorder recordings of the impact were traveling the ship's decks almost as rapidly as the vapor fireball had reached the outer atmosphere all those millions of years ago.

Millions of years?

But it had been only this morning.

Stretched out before him, his body was covered with a thermal blanket, and he could barely feel his feet. Saw them, but didn't feel them.

Scratched by ancient thorns and bruised by ancient blows, his hands rested on his chest.

Before him, several department heads from the ship's labs had gathered to hear Mr. Spock's explanation of what they were seeing on that half-meter-square screen. A couple of interns, one other doctor, and two nurses stood at the perimeter of the briefing. This was only the tip of the iceberg of research that would come from their voyage.

"The cataclysm very quickly became worldwide," Spock said, watching the sprawling white-orange event shudder and balk on the screen. "Only hours for the first shock wave. As we saw, the impact displaced most of the water in the Gulf of Mexico, causing tidal waves in all directions. Of course, there would be a rebound tidal wave as the water rushed back in. Within one day, no part of Earth's surface would be unaffected. A layer of soot found in the K–T layer suggests that molten ejecta raining upon the planet touched off firestorms that burned millions of miles of growth. Excess of carbon-12 in the biomass indicates that fires consumed as much as a quarter of Earth's plants. For a decade or more after, simple lightning would have touched off more fires until finally all the dead plant life was burned away."

"A burning planet," McCoy murmured from Kirk's right side. "Not a pleasant place to live."

Spock nodded. "And a difficult place to live. Only animals of small adult body weight survived. Those that could burrow, hybernate, or otherwise hide and find enough food among the ruined ecosystem. The sun was blocked out for months by a global cloud of soot, sulfuric acid, and debris, possibly thrown outward at the equator by the Earth's rotation. It is speculated that Earth may have been a ringed planet for quite a while."

Through his comfort, Kirk uttered, "Another Saturn . . ."

"Yes. There would have been a total collapse of terrestrial and marine ecosystems. The supergreenhouse conditions in the Cretaceous were too warm for coral reefs, but the loss of sunlight after this event killed all of the Earth's clam reef ecosystem. Reefs are extremely sensitive and delicate and took ten million years to regenerate."

"And ten or twelve million years for mammals to evolve to any appreciable size," Chief Barnes assisted. "Recovery wasn't exactly the next day."

Spock glanced into the crowd of officers. "The expanding curtain of ejecta spread four thousand kilometers, pushing the atmosphere out of the way and leveling everything in its path."

"It's possible the vacuum of space may have been in contact with the molten crater center, Mr. Spock," one of the newly transferred earth science technicians burst in. "It's incredible! To blow the atmosphere away—"

"Possibly," Spock allowed. "It produced the melt-ejecta layer of fused bedrock blasted out of the site. The melt-ejecta layer was overlain by worldwide fallout from the fireball, which preserved the iridium layer. The northern Yucatan at the time was covered with roughly a thousand feet of limestone, or Cretaceous reef rock—calcium carbonates and back-reef evaporites, mainly calcium sulfate. This evaporized over the crater, resulting in high acid rain and enriched CO_2 in the atmosphere. A ring of this debris formed all the way around the planet. Fine dust caused a nuclear winter phase, which volcanoes can never produce, because their dust never leaves the stratosphere. This cloud cut off ninety percent of the sunlight. Trees soon dropped their leaves. Phytoplankton died within a few days. On land, small animals and birds would have found enough food in the cracks to survive, but only species that reproduced quickly and abundantly would have survived. When the cloud cleared, it cleared on a planet with no more giant animals."

His deep voice fell away with a professional finish.

On the screen, a gauze of gray dust began to spread over the planet as the last moments were recorded by the tricorders, seconds before the Guardian snatched them out of hell's bullet hole.

It was hard to believe, even now, that they were watching the real thing and not just a computer-generated animation.

Several members of the starship's officer corp glanced at their captain and first officer with unmitigated awe and respect.

Waxen and drained, Kirk felt inadequate to that respect. The mission had been a success but too close to disaster at every step. He began to comb every detail, now that his head was clear and his pain receding, looking for ways he could have done a better job.

The officers acceded to McCoy's shooing them out of the

captain's recovery chamber. They didn't even excuse themselves to their commanding officer. Already they were muttering to each other about research they couldn't wait to dive into. Physics lab, bio lab, nuclear science, earth science —they all wanted their hands on that tricorder data. It would shoot through the ship, then through Starfleet, then the whole Federation almost as fast as the killer dust cloud had enshrouded the prehistoric Earth.

The room gradually emptied, and there was some comfort for Kirk to see the lights coming on in his officers' eyes. They had something to work on, to be proud of. All across the Federation, their work over the next few months would be famous. Everyone would be talking about the *Enterprise* and her scientists and their fantastic findings.

When they were alone, Spock turned to him, hands clasped easily behind his back as if none of this had happened, as if declaring that they had come full circle and everything was all right. Pretty much.

"A lot of information to distill," Kirk said. "It'll take years to analyze it all. Makes me glad I'm not a scientist, I think."

"I understand," Spock said. "What was your recommendation to Starfleet regarding the Guardian?"

"That we keep our mouths shut about it, as usual; keep its location classified so this kind of thing doesn't happen again. We have the data—but we don't have to tell how we got it."

"Assuming the Clan government agrees?"

"The Clan government doesn't know the location. Oya refused to tell them."

"Indeed?"

"She's a smart girl."

"Apparently." Spock fell silent briefly, then quietly added, "An interesting place . . . the other universe."

Kirk managed a misty grin. "We met some good people in a bad place, didn't we? Temron . . . Roth . . . especially Roth. I'm sorry he had to die that way."

Spock canted his head and gazed wisely at him. "He was not sorry, Captain."

Returning the gaze with a touch of gratitude, Kirk finally nodded. "You did a good job," he rewarded. "I know that wasn't as easy for you as you let on."

Spock pretended not to understand that and skillfully ignored it. "The asteroid collision with Earth is a rare event in the galaxy. Now we have the opportunity to know what really happened. In effect, we shall be confirming sixty-four million years worth of detective work."

The Vulcan's dark eyes gleamed. Under that paragoric mask, he was content as he sighted down his reclining captain, whom he did not have to bury on a world of monsters. He raised a hand to the diagnostic panel and turned off most of the lights in the room, like a father wordlessly instructing a child to get to sleep.

"As you said, Captain," he added, "it is a genuine wonder that life survived at all on Earth."

With tired eyes Kirk gazed up at the angular shadows on the face over him. "Life's stubborn once it gets going, Mr. Spock," he appraised. "Life hangs on."

Epilogue

"Lieutenant."

"Captain!"

"As you were."

The quarters were cool. Appreciation of ship's air-conditioning after a sweltering hothouse planet.

"I said, as you were. Sit down."

"Sir . . ."

"Just sit down, because I'm going to."

Jim Kirk limped to the bare study desk and pulled out the chair, proud that he'd come far enough to get all the way down the corridor and slide into the chair without wincing.

"Not bad," he sighed as he leaned back, "for a man who's been lame for sixty-four million years."

Pale and bruised, Dale Bannon looked as if he were ready to hyperventilate, but he managed to sit down on his bunk.

"Well?" Kirk asked. "Got anything to say?"

Bannon swallowed, blinked at the floor, shrugged. Then suddenly he looked up, and his eyes were ringed with emotion.

"You got us back," he sputtered. "You did everything you said you would do. Even me . . . even Vernon, after we got hurt . . . You didn't leave any of us behind. Sir, I'll never doubt you again!"

The words bumbled around the room, failing in their loftiness and certainly falling on unimpressed ears where the captain was concerned. It was his job to bring everybody back. There shouldn't be such astonishment when he managed to do that.

Kirk glowered at the boy until it hit Bannon that he wasn't going to get anywhere and was trying too hard.

The lieutenant fizzled like a match in a glass of water. "I'm up for court-martial. I understand, sir."

Kirk shrugged. "Court-martial's a pretty stiff penance for a bareknuckled swipe, I've always thought."

Bannon's brows shot together. "I took a swing at you, sir! At a senior officer!"

"I asked for it. Besides, that was a *long* time ago."

The younger man stared at him and shook his head. "Sir . . . how can you joke about it?"

"I've always thought that two men, even two servicemen, ought to be able to punch out their disagreements now and then."

"Oh, my God!" Bannon choked. He shot up. "You can't just let me get away with it! . . . Striking a crewmate . . . That's the lowest act in the whole . . . universe!"

"All right," Kirk allowed. Straightening up, he made for the door. "Someday, when you're a captain, you can do what you want. And so can I. Besides," he said, glancing back as the door panel skidded open, "a little doubt's a good thing now and then."

At the entrance he put his hand on the edge of the door to keep it from closing behind him and looked back at Bannon with the same glint he had given the dinosaurs a few million years ago. "But not too much," he said.

"Good morning, Captain. Welcome back to the bridge. I am pleased you're well."

"Thank you, Mr. Spock, I'm pretty glad myself. Status?"

"We're expected at Starbase 10 in fourteen hours. The Federation will have emissaries waiting to meet the Clan, and Starfleet will take jurisdiction of the assassination of the science team on the Guardian planet."

"Good. I'm glad we won't have to be the ones to sort it out. Now, what else is bothering you?"

"Why would you believe something is bothering me?"

"Instinct. Like the dinosaurs. Well?"

"Yes, sir . . . the paradox of time travel is troubling me somewhat."

"Specifically?

"The Clan Ru, sir. Since the Clan exists here and now, and we know they went back in time to stop the asteroid, then *you* must have been in the past also to keep them from stopping it. The circularity of time suggests that time cannot actually be changed. However, since we have been in the changed time, and we have experienced this kind of anomaly before, we know that it can be. Therefore, is the Guardian of Forever a danger, or is it part of the pattern of time itself? For instance—"

"Mr. Spock, hold on. You know, you're a fine first officer, an exceptional scientist, and by all definitions a decent man."

"Why, thank you, Captain."

"But you're giving me a headache."

"Sir, I fail to see how the extrapolation of theoretical premises can inflict physical pain."

"Easily. If you don't drop the subject, I'm gonna step on your toe. Mr. Sulu, go to warp factor five."

"Warp factor five, aye, sir."

"Steady as she goes."

STAR TREK®

Calendars

STAR TREK®
❑ **30th Anniversary**.................................52929-3/$12.00

Featuring many never-before-seen photographs from the ground breaking
television series that started it all.

STAR TREK
DEEP SPACE NINE®
❑ ....52928-5/$12.00

Kick off the new year with Commander Benjamin Sisko, Major Kira Nerys,
Science Officer Jadzia Dax and the rest of the crew from the hit series.

STAR TREK
GENERATIONS™
❑ ....52938-2/$12.00

Incredible full-color photos from the smash-hit film that brought together
Jean-Luc Picard and James T. Kirk

STAR TREK®
VOYAGER™
❑ ....52937-4/$12.00

A special collection of photos from the dazzling first season of the newest
Star Trek series — includes a phenomenal special effects centerfold!

™, ® & © 1995 Paramount Pictures. All Rights Reserved.

**POCKET
BOOKS**